Charting the Darkness

A Novel

A. C. Geisel

Author photo: Gary Gaudet, Yarmouth County Museum
Cover design: Cathy MacLean Design, Chéticamp, NS.
Edited by Marianne Ward, Dartmouth, NS
Layout: Mike Hunter, West Bay and Sydney, NS.
First printed in Canada.

Library and Archives Canada Cataloguing in Publication

Geisel, A. C., author
Charting the darkness : a novel / A.C. Geisel.

Issued in print and electronic formats.
ISBN 978-1-77206-036-2 (paperback).--ISBN 978-1-77206-037-9 (pdf).
ISBN 978-1-77206-038-6 (epub).--ISBN 978-1-77206-039-3 (kindle)

I. Title.
PS8613.E4437C53 2016   C813'.6   C2016-902115-7
                                                C2016-902116-5
Cape Breton University Press
PO Box 5300, Sydney, Nova Scotia B1P 6L2 Canada

Distributed by
Nimbus Publishing, 3731 MacKintosh St.,
Halifax, Nova Scotia B3K 5A5 Canada

Charting the Darkness
A Novel

A. C. Geisel

CAPE BRETON UNIVERSITY PRESS
SYDNEY, NOVA SCOTIA

Prologue

L ate night. He remembered hearing that when you grow old you require less sleep. It was true. Maybe it was nature's way of stretching the day as one's time grew shorter. He took a deep breath and exhaled air stale with wilted memories and euthanized dreams, yet he was drawn here like the faithful to an altar. Sean Sullivan closed the photograph album and returned it to a steamer trunk tucked beneath bare rafters in a dark corner of the attic. The trunk's bronze hasp was tarnished and the hinge was rusted, but the wood and leather construction was still solid, much like his wiry seventy-six-year-old frame. Sullivan closed the trunk and knelt beside it. The glossy images of all that had been good in his life dangled in his afterthought.

Paint-worn, wooden treads creaked as he descended the stairs to the kitchen. An ancient refrigerator rattled arthritically as Sullivan rummaged for a bottle of Irish stout. Then he walked outside to the beach through a thick coastal fog with his six-month-old German Shepherd, Dutch. A familiar rock, tide worn and even, which had come to rest on this shore of Cape Breton Island long before Cabot explored its shores in 1497, provided a place to sit. A strong hand tempered by the sea reached into the pocket of a worn, checkered flannel shirt and emerged with a cigarette. Sullivan struck a match and watched it cast shadows on the sand as the tobacco began to smolder and then drift into the fog. Between drags on his smoke he sipped on the bottle of stout that he rested in a nook in the rock while Dutch stared into the night and bristled at the sounds of the ocean.

Walking the beach at White Point on Aspy Bay had become a nightly ritual since Sullivan sold his old Cape Islander lobster boat and purchased a fifteen metre ketch-rigged sailboat. The boat had been built before the Great Depression for an American railroad tycoon who had a predilection for the ornate and formidable. Work on the derelict wooden vessel had consumed nearly two years of Sullivan's life so far. It was a labour of purpose, without illusions.

A failing heart would not find him in a hospital or nursing home. It would find him running downwind with his spinnaker filled. His affairs were in order – coiled, wrapped and stowed away except for one matter that was left to the set and drift of circumstance. Another month of repair and outfitting would put him on the threshold of his destination – one that waited in the tropical breezes and tepid azure waters of southerly latitudes.

Sullivan rubbed Dutch's head and conjured visions of distant, paradisical shores that waited beyond the blanket of fog. He stood up to begin the walk home. The dizziness that he had experienced intermittently during the last several weeks returned with a vengeance, but this time it did not relent. Sullivan struggled for a breath that did not come, and clutching his chest he was drawn into the light.

—

Twenty-four hundred kilometres south of Cape Breton, the back door of the Barbecue Pit Tavern in Little Creek, Virginia, swung open, spilling light and country music into the dank twilight. Nick Sullivan timed the arc of the door and catapulted his five-foot ten-inch frame into the gravel parking lot, faltering for a moment before navigating his way toward the water.

The headwaters of the Dismal Swamp were a forbidding place in the summer, and they reminded Nick of another place and time. He walked across the iron footbridge that spanned a narrow canal, concentrating on mastering the alcohol that raced through his veins. He manoeuvred along an uneven footpath that cork-screwed through cut grass, wild grapevines and cattails. The air was seeded with the heavy taste of skunk cabbage, bog and the decay of things abandoned and forgotten.

Footsteps faltered up an anemic wooden ramp to the house-boat where he stayed when he wasn't squandering his meagre pension on hush puppies, barbecue and beer at the Pit. The twisted ropes that tethered the waterlogged timbers and peeled paint to the shore stretched as his shadow merged with the darkness of his two-room shack before light flickered from a dull lamp. He ducked back outside for a moment to retrieve the evening paper and tossed it next to a pile of mail on the kitchen table. Bare feet shuffled across a threadbare carpet of indiscernible colour to a window fan and then to a light switch that fused the room into the night.

The bedsprings retched as Sullivan sat on the edge of his mattress in the darkness. He jabbed a tattooed right arm toward a bureau where a bottle of Jack Daniels waited. He didn't bother with the formality of a glass: Sullivan and Jackie D were old friends. After a brief visit, Jackie was returned to his niche.

Sullivan sank his swirling head onto his pillow. A pair of ocean blue eyes that still saw a dubious world with perfect vision followed slivers of light that reflected off the moon-soaked waters of the canal and danced on the walls. Slightly uneven, the sound of the fan erased all sense of the present and swept in memories from somewhere far beyond the scent of the ocean hiding nearby. When he listened carefully, it was not the sound of a fan at all, but the whirling propellers of a C-130 carrying him into the jungle.

Chapter 1

Mountain air cascaded down from hillsides bejewelled with pink wild iris, purple lupines and blush red wild roses. The gentle scent of blossoms collided with the salty fragrance of the tide that burnished pebbles and washed them onto a beach of pure white sand. Gulls cried out and dropped shellfish that rolled rudely down roofs and into gutters.

In the early morning, before the tourists and locals put down their blankets and baskets like a small army of occupation, he coveted the solitude. He combed the beach for treasures that the surf had plundered: a lobster trap, a glass fishing buoy, an empty wooden crate and a tin of sardines with Russian lettering on it. Along the way he explored the tidal pools for hermit crabs and minnows that swam in circles waiting for the tide to change.

As he walked the beach, he surveyed the houses that dotted the shoreline with hues of blue, red and shades of white. At dawn the first evidence of human intrusion that seeped into the pristine Cape Breton landscape was music. The sweet tones of a fiddle or Celtic air would drift across the Aspy River whose waters flowed into the warm waters of the Gulf of St. Lawrence....

—

Nick Sullivan rolled over on his cot. The rhythm of the surf kept him in the cusp between his dream and truth. He tried to keep his dream alive, but the pylons of war and the steaming afternoon heat were too strong. Sometimes the closing acts of his dreams were filled with dreadful screams that tore him from sleep with heart-pounding terror, but not today. Today his visions were of Cape Breton.

Sullivan stared at the eaves of the tent he shared with three other non-commissioned officers. He felt sunbaked. Sweat had set into a salty marinade that covered his body. He shaved, took a

4

shower, dressed in clean camouflage fatigues and walked over to the mess hall. By the time he reached the mess, he felt parboiled by the Southeast Asian sun.

Technical Sergeant Modesto Martinez shuffled from the oven to a nearby table where the mess staff ate. He carried a plate heaped with fresh baked apple pie and vanilla ice cream and placed it front of Staff Sergeant Nick Sullivan. It was the perfect complement to the steak dinner he had served to Sullivan earlier, pilfered from the base commander's freezer.

Martinez wiped his meaty brow with a bleached cotton handkerchief he kept in the pocket of his white apron. His dark sober eyes were troubled as he watched the sandy haired lad of twenty. He had adopted the boys of Two Alpha, and when one of them didn't return, it was like losing a member of his family.

Sullivan sank a fork into the pie and smiled. "Mo, what's a world-class chef like you doing here?"

"Someone's got to feed you. I've only got two more enlistments before I earn my twenty and save enough seed money to open my own place back home." The burly middle-aged Mexican-American sat down across from Sullivan and pulled a pack of Old Gold cigarettes from his apron pocket.

"Home," Sullivan sighed. He stared at his plate as the ice cream melted.

Martinez lit the Old Gold with a chrome Zippo lighter and took a drag, holding in the smoke before exhaling. "When you going?" Martinez asked.

Sullivan shifted uneasily in his chair. "Sometime tonight."

Martinez knew not to ask where or why. He did know that the men who wore the bush hat and Zap Patch of the First Air Commandos worked in a world of shadows and silence. He also knew that the civilians who ate in his mess hall were sending Sullivan somewhere into the badlands to do their dirty work. The rumour was that there was another war going on across the border in Laos and Cambodia – a war those civilians didn't want the American public to know about. And young men like Sullivan were dying as a result.

Sullivan finished his pie and glanced at his watch. "Time to go. Thanks for the chow, Mo."

He grabbed his bush hat and pushed his chair under the table with his boot. "When I'm in the field, I dream of two things – Sheila and your home-cooked meals."

Martinez's face lit with a smile. "How's she doing?"

Sullivan pulled a picture from his shirt pocket and handed it proudly to Martinez. "Hard to believe she's five months pregnant," Sullivan said with a glow in his eyes, "and she's still taking a full course load at Amherst."

Martinez stared at the photo of a svelte young girl with long blond hair and beautiful features sitting on the breakwater of her parents' summer home in Cape Cod.

"Beautiful and smart," Martinez said. He handed the picture back to Sullivan, avoiding his eyes. And then there was an awkward silence. "You stay safe, son," he said softly.

Sullivan nodded then turned away, disappearing behind the swinging doors that hid the kitchen from the mess hall and the killing fields beyond. Martinez made the sign of the cross and finished his smoke.

Forty-five minutes later Sullivan left the briefing room at base intelligence carrying a green canvas map case, and walked toward the hanger where his gear was stored. The sun had been down for an hour, and blue runway lights sparkled in the shadows of the mountains. His buddy, Tony Capello, a two-striper, was waiting for him, leaning against the fender of a Dodge Power Wagon and chewing on an empty lollipop stick. He was two inches taller than Sullivan with a trim frame that rippled with muscle. Camouflage paint covered his face, which narrowed to a dimpled chin. His bush hat was pushed forward on his buzz cut black hair, keeping the sweat out of his eyes.

"Nice night for a plane ride," Capello said, glancing at the sky while he followed Sullivan.

Sullivan glanced at the sky too. He could see the muted glow of stars through scattered clouds.

Capello looked at the tarmac where mechanics were performing the pre-flight on the F-4s that would fly their cover. "Where are they sending us?"

"We've lost two O-2s in the last three weeks," Sullivan said referring to the single-engine, propeller-driven plane used to spot the enemy and call in air strikes. Sullivan stopped and faced Capello. "There's something big going on over the border and the boss doesn't want to risk losing another."

"So they want to insert us?" Capello asked.

Sullivan nodded his head and continued walking. The two men entered a side door of a hanger and slid through the cavernous interior. They walked past the C-130 that would be their ride and into the ready room that housed all the wares needed for a week-long trek in the jungle far behind enemy lines.

Forty minutes after the C-130 was airborne, Sullivan began slipping into his gear under Capello's watchful eye. The weight increased as the olive drab tools of war were stacked on his back. He bounced the load a few times and tightened the straps. Then he helped Capello with his gear. The two men pulled black helmets over their heads, sat down and took long deep breaths.

The jump master raised his index and middle finger and yelled, "Two minutes."

Sullivan stood, hooked into the static line and adjusted a black rubber oxygen mask over his face. He took several deep breaths and nodded his head, looking into Capello's dark eyes. Sullivan set his jaw. A buzzer sounded and a red light blinked as the C-130's cargo door slowly lowered, letting in cold gusts of reality.

Capello stood behind Sullivan with his hand on Sullivan's shoulder. The red light turned to green. Sullivan's senses went numb as he walked to the end of the cargo ramp and disappeared into the night ten kilometres above the earth.

Chapter 2

Little Creek, Virginia

Sullivan's nightmare ebbed into the Virginia dawn. It came less often now, sometimes not visiting for months, but it always returned slithering into his head from a dark place. He slid his legs over the side of the bed, shuffled across the floor in his boxer shorts, turned off the fan and raised a torn, yellowed shade.

After swallowing a handful of Aspirin with a swig of beer, Sullivan set off on his morning walk on a path that ran along the canal before the sun had a chance to sear the morning air.

He stopped at a donut shop for coffee then took the same route back home. After a cool shower and shave, he poured milk over a bowl of bran flakes, hovered over the pages of a day-old newspaper and then started on the mail, again. It had been nearly six years since he had stopped at the Barbecue Pit for a beer and ended up staying .

The scant tenders from the postal service were something he looked forward to like the token prize in a Cracker Jack box. He looked askance at the return address on an officious looking envelope and ripped off the edge, wondering for a moment what reason a law firm in Nova Scotia, Canada, would have to contact him. But even before he unfolded the single sheet of paper inside, he sensed the reason. Glancing at the words from the Cape Breton barrister, he walked out onto the deck of the houseboat and gazed across the canal. A boat motored past, heading north from wintering in Florida or the Islands, the wake slapping against the shore as it receded. He crumpled the letter in his hand and then straightened it and, after a moment, read it again more carefully.

"Dear Mr. Sullivan: As the appointed representative of the Crown, it is with remorse that I must inform you of the passing of Sean Patrick Sullivan on the eighth day of June of this year. I regret that this news must come in the form of a letter as there was no other way to contact you. Mr. Sullivan's remains have been remanded to the Office of the Chief Medical Examiner until such time that you decide on his final disposition. Such disposition must be made on or before July seventh. Failure to make said provisions by the requisite date will be determined to be an abandonment of any and all rights regarding said final disposition...."

Sullivan folded the letter so that it fit in the pocket of his shorts and walked over to use the phone at the Barbecue Pit. He stopped along the way to pick some wildflowers from the riverbank. As he walked across the short span of the metal footbridge over the canal, he could see the Pit owner's son, Rocko, unloading cases of beer from a truck.

Sullivan paused as he approached the rear door to the kitchen. "Don't go short on the Corona Light," he said.

Sweat trickled from Rocko's curly black hairline. His frame was rounded, hardly concealed by the grey T-shirt over his belt buckle. He brushed his forehead with a work glove before the salty beads of toil ran into his dark eyes.

"Light Mexican beer is for wimps." He looked at the flowers in Sullivan's hand and winced. "I hope those aren't for me."

Sullivan cocked his head and held the door open for Rocko as he pushed a hand truck loaded with beer inside.

Sullivan pointed to Rocko's paunch. "And as for the light beer, you might consider putting more low-cal in your feed bag, muffin top."

Rocko winced again.

Sullivan asked, "Is Ma in? I've got to use the phone."

"In the office," Rocko said.

Sullivan walked through the kitchen and down a set of concrete stairs to a basement office. The door was open. He rapped on the doorframe and walked in.

Ma Puglise was sitting behind a metal grey desk tapping on the keys of a calculator. She tilted her head and squinted through the bottom of her bifocals at the paper tape spewing from the machine. Ma was a few months shy of seventy, abundant, with the face of a saint. She pulled a pencil from behind an ear hidden by wispy silver hair and scribbled on a white pad of paper.

Ma looked up at Sullivan and smiled. In the glare of the fluorescent lights, Sullivan could see the crow's feet around her ebony eyes and light liver spots on her face.

"In kind of early, aren't we?" Ma asked.

Sullivan leaned against the doorframe. "I'm not here as a paying customer. I just thought I'd show up and make people's lives interesting."

Ma smiled wide.

Sullivan said, "Actually, Ma, I need to use the phone for a long-distance call. Make sure you put it on my tab."

"I can step out if you want," Ma said.

Sullivan handed her the flowers and kissed her cheek. "I don't keep any secrets from you, Ma."

She looked at him deeply. In addition to her two sons, Rocko and Joe, both of whom worked at the Pit, she had adopted scores of others. The Pit was home to the personnel stationed at the nearby Norfolk naval base as well as to the veterans who parked their duffel bags and settled in the area. And she had a place in her heart for every one of them. But she loved Nick Sullivan as if he had come from her own womb.

She listened to his conversation. She didn't know Sullivan had an uncle. But she did know he had lost both his parents, that his wife and daughter had deserted him while he was rotting in a prisoner of war camp and that his best friend died literally in his arms. He was an orphan from everyone he had ever loved. And now he was slowly dying from a disease that he brought back from the jungle. It wasn't a disease of the body. Something worse ate away at the core of his soul. He hid it well with counterfeit repartee, but Ma knew there was no inner glow; the light that made eyes sparkle and smiles gleam was snuffed out long ago. It was her mission in life to keep him from more hurt, or at least to try. And while she cut Sullivan off while he was at the Pit before his brain cells drowned in Corona, she could not the curb the onslaught of eighty-proof when he left.

Sullivan scribbled a phone number the coroner gave him. He made a second call to a funeral home and another to the attorney handling his uncle's estate. Then he hung up the phone and sat in a chair next to Ma's desk.

"My uncle died," he paused and added, "in Canada."

Ma patted Nick's hand. "I'm so sorry, Nick. Were you close?"

"I haven't seen him in a long time, since I was a kid actually, and I'm not the best at keeping in touch. But yes, we were close at one time."

"Where in Canada?"

Sullivan smiled. "Nova Scotia."

"Has it been a long time, I mean, since you were there?" Ma asked.

"God, it been so long. Last time I was there was when I graduated high school. But you know, Ma, I can still picture it. Our family used to visit Uncle Sean, Aunt Ann and my cousin Richie summers when I was a kid. Uncle Sean taught me how to fish, how to tack and jibe under sail. He spent some one-on-one time with me when my dad was dying." Sullivan's voice trailed to a whisper. "I was visiting when my cousin Richie died."

Sullivan closed his eyes and took a deep breath.

"You know, Nick, I discovered a long time ago when I lost my husband that good memories exist independently of darker times. We do a disservice to those kind recollections when we don't let them shine."

Sullivan thought about it, his eyes distant. "Not easy to do. But there were good times. You know, I experienced my first love with a local girl there on Cape Breton Island. Funny, I can't see her features clearly anymore."

"Time will do that," Ma said. "But it seems you had good moments there, things worth remembering."

Sullivan smiled at some memory and then retracted it. "He doesn't have anybody else, so I'm going up to Nova Scotia to bury him."

Ma reached over and took Sullivan's hand again. "Is there anything I can do?"

"No thanks, Ma."

"Sounds like there's someone taking care of the funeral arrangements?"

"Yeah, the attorney handling my uncle's estate and the funeral home director both said they were taking care of the preparations. From the way they talked it seems as if he had a lot of friends there."

"Well, less for you to do then, dear."

"I'll pack and be leaving in the morning, Ma."

"How are you going to get there?"

"The pickup."

Ma shook her head. "That rusted piece of junk hasn't run in months. It's got a flat tire and the bed is filled with rubbish."

"Better get cranking. I'll be back tonight." Sullivan stood up and kissed her on the cheek.

He stood outside in the far corner of the Pit's parking lot with his hands on his hips. The rusted, faded-red, 1975 Ford F-150 with its camper top seemed to be hiding from him. It rested off the pavement in tall grass and was tilted to one side as if it was trying to look casual.

Sullivan opened the Ford's hood and made some notes on the back of the attorney's letter. Then he borrowed Joe's old Cadillac and drove to an auto parts store. An hour later he returned and spent the rest of the day crawling through the wretched piece of machinery. It was old and used up just like he was.

Later when he crawled from beneath the Ford, he yanked at the driver's door and slid across the torn plastic upholstery patched with duct tape. He turned the key in the ignition and the engine coughed and groaned and then came to life, expelling a cloud of blue smoke. Sullivan drove the relic to a repair shop, where a steel plate was welded over rotting floorboards, returned home and washed up.

An hour later at the Pit, the happy hour crowd was dwindling and he took a seat at the bar. Suzie was running the register and brought him a Corona Light. She was everyone's sister. Her thirty-something big doe eyes matched her dark brown hair. Suzie had never married and had seldom been cherished, at least in the romantic sense. But she was loved by every heir to her smile, and her gentle words soothed the souls who came to the Pit to dull their pain.

Suzie patted Sullivan's hand. "I heard. I'm sorry." She rushed over to a customer waving his hand and came back a few minutes later. "Dinner?" she asked.

"Fish and chips, puppies and another Corona."

She nodded and rushed off again.

The night crowd had just begun to dribble in when Ma arrived with a cake. She nodded to Joe and Rocko, and they went behind the bar to relieve Suzie.

"Happy birthday," Ma said to Sullivan. "I know it's not for another two weeks, but you may still be up north, so we thought we should celebrate it now ."

Suzie said, "We pitched in and got you few things for your trip."

She handed Sullivan a package gift-wrapped with little red sailboats sailing across a sea of blue paper. Sullivan tore off the paper revealing maps, complete with an AAA membership. It was perfect for someone broken-down or lost, or both.

"Thought you might need it," Suzie said.

Sullivan gave Suzie a hug.

"Something for my boy," Ma said handing him another envelope, smaller than the first with just a ribbon around it.

Sullivan opened it and Ma explained the contents. "It's a reservation on the Portland ferry. It sails overnight from Maine to Yarmouth, Nova Scotia, and will save you twelve hours of driving."

Sullivan bit his lip and looked down for a moment. Then he gave Ma a long hug too. "Thanks, you guys. I'm going to miss you. Early to bed. Early to rise. I have to leave before the sun comes up."

His friends watched as Sullivan handed Rocko an envelope stuffed with cash to settle up his bar tab for the month and to pay for the houseboat's electric bills and any other expenses that arose in his absence. Then he walked out through the kitchen door just like he had every other night for the last six years.

The canal was quiet when he returned to his shack. In the mist he thought he could almost see George Washington surveying the twists and turns of Dismal Swamp before the Revolutionary War.

Inside, Sullivan rummaged through his locker, pulling out old clothes and uniforms until he uncovered an old suit. He pulled it out and placed it in a suitcase. Hidden in the dark shadows of the locker were relics – breadcrumbs scattered on life's path that reminded him who and where he had been.

He removed a photo album and held the leatherette cover in his hand. He hesitated and then opened it. Each turn of a page dragged him through the briars of his past. The pictures chronicled his life: baby pictures, birthday cards from his parents, photos of his summers in Nova Scotia and the girl he fell in love with there, when he was sixteen.

He turned the page and his finger trembled as he ran it over a picture of Sheila, as if he could somehow reach beyond the coated paper and touch her. He remembered the day the picture was taken.

Sullivan had met her at a party that a college friend had invited him to, and they began dating soon after. He had picked her up from her dorm one Friday in early spring and they drove to her parents' cottage on Cape Cod. The cottage had been cold and dank. They started a fire in the stone fireplace and purloined a bottle of wine from her parents' liquor cabinet. They found some heavy blankets, and huddled in front of the hearth, sipping wine, laughing and making love. Then they talked until morning about everything.

She was so beautiful. He still loved her so much.

The last pages of the album were the darkest . The camera had been a Christmas gift from Sheila. From a distance he had captured images of his daughter at a playground.

Sullivan hauled the suitcase out to the Ford. When he returned, he uncapped the bottle of Jack Daniels he had started on the night before, and emptied it. Jackie D numbed the pain and delivered him to a place that was warm and safe. But somewhere in the night, almost every night, Jackie retreated and Sullivan was naked and alone – almost.

Jackie had acquaintances that loitered just on the edge of sobriety and who spoke with the hushed hiss of a serpent. *Nick, we're over here Nick. You'd like it here.*

Sullivan smiled and considered it.

He turned on the window fan and stumbled to his bed, forgetting the bedside lamp. He closed his eyes and hurried to sleep where a plane was waiting to take him back into the jungle.

———

Sullivan winced as his chute caught in the jungle canopy and wrenched him to a sudden halt. A few moments later he cringed as Capello's body plummeted through the dense foliage, snapping tree branches and finally coming to rest with a thunderous thud on the ground. Then there was silence. Sullivan listened, focusing on each sound that penetrated the moonless night until he was assured that there was no immediate danger lurking in the bush. He pulled his Randall fighting knife from its leather sheath on his shoulder harness and quickly sliced through the nylon webbing that held him captive. As he lowered himself to the ground, he caught a glimpse of Capello crouched and slowly turning in a circle with his M-16 rifle pressed against his shoulder.

Sullivan took a compass bearing and tapped Capello on the shoulder. The two men stepped silently into the shadows.

Sullivan glanced at his watch. It was almost two o'clock. He grabbed Capello's shoulder and whispered into his ear.

"Let's find a spot to settle in."

Capello nodded and followed Sullivan as the two crept through the tepid jungle where they were swallowed by the darkness.

Sullivan's eyes flickered as a beam of sunlight broke through the tangle of brush where he had slept. Each of them had managed a few hours' sleep as the other stood sentinel. Sullivan blinked sleep from his eyes. He watched Capello slowly chewing a piece of beef jerky while peering through an opening in the jungle canopy, his weapon at the ready.

"Morning, Sulli. I made breakfast," Capello said, tossing a piece of non-government issue jerky to Sullivan.

Sullivan said nothing as he took a bite of the spicy dried meat and walked a short distance to a clearing on the mountainside near where they had camped. The sun, still rising, began to brush the landscape with colour. Through binoculars he could see birds flocking high in the tropical canopy and orchids and rusty brown trails that stained the lime-coloured jungle. He wanted to believe that he was on some tropical island and that Sheila was holding his hand, but the raspy nylon sling of the M-14 rifle he was clutching reminded him where he was.

Sullivan motioned Capello to join him as he knelt and opened his map case. On a nearby tree branch, a douc monkey sat, watching. The men talked in whispers.

"I figure we're eight miles from where the first O-2 was killed," Sullivan said. He jabbed his forefinger at a contour line on the map. "We should make it to this ridge by nightfall, set up a perimeter."

Capello scratched at an insect bite on his neck while studying the map. "There are a lot of places to get killed between here and there. We'll need to stay off the trails and bushwhack our way there."

Sullivan nodded and stood up.

Capello squeezed into his pack and bounced a few times before adjusting the straps. Sullivan looked at his compass again and motioned Capello to follow. The jungle canopy hid them from the blazing sun but sealed in the humidity. The camouflaged tiger suits they wore hung over their bodies like wet rags. They moved slowly, taking only a few cautious steps at a time before stopping and listening. At times the thick jungle foliage looked to be an indiscernible blur. The first three hours seemed like days. Then there was no sense of time at all.

The murmur of fast water could be heard for a half-hour before they came upon a stream swollen from the daily afternoon deluge that kept the jungle a sauna of sweat and bugs. They surveyed the stream for fifteen minutes before crawling, one at a time, to the water's edge to dip their heads in the clear, cool liquor of life and to fill their canteens. Then they retreated back into the jungle.

Chapter 3

The din of the alarm clock paused Sullivan's nocturnal torment. He sat on the edge of his bed and spun the cap off of Jackie D to stop the shakes and then took the bottle with him into the shower to sluice the sweat and scour the stains of his dreams.

Forty minutes later, he fastened the houseboat's door hasp with a padlock. Sullivan walked to the Pit using a flashlight. He shined the light over the pickup and removed a note from behind a wiper blade. He opened the tailgate and lifted the lid on the cooler that Rocko and Joe had filled with Corona Light, ice and enough food for a week.

Sullivan turned over the Ford and let it idle. He unfolded a map and traced a route with his finger. The Timex on his wrist said it was two and a half hours past midnight. If all went well, he would arrive in DC by five, when the city would be quiet and he could be alone. He took a last look at the Pit and headed for the highway.

—

Leaning against a tree, Sullivan opened his map.

Capello knelt next to him. His throat felt harsh and dry and he had to raise his voice in order to whisper. "Looks like we're about three quarters of the way there," he said, pointing to a gaunt blue line that snaked along the map.

Sullivan studied the map for several more minutes before folding it and putting it away. "Let's have some chow and rest up," he said.

Capello reached into his pack and retrieved a C-ration and a package wrapped in aluminum foil. He folded back the edges of the foil to reveal a slab of apple pie.

"Mo wrapped this up for us. Best we eat it now before it goes bad," Capello said as he pulled out his knife, opened the rations and sliced the pie into two portions.

Sullivan grabbed a piece of pie. Some of the filling dripped though his fingers, wasted like everything the war touched. When he finished his rations of franks and beans, he rested his head against the tree trunk and closed his eyes. Mo's pie reminded him of home and of Sheila and of his mother.

Sullivan lifted his eyelids instinctively and looked over at Capello. Capello spit a wad of half chewed food from his mouth, his eyes wide and searching. He tapped his ear. Sullivan heard it too – voices coming from the stream.

The two men quickly covered their spent ration cans and slipped on their packs. They moved cautiously through the jungle and upstream of the intruders. When they covered a safe distance, Sullivan crawled, a hands length at a time, to the water's edge. Capello followed a safe distance behind.

Thirty metres away, a teenage boy sat on a rock across the stream with an AK-47 held limply in his hands as he listened to two uniformed NVA soldiers. The boy was ragged and wore sandals. He must be a local kid from a village somewhere nearby, Sullivan thought, paid by Hanoi to guard the far approach to someplace important. The soldiers disappeared into the bush. Twenty minutes passed. The kid looked bored, untrained and undisciplined. But the automatic weapon in his hands was deadly serious.

Sullivan began to slip back into the jungle. Nearby, a hornbill cackled a warning. Sullivan could see the boy tense and stare in his direction. He felt naked and his whole being tingled in fear as he lay still on his stomach. He reached for the Colt .45 automatic holstered on his side and slowly removed it. He could hear the sound of the boy splashing through the water toward him. Still invisible to the boy, Sullivan counted the steps as they grew more intense. His right hand moved the pistol in front of him and pushed the safety off the Colt, his entire body beginning to tremble.

Suddenly the boy's feet churned the water into a maelstrom. Sullivan sprung up into a crouch. His world began to move in slow motion as he swung the big Colt. In an instant he leveled the .45 on his target. But he lowered the pistol, as crimson stained water flowed past him.

Capello held the blood-stained body of the boy with his hand under the boy's chin. His other hand clutched the carbon steel blade of a custom-made fighting knife.

Sullivan was close now, close enough to see the boy's eyes following his advance. Those eyes, filled with terror, blinked and darted for what seemed an eternity. Even as the blood stopped flowing from his wound, his eyes moved and then stared lifeless. Sullivan vomited and then holstered his weapon and grabbed the boy's feet. In another ten minutes, the body was part of the jungle.

—

The balding tires of the Ford squealed as it turned off Route 64 and onto the Interstate. A light rain began to fall, fogging the windshield. Sullivan rolled down the driver's window, finding the cool morning air sobering. He wanted a drink, but he would wait until after his visit, when he would need it most. The rhythm of the highway and wipers counting time lulled him into daydreams: a young boy in the family station wagon heading north through Maine to Nova Scotia for the first time; a young man leaving there never expecting to return.

Sullivan parked the pickup in an empty lot at the National Mall a few minutes before five o'clock. The rain was heavier now. He donned an olive drab poncho and a ragged bush hat and stepped out of the Ford. The path to the Wall was familiar. He had walked it every year since it was erected. Mute bronze figures watched him as he walked to the polished black monolith and ran his eyes down an endless roll call of names. Sullivan pressed his fingers against the etched letters that spelled "Capello, Anthony M." and knelt so that he was at eye level.

He whispered, "Hey, Cappy. How you doing, buddy? I was passing by on my way north. My uncle died, and I have to take care of things. Not much happening in my life. I'm just hanging around, marking time."

Sullivan paused, looking to see if anyone was listening but at the same time not caring. All he saw was the rain running down the wall.

"I think about you a lot, Cappy. I wonder what it's like where you are. I wonder why I'm here and why it turned out the way it did. I wish I could have traded places with you, buddy. You would have done a better job of things, become someone, made a difference. I love you, brother."

Sullivan leaned his forehead against the cold stone wall that hid him from Capello's world and wept until the tears ran dry.

As he retraced his steps to the parking lot, he felt Capello's presence walking beside him. But the apparition stopped where the grassy grounds to the Vietnam Memorial ended.

Sullivan reached under the seat of the Ford and pulled out Jackie D dressed in a brown paper bag. He raised it in a salute, took a large swallow and then another. He could feel Capello's stare as he drove away; the Interstate north was beginning to choke with commuter traffic. A half-hour out of DC, the rain began to come down in torrents.

Sullivan could barely see the figure wrapped in a light blue raincoat waving from the breakdown lane. It was too late to manoeuvre into the passing lane, and the Ford threw up a geyser of water that momentarily obscured the figure. Sullivan slowed to a stop, ground the gears into reverse and backed up. The blue raincoat tapped on the window and Sullivan reached over to crank it down.

"You. Stupid. Son. Of a bitch." On the decibel scale of displeasure, Sullivan thought the female voice might be an eight out of ten. But then it was 6:45 a.m., and one's decibels were usually not up to par so early in the morning, so he gave it a nine with a handicap.

Sullivan shrugged his shoulders. "Sorry, I didn't see you."

She repeated her greeting, but added a few cuss words. This time it was a ten – no handicap.

"Look, lady, I said I was sorry! And as for stupid, you rack up big points for hitchhiking on the Interstate dressed like a raindrop."

"I'm not a raindrop, and don't call me lady."

Sullivan rolled his eyes. "Listen up. You can either grab a ride with this stupid son of bitch, or not. You have to the count of five."

She got in at four and a half, preceded by a backpack and a guitar case wrapped in green garbage bags. She screwed her face into a pout. "That's better. I accept your apology. Now, what are you going to do about my clothes?"

He said, "I plan to get off at the next exit in Aberdeen for gas and coffee. You can change into a dry set of clothes in the restroom."

She folded her arms with a "humph."

Sullivan pulled into a truck stop that included a motel, diner and gift shop. He fuelled the Ford while Raindrop changed her clothes. Sullivan waited for her in the diner and waved to get her attention when she emerged from the restroom. He watched as she walked toward him dressed in dry jeans and a brown knit pullover shirt. She had long blond hair that flowed past broad shoulders, a pretty face and an hourglass figure that could grace a magazine cover. Sullivan pegged her at twenty-something going on forty.

She sat down across from him and slid across the bench-style seat, laying her raincoat next to her. Sullivan looked into brown eyes that sparkled with defiance and blush of crimson. A hint of darker roots betrayed her real hair colour.

"Coffee?"

"Please."

Sullivan motioned to the waitress and ordered two coffees. He studied Raindrop again.

"Feeling better?"

She smiled. "Ya, I'm sorry I yelled at you back there. Getting soaked was the last straw in what has been a shitty twenty-four hours."

Sullivan extended his hand.

"Nick Sullivan."

Her grip was feminine. "Deanna. You can call me D," she said.

"I kind of liked Raindrop."

She smiled.

"So D, where are you headed?"

The coffee came in cardboard cups to go. She took it with cream and sugar and sipped before she answered.

"Boston, maybe Cape Cod. And you?"

"Portland, Maine, to catch the boat to Nova Scotia. I can drop you off on the Massachusetts Turnpike just outside of Boston."

She nodded. "Thanks."

Sullivan looked out the window as the rain dimpled puddles and then he glanced at his Timex. "I hate to rush, but I've got to be in Portland by eight tonight."

They both ran to the Ford, trying to escape the rain.

Back on the Interstate, D wiped away windshield haze and asked, "What will you be doing in Nova Scotia?"

"My uncle died."

"Sorry. I saw a travel magazine article about it once. It's supposed to be nice."

"It is. And at Cape Breton Island the waters are the warmest anywhere north of the Carolinas," Sullivan added.

She turned in her seat and leaned against the door. "Tell me about it."

The traffic slowed in the rain. Brake lights blinked and hovered. The Ford's wipers squeaked against the windshield.

"I haven't been there since I was a teenager, but what I remember is green mountains that seemed to rise from an ocean you'd expect to find on some tropical island. And the water was crystal clear. My Uncle Sean had a house on the bay near the Aspy River. What I remember most, though, is the music. Nova Scotia has a big Celtic influence. Everyone danced, sang or fiddled."

"That's what I want to do, sing," she said.

Sullivan nodded. "What do you do now?"

She tossed her hair back and her face tensed. "Model – freelance," she said abruptly.

Sullivan's eyebrows arched. "That must be exciting. Who do you model for?"

She paused. "You know, car shows, boat shows, stuff like that. Anyway, I'm ready for a career change."

He wondered about the other stuff.

She clenched her jaw, then turned on the radio too loud to talk over.

Two hours later Sullivan pulled off the highway and rolled into a service area with a McDonalds in Trenton, New Jersey. The rain had stopped and sheets of dark clouds raced overhead.

"Want some lunch? I've got sandwiches in the cooler," he said pointing to the pickup bed.

"Sure. I need to use the restroom."

She picked up her pack and disappeared under the golden arches.

Sullivan opened the camper body and pulled the cooler to the tailgate. He was chewing on a ham club sandwich Rocko had made and sipping on a Corona when D returned.

He swallowed. "Help yourself."

She giggled, and then took the Corona from Sullivan's hand and took a long gulp. She giggled again and rummaged through the cooler pulling out a Ziplock marked "tuna." She sat on the tailgate eating her sandwich, swinging her legs and blinking her bloodshot eyes to an unheard rhythm. The abrupt change in her behaviour didn't go unnoticed.

Sullivan grabbed a fresh Corona and finished his sandwich, then used the restroom. When he returned to the Ford, D was sitting in the cab wiping her nose with a napkin. The radio was blaring and Sullivan turned it down a notch. A while later he turned it off.

"It's giving me a headache," Sullivan said.

The giggle was gone.

He shifted in his seat. "How long have you been riding the white horse?"

Her features corkscrewed into a question mark. "What?"

"The Bolivian marching powder. You hitched up the reindeer back when we stopped at Mickey D's."

"Did what?"

"Come on, you're wasted."

She clenched her teeth, trying to crush the truth.

"Go to hell! Who do you think you are, judging me? Let me guess: divorced, burnt out, unemployed, over the hill alcoholic, right?"

Sullivan thought about it. "That's about right."

He turned his head and saw tears run down her cheeks, but otherwise her composure was intact.

She blew her nose in the napkin. "You haven't a clue about who I am, so you can take your frigging opinion and shove it."

Sullivan's tone was supple. "Ditto."

"Ya, well at least I'm trying."

Sullivan sighed. "Maybe you need some help. You have family, friends?"

She sniffed. "Only my mom. I only bring her grief. People just use me."

"Because you let them?" Another sniff.

There was an anxious pause. Sullivan looked at his watch.

"We're almost in Connecticut. It will be another two and half hours before I drop you off on the pike. I've got some time. What do you say we stop and have an early dinner? On me. No sense parting company enemies."

She shrugged her shoulders and blew her nose again.

Sullivan stopped at an inn just shy of the Massachusetts border that proclaimed it had been serving travellers since before the American Revolution. It was quaint with replica period furnishing and waitresses that dressed in eighteenth-century costumes. They both ordered the special.

Sullivan asked, "Where will you stay tonight?"

D's voice was thin and her gaze was flat. "Boston. I'll get a room."

Sullivan stirred his glass of ice tea with a plastic straw. "And then?"

"I don't know."

"You have money?"

She lowered her eyes and nodded. "I'm sorry I was such a bitch. I didn't mean the things I said before. I was, you know, not myself."

Sullivan reached across the table as though to touch her. Their eyes met. "You're young. Maybe you think you've been all the way around the block and got it all figured out." Sullivan shook his head. "Dream. Don't look back. And take baby steps. Most of all, be kind to yourself ."

D took his hand and held it to her face. She blinked away a tear and nodded.

Sullivan went out of his way and dropped D off at Boston's Copley Square. She gave him a peck on the cheek and then pulled her guitar and pack from the Ford. Sullivan watched her disappear into the crowd. She never looked back.

Two hours later, and in plenty of time, Sullivan drove into the Portland ferry terminal, reported his name and reservation number, and was directed to a line of cars. It was eight o'clock when he boarded. He shoved a change of clothes, some food, and a couple bottles of Corona into an overnight bag. Then he made room for his buddy Jackie D and zipped the bag shut.

A steward directed him to his cabin. It had a bunk bed, writing table and a full bath. Sullivan glanced out the cabin's one porthole at the lights of Portland Harbour. There was a postcard with a picture of the Portland ferry on the desk. He wrote a brief note to Ma and the others at the Pit, thanking them again for the ticket and other gifts. Sullivan sat at the writing table and finished off two Coronas and one of Rocko's club sandwiches. He felt the ship begin to move and watched the harbour disappear through the porthole.

Grabbing a jacket, Sullivan walked up a flight of stairs to the purser's office on the main deck and mailed the postcard. Then he followed the sound of live music to the ship's nightclub. He grabbed a stool at the bar that he kept until it closed six beers later.

It was one in the morning when he strolled out onto the deck. The ship's lights formed halos in the battleship grey mist. Sullivan turned up his collar and followed the empty deck toward the stern. Every two minutes the foghorn called out a deep baritone warning.

He hadn't gone far when his eyes caught the silhouette of someone standing by the railing. Sullivan watched the figure reach into a coat pocket and retrieve a plastic bag that was tossed into the sea. He drew closer and stopped.

Sullivan put his hands on the railing and looked out into the darkness. "Quiet night."

The figure didn't falter from her gaze. "It's the kind of night when the blues can creep in if you're not careful."

"I know what you mean." He glanced at her and then fixed his eyes back on the fog. "I once knew a girl that looked a lot like you."

The figure turned toward him. "What was her name?"

"Raindrop."

"Sorry, don't know her. My name is Deanna, Deanna Beutel. My friends call me – they call me Deanna."

She offered her hand. Sullivan took it and gave it a squeeze.

She said, "You look familiar too. You remind me of a man that spoke to me about baby steps and about not looking back. That first step is the hardest."

She stepped away from the railing. "Maybe I'll see you again."

"It's a small world," he said .

Sullivan watched her leave. He returned to his cabin and sat on the edge of his bed. His hands felt clammy and he wiped them on his pant leg. It was sad saying goodbye to an old friend. Sullivan took a deep breath and grabbed a brown paper bag from his luggage. He stepped to the sink and Jackie D quivered in his hands. But, when it came down to it, he just couldn't let an old friend go down the drain.

When Jackie D was gone, the room began to carousel. Later, when Jackie had said good night , Sullivan could hear whispers, hope of another kind. He closed his eyes and listened.

When his eyes blinked open, he could see Capello's ghost chewing on a lollipop stick and leaning back in the chair across the cabin. Sullivan glanced at the worn soles of Capello's jump boots propped on the edge of the writing table. Sullivan nodded and Capello nodded back.

"If you'd come earlier, we could have shared a drink."

Capello shrugged.

Chapter 4

They washed blood from their hands in a runoff of the stream. Sullivan could see the reflection of Capello's face in the still waters, a reflection that carried an expression that said Capello's life would never be the same again.

They hiked cautiously uphill for nearly an hour, pausing only to take compass headings . Then they stopped to rest behind a thicket. Sullivan's breath slowed. His face was drawn. His eyes carried as much worry as horror.

"Thanks for what you did back there, Cappy."

Capello looked away and sniffed tears from his eyes.

Sullivan said, "When they discover him missing, they'll come looking for us."

A spotted pit viper slithered across the jungle floor and into a hole. Sullivan watched it disappear and then pulled the map case from his pack and spread it out on the ground. He measured distances using the joints in his index finger as a scale. "We should reach the ridge within two hours, find a good spot to set up and maybe settle in before the rain," he said.

Capello had taken his pack off and was lying on the ground. He looked at the clouds building and then glanced at his watch. Sullivan put on his pack, slung his rifle and offered Capello a hand getting up.

Reaching the top of the ridge, they found the sun again resting on the edge of the horizon and casting a golden hue on the valley below. Capello scouted out a place to set up camp while Sullivan scanned the terrain. Capello found a clump of conifer and melaleuea bushes next to a large fallen broadleaf evergreen. He cut out a space in middle of the cluster of bushes and laid the branches down for ground cover. Then he set up a tent half as a rain shelter.

A half-hour later the two men huddled together listening to sounds of the rain. Capello caught the rain in his canteen as it cascaded off the tent half. Then he poured cherry flavored Kool-

Aid into the canteen from a plastic bottle. He took a swallow and passed the canteen to Sullivan.

Sullivan smiled. "When I was a kid we would freeze Kool-Aid in an ice cube tray and make Kool-Aid pops," he said in barely a whisper.

Capello nodded. "We would wait for the Good Humor man to make his rounds. You could hear that bell ringing on the truck a mile away."

"Toasted almond," Sullivan said.

"Strawberry shortcake," Capello replied. "Or sometimes a Fudgsicle or ice cream sandwich."

"Yeah. And if I had enough money from mowing Mrs. Griswald's lawn I'd spring for a sundae."

"Hot fudge," Sullivan continued, reading Capello's mind. "Then we'd ride our bikes or play ball in the street. Or play good guys bad guys."

"What I wouldn't give," Capello said. He stared up at the camo-coloured tent half. "Who are we, Sulli? We the good guys or the bad guys?"

Sullivan shook his head. "We're just the guys that are going back home. We'll put our uniforms in a trunk in the attic, along with everything that happened here. We'll watch our kids listen for the Good Humor man ringing his bell like none of this shit ever happened."

"Sulli."

"Yeah?"

"How come there was no Good Humor woman?"

Sullivan punched Capello in the shoulder. Then he reached into his pack and retrieved a poncho.

Sullivan glanced at his watch. "I'll do the first watch. Chow down and get some sleep."

Capello nodded. His lips were stained blood red from the Kool-Aid.

Sullivan crawled to the edge of the fallen tree. The rain beat on his poncho and he cradled his M-14 under it to keep the wood stock from getting wet and swelling. Night set in. The rain stopped. The bugs came out. Sullivan rubbed fly dope on his face and hands, but the bugs ignored it. Somehow the man-eating insects managed to find a path up the legs of his trousers and under his bush hat. The bugs continued to feast on his body until the cool night air collided with the hot jungle creating a breeze that kept the swarms at bay. Sullivan opened a can of rations. The hash and potatoes and chalky chocolate bar tasted the same. The food in his stomach made him tired.

Suddenly a lightning bolt of primal fear coursed through his body, rousing him. It was a single consonant of noise that didn't belong. Then he heard another. The hunters shattered branches and sniffed the forest for their prey. Then they moved on and repeated the ritual until the sounds grew dim. He mentally marked the path of their intrusion.

Sullivan waited long after his watch was over. Assured the danger had passed, he crawled into their lair and shook Capello's shoulder. He was awake instantly. Sullivan whispered in his ear that death was hiding somewhere nearby. Capello crawled away. Sullivan inhaled the stench of sweat and bug dope that Capello left behind. He thought that he could not rest, but he fell asleep instantly, unaware that his life would soon change forever.

The jungle was still dark when he awoke. He grabbed his rifle and pulled his body through the tangle of bush that concealed him. Capello was nowhere in sight. Sullivan stared intently into the bush, but he could not see his partner until he was just yards away. Capello climbed behind the fallen tree next to Sullivan. He leaned his back against the dead tree stump and took a deep breath before he began to speak.

"They came through here last night," Capello whispered. "I mapped out where they placed the booby traps."

Sullivan looked into the pre-dawn light. Rainwater that had pooled on leaves dripped onto the forest floor. Clouds of bugs cruised, looking for a meal. Sullivan and Capello ate and then checked their gear.

By daylight they had crawled a mile and set up an observation post in a shallow cave just below a clifftop. Far below lay a ravine with a worn dirt trail winding through it. They took turns searching the valley through binoculars. It wasn't long before they saw movement.

Capello handed the binoculars to Sullivan. "Looks like a squad-strength scouting patrol of NVA," Capello said.

Sullivan watched as the patrol emerged slowly from the bush and followed the trail off to the left of their position. After five minutes, the enemy disappeared.

"Routine patrol," Capello whispered. "Probably the same route every day. The boys that paid us a visit last night were most likely from the same unit."

Sullivan adjusted his bush hat to keep the sun out of his eyes. "Might as well get comfortable," he said. "It's going to be a long day."

Early afternoon the sky clouded over and the rain came. Instead of a quick, short-lived deluge, the rain persisted. Capello and Sullivan rarely spoke when they were in the field, and when they did it was furtive and imperative. But in the shelter of the cave and with words muffled by the storm they talked in whispers.

Capello opened a C ration, sampled it and made a face.

"What is it?" Sullivan asked.

"It says 'spaghetti and meatballs,' but I'm not really sure."

Sullivan smiled.

"Someday I'd like to meet the guy who invented this shit," Capello said.

Sullivan said, "You and me both. I'll hold him and you can feed him a spoonful of that spaghetti and let him guess what is."

"Let's do that," Capello said. He was quiet for a moment. Then he said, "There was this place on the eastern end of Long Island called the Casa Loma. Best pasta anywhere on earth. And they had a pizza pie to die for."

Sullivan rested his head against the cave wall and closed his eyes. "Yeah, there was a place that Sheila and I use to go to like that in South Boston. It was way out of our way, driving to Cape Cod, but like you said, the food was to die for."

"Yeah, to die for. What are we doing here, Sulli? And don't give me that crap about fighting for freedom and the American way. The little people here don't give a shit."

Sullivan shook his head. "Doesn't make a difference what the reason is – we're here. Our recruiters lied to us."

Capello let out an audible laugh.

"Like I said, we're here," Sullivan continued. "We fight and die for each other. Any reason beyond that is above our pay grade."

"I'd like to mail this spaghetti and meatball to General West-moreland and ask him what he thinks it is."

They both laughed.

"You know, Sulli, when I get back to the world I'm going back to that Italian restaurant on Long Island. I'll be driving a brand new Pontiac GTO convertible. I haven't decided on the red or black."

"Go with the red," Sullivan said. "Black shows dirt more."

"Yeah, red with a black rag top. And I'm getting the four hundred cubic inch that puts out 366 horses and the optional Muncie 4 speed."

Then Capello went quiet.

"You okay?" Sullivan asked.

Capello shook his head. "I got a bad feeling, Sulli. I don't want to die here or even worse go back home an LBJ special with-out any limbs."

"I won't let it happen," Sullivan said.

"You can't make that a promise," Capello said.

"I just did," Sullivan answered.

———

Sullivan awoke feeling that he hadn't slept at all. But traces of a lingering dream and an empty bottle lying next to his bunk told him that he had. He peeled off the sweat-soaked bed sheets that covered him and sat on the edge of the bed. His mouth was dry with the taste of the previous night's bar snacks, beer and Jackie D. A funky odour of alcohol and sweat filled his nostrils. He stepped into the shower and let the hot water trickle over his body, sobering his flesh.

Sullivan dressed and walked to the main deck and into the duty-free store. A new country deserves a new friend, he thought. So he purchased a bottle of Glenora single malt whisky distilled in Cape Breton and returned to his cabin for a quick introduction.

He then returned to the main deck where breakfast was being served in the restaurant. He grabbed a cup of coffee and a Danish and looked around the room for a seat. He saw Deanna sitting in the corner.

He pulled out a chair across from her. "How'd you sleep?"

She lifted her head from a travel magazine. Her face was bloated and her eyes were dark and puffy. Sullivan noticed the magazine tremble in her hands.

She managed a smile. "It was a long night." Deanna ran her eyes over Sullivan. "And you?"

Sullivan shrugged his shoulders. "Just another night."

Deanna saw the familiar distant look of self-betrayal in his eyes that only another addict could detect.

A voice blared from the loudspeaker, saying that the ship would be docking in one hour.

Deanna's features brightened. "Come on, let's go on deck."

She wrapped herself in a fleece jacket embroidered with a sailing ship purchased from the ship's store and grabbed Sullivan's arm. They walked to the stern of the ship in the lee of the morning breeze chilled by the deep Bay of Fundy waters. Her eyes seemed to sparkle as the sun rose over the Tusket Islands that loomed in the distance.

For a moment there was silence, then Sullivan asked, "Where will you be going?"

"I was up reading travel brochures most of the night. I'll probably wander up the coast along what is called the Evangeline Trail today, and then I'll see."

"I'm going that way before I pick up the highway to Cape Breton. You can tag along for a while if you want."

She considered it and said, "Okay."

They watched as the ship drew closer to land past barren islands and expanses of deserted sand beach. As they approached the port of Yarmouth, seagulls swept from the sky looking for an easy meal.

Sullivan gathered his belongings from his cabin and met Deanna in the main salon. They descended to the car deck and tossed their bags in the back of the Ford.

A border services agent checked identification and asked a few perfunctory questions. He looked at Deanna and then examined Sullivan with a look of disapproval. After a quick perusal of the truck's cargo bed, the agent waved them through. The Ford manoeuvred through the quaint town of Yarmouth and onto the Evangeline Trail.

Deanna read from a travel brochure. "This area inspired Longfellow to write 'Evangeline.' It's a story about two lovers separated when the English expelled the French in the eighteenth century." She looked at Sullivan and giggled. "The customs inspector thought we were together."

Sullivan smiled.

Deanna asked, "Do you have kids?"

His smile crumbled. He nodded his head. "A daughter."

Deanna turned in her seat. "Tell me about her."

Sullivan took a deep breath. "Nothing to tell. Never met her."

Her expression clouded. "I'm sorry. What happened?"

Sullivan gripped the steering wheel. He wished Jackie D was there. "Vietnam."

The Ford slowed as a farm tractor crossed the road.

"I was a prisoner of war for over three years. The Air Force listed me as missing in action. She remarried. When I returned home, her father, a judge, got a restraining order against me. They said I was an unstable influence. I tried to reconcile, but my ex wouldn't talk to me let alone meet. I tried to get visitation rights, but the court nixed that. All my letters to my daughter were returned – hundreds of them. Maybe my ex was right. Maybe they were better off without me."

"You know that's not true," D said.

There was an awkward silence. Quietly Deanna asked, "You really mean you never met her?"

Sullivan shook his head.

"I'm sorry," she whispered.

"Me too."

"Hey, look," Deanna said, clearly seeking a diversion, "an ice cream store. It's not too early. My treat."

Sullivan pulled in. They both ordered hot fudge sundaes, ate them then got back on the road. They spent the next half-hour driving slowly and gazing at the landscape of old farms, quaint churches and glimpses of the ocean beyond.

Deanna suddenly grabbed Sullivan's arm. "Turn here," she begged.

Sullivan wrenched the wheel, and the Ford's tires squealed as they made the turn past a sign announcing a provincial beach.

Deanna bristled. "Can we stop just for a moment?"

Sullivan looked at his watch. "Sure."

He pulled the Ford off the narrow road and they walked over the top of a sand dune. Neither said a word for several minutes. The deserted, wide, sandy beach stretched forever toward a lighthouse perched high on the cliffs beyond.

Sullivan broke the spell. "Melville called it water gazing. It's like looking through a portal into your soul."

Deanna pulled the pink sneakers off her feet and walked toward the waves. She stopped, and it took several paces for Sullivan to catch up to her.

"It's magical," she whispered.

They walked for a couple of minutes.

Finally she stopped and looked at him. "This is where I need to be for a while."

Sullivan nodded.

They walked back to the Ford, and Sullivan dropped off Deanna at a motel not far from the beach. She registered and he helped her with her bags.

"Baby steps," he said.

She hugged him.

"Goodbye, Raindrop."

She held up her hand and watched as Sullivan drove away.

Chapter 5

Deanna's features ebbed from Sullivan's memory somewhere along the windswept Fundy shoreline. As he crossed the causeway that held Cape Breton Island away from the rest of the world, he sensed a change. It was as if he were being absorbed beyond the ink and cotton-fibre pages into a fairytale. The farther he travelled into the seemingly imaginary landscape, the more illusory it became. In his dreams he had visited the Ceilidh Trail that curled through Norman Rockwell villages on their way to the sea.

He followed the road east and then north for hours through foothills and places with names like Whycocomagh, Wagmatcook and Baddeck that defied the stereotype that Cape Breton was all Celtic. Each place and name brought with it a wave of memories. He wanted to reach out and embrace the innocence of the boy that had first visited here so many years before. The image that stared back at him in the Ford's rearview told him he could not.

Sullivan steered the Ford through the village of Cape North, knowing that the town of Dingwall was not far. He gripped the wheel, hoping it hadn't changed, that something of his past still remained that was worthy of remembering. He passed the small grocery store where as a youngster he bought bubble gum and ten-cent candy bars. The road forked and then wandered on toward a panorama of scattered houses, barns and untilled fields of wildflowers.

Sullivan parked the Ford on the street in front of St. Joseph's church. It was as he remembered it. The facade was painted the same shade of white as the rectory next to it, and the doors were finished with a coat of glossy red paint.

Sullivan pressed the rectory's doorbell and summoned a matronly woman who said her name was Maggie. Her nickle-coloured hair was spun in a bun and she was dime thin. Her voice barely registered when she asked him to wait in the parlour while she went to fetch Father O'Malley.

Sullivan's eyes scanned the room where a crucifix and a picture of the pope were fastened to a white plaster wall. The floor was covered with a dark woolen rug that didn't quite cover the wide pine floorboards that hinted at century-old wood. He lifted a photograph from an end table and gazed into the picture.

"That's me and your uncle."

Sullivan was startled by the voice. He turned and was met by a wide smile and blue eyes that danced through a pair of gold wire-rimmed glasses. Father Michael Patrick O'Malley was a diminutive man with wire brush grey hair and fleshy bulldog jowls.

The priest stood next to Sullivan and gazed at the picture of two men posing with a string of trout. Sean Sullivan was a tall man, wiry and well muscled. His full head of wavy hair was silver and peppered with black. His weathered face, with rivulets carved by the elements, seldom revealed his emotion, and his mouth rarely widened in a smile. His hazel eyes stared out at his nephew.

O'Malley's voice sang like an Irish pennywhistle. "We would get up the crack of dawn the opening day of trout season. Then on the way back we'd stop at Timothy Kerr's pub for a pint. It was a fine time, it was."

Sullivan returned the picture to the table.

The priest smiled and examined Sullivan. "It's been a long time, Nick Sullivan. Welcome home, lad," he said patting Sullivan on the back. "Come and sit awhile. You'll be having dinner with me tonight. I told Maggie to fix something special, it being your homecoming. Afterward, I'll take you to your uncle's. I have a spare key that he left with me. It's not right to let a man return home after so many years to an empty house, you see."

The priest peeked over the rims of his bifocals and squinted. "How long has it been now, lad?"

"The last time I was here was when I was eighteen. It was the summer before I was supposed to start college." Sullivan's voice became thin and shredded. "It was the year Richie died."

Father O'Malley watched the muscles in Sullivan's face twitch and his jaw set. O'Malley stood and walked across the room to an oak cabinet and returned with two small glasses and a bottle of Irish whisky. He filled both and handed one glass to Sullivan. The priest took a swallow.

"There wasn't a dry eye in heaven when they dragged Richie's body out of the water," the priest said. "I'll never be forgetting that day, though God knows I've tried."

Sullivan's hand trembled as he emptied the glass with a quick gulp. Father O'Malley eyes narrowed as he passed Sullivan the whisky and watched him refill his glass.

Sullivan took a large swallow and held the glass in both hands. He felt as if he was being dragged toward some dark distant place, and from somewhere deep inside of him there were screams.

"I told him not to go. He wanted to sail out past the breakers into deep water to go fishing. I told him it was too rough."

Sullivan remembered. It had been mid-August. It was the summer that his uncle taught him about the intricacy of wind and sail, of things man-made and not.

A summer hurricane raced north from the Caribbean Sea and danced along the eastern shores of the Maritimes before it began to wither. "The storm might bring big fish into Aspy Bay," Richie had said. They had loaded the dory with cut bait and handlines and pushed off the dock. Richie had lowered the centreboard and reefed the small mainsail, but even inside the breakwater the wind pushed the boat off course. As they approached the inlet, Nick had bailed water that crept through tiny cracks in the hull and washed over the gunwales.

A gust of wind tossed the dory against the tip of the breakwater and Nick leaped ashore to fend off the wooden hull before it tore against the rocks. He looked at the seas building in the bay and begged Richie to turn back. But Richie taunted him and challenged his manhood.

Suddenly, the sail caught a gust of wind and lifted the dory off the breakwater, and the tide carried it out into the bay. Nick leaped from the boulder-strewn jetty and ran along the beach, chasing the dory as winds and currents carried it into the open sea.

He found his uncle at home repairing lobster traps. Nick would never forget the fiery anger that burned in Sean Sullivan's blue eyes – they spoke of betrayal. Nick was two years older than Richie. He should have stopped him.

—

Sullivan gazed into depths of the liquor in his glass. "I remember every boat between Cape North and Neils Harbour went out looking for him. They finally found him off White Point the next morning."

Father O'Malley lowered his eyes and let out a sigh. "That was a long time ago, my son. Don't you go blaming yourself now. It happened when God wasn't looking. Besides, Sean, young Richie and your aunt are together now."

The priest leaned forward. His face was screwed into a question mark. "Is that why you never returned?"

Sullivan didn't answer.

"What a pity," the priest said. "Sean Sullivan blamed only himself, you hear? If there was a hell on earth, he found it especially after his wife died – just three years after Richie. It wasn't until he bought that old derelict of a boat that I saw something positive in him. He seemed content, though not what I would call happy. Sean was planning to sail off to some tropical island. I think, too, he thought in terms of numbered days and of finally going home to his wife and son. I imagine the scow will be yours now."

Maggie materialized to announce dinner and then disappeared into the shadows. The priest cinched the whisky away in its nook and led Sullivan into the dining room.

After dinner, Sullivan followed the priest's car to Sean Sullivan's house. Mantles of clouds were silhouetted against a crescent moon, just enough so that Sullivan could discern images of the old homestead. He parked the Ford behind his uncle's dark blue Chevy pickup. It made his Ford look new in comparison. The heels of Sullivan's shoes crunched on the gravel driveway, which sprouted a field of weeds. In the distance, the silhouette of sand dunes sculpted by the wind spread across the landscape toward the Aspy River.

Sullivan's eyes traced the weathered cedar shingles along the roofline and down the upstairs dormers to the front porch of the two-storey farmhouse, looking for things that were familiar. The lawn was an overgrown meadow of dune grass. Once there had been a flowerbed along the foundation of the house – now nothing but dry earth. A barn that sagged and spilled moonbeams through missing siding stood nearby. The barn had been a rainy day playground during the summers of his youth.

Father O'Malley walked heavily up three steps to the front porch and turned the key in the lock. He fumbled for a light switch while Sullivan stood at the doorstep. The priest took several steps into the room and removed his Donegal tweed cap. He looked beyond the varnished wainscotting of the walls for a moment and then turned his head toward Sullivan.

Sullivan stepped into the living room, leaving the door open. The furniture, two upholstered chairs set on either side of a coffee table and a couch, were worn and dull. The only light in the room came from a plain glass overhead fixture.

Father O'Malley nodded his head in the direction of the door and then pointed to a woodstove set into the fireplace.

"It's cold for June. The place could use a wee bit of heat."

Sullivan drew kindling from a stack of wood on the porch, heaped it into the cast iron stove and set it ablaze.

O'Malley warmed his hands over the hearth. "I had Maggie come by and tidy the place before you arrived."

"Thank you, Father."

"Least I could do. You'll be staying for a while after the funeral?" O'Malley asked.

"Just until the estate is settled. Not long, I expect."

The priest nodded. "Best I be off. I'll be seeing you Saturday at the funeral." He took a step for the door and turned back. "Sean Sullivan was a fine man, he was. And he loved you."

Sullivan listened to the door close and the car drive off. Then there were only ocean sounds. He went to the Ford and gathered his bags. He climbed the stairs opposite the entrance to three small bedrooms and a bath. He pushed open the door to the bedroom he once shared with Richie. The room was bare except for twin beds, a plain pine bureau and a single chair.

He groped in his suitcase for the last bottle of Jackie D he had squirrelled away and crawled into bed. The wind shrieked in eddies around the dormers, and when he closed his eyes he could hear Sean Sullivan's screams the night that Richie died. And if life was fair, he would have been in the boat with Richie that day.

The next morning Sullivan drove to the funeral home and make final arrangements for the funeral. Then he fuelled the Ford and poured two litres of oil into the crankcase for the long drive south to the barrister's office in Sydney.

Sullivan arrived at a modern office building and rode the elevator to the third floor. An attractive young secretary smiled and told him that attorney Boudreau would meet with him shortly. Moments later, Leonard Boudreau greeted him.

He was the same height as Sullivan but was leaner and had short dark hair with greying sideburns. He was dressed in a conservative, dark suit, white shirt and dark blue silk tie.

Sullivan followed him into an office furnished in rich solid woods. He took a seat in a heavy leather chair. Boudreau sat behind a mahogany desk and examined a manila folder. The attorney smiled and looked at Sullivan through a pair of dark-framed glasses.

"Your uncle was a client of my father's when he had his practice in Ingonish. I took over most of his clients and moved his office to Sydney when he retired three years ago. I'm sorry to hear of your uncle's passing. My father sends his sympathy and asked me to tell you that your uncle was well thought of."

"Thank you."

Boudreau sat back in his oxblood leather swivel chair. "Your uncle left a will," he said as he handed a document printed on heavy linen paper to Sullivan. "I'd like to review it with you and encourage you to ask any questions you might have regarding its contents."

Sullivan nodded.

"In brief, Mr. Sullivan, my father has been named the executor of the estate. You have been named sole heir of your uncle's holdings, which are comprised of those real and personal assets detailed in Appendices A and B, and any debt. As for the latter, I know of nothing other than funeral expenses, and of course, estate taxes. As for the assets, I must tell you that the gross value of the estate amounts to some four hundred thousand dollars. However, your inheritance is conditional. Furthermore, a special trust fund was established in the amount of twenty thousand dollars on behalf of a third party."

Sullivan's eyes narrowed. "I beg your pardon?"

Boudreau leafed through the document and straightened in his chair. "Your uncle amended the will six months ago. He met with my father, actually, and filed the amendment with him."

"And?"

"And your inheritance is conditional upon the completion of certain events. Let me be direct. Sean Sullivan has stipulated that your inheritance is subject to the completion of the restoration of a vessel further described herein as a ketch-rigged sailboat of some fifteen metres in length. Of course all restoration expenses will be covered from available cash assets. ”

Sullivan digested the attorney's words in silence. His lips spiraled into a question mark, but he was speechless.

"There's more, Mr. Sullivan. The will stipulates that once the boat's restoration is complete, you must sail the vessel to the Island of St. Christopher, one of the islands in the chain of the Windward Islands."

Sullivan smiled and then laughed aloud. "You've got to be kidding me."

Boudreau leaned forward in his chair. "I'm quite serious, Mr. Sullivan. Actually, the will provides for several contingencies had your uncle actually begun his intended journey but was unable to complete it, that being irrelevant now. Furthermore, it allows you to sail with crew, if you wish, but you must carry one passenger, Dutch Sullivan, a six-month-old, purebred, male German shepherd."

"And the trust fund?"

"For the dog," the attorney replied.

Sullivan lost his smile. "I didn't know my uncle had a sense of humour. I'm afraid this charade can't play out."

"I assure you, as your uncle's attorney, the stipulations are legal and binding. If these conditions are not met within two years of the filing of this will with probate, the estate will be remanded to a charity."

"Well, the charity sounds like a good bet. The island cruise actually sounds nice but not in a boat that doesn't have a restaurant and a bar," Sullivan said. He sighed.

When Boudreau's eyes made contact, they were filled with regret. "Mr. Sullivan, I wish I had something positive to offer you. Unfortunately, the stipulations in the will are binding."

Sullivan nodded.

"For what it's worth, I've printed directions to the yard where the boat is stored and to the kennel that is caring for your uncle's pet. As for the dog, the local SPCA will do their best to find a good home for him, if you so desire."

"That would be best," Sullivan said. He looked at his watch. "Mr. Boudreau, I've taken enough of your time. I want to thank you for honouring your obligation and the trust you have shown regarding my uncle's wishes."

Boudreau took Sullivan's hand. "If you change your mind, please contact me. I truly hope you do, Mr. Sullivan."

Sullivan tossed the will on the seat of the Ford and made a U-turn to pick up the highway out of town. He mused on his day, smiled at his uncle's whimsy and backpedalled to pleasant memories before Richie died.

Suddenly, Sullivan pulled to the side of the road and unfolded the directions Boudreau had given him. An hour later he was back on the road to Dingwall. On the seat next to him, a pair of warm brown eyes watched him. Sullivan glanced at his uncle's German shepherd, Dutch.

"I want you to know why I sprung you from canine prison."

Dutch straightened his ears and tilted his head.

Sullivan said, "Don't go thinking we have something permanent going on here. It's just that, well, I've been there."

Chapter 6

Sullivan filled a bowl with dog food purchased from the kennel and placed it on the front porch. But Dutch ignored it and sat quietly staring into nightfall.

Sullivan put away the groceries he purchased while he was in Sydney. Grabbing a Corona from the ancient Frigidaire that hummed and rattled incessantly, he put a TV dinner in the oven. After waiting the requisite twenty-five minutes, he sat at the kitchen table picking over the uninspiring morsels on his plate.

After dinner Sullivan picked up the receiver of the old rotary dial phone that hung on the kitchen wall and dialed the bar at the Barbecue Pit.

Suzie answered. "Well, if it's not the prodigal son. How's Canada?"

Sullivan said, "The funeral is tomorrow. In the meantime, I've inherited a dog and a derelict boat that I'm supposed to sail to some island in the Lesser Antilles. If that isn't enough, I can't find Corona Light locally up here. On the bright side, the Ford hasn't broken down, although it's keeping an oil refinery working overtime. Is Ma there?"

"Nope. She's gone home for the night. Look, Nick, it's crazy busy. I've got to run. I'll tell everyone you called. We miss ya."

"Me too."

Sullivan gave Suzie his number, hoping for a call later from a familiar voice, and hung up the phone.

The night ebbed. The phone was silent. Loneliness seeped in like a cold draft. Sullivan poured the Glenora whisky he had purchased on the ferry into a water glass and walked out onto the front porch. He took a seat in an old wooden rocker, wondering if it was the same one that he sat in as a boy. Dutch watched him as he took a long swallow from his glass.

"I guess I feel a bit like you," Sullivan said. "We're marooned on an island of circumstance. You're young though, so there's hope. Me, I was washed up a long time ago." He drained the whisky. "I should have died back there with Cappy. You didn't know him. He was a hell of a stand-up guy."

Sullivan let the liquor work. He lingered in the chair, listening to the surf and watching the stars. Later he stumbled upstairs to bed with the bottle in his hand.

Waking to the sounds of crashing surf, Sullivan could feel the warmth of the sunlight as it leaked past the window shades. He opened the shades and sat on the edge of the bed for a moment. There were still a couple of fingers of whisky left in the bottle sitting on the night stand. Sullivan reached over and took a long pull. Then he walked to the bathroom to shower and shave. The bottle came along for company.

Dressed in his only suit, a three-piece charcoal pinstriped ensemble, he arrived at the funeral home. The age-ripened funeral director narrowed his sunken eyes and pressed his lips paper thin as Sullivan entered with Dutch following closely behind. Sullivan explained that his uncle's pet hadn't eaten since his rescue, and that seeing his master might, in some canine way, untangle his despair if not his confusion.

The director closed the door to the room where Sean Sullivan was laid out in a navy blue suit purchased for the occasion. Dutch put his front paws over the edge of the casket and peered inside. He lowered his ears and looked at Nick Sullivan for help.

Sullivan stroked Dutch's head, closed his eyes and plugged in memories: Aspy Bay in summer, still water catching the morning sun, the sounds of wind and rigging, the tug of tackle as fish and bait collided. He could almost taste the aroma lifted from pot and pans and a squeaking oven door of his aunt's kitchen. He recalled laughter, the sounds of his uncle's voice and the feel of a strong hand on his shoulder. His childhood summers on Cape Breton radiated light.

"Thank you," he whispered.

Nick and Dutch Sullivan both took one last glimpse of the one they loved then drove to the church. Dutch watched from the Ford as Sullivan entered St. Joseph's. Sullivan sat in the front pew and looked over his shoulder. The church was nearly full.

Father O'Malley celebrated Mass and offered kind words. He told some humorous stories about his fishing adventures with Sean and about Sullivan's life. Sean Sullivan had come to Cape Breton Island from Connecticut as a young man. He was smitten with the natural beauty of the majestic hills and mystical shores. But it was the people he loved most. And so it was he made Cape Breton his home. There he met his wife, bore a son and buried both.

There were more words at the small cemetery that stood on a wooded knoll that swept toward the sea where Sean Sullivan was laid to rest next to his wife and Richie. His friends took handfuls of earth and tossed it on his casket.

The funeral director announced that friends were invited to the Celtic Pub. Then the cemetery slowly emptied, leaving only the gravediggers. It was Sean Sullivan's own idea to have an Irish send-off at the pub; he had put this last request in his will.

Sullivan's Ford seemed to fit in with the rusted sedans and dented pickups as it rolled to a stop in the gravel parking lot of the Celtic Pub, which was owned by the Kerr family. Sullivan listened for a moment to the tones of fiddles and flutes that seeped from the tavern before he walked inside with Dutch.

Once through the front door, Sullivan seemingly crossed through a portal into the past and arrived in some obscure Celtic hamlet. It was in fact, he later learned, a replica of the Kerrs' great-grandfather's tavern in Coleraine, Ireland. The wood floors were wide and worn smooth. White plaster walls rose four metres to meet old beams. Round tables large enough to seat four in captain's chairs were cloistered in subdued light tinted with blue tobacco smoke. Left of the solid wood front door, whose timbers were lashed with wrought iron straps, was a spar varnished bar with brass foot rails. The bar had been disassembled and shipped from Ireland.

On the other side of the room, music flowed from a fiddle, guitar, double bass, an Irish flute and a mandolin that provided a counterpoint to loud conversation. At the far end of the pub, serving tables stood ready for a buffet-style meal that was being readied in the kitchen.

Father O'Malley saw Sullivan and motioned him over to where he was standing at the bar. Sullivan shook the priest's hand, which was cold from the ice that floated in the amber liquor in his glass. O'Malley ordered a whisky for Sullivan and then raised his voice above the bar noise to introduce him to those within earshot. They nodded and raised their glasses.

"That was a fine service," Sullivan said. "I know my uncle would have appreciated it."

The priest blinked his eyes and forced a smile. "It came from my heart. I'll be missing that man. But now he's home with his wife and boy. With wings he'll be watching us now," he said, lifting his head. He swept his free hand across the room. "Look around you. There was no man here who was more respected. If someone should be needing an extra hand or fell on hard times, there you'd find Sean Sullivan."

The priest had the bartender freshen their drinks and then led Sullivan to an empty table. The tavern's owner brought plates from the serving line and sat with them for a moment before disappearing back into the kitchen. Dutch lay next to Sullivan content with a stew bone.

O'Malley looked down at Dutch. "Sean loved that dog. When they found Sean on the beach, the tide was rising and that young pup was trying to pull him above the high water mark."

O'Malley could read Sullivan's face. "He didn't suffer a moment. God took him right away. Massive coronary. I believe he knew his time was near. He complained about a tightness in his chest and dizziness, but he refused to see a doctor."

Sullivan nodded, tried to think of something appropriate to say, but couldn't. He cut into the roast beef on his plate and put a piece in his mouth.

As Sullivan ate his dinner, the people of Dingwall visited his table to introduce themselves, pat Dutch on the head and relate some special connection they had with his uncle. The afternoon wore on and the alcohol made the music seem more melancholy, and the more pensive it became, the more people drank.

Father O'Malley was the first to leave when his cheeks became rosy and the twinkle in his eye betrayed more than his sparkling Irish personality. Others followed when the open bar closed. The bartender brought a cup of coffee over for Sullivan. He stirred a spoonful of sugar into the cup and when he looked up he saw that he wasn't alone.

"It's been a long time, Nick."

Sullivan lifted his gaze to a woman with hazel eyes and high cheek bones and long, light brown hair."

"Hello, Liz."

"I was hoping you'd remember," she said.

Nick did remember. Liz was a local girl. They had met the summer before Richie died. He remembered how they had held hands, walked the beach at night and shared kisses. When Sullivan returned to the States, they exchanged love letters and photographs that spurred Sullivan's imagination when he was alone. She was only fifteen when they met – two years younger than him. But she matured into a beautiful woman well in advance of her age. He remembered her summer-coloured hair that fell past her shoulders and the way her peaches and cream complexion bronzed in the summer sun and felt hot to the touch. He remembered the night the following summer when they walked around White Point when the tide was low to a deserted niche the surf had carved in the cliffs. They probed with their tongues and explored with their hands. He remembered how their clothes were abandoned in a bed of sand. The surf swallowed cries of pain and then moans of pleasure. In the moonlight, they swam naked and washed away the sand and aftermath of their passion. Later that summer when Richie died, he remembered how she had held him while he cried. He remembered how their passion became distant in the sea of space and time that separated them, until one day it was lost.

He remembered it all again in a sudden rush of memories now that she was close again. Sullivan tried to coerce a smile, but something broke deep inside. He hid his eyes with a wayward glance at the table. When he looked up, he saw her, still sitting across from him.

She said, "We were visiting here at our summer home when we heard the news. We were all saddened when Sean died. He was such a wonderful man."

She read the uneasy look on Sullivan's face. "I ... I wasn't sure if I should have come here or not. I didn't want to intrude on...."

"On old memories," Sullivan said.

"I guess. But I realized that memories, especially goods ones, are forever. They will always be locked up in a safe place where you can visit them." Her face lit with a smile.

Sullivan's mouth spread into a smile too. "You're doing it again."

"What?"

His voice was soft. "Remember how we always knew what the other was thinking even when we tried to hide it? If one of us was sad, the other cried."

"I remember. I said you were contagious."

They laughed.

She said, "We shared a wonderful time in our lives."

Her eyes sparkled and ignited feelings he had long forgotten.

"I thought of you, Nick, after you left that summer. I learned that you married, and ... and I heard about Vietnam. I cried for you when I heard that you were missing. I went off to college where I met my husband, Charles, a law student. We moved to Ottawa and had three children. The youngest starts college next year."

She reached over and placed her hand on Sullivan's. "Life's been good to me, Nick. From time to time my parents would tell me news they heard about you. You know how Island folk gossip. I'm sorry about some of the difficulties you've had."

"Well, Island gossip aside, it's not the life I wanted, but you play the cards you're dealt."

She took her hand away and he felt hollow. She read the lie in Sullivan's eyes and then looked at her watch. "I've got to go. We're going back to Ottawa day after tomorrow."

"Have a safe trip. And Liz," Sullivan hesitated. "Thanks for taking me to that place where those kind memories are locked up. I'll visit there from time to time."

"Me too, Nick," she whispered.

He stood up and offered his hand. She stepped toward him and embraced him. He buried his head in her long hair, still summer coloured, and for a moment he stepped back to a time filled with promise. Then she was gone.

It was the cry of the gulls and the narcotic sound of the surf that Sullivan loved most about mornings on Cape Breton.

He sat on the front porch. The sun was warm on his face. He had finished what he had come for. He was running short on funds, and he felt alone here with so many ghosts.

Dutch's bark forewarned Sullivan of the approach of a Mercedes sedan. He turned in his chair and watched as the sun bounced off the polished chrome and shiny silver paint of the big sedan that looked every bit as new as the day it left Stuttgart, probably twenty years before. A trail of dust lingered as the big sedan rolled to a stop. The door swung open and a pair of polished black oxfords and light charcoal suit pants appeared. Then the whole being emerged, dressed in a white short-sleeved dress shirt, black bow tie and clutching a cane. The figure walked toward the porch with a gait unexpected for a man who appeared to be eighty, at least. His thinning hair was brushed back and white as mountain snow. His jaw was set and his eyes were skewed in an unwavering gaze.

Sullivan involuntarily stepped back as the figure stood before him. He looked a bit like a late Spencer Tracy, Sullivan thought. The man thrust his hand at Sullivan and pressed Sullivan's fingers in a vice.

"Clarence Boudreau," the man said in resonant baritone.

Sullivan nodded his head.

Boudreau pointed his cane at the door of the house and raised his eyebrows.

"Oh, I'm sorry. Please come in," Sullivan said.

Boudreau followed Sullivan inside and stabbed his cane in the direction of a chair. Sullivan sat down while Boudreau paced.

"May I offer you a cup of coffee, I just brewed—"

"What I have to say won't take but a minute," Boudreau snapped. "I understand that you spoke with my son the other day. He told me that you were indifferent. Let me get to the point. Sean Sullivan was my client. He was also my friend. Sean's last wish was to have you fulfill a dream he had. I came here today to urge you to reconsider your position regarding the fulfillment of the conditions requisite to the inheritance of your uncle's estate."

Sullivan stood. "Mr. Boudreau, the fact is that I have accomplished what I came here for, and that was to bury my uncle. I'm short on funds, and quite frankly want to return to Virginia. So if you don't mind—"

"I have a resolve to the money issue, if that is your concern. I believe it would not be a breach of the conditions of the will to provide you with, let's call it, progress payments. As you progress toward the fulfillment of these conditions, I'll see to it that payments commensurate with your progress are made. Furthermore, I don't see why some of the more difficult work regarding the restoration of your uncle's boat, which may be beyond your capability, can't be contracted out."

Sullivan shook his head. "I'm sorry—"

Boudreau tapped the tip of his cane on the floor. "Mr. Sullivan. You certainly fall short of the man your uncle had so much faith in."

Sullivan folded his arms. His lips were zipped tight as he stared down Boudreau.

Boudreau wasn't intimidated. He reached into his pocket, and his hand emerged with a business envelope. He tossed it to Sullivan. "Open it," he said.

Sullivan lifted the envelope flap and stared at a stack of hundred-dollar bills.

"There's a thousand dollars in that envelope, Mr. Sullivan. Consider it the first progress payment. All you have to do is stay here another week."

Sullivan threw up his hands. "Okay, Mr. Boudreau, one week. That's all I'll promise."

Boudreau raised his chin. "Very well, Mr. Sullivan. I'll see myself out."

Boudreau began to leave but stopped and turned around. "By the way, there is no stipulation regarding your uncle's personal affects. Therefore, they belong to you," he said swinging his cane around the room. "This place could use with a bit of tidying up."

Sullivan stood in the doorway and watched the Mercedes disappear in a cloud of dust.

He looked at his watch. It wasn't yet nine o'clock. He made a list, hustled Dutch into the Ford and drove to town. An hour later, he finished unloading a week's groceries, Glenora, beer and an assortment of cleaning supplies.

Swinging a broom, then a mop, he began downstairs and worked his way up toward the attic, filling two trash barrels with old magazines, stale food and tattered work clothes. He discovered that Sean Sullivan was a frugal man. The good clothes he bundled for the needy of St. Joseph's.

It was mid-afternoon when he walked the stairs to the attic. He pushed open the door and was battered by a wave of heat. The beams of the attic rose to a peak in the roof that was high enough so that Sullivan could stand. Light streamed through two windows, one at each end of the room, which edified boxes and ghostly protrusions covered in yellowed bedsheets. After some effort, he managed to open both windows and stood by one for a moment to mop the sweat from his face with the hem of his T-shirt.

Sullivan began to work his way across the room through broken chairs and past a lampstand, fishing gear and an old hunting rifle propped in the corner. When he reached several cardboard boxes, he lifted the lid of one and took away his hand covered in grime. It was filled with woman's clothes and the next box was crammed with old toys.

In the corner was a streamer trunk. Sullivan rattled the worn clasp and pushed the top over on its hinges. The contents were neatly packed. Sullivan lifted a bundle of envelopes tied with a string. He read through several love letters between his aunt and uncle before they were married. Underneath was a photograph album with pictures of his aunt and Richie as a baby. He turned pages that chronicled a man's life until he came to a picture that stopped him.

It was the summer he first came with his parents to Cape Breton. He remembered the picture. The Sullivan clan was enjoying a cookout of lobsters and clams. Travelling the seemingly endless stretches of highways and a ferry crossing was a great quest. But it did not compare with the adventures of exploring the Aspy River or getting caught offshore in a sudden thunderstorm when his father and uncle took Richie and him along to pull traps.

He and Richie had returned from a day of sailing the dory when he overheard the whispers between the two brothers. He heard the words spelling out the deadly disease that would take his father away from him.

—

Sullivan closed the photo album realizing that he was the only one in the picture left alive. In the bottom of the trunk there was an old revolver and a box of ammunition. Sullivan wondered if there were nights when his uncle climbed the stairs to the attic to turn the pages of the photo album, to turnover memories. He wondered if his uncle also heard whispers from Jackie D's friends in the night.

Sullivan finished his work in the attic. Dutch followed him as he walked to the barn. The hasp on the two large doors was secured with bailing wire. He and Richie referred to the dilapidated structure filled with lobster pots as their clubhouse. They would go there to hang out, smoke cigarettes and talk about girls.

He pushed opened the door. Light seeped in from a hundred breaches in the old wood. Barn smells still lingered, but now it was empty except for an assortment of tools, an old aluminum canoe, a handful of lobster traps and nesting birds. Sullivan ran his hand over the old canoe and remembered when he paddled it down the Aspy River, exploring the shoreline and tossing a fly line for trout.

Sullivan's exploration of the barn was interrupted as Dutch sniffed the air and ran from the barn to bark a warning. Through the barn's open doors, Sullivan could see a man standing on the porch of the house. Dutch ran over and licked the man's hand. The man noticed Sullivan walking toward the house and raised a hand. The other hand cradled a cardboard box. He was of average height with coal black hair tied back in a short ponytail. As Sullivan moved closer he could see the man's bronze complexion and agate eyes. He had the rugged build of a man who used his muscles to make a living.

The man nodded. "John Sylliboy," he said. "I stay in the house just on the other side of the river," he said, nodding toward a distant speck of shoreline that was home to a single storey white structure. "Came over in the skiff. The wife fixed a pot of seafood chowder and an apple cake for you."

"Nick Sullivan. Nice to meet you. I was just finishing some chores." Sullivan held the screen door open. "Come on in. I could use a cold one. How about you?"

Sylliboy nodded and took a chair at the kitchen table while Sullivan washed his hands at the sink, put away the chowder and pulled two beers from the Frigidaire.

Sylliboy took a long pull from the bottle. "Sorry I missed the funeral. I was out fishing. The wife radioed me that Sean passed. She said that his nephew was in town and staying in the house. Sean and I go way back. He fished with me just last fall to get some extra money for a new diesel for that rag boat of his. Damn shame he'll never get to see it sail."

"A fact that Clarence Boudreau and his son keep reminding me of," Sullivan said.

"Ahh, that old coot. His bark is worse than his bite. What's he on about?"

"He wants me to finish restoring my uncle's ketch and sail off somewhere."

Sylliboy shrugged his shoulders and took another gulp from the bottle. The throbbing engine of a fishing boat echoed across the bay as it headed out to open water.

Sullivan looked at the man across the table. "Sylliboy. Is your family from the Island?"

Sylliboy laughed. "Mi'kmaq. We'd been fishing these waters for thousands of years before you bagpipers and potato farmers got lost and ran aground here."

Sullivan smiled.

Sylliboy finished his beer with another marathon swallow.

"Stay for another?" Sullivan asked.

"No thanks. Got to get back. Just on a quick turnaround. Lots to do. If you need anything, you can find me down at the boat. The *Aspy Lady* is her name."

Sullivan walked Sylliboy to the door and thanked him and his wife for thinking of him. A few minutes later he could hear the faint sound of an outboard motor.

Sullivan took a shower. When he finished, he put a roast in the oven and a twelve pack of pale ale on ice. He was just starting on the first one when the phone rang.

"How's my boy?"

Sullivan's face lit up. "Hi, Ma. How are things back at the ranch?"

"You're not missing a thing, dear. I had Joe check on your floating palace, and I went through your mail like you asked," Ma Puglise said.

"And?"

"And that waterlogged derelict you call home is still above water, but a zoning enforcement officer stopped by and asked me if I knew who owned it. I told him he should check with the tax assessor's office."

"And it's not on the tax books," Sullivan said.

"I know that, dear. As for the mail, I sorted it into two categories, junk and more junk."

"That sounds about right," Sullivan said. "How are you feeling, Ma?"

"Very tired. I keep on thinking about the house I bought in Florida for retirement."

"Maybe it's time to turn the keys over to Rocco and Joe?"

"Or sell it," Ma said. "I'll think on it. Suzie's going on break so I've got to fill in. You'll call me soon, won't you?"

"I will, Ma."

Sullivan felt the lines that tethered him to Virginia unravel a bit. Little Creek held the net contents of his life – a place with walls and a roof and people that helped keep his demons at bay. He poured a whisky, threw it back and washed it down with a pull of ale.

Chapter 7

Sullivan wiped the remnants of a soft-boiled egg from his plate with a piece of wheat toast. From his table at the window of the small café, he watched the fleet of longliners, draggers and lobster boats set out from Lochinver Harbour for Cape North and the fishing banks beyond.

He turned his gaze to the sailboat suspended on jack stands above the gravel parking lot located next to the ship's store and marine repair shop that shared the harbour complex with the café. Up close the ketch looked forbidding. The hull had been sanded to the dull bare oak planks scarred with black patches and white caulking. The teak deck, brass fittings and brightwork waited for a patient hand to reveal their beauty. Sullivan had found the boat's cabin littered with tools and boxes of supplies layered in dust. But from the window of the café, the imperfections were absent and the ketch looked as if it wanted to break its earthbound shackles.

Sullivan paid his bill, crossed the parking lot, and let Dutch out of the front seat of the Ford. Together they took another walk around the ketch, eyeballing it with cavilling glances.

"It's not the fankle it looks," exclaimed a voice with Scottish roots.

Sullivan glanced over his shoulder. Pinwheels of sunlight spun off chromium and stainless steel. He blinked away images of veteran hospital orderlies pushing bodies with severed limbs and truncated lives down polished linoleum hallways. If the wheelchair had been a sleigh, the old man speaking to him might have passed for Santa Claus.

"Name's Calum Baird. I saw you at Sean's funeral." Blue veins rippled on his hands as he stroked Dutch's mane. The man's head was wrapped in a blue baseball cap emblazoned with a Caterpillar equipment logo, and his puffy shopworn face was covered in a storm cloud of bearded white down.

Sullivan stepped forward and grasped a large callused hand. "Nick Sullivan. Sean was my uncle."

Calum nodded. Bushy eyebrows sprung like a bird's nest above a pair of brown eyes that squinted against the summer sky.

"I've been sitting here every day since Sean hauled her out," he said pointing to the ketch. "I spent most of my life walking the decks of wooden boats, so I know a thing or two. The next thing Sean planned to do was epoxy the hull. Then the new engine and shaft were going in. Inside of a month or two she'll be ready for sea trials. Caitlin got the epoxy in the other day. It's sitting up in the store already bought and paid for," he said, pointing a finger at the ship's store.

Sullivan ran his hand over the bare wood.

Calum pulled a pair of telescopic crutches from a pouch attached to the back of his chair and hobbled to the ketch.

"I've been imagining what she'd look like with a shiny dark blue finish on her," Calum said. "That's the colour Sean picked out, hey."

Sullivan let out a deep breath. "You'll have to let me know how it turns out. I'm leaving in about week."

"Och, then we have plenty of time. You'll just be needing a week or two to brush on the epoxy resin, then a primer, some light sanding and two finish coats of paint and she'll be done. Mon, with me helping it won't be taking much time at all. Come on now, I'll take you up to the shop and introduce you."

Before Sullivan could object, Calum shuffled back to his chair, spun it around and pointed it toward a building with a wheelchair ramp and a sign announcing it was the home of Lochinver Marine Supply. Sullivan had to pick up his pace to catch up with Calum and Dutch.

When they entered the shop, Calum bellowed, "Caitlin!"

A voice replied from somewhere beyond a set of stairs. "I'll be a minute, Calum. Get yourself some coffee."

Calum navigated his wheelchair down a narrow isle of shelves filled with fasteners and fittings to the back of the store where a coffee pot was warming. He poured a cup and offered it to Sullivan who waved it off. A marine sideband radio crackled from somewhere behind the counter.

Calum said, "Caitlin passes traffic for the boats in the fleet to the homes of the crew during the day. I've got me one home too, and I talk to the lads at night."

Sullivan nodded and smiled.

Marine supplies of every variety filled the space within the wood clad walls of the store. Cordage of various sizes and types dangled through a hatch in the ceiling, attesting to a second storey similar to the first.

Sullivan's eyes followed the sound of footsteps as they made their way across the floor above and down the stairs. A pair of white sneakers attached to long legs covered in denim materialized into a near perfect form. Sullivan held his breath. At a distance, the woman looked like Sheila: tall, lithe, straight blond hair cut in pageboy style – and freckles. Sullivan thought she might be on the far end of her thirties. Dutch scampered down the isle and she knelt down.

"Dutch, you handsome boy." Dutch licked her face and got a hug in return.

Calum said, "Caitlin, I want you to meet Sean Sullivan's nephew, Nick."

The smile returned. Her eyes were a cobalt blue that sparkled like her smile. "I'm sorry about your uncle. I miss him a lot."

"Nick is here to pick up that epoxy resin Sean ordered. We're going to finish the hull," Calum said.

"Well I didn't say that I was—," Sullivan began.

Calum interrupted. "Nick, why don't you back your truck up to the loading dock? That way you won't have to lug the five gallon pails by hand."

"I'll meet you there," Caitlin said.

Sullivan walked to the parking lot. His breathing quickened. He felt uneasy. He wanted to look into those blue eyes again and see Sheila's smile, her eyes and her form. He wanted a drink. Sullivan backed the Ford to the dock, and Caitlin dropped two pails of resin on the tailgate.

She said, "I have a list of items that I was holding for Sean. Drop by later and I'll make a copy for you."

Sullivan thanked her and took her hand. It was warm and slender and callused. He embraced it and was sorry when he let it go.

Sullivan found some old coveralls in the ketch that he pulled on and an old bed sheet to wrap around Calum who insisted on wielding a brush. Through the remainder of the morning, Sullivan learned how Calum became crippled in a car accident. He listened intently to the story of how Caitlin became a widow when the boom of a sailboat her husband was racing on knocked him overboard, how his body was never found and how she now ran the marine supply business on her own.

By mid-afternoon their work was complete and there was nothing to do until the next day while the resin hardened. They washed up with water from a hose and hand cleaner Sullivan found aboard the ketch.

Calum wouldn't take a cent for his labour but wouldn't refuse an offer of a pint and some of the Celtic Pub's fare. The pub was a second home for the mariners of the area, and when they weren't fishing they could be found there embracing a mug or a tall glass.

The bar was lined with fishermen. An exhaust fan drew the scent of tobacco smoke and bait into a ceiling vent, and open doorways snatched the tepid summer air into a pleasant breeze.

Calum and Sullivan grabbed a table and spent time with a pint and shot while waiting for a bowl of fish chowder. Dutch's attention was focused on a soup bone courtesy of the kitchen staff.

John Sylliboy was hunched over a tall-necked bottle when he saw Nick. He slipped off his bar stool and sat down heavily. Sylliboy's eyes were fleshy and they wandered before they focused. He took a long swallow of beer and wiped the back of his hand across his mouth.

"The Ella Rose was lost sometime yesterday." He drew a breath and pushed out the words. "The entire fleet was out looking for them. They found debris, no sign of Henry and the others. Father O'Malley is out telling their families."

Sylliboy read the question mark in Sullivan's eyes. "They were out setting lines for sword just like the *Aspy Lady*. The seas were calm, heavy fog but no sign of trouble when Henry called his wife on the sideband last night. Nobody heard from him since. Second boat lost in less than a year."

Dutch stood up and walked to the side door with the bone in his mouth. He watched the gulls picking at scraps from the dumpster and decided what he had was better. He went back to Sullivan's table.

Calum shook his head. "I knew those lads. Drowning in a cold sea is a bum way to go."

Sullivan thought about it. The recollection of North Vietnamese prison guards pouring water through your nose until you choked and coughed your lungs out seemed about as bad as he could imagine.

There was a commotion. A man stumbled from the bar, but two others caught him before he hit the ground.

Sylliboy glanced at the ruckus. "Henry's brother. He's got the right."

The sun dimmed and the lights in the pub had grown brighter when Sullivan drove Calum to the modest five-room house on the periphery of Lochinver Harbour that the old man called home. The driveway was a rutted path of gravel and crushed seashells being invaded by tall dune grass. The house was dark, paint bare and weathered grey and had every appearance that it was empty of life. An outbuilding that Calum called his workshop stood next to the house.

Calum invited Sullivan in for a nightcap. Sullivan lifted Calum's wheelchair from the back of the Ford as Calum walked on his crutches up a ramp to an enclosed porch and balanced himself as he turned the doorknob. Dutch nudged in after him.

Inside, in dim light, the home might have once been cozy, but now it just seemed solitary. In the living room, a clock marked time on the fireplace mantel that was home to framed pictures of Calum and his wife. And next to it was a ceramic urn, hand-painted with flowers and doves and a sky backlit with a ray of heavenly hope. The fireplace was blocked in with brick surrounding a wood stove insert.

The room held a couch covered with a red wool throw, and two worn easy chairs surrounded a coffee table that was home to a brass telescope and a bottle of Irish whisky. Hand-embroidered, faded white curtains were drawn tight around the windows as if to keep memories from escaping. The room tasted of burnt wood and of musty furnishings that came with living near the ocean.

Dutch sniffed the periphery of the room.

Calum limped off his crutches and onto an easy chair with lumps and curves moulded by a lifetime of sitting. His drew Sullivan a shot of whisky and then poured one for himself.

Sullivan settled into the other chair. His eyes were drawn to the telescope. "That looks like an antique."

Calum leaned over and lifted the telescope into his hands. "It came down from me grandfather on me mother's side. Story was, someone that owed him money was short on paying up, so he got the telescope in lieu of some of the cash. A fella in town that knows something about antiques said it dates back to the seventeen hundreds."

Calum handed the telescope to Sullivan. "It works mighty fine looking at the night sky and trying to see beyond the curve of the horizon. It makes you think about what's out there waiting for you, makes you want to stick around just to find out. That's the wonder of life, hey." Calum winked.

Sullivan closed one eye and looked through the telescope. There are two ends of a telescope, he thought silently. He placed it back on the table.

While Calum freshened Sullivan's drink, Sullivan lifted a picture from the lamp table next to him. An image of a young private dressed in the brown winter wool uniform of the Canadian infantry smiled back at him.

"You were in the service?" Sullivan asked.

Calum grew quiet. Then he said, "It was taken in Halifax before I left for England. My parents came out to see me off. When I visited them in late forty-four, they barely recognized me." Calum shook his head.

Sullivan asked, "Where did you serve?"

He watched Calum's face change. Something lurking behind his eyes drained the colour from his face. "Normandy. Juno Beach with the Third Infantry, Nova Scotia Highlanders. "

Sullivan nodded.

"Then you know. A third of us were slaughtered before we hit the beach." He paused. His voice grew thin. "I lost me good friend Seamus Muir there. One of those fast-firing German thirty-seven millimetre guns chewed him to spit." He drew a shaky hand across his beard.

Sullivan thought of Capello. The tools of war chewed up more than flesh, he thought. They gnawed through chunks of your life like a meat grinder. The gnawing stopped when your breathing stopped. Until then there was Jackie D. Sullivan's mouth went dry. He gulped the remainder of his drink and Calum poured him another.

Sullivan's head was whirling when he arrived at home, and he could hear faint whispers from a place distant and dark. He sat at the kitchen table and made himself a nightcap. Blinking sleep from his eyes, he saw Capello leaning against the kitchen counter.

Sullivan looked at Capello who nodded his head, and Sullivan nodded back. He took another sip from his glass and leaned back in his chair.

"What's it like where you are?"

Capello smiled.

"Yeah, I thought so."

Sullivan became fixed on a distant thought. "I should be there with you. That woman, Caitlin, reminds me of Shelia, made me think about her all day. The best thing that happened to Sheila was getting rid of me. There's nothing left for me on this side."

Sullivan stared at the linoleum floor. A tear ran down his cheek.

"I can't take any more, Cappy. I can't!"

His voice faded to a trickle. "I can't."

Sullivan staggered up the stairs and into bed where there was a war waiting for him in his dreams.

—

It was early evening when Capello roused Sullivan from a catnap.

"It's NVA , company strength, " Capello said, unable to pull his eyes from the binoculars.

Sullivan didn't need help to see the spectacle below. The road was filled with scores of troops, bicycles draped with supplies, and field artillery towed through the mud by oxen. They watched as the seasoned enemy troops led the column with a half-dozen trucks and a Soviet T-34 tank.

"We can't get any aircraft up in this weather," Sullivan said.

He closed his eyes and listened to the rain shake from the sky. "Let's backtrack their route and scout for a staging area. If we're lucky we can get this over with and get back to base."

The rain stopped at dusk. They descended the ridge and by midnight they had crossed the valley. Searching the area where they observed the scouting party emerge from the bush earlier in the day, they found a worn footpath that they paralleled through the jungle. In the middle of the night they paused by a stream, drank from their canteens and refilled them.

Capello knelt next to Sullivan, exhausted. "Where to now?"

Sullivan folded his map and looked at Capello with bloodshot eyes. "We rest up and wait for dawn."

They found a cluster of dense foliage that hid them well. The morning sun quickly rose in the sky and slowly arced through the afternoon and into the evening. Sullivan stood watch while Capello slept. Once Sullivan dozed off for a moment until his head dropped to his chest, awakening him. Later Capello relieved him.

It was dark when Sullivan awoke suddenly with a gasp. His mind not registering where he was, he blurted out Sheila's name. A hand clamped over his mouth.

"It's okay Sulli," Capello said quietly. He relaxed his grip.

"Sorry." Sullivan tried to rub the remnant of sleep from his eyes. His right eye continued to twitch.

They decided to eat, to build up their strength, then cleaned their weapons, wiped down their ammo and refilled the magazines. They smeared on fresh camo paint, checked the radio and walked out into the moonless night.

They crawled perpendicular to the trail and then paralleled it to where the map showed a slight elevation in the terrain. Finding cover, they sat and waited, looking through the Starlite scope. They didn't wait long. Movement, slow at first, filled the scope. Then the jungle filled with activity. It reminded Capello of a swarming anthill. Sullivan turned away, and with a red penlight, verified target grids from his map. He wrote them in ink on his forearm and then moved closer to Capello so that their bodies touched.

Capello said, "Looks like battalion strength, maybe more. It seems like they are materializing out of nowhere. They probably have tunnels dug from here to Hanoi."

"Let me look," Sullivan said. Capello passed him the Starlite scope. Sullivan squinted through the single lens optic. His lips quivered and he locked his jaw so Capello wouldn't notice.

"I hear armour but can't see it through the canopy. We need to get closer," Sullivan said.

They crawled downhill and then slid on their bellies to the perimeter of the camp, setting up two claymore mines along the way to cover their escape route. Then they stole past sentries and drew even closer.

Capello stared intently through the scope. He grabbed Sullivan's arm, whispering "follow me."

They scampered to the edge of the compound and hid underneath an abandoned truck parked in tall grass. The hood was open and engine parts were scattered about. They pulled off their packs. Gazing into the compound, Sullivan could see that he had been right. Supplies were being unearthed from underground catacombs. Scattered under the jungle canopy and hidden under camouflage nets stood trucks and Soviet T-62 tanks that spewed exhaust and filled the dank air with a thunderous rumble. Trucks, armour and troops on foot and bicycles began to line up in what appeared to be three different convoys that would eventually leave in different directions.

Sullivan grabbed Capello's collar and pulled him close. "I'm going to call it in," he said.

He crawled to the flattened rear tires of the truck and extended the radio antenna away from the metal frame. He twisted a tiny microphone into his ear.

"Hornet, Covey One."

There was an immediate reply.

"Covey One. Hornet. Go."

Sullivan grasped the radio in both his shaking hands. "Hornet, need fast movers on coordinates Romeo Charlie 375990 slash

Mike Hotel 177326. Target battalion-strength NVA, tanks, field artillery. How copy?"

"Have you five square, Covey One. Stand by."

He waited, stared at his watch and then at the radio. A hand pulled him back underneath the truck. Capello motioned that they were not alone. Feet walked past. Words were exchanged. More feet passed and then it was quiet. The radio crackled static in his ear. He rolled to the edge of the truck again and extended the antenna.

"Hornet, Covey One, say again."

Sullivan screwed the earphone more tightly into his ear and plugged his other ear with his index finger. The sound of engines grew louder.

"Covey One, Hornet. Sortie approved. Verify your target grids and your position."

Sullivan repeated the target coordinates. Hornet confirmed that the ETA for the air strike would be thirty minutes and recommended that they clear the area and arrange for an extraction point. The radio hissed and Sullivan shut it down.

Sullivan crawled to Capello.

"The Thuds will be on top of us in thirty minutes," he said, referring to the F-105 Thunderbirds. "It's time to get the hell out of here."

Capello lowered the Starlite scope from his right eye and handed it to Sullivan. "We have a problem. They won't have a solid target in thirty minutes."

Sullivan raised himself on his elbows, grabbing the scope and twisting it against his eye. The convoys were leaving. Sullivan buried his brow in his hands.

Sullivan said, "Okay, we can do this." As he spoke he rummaged in his pack for an explosive charge and armed it with a five-minute fuse.

"We split up, find a good shooting position and engage. That will stop the convoy from moving and draw troops from the tunnels. Our guys will catch them in the open, if we keep them busy. We back out of the perimeter in fifteen minutes. There's a clearing on the other side of the ridge. I'll meet up with you there and call in an extraction."

They lightened their packs, leaving only the essentials. Then Sullivan stuffed the explosive charge under the truck's fuel tank and looked at his watch. "I'll see you in fifteen minutes, Cappy."

They crawled from underneath the truck and scanned the darkness. For a moment Sullivan caught Capello's gaze. Capello opened his lips but no words came out. Sullivan forced a smile, turned and was swallowed by the night.

Sullivan moved quickly to the edge of the encampment. He set his pack between the trunk of two trees, attached the Starlite scope to his M-14 and set the cross hairs on a figure standing in front of a platoon-size column of troops. The 172 grain boat-tail bullet loaded at the Lake City Arsenal struck the figure square in the chest, knocking him over as if he had been hit by a bus.

—

Sullivan's eyes were heavy when they opened the next morning. It was the promise to meet Calum at ten that put him in motion, the progression of a hot shower and hot coffee calling a truce with his hangover. Calum was waiting for him with a thermos of coffee and box of muffins. The glucose and caffeine coursed through his body and helped level the playing field.

Three hours later, Sullivan grabbed two beers from a Styrofoam cooler and sat with Calum in the shade of the boat with Dutch while they waited for a coat of primer to dry on the hull.

Calum pulled off his cap and blinked at a sky filled with billowing knots of clouds. "Where will you sail her when we're done?" Calum asked.

Sullivan shrugged his shoulders. "Don't know if it will ever get in the water."

Dutch took a drink of water from a metal bowl and watched a car drive to the dock.

Calum shook his head. "That's not right. Sean, why he was going to sail right down the coast to Key West. He told me so."

"So, he was going to sail solo?"

"No, one of the young lads that works for a sailmaker in Halifax was going to tag along as far as Virginia and maybe go the whole distance if Sean couldn't find new crew."

Calum shifted in his chair and looked toward a distant spot on the horizon as if he was going there. "And then he was going to Cuba, the Bahamas and someplace called St. Christopher and Nevis. He promised he would call me on the sideband every night. He would've, you know."

Sullivan smiled, nodded his head and looked out at the same horizon Calum was watching. He couldn't see prospects past the breakwater. Then Sullivan looked toward the ship's store where he could see Caitlin watching from a window. Her gaze remained focused somewhere Sullivan could not see. Sullivan looked away when she discovered him staring, and when his gaze returned to the spot, she had disappeared.

Sullivan stood up and touched the hull with his finger. The primer was dry. Another three hours and a dozen empty beer bottles later, the first coat of cobalt blue paint shimmered in the sunlight.

Sullivan stood back and dabbed sweat from his brow with the hem of his T-shirt.

"Some sailor is going to fall in love with this lass when we finish with her," Calum said.

Sullivan thought so too. He had forgotten what pride felt like. The kind of pride he felt when he had a silver star pinned to his uniform and later the wings of a pilot. That was before Jackie D and his friends came to stay. They started out as acquaintances. He could control them at first, hide them from the flight surgeons and the instructor pilots. But later they became extended family, characters in the war movie that played in his head.

His military career had ended one day when he took an unscheduled flight in an F-4 out of Langley and flew over Sheila's house at treetop level. It had happened when a letter he had sent to his daughter, Jessica, was returned just as a hundred before it had been. He wanted her to know that he existed and that he loved her. The Air Force couldn't court-martial a war hero. But what they could do was hospitalize him, drag him through detox and ground him for life. They offered him a desk job or a medical discharge with a monthly disability cheque. He grabbed the cheque.

Sullivan had left the service and wandered around Alaska flying for an oil company and then another company that flew freight to the Arctic until he was fired for reporting to the flight line drunk. Tired of eternal winters, he travelled south along the Atlantic coast until he discovered Little Creek, Virginia.

—

Sullivan dropped Calum off at the Celtic Pub and bankrolled him with the bartender before he returned to the house. He found a gift basket of fruit on the doorstep. He ripped the end the envelope taped to the cellophane wrapper and slid out a card. It was one of those greeting cards without the store bought message. It read, "Nick, meet me tonight at nine where you first told me you loved me. Liz."

Sullivan went to the kitchen. He tossed some leftovers in the oven and then sat at the kitchen table with a bottle of Glenora.

Sullivan read the note again. The place where he uttered those words to his first love visited his thoughts from time to time. It had been the first summer they met. They had held hands and walked the flats that the tide left bare to a notch in the cliffs that held a sand beach. It had been a place that kept secret their kisses and whispers, and it was there that he had chiseled their initials into a rock.

At twenty to nine, Sullivan fed Dutch and then walked over the dunes to the beach. The tide was low. The sea was moonwashed. Spent waves warmed by the Gulf Stream lapped at his bare feet and washed away his footprints.

He could see her silhouette watching for him from the nook that was the sovereign territory of their youth. He sat next to her in the sand. Her hair was tied back in a ponytail.

"I didn't know if you would come," she said.

"I thought you went back to Ottawa."

"I changed my mind. I guess I needed to be alone for awhile."

"What about that terrific life waiting for you there?"

She looked away. Her eyes met the ground. The sand soaked up her voice.

"I meant what I said. Charles has given me a wonderful life, a wonderful home, three beautiful children. But there is something missing, something that I had forgotten about until I saw you the other night." She turned to him and took his hand in both of hers. "Don't you remember what we dreamed about?"

Sullivan's eyes grew distant. His mind wandered beyond the alcohol fog and through the haze of a hundred soiled chapters in his life until he came to the right page. He smiled at the revelation. "I remember that you wanted us to join the Peace Corps and change the world. Then later we would live in some obscure place where summer never ended. We'd always wear shorts, and our children would play under palm trees. We would never be rich or poor, just happy."

She squeezed his hand. "Now I live in a world of country club socials where people are a thing you step on to get to the top. But there is no top. Along the way all you find are things: bigger homes, bigger cars, bigger egos. Then one day you wake up and find that there is a hole in your life. You make babies, you make dinner, you make excuses and you wake up the next day and do it all over again. I don't know who I am anymore. Nick, I've forgotten what it's like to be in love, to laugh, to wake up excited about life."

Liz's voice dissolved. She took a deep breath. Her words trickled from her lips. "Nick, I'm thinking about leaving Charles."

Sullivan looked into her eyes. He remembered how strong she was, how hard it was to make her cry. He wiped a tear from her cheek with the back if his hand. She took his hand and kissed it.

"Why did you ask me to come here tonight?" Sullivan asked.

"We loved each other once, Nick. We were best friends. I needed to find out if ... someone could still love me."

Sullivan closed his eyes. He painted a picture of her life full of giggling children, Sunday dinners, Christmas mornings, family things that he dared not dream of but were all he had ever dreamed of when he had married Sheila.

He said, "I live in a houseboat that makes a homeless person's refrigerator crate look good. I drive a derelict truck held together with bailing wire. My extended family lives in a saloon, which is where I spend every night and most afternoons. I've seen a lot of landscape. The paradise we dreamed about when we were teenagers just isn't out there. Charles sounds like a good bet."

Sullivan stood up and walked to the water's edge. The Gulf Stream water lapped at his ankles and pulled at the sand around his feet. Liz walked up behind him. He could feel her breasts against his back. She rested her chin on his shoulders and whispered in his ear.

"I need to find those things out for myself," she said. "I need you to show me."

"I'm not a piece of litmus paper."

"Nick, our lives will be different, better together."

She took his hand and urged him to follow her. He considered it, thought about how wrong it was and thought about how nice it would be.

They walked back to Sullivan's house. He had forgotten what intimacy was. Later, she slipped her legs between his. They talked, slept, gave each other back rubs and made love again.

When the moon was just becoming dim, he drove her to her car. He promised he would be thinking of her and that he would phone her that afternoon. She promised she would be waiting.

Chapter 8

The phone rang early. It was Calum. He said the sky was the colour of printer's ink and that the second coat of paint for the hull would have to wait. Sullivan was awake now, so he told Calum he would meet him for breakfast.

He climbed in the Ford. Dutch leaped in beside him. By the time they arrived in Lochinver Harbour, it had started to drizzle.

"It will be over by evening," Calum said to Sullivan who was on his second cup of coffee. "We'll need to wait a day for things to dry up. It'll give us time to talk to the yard about scheduling the installation of the diesel."

Sullivan nodded. He wasn't thinking about the ketch. He wondered what Liz was doing, what she was thinking.

"Lad, you hear what I'm saying?"

"The motor," Sullivan acknowledged.

Calum squinted then smiled. "You're thoughts are out to sea. Must be a woman."

"Isn't that John Sylliboy's truck?" Sullivan asked, changing the subject.

Calum turned his head and looked out the window. "That it is. He's trying to turn around the *Aspy Lady*. The word at the pub is that he's looking for crew. It seems that one of the young lads who was fishing with him up and quit. When you sail short, you lose a set a hands and eyes. The crew has to work harder, they get tired and mistakes happen."

Sullivan followed Dutch down the concrete quay to visit with Sylliboy while Calum finished breakfast. The *Aspy Lady* was rafted on the inside of two other boats. Brown spots of iron cancer seeped through the bright red hull and black gunwales. White lettering on the bow and stern proclaimed the vessel's christened name.

Sylliboy was on the deck of the twenty-five metre boat, watching over a mechanic who was overhauling a winch motor. Sylliboy was dressed in ragged jeans and a worn T-shirt with stains that would mock a box of Arm & Hammer. His head was adorned with a sweat-stained red bandana. He saw Sullivan and waved.

"I'm going to have to set the market next trip to pay for all this," Sylliboy said, raking his eyes around the boat while wiping his hands with a rag. "First the gen-set needed an overhaul and now the winch motor is on the bum. And the wife wants to know why we can't go to Cuba for vacation next winter."

"I'm sure your luck will turn," Sullivan said.

Sylliboy tossed the rag on the deck. "That's what it's going to take." He looked hard at Sullivan. His brilliant white teeth glistened behind a smile. "You ever do any fishing?"

Sullivan smiled back. "As a boy I pulled traps with my uncle. But not the kind of fishing you're thinking of."

It had been the summer before his father died. He and his father launched a canoe in the Aspy River. His father taught him how to cast a fly line. He made Nick stuff the butt of the rod up his sleeve to stiffen his wrist and coached him in the art of delivering a tippet so naturally that it looked like a real insect alighting on the water. He talked to Sullivan about the natural order of life, told him how all living creatures had a life cycle, and confessed that his own time was coming to an end. There had been no look of fear on his father's face, and when tears had pooled in Nick's eyes, a stern look told him that such displays of emotion would not be tolerated.

Later that summer, when he helped out on his uncle's lobster boat, he hauled lines until his hands bled raw. The salt water had seared his torn flesh, and the pain had taken his mind away from the nightmare that his father had promised.

—

Sullivan wondered what it would be like to feel the roll of a deck beneath his feet again, to steam beyond the edge of the horizon to a place where there was nothing but the sea and stars.

"I'm looking for crew ," Sylliboy said. "Rookies get three quarters of a cut, but you can make a thousand a week if it's good."

Sylliboy had cast the bait. He watched as his mark sniffed it and rolled it over.

"Thanks, John, but I think I'll pass."

The skipper nodded his head and gave a shrug. "Think it over. If you change your mind, let me know," he said, turning his attention back to broken winches and unpaid bills.

Sullivan sealed up the ketch from the threatening sky and saw Calum off. Ten minutes later he pulled the Ford to a stop at his uncle's house. From the porch he watched black clouds that glowered and rumbled in the distance. He lifted the phone and spun the rotary dial. He took a deep breath. It rang. A woman's voice answered.

"Hello, Liz?"

There was a pause, a sense of foreboding and an unfamiliar voice.

"I'm sorry, Mrs. Moran isn't here. May I take a message?"

"No, thank you. I'll call back later. Can you tell me when she will return?"

Again there was a pause. Sullivan's heart raced.

"I'm sorry, but Mrs. Moran has returned to Ottawa."

Sullivan gripped the phone. He whispered, "Thank you" and listened to the dial tone for a moment before lowering the phone to its cradle.

"Litmus paper," he said.

The bottle of single malt he opened the night before was three-quarters full. He pulled it from the shelf, dismissed any thought of a glass and sat on the back porch. He watched the rain fall in sheets. The wind bent the tall dune grass and tossed the ocean against the beach.

Sullivan was a sober drunk. He stumbled, but never fell, and in the morning he could recall the receding night with clarity and introspection. His addiction maintained equilibrium between utility and mitigation, but not today, not when he had been gutted and left to bleed out.

The single malt warmed him and turned his pain to anger. Later, when the bottle fell off the porch railing (he had been lecturing it on the corruption of trust specifically and humanity in general), he wept at the loss. But Sullivan was not a quitter. He discussed the matter with Dutch, who was young and indecisive in such matters; receiving no dissention, they drove to the Celtic Pub.

Sullivan had pride. He didn't falter when he walked up to the bar and occupied a vacant stool. His words weren't slurred. He laughed at the bartender's jokes and told a few of his own. Dutch sought anonymity under an empty table.

Three hours later, when John Sylliboy stopped at the pub on his way home, Sullivan's face was numb and he had to concentrate to coordinate his lips and tongue to produce a coherent word. Sylliboy asked him how things were going.

Sullivan smiled and said "maaaarvelous."

An hour later, before he fell off his stool, he wasn't saying anything.

Sullivan waved off any assistance, picked himself up off the floor, and regained his seat. He shrugged, smiled and ordered another round. Sylliboy looked at the bartender and shook his head.

"Come on, Nick. It's closing time."

Sullivan squinted at the clock, cocked his head and fell off the stool again.

When Sullivan woke up, he was in bed and Sylliboy was sitting in a chair next to him. Dutch looked up over the foot of the bed with his ears down. Sullivan sat up. The smell of vomit flowed from a plastic bucket. His mouth was gritty and dry.

"Pretty bad, huh," Sullivan said.

Sylliboy leaned back in the chair and rubbed his eyes. "Oh, I don't know. I've seen worse. You actually made it out to my truck on your own two feet and you managed to crawl upstairs to your bed. I gave you a bucket. You took care to use it. The bartender said you put down over two hundred in cash on the bar, killed a half-litre of the finest Irish whisky he had, bought the bar a few rounds and left him a nice tip. That was big of you. You do this often?"

Sullivan let his head fall back on the pillow, too embarrassed to answer.

Sylliboy said, "You kind of mumbled the story in bits and pieces. My lips are sealed." He got up from his chair and set his agate eyes on Sullivan. "I'll be on my way. I think you're going to be okay now. You went through the ritual purging," he said, cocking his eyes toward the bucket. "My advice is that you be done with her, brother."

Sullivan put his hand over his forehead and winced. "Thanks," he whispered.

"We take care of each other here."

Sylliboy began to leave, but stopped short of the door. "Oh, a couple of the guys at the pub drove your truck back. And a lady called asking for you. I said you weren't in, but I think that somehow she knew the truth. She said she would call back."

Sullivan propped himself up on his elbow. "What was her name?"

"She didn't say."

—

The next morning Sullivan listened to raindrops waltz on the roof over his bedroom long before he opened his eyes.

Dutch had sat by Sullivan's bedside, keeping vigil through the night. When Sullivan stirred, Dutch rested his head on the edge of the bed and looked into his master's eyes with a wisdom that said stupidity could be forgiven. Dutch tugged on Sullivan's bed sheet, sending a clear message that someone's misery would continue unless immediate steps were taken to allow the due course of nature to occur outside instead of bedside. Sullivan was a responsible drunk. He tended to canine needs, cleaned up the aftermath of his indiscretion and only then ministered to his own necessity – a hot shower, a hot cup of tea and a piece of toast that remained only partially eaten.

The need for the warmth of a caring soul found Sullivan spinning the dial of the old rotary phone.

"Nick," Ma said.

"It's me. You must be looking at your caller ID."

"How are you, dear?"

"Hanging in there, Ma."

Ma Puglise let out a breath of air. The pause in her voice made Sullivan's heart skip a beat.

"I was going to call you later today, but you beat me to it. I've got some good news and some not so good news."

Sullivan held his breath.

"Suzie is in the hospital. She's needs a hysterectomy ... ovarian cancer. Her oncologist is starting chemo. He wants to shrink the tumor before they schedule surgery. The good news is that the prognosis is hopeful."

"How's she taking it?"

"As you might expect," Ma said.

"Life's not fair, Ma. Not fair at all. Why does shit like this happen?"

"It just does, dear. So, things here are busy with Suzie out."

Ma said that a former worker, Ginny, was coming back to work part-time and that last night the twins, Samantha and Sarah, and Gene, all patrons, helped out with the registers.

"Can I do anything to help, Ma?"

"I'm sure that Suzie would like to hear from you."

He wrote down the number of the hospital.

"Oh, I almost forgot. Someone came in the Pit asking about you. He looked and talked like a cop."

"What did you tell him?"

"Not a thing. Anything I should know, Nick?"

"I don't have any secrets from you, Ma – you know that."

"I do, dear. You stay well."

Sullivan took a long pull of eighty-proof from a bottle in the kitchen cabinet, took a moment to find a happy voice and dialed Suzie's number.

"Hey, Suzie," Sullivan said.

"Oh, Nick, it's so good to hear your voice."

"The pleasure is all mine, sweet stuff. Ma said you're a bit under the weather."

"Freaking hurricane. They want to neuter me, Nick." Her voice was heavy with every woman's nightmare.

"Any second opinions?"

"Maybe a partial hysterectomy. I'll never have kids."

"You can adopt me," Sullivan said. "But I'll never be properly potty trained."

"Maybe I can teach you to fetch the morning paper," Suzie said.

They both laughed for a moment.

"Oh, Nick. Why is this happening to me?"

Sullivan cleared the lump in his throat. "I don't know, babe. I want you to think positively."

"Will you be coming back soon, Nick?"

"Soon, babe. Soon."

Sullivan set the phone in its cradle and sucked in air that turned into a tempest of tears. The rain had stopped and the air was raw. He pulled on pants and long sleeves. He walked over the dunes to the beach. The wind picked up the sand and spun it in whirlwinds.

Later, he sat on the porch. He couldn't remember a time in his adult life when the blues didn't play. But it was on the downside of a distilled grain high that he felt misery so unbearable that he wished he could smother it forever.

The doctors at the VA hospital had prescribed medication years before. The drugs might have quieted his demons some, but it didn't banish them. And the pharmaceuticals were expensive and made him lethargic. Booze, in the company of a good crowd, worked much better. But when the doors of the Pit closed for the night and Sullivan was alone, the gloom seeped into his pores, and he could hear Jackie D and friends whisper that letting him survive the war had been God's cruellest mistake.

Sullivan's constitution wasn't ready for hard liquor, but there were still two six-packs of beer in the refrigerator that would do nicely in the interim. He took a six-pack from the fridge, grabbed an opener and walked up the stairs to the attic. He opened the window. The wind rushed in, rattling cobwebs and scattering dust. Sullivan sipped his beer, closed his eyes. The narcotic tempo of the rain mixed with the beer and the odour of things stored away and long forgotten reminded him of a dark day in April.

Sullivan recalled another attic. It had been Easter morning when his father whispered in his mother's ear that it was time. His father had refused the suggestion of an ambulance and had stumbled in his slippers and pajamas to the car. His grandmother, who lived down the street, had come to stay with him. He paced and watched the hands of the clock move slowly. In the afternoon, the phone rang. His grandmother answered the phone, mumbled a few words and hung up. She told him that his father had died and she went to hug him, but he ran away. It had been a bitterly cold day for the middle of April. His father had warned him that a man shouldn't shed tears. He hadn't lived up to his father's expectations. He hid in the attic and had wept in private.

—

Sullivan walked over to the steamer trunk discovered when he was cleaning the attic. He lifted the lid and removed a stack of envelopes tied with a withering yellowed string. He read a few of the love letters between his uncle and aunt. The letters held the private thoughts between two lovers who had charted their hopes and dreams. He tried to recall his own. They were there, ready to taunt him.

Dreams: He remembered how Sheila had written him about finding the perfect little starter home in town and not far from campus. It was a small two-storey with two bedrooms located on a side street canopied with old elms. She hurried to move in before Christmas and to remodel before the baby came – she was due in

February. Sheila sent him pictures of each room and he imagined himself there. Her father agreed to help with the mortgage until Sullivan returned home. He had planned to go to college under the GI bill and get a part-time job.

———

There was a sudden and overwhelming realization that he was imprisoned in a hopeless place.

Sullivan rummaged through the trunk, and his hand touched the cold steel of his uncle's revolver. He studied it. It was a Smith and Wesson .45 A.C.P. Stamped on the black military finish of the barrel were the words "Property of the U.S. Government." He opened the cylinder, spun it like a carousel and snapped it shut with a flick of his wrist. The hammer set with a click. A metallic clack shattered the stillness when he squeezed the trigger on an empty chamber. In the bottom of the trunk he found a plain brown cardboard box of cartridges.

Leaning against the rafters, Sullivan closed his eyes and felt a shiver. In the last several days, events had unearthed what he had spent a lifetime burying. He was alone. His life was anorexic. His only links to the past were pain and guilt. The revolver was clutched in his left hand. He finished the last of the beer with his right.

The more he drank the more he hurt and the more he wanted it to stop. The face of the young boy whose throat Capello slit open floated into focus. He blinked his eyes, but the image kept staring at him. Then others came: Sheila, Capello, Richie and Liz. He summoned them all and they all came. His heart raced. Sweat beaded on his brow.

He wept, but it did not purge the pain. The thought of dying crept from a dark place and into his head. It was spiritual and bright and spoke of healing the hurt.

Redemption was a two-hundred-thirty-grain, full metal-jacketed bullet that slid easily into the chamber of the revolver. Some unseen force moved his fingers and closed the cylinder. He was no longer in control, but he felt at peace. The barrel felt cold against his temple. He could feel the vibration in his skull as he cocked the hammer. The serrated groves of the trigger held his finger secure as he tightened it. Sullivan squeezed his eyes shut so tightly that the flesh on his face twisted into a ball as he anticipated the microsecond of pain that was to follow.

Chapter 9

Dutch's bark brought him back from the dark place where his soul was about to be launched. He blinked his eyes and screwed the barrel harder into his skull. Jackie D's friends were cheering. There was another bark and then a voice.

"Nick. Hey, Nick, you there? Nick, it's raining out here. Nick, if you don't come out here right this minute, I'm going to drown. Nick!"

Sullivan's hand was shaking as he lowered the revolver. He made it safe and placed it deep in a corner of the trunk. He knocked over empty beer bottles when he got up and had to hold onto the railing going down the stairs.

"Niiiiiiick!"

Sullivan held Dutch's collar and stared through the wire mesh of the screen door.

"Raindrop?"

"You've done it to me twice now. Either let me come in or throw me a life preserver."

She was dressed in wet shorts and sneakers and wrapped in her hooded, blue raincoat. Her hair was a sodden mass of blond. There was a pack on her back. She held a guitar case wrapped in plastic bags in one hand and a six pack of Corona Light in the other.

Sullivan introduced her to Dutch and led her to the kitchen. He set a teapot on the stove and went upstairs for a towel. When he returned she had already pulled off her wet shorts and T- shirt and replaced them with a dry pair from her pack.

"What the heck were you doing? I was going down for the third count. It's been raining ever since I crossed the causeway," she said.

Sullivan's body was shaking and he wondered if she noticed. "I was in the attic."

She dabbed her hair with the towel and then shook her blond locks like a wet dog.

Sullivan asked, "How did you find me?"

"You told me your uncle's name was Sean , so I stopped by a visitor's centre with Internet access and found your uncle's address. I tried to call you really late last night. I left a message with some guy."

Sullivan sat across from her at the kitchen table. She had her hands wrapped around a mug of hot tea. Sullivan started on a beer.

She gazed into her teacup for a moment and then looked at Sullivan with her fawn eyes. "Nick, I hope it's alright that I came here. I had no place else to go. And I had things to tell you."

Sullivan raised his eyebrows.

"After you dropped me off, something incredible happened, and I owe it all to you."

Something had happened. Her eyes were clear, she was poised and she was smiling.

"A couple days after you dropped me off, I took a walk. It was early in the morning and I wanted to see the sunrise. It was spectacular! Anyway, I walked to the end of the beach and up to this lighthouse and I found an old trail. I followed it along the cliffs for almost an hour until I came to a gravel road. Then I followed the road and that's when I found it. There it was. This church right in the middle of almost nowhere. Nick, it was incredible!

It was old and painted white, and like really quaint and quiet. Something told me to go inside, and I did and I was all alone."

She took a breath. "Inside there were wide planked floors and old wooden beams. There was a smell of wood and salt air. I sat there for a moment watching the sunlight shine through the stained-glass windows. And then all of sudden, poof, there was this feeling like I was hit by lightning or something, this wonderful feeling."

Her eyes began to well up with tears. "Later this priest came in and we talked for an hour, a whole hour. And there it was, all laid out in front of me, my horrible, putrid, wasted life. He told me that I needed help and then he made some calls. I went to this clinic and got some help for ... uh, you know ... for my problem."

"I'm proud of you, Deanna."

"You can call me D again."

D warmed up leftovers for dinner. Afterward they sat in the living room. D was curled up on the couch next to Dutch and Sullivan was in an easy chair with his hands around a Corona.

"People are a bit old-fashioned here," he said, "and I imagine the two of us living under the same roof, well, people might—"

"Raise some eyebrows," D said with a giggle. "I think that's so cool."

"I have a better idea," Sullivan said

D would become the daughter of a cousin on Sullivan's mother's side, visiting Cape Breton on vacation. He would be Uncle Nick – the title uncle only in respect to their age difference and familiarity. D thought it would be much more theatrical if she was billed as a sultry mistress in the drama, but the rigid expression on Sullivan's face told her otherwise.

Small talk was spent. The evening became quiet. In the shadows of the dimly lit room, D looked like a child curled up in a bundle on the couch. In his alcohol fix, Sullivan imagined his own daughter into existence.

D asked, "Do you believe in dreams, Nick?"

"No," Sullivan said.

"Well I do. I think this place is full of dreams. I felt it when I crossed the bridge to Cape Breton. There are argons from the past here. I can feel them."

Sullivan smiled. "Argons?"

"Yeah, argons. Argon is the only element that doesn't break down." She propped herself up on her elbows. "It's a part of the air we breathe. So a breath that someone exhaled a million years ago is still out there. It might be here right now in this room, waiting to become part of us."

Sullivan considered this for a moment. "Like a ghost?"

"No, but I believe in those too. It's more a living thing, but eternal. What do you believe in, Nick?"

"Not a whole lot."

"Are you afraid of dying?"

"No."

She examined Sullivan. "What's the tattoo on your arm?"

"It's the insignia of my old unit."

"You were in the war?" she asked, sensing a revelation.

"If you mean Vietnam, yes."

"I've seen documentaries."

"It was a lot different being there."

"Did you ever like, kill someone?" she asked in a whisper.

He nodded his head.

"Is that why you drink so much, Nick? Is it because of what happened to you over there?"

Sullivan's eyes blinked and widened, his lips quivered.

D's lips were opened, her eyes looking for answers. He could see her swallow hard.

"It's been a long day," he said. "Come on, grab your gear. I'll show you the spare bedroom."

Sullivan got D settled in and then went to his room and shut the door. He had a high working but not a head spinner like the night before. He closed his eyes and could hear the faint whisper of his demons

"I was almost there, Cappy," Sullivan said. "I've made a decision, buddy. It's time for me to fly away. It's funny, but I feel good. Okay with things. You'll be waiting for me, won't you, Cap? That's what they say, that someone you love will be waiting for you in that bright light. I love you, buddy. I'll be coming soon."

Sullivan had failed at suicide before. Once, when he was in a North Vietnamese prison, one of his interrogators taunted him by fabricating a story that Sheila and his daughter, Jessica, had been killed in an auto accident. He tried to starve himself to death, but they told him that one of his fellow prisoners would be executed for each day that he refused to eat.

There were other attempts, cloaked so well in bravado that he himself did not recognize them. There were times when he took insane risks flying the F-4 and times, too, when on a Saturday night he would get roaring drunk and bury the needle on his motorcycle's speedometer. But this time it would be different. For once in his life he would do something right. He thought about how and when. It made him feel settled and cozy inside. It would be soon and away from prying eyes. Suicide was not a spectator event. Then it came to him. It would be perfect. The warring factions in his brain had finally reached an understanding.

He woke the next morning breathless, his bedsheets soaked in sweat. The house was filled with the aroma of fresh brewed coffee and food mulling on the stove. His Timex said it was seven-thirty.

Sullivan followed soft alto tones and arpeggios into the kitchen. The windows were open, letting the taste of high tide spill in. Sullivan glanced at a radio on the countertop that had a glue-mended chassis. But the music didn't come from diodes and transistors. D sat in a kitchen chair facing the open door. Dutch was sitting at her side, an attentive audience as her fingers glided along the neck of a guitar. She had on the same salmon-coloured shorts as the day before with a white, three-button pullover shirt and leather sandals. Her hair was in a ponytail.

She looked over her shoulder. "I was wondering when you were going to get up," D said.

"I didn't sleep too well," Sullivan said.

"Bad dream?"

"Something like that."

"Where did you learn to play the guitar?" Sullivan asked.

D placed the Martin Bellezza Bianca concert guitar in a velvet-lined hard case and closed the lid. "I've been studying since I was nine. My teacher studied with Segovia."

"You're just full of surprises."

"Keeps them guessing," D said.

Sullivan poured himself a cup of coffee. On the stove, thin cuts of steak were sizzling next to a pan of omelette.

"Where did you get all this stuff?" Sullivan asked.

"I was up to watch the sunrise. Dutch and I walked the beach for a half-hour, and then I borrowed the truck and we went to that little grocery store up the road. You know, they say that breakfast is the most important meal of the day."

D dished toast, steak and omelette onto Sullivan's plate, and they sat across from each other.

Sullivan took a bite of omelette. "Very good. Where did you learn how to cook?"

"In a little town outside of San Diego. My mom had a catering business. She was only nineteen when I was born."

"And your dad?"

"He was a promising attorney who liked to screw his female clients. Mom kicked him out. Last I heard he was chasing ambulances in Escondido."

D smiled. Her eyes danced with mischief. "You know, my mom just turned forty-three. She still turns heads. In fact we entered a daughter and mom beauty contest and won first place a few years ago. I could set you up."

"Not if you love your mom," Sullivan said.

"Come on, you're a handsome guy. And a nice guy too. A good woman could straighten out the rough corners in your life."

Sullivan grew quiet. He sipped his coffee.

D said, "I hit a nerve. Didn't mean to."

The phone rang. D jumped up and answered it. "Hello. No, you have the right number. This is Nick's niece, D. Hold a sec. Uncle Nick, it's Calum."

Sullivan went to the phone. D gave him a wink. The conversation was short.

Sullivan began to clear the dishes from the table. "Calum has been helping me with the ketch."

D's eyes widened. "You've got a boat?"

"Not one in sailing condition. Come on, let's take a drive up the coast, and then we'll stop by at Lochinver Harbour on the way back and I'll introduce you. You can see the ketch then."

They cleaned the kitchen together and then piled into the Ford with Dutch. The sun was pouring through the windshield, and the windows were cranked down, pulling in the fragrance of tidal flats and dune grass.

Sullivan drove all the way up the coast to Meat Cove past paint-worn weathered grey barns and small harbours dotted with boats with a rainbows' assortment of coloured hulls.

D asked Sullivan to stop at a field, next to an old cemetery that bloomed with wildflowers. D gathered a bouquet of wild roses while Sullivan walked among the tombstones. Dutch sniffed the tall grass, hoping to flush a bird or rabbit.

Sullivan knelt next to an old headstone bleached by a century of sunlight and fixed unevenly in the ground by countless winters and frost heaves. There would be no one to visit his grave, he thought.

Sullivan watched D as she laced a wild rose in her hair.

His eyes drifted beyond her and settled on a summer day when he had been released from a North Vietnamese prison.

—

He and thirteen others had been handed over to American dignitaries and shuffled off to an army hospital in Japan. There, doctors and nurses probed them with medical instruments and questions. Over the next few days, they were allowed to phone their families back in the States. An army psychiatrist led Sullivan into a private office when it was his turn. The doctor sat in an armchair directly across from him. The doctor's uniform was limp and his shoes dull. He wore the insignia of a lieutenant colonel on his epaulets.

The doctor asked Sullivan if there was anything he wanted – a cigarette or cup of coffee. Sullivan shook his head. The doctor told him that he had good news and bad news. The good news was that he was going home in two days and that his mother was going to meet him in California when his plane landed. The bad news was that his wife and little girl would not be there. He took Sullivan's hand in his. The doctor's hand had felt soft and fleshy. Sullivan's mouth opened, drawing in deep breaths. His neck and ears had turned red as if he had prickly heat.

"Sometimes bad things happen," the doctor explained. "When you were classified missing and presumed dead, your wife remarried. She thought that it would be best for her and your daughter. I've spoken to her and encouraged her to speak with you. She declined. You've been through a lot, Nick," the doctor said, gripping his hand tighter. "There will be help for you when you get home. It's going to take a while, but you are going to get through this. I promise you."

The doctor had lied. But Sullivan had failed at his share of promises.

Sullivan had been numb when the commercial flight landed at the airport in California. He and the others paraded off the plane in clean uniforms and spit-shined shoes, past generals, politicians, television cameras and a military band. A small crowd of onlookers, mostly military stand-ins, cheered from behind a rope barricade. Sullivan's eyes looked blindly ahead; it was momentum alone that moved him. A college-aged girl with a flower in her straight, long, brunette hair yelled something at him. He didn't hear her over the sounds of the band and the shouting. Spittle struck his face. He turned and looked at her. Purple veins swelled from her throat as she cursed him. Her face was twisted. Her eyes raged with hate. He wiped the spit from his face. It hung on his hand and dried into a silky crust that became a part of him.

—

They got back in the Ford. D bundled the flowers with an elastic band she found in the glove box. The steering wheel gravitated toward Lochinver Harbour, where the parking lot was dotted with the cars of fishermen and café patrons. Miniature ponds from yesterday's rain filled potholes in the gravel. The Ford pulled in next to the ketch. D's jaw unhinged like a child's delight at a birthday surprise. She jumped from the Ford, Dutch at her heels, and walked slowly around the sailboat. Her eyes scanned the boat and charted unseen cerulean waters.

"Nick, oh Nick, it's beautiful! Can I go aboard?" she asked.

"Don't fall," he warned as she climbed a wooden ladder to the cockpit.

Sullivan caught sight of Calum in the doorway of the ship's store, waving him inside.

Sullivan walked up the steps. A bell chimed over the door. Calum had a cardboard box on his lap. He was dressed in paint-stained denim coveralls and a worn blue short-sleeved work shirt.

"I got bored of playing Tarbish," he said, "so I had John Sylliboy gather up the brass fittings from the ketch and bring them over to my workshop."

He opened the flap on the box and handed Sullivan a brass cleat. Sullivan turned it over in his hand. It was as smooth as talc and shined like bullion.

"Calum," he said, "if you burnished these any more, they would put a man's eyes out. I'll be owing you something for this."

"No need for that," Calum said. "But if you'd be needing crew for her first cruise out of the harbour, I'd be honoured."

"You can count on it," Sullivan said.

Calum's mouth turned up wide. "If it's going to be in my lifetime, we'd better get to work. I'll run this down to the boat," he said patting the box, "and introduce myself to your relations."

As Calum opened the door to leave, Dutch squeezed through, anticipating a treat.

Caitlin was leaning over the counter looking at paperwork. She was wearing a powder-blue polo shirt a shade lighter than her jeans. When she looked up, her blue eyes danced in the glow of the overhead fluorescent lights that highlighted her freckles.

Her smile was shy and unrehearsed. Caitlin dropped to her knees when Dutch scampered around the counter.

"I got these just for you, sweetheart," she said, pulling a treat from a box underneath the counter.

"He's going to be a spoiled boy," Sullivan said.

Caitlin stroked Dutch's head. "Your uncle loved him. Dutch gave him great comfort. He would spend his last loonie on some expensive food for Dutch while he ate mac and cheese."

"That was Uncle Sean," Sullivan said.

He wanted to confide that he wished he hadn't abandoned his uncle. Instead he said, "I remember you said you had a list of items that my uncle had ordered."

"Got it right here," Caitlin said.

She walked to filing cabinet, pulled out a manila folder and placed it on the counter. Caitlin read from a two-page list of items that Sean Sullivan had ordered. But Sullivan wasn't listening. She handed him a copy of the list, which he placed in his pants pocket.

"I've been watching your progress on the ketch," Caitlin said. "It's nice that you are letting Calum help. He lost his wife to cancer four years ago. And when he lost his border collie last year, he almost gave up on life." Caitlin lost her smile and lowered her eyes.

Sullivan understood what it meant to give up. He sensed that Caitlin might have waltzed with that spectre too.

Sullivan stepped outside. The feel of Caitlin's handshake lingered. He watched as D entertained Calum with her charm. Then he turned and scanned the harbour. He could see John Sylliboy on the *Aspy Lady*. Sullivan walked to the ketch. D called Dutch and he ran to her side.

D said, "Calum said I could help paint."

"Why don't you go see Caitlin and ask her to fix you up with a brush and disposable coveralls while I talk to John for a minute," Sullivan said.

Calum watched as D walked away and then he turned to Sullivan. Sullivan stood rigid, looking out at the harbour with his back to Calum.

After a moment Calum said, "You're thinking about taking John up on his offer aren't you?"

Sullivan hesitated. "I'll be back in a few minutes."

His legs felt weak, as if he was struggling against a rip tide as he walked down the dock. When he arrived at the *Aspy Lady*, his face glistened with perspiration. John Sylliboy was in the pilothouse. Sullivan called out his name and the skipper waved him aboard. The climb up the steps to the pilothouse seemed like an eternity.

Sylliboy was leaning over a chart table with a pair of dividers in his hand. He smiled when Sullivan came through the door. "I saw you drive in," he said. "People are beginning to believe that your ketch may actually make it into the water."

"Just maybe," Sullivan replied. Then he said, "I've been thinking about your offer. I'd like to crew up with you, if the job is still open."

Sylliboy turned his head and looked out the window of the pilothouse for a long moment. A boat was clearing the breakwater amidst a swarm of gulls. The bell buoy marking the channel rocked in the boat's wake. When Sylliboy looked back, his smile was gone. He looked hard at Sullivan and tapped the dividers on the table.

"What made you change your mind?" Sylliboy asked.

The lie was easy. "I could use the money," Sullivan said.

Sylliboy thought about it and then nodded. "Okay, but I've got some conditions. No booze on board, understand? You're the new Joe so you'll be deck slave to every man on board —when you're not running the galley, that is. You agreeable?"

Sullivan nodded.

"Okay then," Sylliboy said. "Welcome aboard. We're leaving Tuesday, so come see me in the next few days and I'll get you squared away with the boat."

Sullivan shook his hand. "Thanks, John."

Sylliboy's hand felt like a vice. He looked hard into Sullivan's eyes. "Don't let me down."

Sullivan walked down the dock. He felt lightheaded and free. It was done. In a just handful of days, he would slip over the side of the *Aspy Lady* in dark of night. He would pull the cold waters of the Atlantic over him, and, in a few moments after inhaling the brine, the pain would be gone.

Work on the ketch continued through the afternoon. Sullivan found himself laughing at Calum's jokes and D's banter. The deep ocean blue tint of wet paint on the ketch's hull gleamed as the sun tilted toward sunset.

Sullivan dropped Calum off at his house. On the way home D said, "There's a Celtic band playing at the pub tonight. Calum said he wanted to go. I told him we could pick him up, that is assuming you want to go?"

"Sure," Sullivan said.

D looked at Sullivan with an impish grin.

"What's going on?" Sullivan asked.

"Umm, I had a long chat with Caitlin. She's really neat."

"So?"

"So, we talked about girl stuff."

"Why is it that I'm thinking I'm not going to like the rest of this story?"

"Nick, she's a fox and she's available. What's not to like? And I think I saw some chemistry working when I mentioned your name. So I told her I'd meet her at the pub at eight tonight."

Sullivan's lips twisted into a knot. His words were slow and deliberate. "I don't want you getting involved in my personal affairs. Is that understood?"

D dropped her eyes and took in a breath. "I'm sorry, Nick. I didn't mean to upset you. It's just that I know that we're connected somehow, like in a spiritual way, and I want to see some real happiness in your eyes for once."

Sullivan was silent for what seemed like an eternity. When he spoke again his voice had lost its edge and it sounded like he was talking from a different place. "I'm going out on John Sylliboy's boat in a few days. I'll be gone for a while. I need you to take care of Dutch. Can you do that for me?"

Lines formed on D's brow like a line of breakers. "Sure, Nick. When will you be back?"

Sullivan didn't answer.

Chapter 10

The July sun poured through the windows of the Celtic Pub. A sea breeze swept the rafters clean of old tobacco. It was eight o'clock on a Friday night.

A Celtic band from Judique, touring the province for the summer, had just started a set. The pub was overflowing and D looked for a place to sit. Her smile caught the eyes of two fishermen who gave up their table for them and took a seat at the bar.

Calum had decided to stay home. He looked tired and pale when Sullivan saw him off earlier in the afternoon. Dutch came along for the ride and was taking a nap in the Ford.

The band was good. The patrons, mostly couples, listened quietly and applauded loudly. People gave a polite stare at Sullivan and D noticing the difference in their ages. D stared back and giggled.

Sullivan's mind was occupied. There were loose ends that needed to be tied neatly. Sullivan saw D smile and wave. By the time

Sullivan looked around, Caitlin was already pulling up a chair. She let out a nervous puff of air and smiled. Her eyes wandered.

"I wasn't sure that I was coming until the last minute," Caitlin said. "We had a shipment come in that wasn't due until next week."

She looked around. Her faced was flushed. It was probably the first time she had gone out socially since her husband died. She was overdressed in a plaid skirt and ivory blouse that was buttoned high. A simple gold chain with a ruby stone hung around her neck. She didn't wear any makeup – her light freckled complexion was perfect. Sullivan thought her even more beautiful.

He smiled and asked her what she wanted to drink.

Caitlin looked at the drinks on the table and thought for a moment. "A tequila sunrise, please," she said.

Sullivan flagged a waitress. When Caitlin's drink arrived, she finished it in frequent sips.

D told Caitlin how different life was on Cape Breton as compared to California and engaged her in small talk. Somewhere into her second drink, Caitlin revealed snapshots of her life growing up in Montreal. Her voice grew overcast as she talked about attending college in Vancouver and meeting her husband there. He was from Cape Breton and they moved to the Island after they were married during their senior year. Sullivan ordered her another drink.

The band took a break, and D left the table.

Caitlin sipped her drink. Then her eyes settled on Sullivan. "The ketch is really taking shape. The whole village has been asking when she'll be commissioned."

"If Calum has his way, it will be sooner than later," he said.

"I'd love to go for a ride, even if it's just around the harbour."

"Sure," he said. "I'd like that."

Her words took Sullivan by surprise. He felt a tinge of expectancy. But, hope was a curse, like a binge on cheap booze. It gave you a lift but always let you down when it washed off and left you spun dry.

D returned to the table full of smiles. She ran her hands along the sides of her pants and blew out a puff of air. "They're going to let me sing."

A moment later, the band's fiddler announced that Deanna, a relation to the Sullivan clan, was going to sing. D walked to the microphone on the small platform stage at the back of the pub. A band member adjusted a portable spotlight. She looked stunning in designer jeans with pink embroidered long-stemmed roses on the sides and a pink blouse.

D took the microphone and announced she would sing an ancient Irish ballad entitled "Maighread Ni Dhomhnaill" that originated on the Island of Tory. She stood for a moment just looking at her audience. The first golden alto tones of her voice grabbed at heartstrings and never let go. To everyone's amazement she sang the ballad in Gaelic. When she finished, she stood in hushed silence. Someone cleared their throat, another sniffled.

Sullivan swallowed an emotional knot with a gulp of Glenora.

"That was so beautiful," Caitlin whispered.

The applause lasted long after D took her chair again at the table. When the clapping continued, she stood up and curtsied and begged with her hands for the pub's patrons to stop. They did, but eyes watched her long after.

Moments later the bandleader came to the table and asked to speak with her. When she returned, her smile was so wide Sullivan thought that it might hurt.

"I've got a job," D announced. "I'm going to sing and get paid for it."

"I'm proud of you," Sullivan said.

"I owe it all to someone special," D said.

Toward the end of the night, the band lightened the mood with jigs, reels and modern Celtic songs. A space was cleared and the audience was encouraged to dance. Caitlin looked around nervously.

D said, "Okay, Uncle Nick. It's time."

"For?"

D pointed to the dance floor. Sullivan shook his head.

D rolled her eyes. "You're Irish and you can't jig?"

"Only on my father's side," Sullivan said.

"Caitlin, how about some help here," D said, pulling Sullivan forcibly from his chair.

"It's really not hard, Nick," Caitlin said. "I'll show you."

D and Caitlin each took one of Sullivan's hands and walked him clear of the tables.

"Watch my feet," Caitlin said. Sullivan did, and when he tried to imitate her steps he nearly tripped. Caitlin caught him and laughed.

Sullivan smiled at her. "It's nice to see you laugh."

Caitlin looked around nervously. "Where's Deanna?"

"I think she disassociated herself from me," Sullivan said. "What do you say we give it another try?"

They did, and spent the next hour dancing, laughing and finally in one another's arms as the night ended with a slow dance.

D reappeared and motioned to Sullivan. "I'll be waiting in the truck with Dutch," she said.

Sullivan walked Caitlin to her Jeep. She groped in her purse for her car keys and opened the door. "I had a nice time. It was kind of you and Deanna to spend the evening with me."

Nick held the door while she slipped behind the wheel. "You're good company, Caitlin."

"You too, Nick."

Sullivan closed the door of her car and watched her drive off. He was quiet during the drive home.

"So?" D said. "Do I have to drag it out of you? I told you there was chemistry there."

"She is a nice lady," Sullivan said. "But the timing is all wrong."

"What timing?"

Sullivan didn't answer.

The next morning at breakfast, D's excitement about the debut of her musical career was met with distant staccato replies. Sullivan made a phone call, and later, when D was washing the dishes, she watched Sullivan make notes on a scrap of paper. He stuffed the paper in the breast pocket of his shirt and told D that he had to run some errands.

Sullivan drove to Lochinver Harbour and parked the Ford so that Caitlin could not see it from the window of her shop. He knew John Sylliboy would be aboard the *Aspy Lady* making her ready for her trip offshore.

Sullivan found Sylliboy below decks in the crew's quarters. Sullivan gave him a neat salute.

Sylliboy smiled. "Your timing is good, Nick. This is where you are going to start your day at dusk and end it after your watch," he said, pointing through an open doorway toward a stainless steel stove with four burners, a grill and large oven. "The cook's watch starts when he's cleaned up the galley after dinner 'cause he's up early. I suggest you come up with some decent recipes for a crew of five that eat like a group of ten. Life can be pretty miserable for a cook that can't turn out some good chow."

Sullivan nodded and peeked in the oven.

Sylliboy took him on deck and showed him how to bait a long line. "You won't be tending line as much as you'll be hauling frozen bait from the hold and cleaning the deck. Should we have fish on, you'll help with the gaffing, hauling line and staying clear of hooks, thrashing fish and falling overboard. It's hard work, but I think you'll do just fine."

"Who orders the food?" Sullivan asked.

"Normally the cook, but I'll take care of it. I'll drop off a list tonight so you'll have a chance to get a meal plan together."

Sullivan took a deep breath. "Thanks for taking a chance on me," he said.

Sylliboy chuckled. "You won't be thanking me, Nick. You can bet on that."

But he would be thanking him, Sullivan thought, in a way Sylliboy could never imagine.

After he left the *Aspy Lady*, Sullivan and Dutch walked over to the marine repair shop and made arrangements to have a new engine installed in the ketch. It wasn't a matter of tying a knot in a loose end – it was planting a seed of deceit.

Then Sullivan drove up the coast to a lookout with views of the deep ocean waters that spanned the horizon beyond Meat Cove. It was one of the most desolate stretches of coastline on the Island. The sun was bright and his brow glistened with perspiration. The rumble of a trawler's engine making its way into port below reverberated off the walls of the cliffs and harmonized with the sounds of breakers exploding on the rocks.

Sullivan felt compelled to spend the last remaining days in some splendid way, but he could think of nothing splendid to do. It was like the end of a long trip, when all you want to do is end the journey and return home. He had arrangements to make.

Sullivan reasoned that he had an obligation to John Sylliboy – Sullivan's word was his honour. There would be no breach of promise. Sullivan would remain sober, he would discharge his responsibilities and he would take his last breath at the end of the tour. The last night before returning to port would be the moment. Sometime during the dogwatch, when eyes were faltering, he would slip from his berth and make his way to an opening in the railing along the side of the boat. He had seen some heavy chain on the deck of the whose weight would take him quickly into the depths and thwart any instinct for survival. The agony of those final moments troubled him, but it would be brief and modicum in the scheme of things.

Sullivan drove to Ingonish and stopped at a small eatery for lunch. He ordered two burgers, fries and a vanilla shake – the kind made with real ice cream. When he was starving in prison, he would fantasize about a meal, just one, for an entire day. A burger covered with fried onions, peppers and ketchup was one of his favourites. Fried chicken, roast turkey or meat loaf with gravy and mashed potatoes were close behind. He would make sure that he made several of those favourite meals while he was the cook aboard Sylliboy's boat.

After lunch, Sullivan drove to the home of Clarence Boudreau in Dingwall . He saw Boudreau's Mercedes in the driveway and parked next to it. The house and wide veranda were whitewashed and meticulously maintained. The windows had dark green shutters, and the heavy front door had a transom light. A large barn, now a garage, was attached, hinting that Boudreau's home probably belonged to a farm at one time.

The grounds of the two-storey structure were well kept, and green grass flowed to a post fence that separated old pasture land that had been overtaken by hardwood years ago. Rose beds wrapped around the house, and the veranda was festooned with flowerpots spilling over with red geraniums and pink, yellow and white begonias. Sullivan took in the scent of cut grass as he walked to the door.

He hadn't made an appointment. After all, Boudreau had arrived unannounced at his doorstep. Sullivan pressed the door buzzer and waited for what he thought was several minutes before he pressed it again and held it a bit longer. He heard footsteps and saw the doorknob turn. He stepped away from the door as it swung open.

Boudreau peered through the mesh of the inner screen door. He was dressed in a white short-sleeved dress shirt, unbuttoned at the top, and grey dress pants with suspenders. His mouth curled as if he was displaying his dentures in a pre-emptive warning. He looked Sullivan up and down with the disdain of greeting someone harbouring a pestilent disease. Boudreau's steadfast eyes settled on Sullivan's.

"I'm sorry to intrude," Sullivan said.

Boudreau snapped, "No you're not. Otherwise you wouldn't be here."

"Believe me, Mr. Boudreau, I wouldn't be here if it wasn't important, and as you don't have an office, this was the only place I could reach you."

Boudreau closed his eyes as if it would make Sullivan disappear. "Well, you're here. What is it?"

"I need to make out a will," Sullivan said.

"Now, on a Saturday afternoon? I suggest that you call my son and make an appointment with him."

"I called his office," Sullivan said, "and there was a recording saying that he would be in court all next week. And there is some urgency. I'm going to work on John Sylliboy's boat in a few days. I thought it might be a good idea to, well, cover contingencies."

Boudreau sighed. "Come back Monday at nine a.m. sharp with a list of your assets and names and addresses of any beneficiaries." Then Boudreau slammed the door.

D was making dinner when Sullivan returned home. At the dinner table he ate silently. When D asked him if he wanted a beer, Sullivan said, "I've had my last one for a while. I want to shape up for my tour with John."

Did they have Corona Light in heaven, he wondered? Then he asked himself what they had on tap in hell.

After dinner he crossed over the dunes to the beach. It was the first time he'd walked the beach since he had met Liz there. The sun was low in the sky and it painted the water with sparkling hues of gold and crimson. The heat of the day had fled and the sand felt cool on his bare feet. It occurred to him that this would probably be his last walk on this beach. He sat on the sand until the sun wilted and the sky turned tarnished nickel. He said "goodbye" in a shallow voice to the shores he had dreamed of so many times while in Southeast Asia.

Sullivan hadn't had a drink all day and now he was craving a fix. It wouldn't take much, just a six pack to take the edge off, but he knew it was time for a reckoning. He felt edgy and chilled when he reached the house and entered the kitchen.

John Sylliboy and D were sitting at the table. Their eyes swept quickly over Sullivan, dissecting him.

D said, "Uncle Nick, John stopped by with a grocery list for your fishing trip."

"I thought you might like to look it over before I go into Sydney on Monday," Sylliboy said.

Sullivan knew the look. He hoped they didn't see the first signs of withdrawal as beads of perspiration welled up on his brow and upper lip. "I'm a pro at pork and beans, anything else gets iffy."

Sylliboy looked at D and then smiled. "The crew is kicking money into a pool to wager whether or not you'll still be aboard when we return to port in two weeks."

Sullivan choked back his smile for good reason and glanced over the list. "I'd add a serving of ice cream per man per day. It's a good afternoon treat that will cool down a man's body core temperature on a hot day. And get some frozen pizza dough and toppings – pepperoni, anchovies, mozzarella and the like, so the guys can top their own pizza the way they like. Otherwise it looks like you've done this before."

"Then we're finished," Sylliboy said. "Best I head back to the house before my wife forgets who I am. Nice meeting you, D." He held D in the crosshairs of his agate eyes, passing some secret telepathic code to her. Sullivan saw him to the door.

When Sullivan returned to the kitchen D said, "John is nice."

Sullivan said, "Yes he is." He made a pot of coffee as D watched.

D said, "Hey, don't make believe that I don't know what's going on. I've been there when people I know have tried to kick a serious habit. They thought they could do it alone. They couldn't."

Sullivan's ocean blue eyes levelled an iceberg stare. "When you're a prisoner of war, willpower takes on a whole new dimension. You either have it or you die."

D started to speak but stopped and nodded.

Sullivan gave her a smile. "Thanks anyway. Maybe you can give me a hand with some meal ideas. I think John was serious about that pool."

They looked through a cookbook that D found in a kitchen drawer and copied down recipes on a piece of notebook paper. D offered a few menus that her mother used in her catering business. An hour went by, then another. The sweating was more profuse. Sullivan's shirt hung damp on his chest. He went upstairs to take a shower. Later, D could hear him retching in bathroom.

It was after midnight when D went to bed. She stopped at Sullivan's door on the way to her room and cracked it open. Sullivan was shivering. She went to the linen closet in the upstairs hallway and returned to Sullivan's room with an extra blanket. Light from the hallway shed a beam over Sullivan's bed.

"Nick," D whispered. "Are you okay?"

Sullivan turned over. His face was ashen and his eyes were hollow. Dutch was lying on a rug by his bedside watching Sullivan with his ears lowered.

"I'm fine."

"Can I get you something? How about a glass of juice?"

"It's just my stomach. A glass of water with an Alka Seltzer would be nice, thanks."

"I'll get it," D said. She returned a few minutes later and handed a glass to Sullivan. He emptied it slowly.

"Thanks. I'll take it from here," Sullivan said.

The next morning, D remembered hearing Sullivan in the bathroom during the night. She looked in on him. He was motionless in his bed. She opened both windows in his room, purging the iniquity. She left a note on his pillow saying that she was going to church.

When D returned, Sullivan was at the kitchen table holding a cup of tea with both hands. He was dressed in grey sweat pants and a worn T-shirt of the same colour. Sullivan had spiritless eyes and a vacant face that reminded D of an unfinished clay sculpture.

She dropped a bag filled with groceries and the Sunday edition of the Halifax Herald on the kitchen counter and sat across from him.

"Can I get you anything?" she asked.

He shook his head.

"I'll make some toast."

She did and sprinkled cinnamon and sugar over the melting butter. She went upstairs to change into a bathing suit, and when she returned the toast was untouched and Sullivan was sitting in an old slat-built wooden chair on the back porch, looking at the water.

Dutch followed D into the water and they swam in the Gulf Stream warmed surf for almost a half-hour. D sat down next to Sullivan after the swim. She mopped her hair with a towel. Sullivan still wore a plaster pose, and it startled her when he spoke.

"When we were kids, Richie and I would play in the surf all day. We came out looking like prunes."

"Sometimes I think that I'd like to turn into an eight-year-old again," she said.

Sullivan nodded. "Me too."

D said, "It looks like you might be feeling a bit better. Can I get you something? Coffee, tea?"

"Tea, thanks."

She made a cup for herself too, and they sat together talking about what life was like when they were children. He was reliving his life, leaving pages blank where they were stained by some dark memory.

Sullivan helped D make dinner that evening. He ate in disinterested small bites and went up to bed early. That night D listened as Sullivan tossed and turned. He was mumbling the same word again and again in his sleep. The word she thought she heard gave her nightmares.

Chapter 11

The next morning Sullivan was up early. The reflection in the bathroom mirror shocked him. His eyes were puffy and his skin was the colour of dusk. Sullivan walked to the sand dunes and watched the sunrise over the Aspy River on what would be his last day on dry land.

There was still a trace of twilight showing when he drove to Lochinver Harbour and walked down the dock to the *Aspy Lady*. His body was still on the roller coaster ride of withdrawal. He wanted a drink to take the edge off.

Boats had already returned from a night of fishing and were unloading their catch of herring onto conveyors that rained fish into plastic tubs on flatbed trucks.

No one was aboard the Lady. It was low tide so Sullivan had to climb down a ladder on the dock to reach the deck. Dutch waited in the Ford, his head out the window, watching seagulls.

Sullivan walked around the deck, choreographing the steps that would free him. So it's come down to this, Sullivan thought. He could have died in Vietnam, but God let him fester for a lifetime. Now he had to drown the pestilence. The oil-stained waters of the harbour clapped against the concrete pier as if signalling him to follow. Sullivan recoiled at the reflection on the water that watched him.

"Some say it is bad luck."

"What?" Sullivan looked up.

A dark-haired man stared down at him. He was dressed in blue jeans, rubber boots and a tan work shirt with the sleeves rolled up to reveal well-developed arms. The man's face was narrow with a prominent chin and weatherworn vales and knolls that were landscaped with day-old whiskers. Perhaps he was a dozen years or so his junior, Sullivan thought, and a few inches shorter.

The man said, "I was saying that some believe that looking at your reflection in the water is bad luck, that the spirits that live there will drag your soul into the depths."

"Sorry, I guess I was daydreaming," Sullivan said .

The man nodded and then descended the ladder and leaped aboard the *Aspy Lady* like a cat. "My name is Todd Sipu. I'm John Sylliboy's cousin."

"Nick Sullivan."

"I know," Sipu said.

As they shook hands, Sipu's raven eyes looked past Sullivan. But Sullivan felt as if Sipu was looking directly at him, like an eagle that watches prey in its periphery.

"John told me about you," Sipu said. "You're the new cook." He pulled a pipe from his pocket, packed it with tobacco, and struck a match on the boat's railing, cupping the flame in his hand.

"I just stopped by to check on the ketch," Sullivan said, "and thought I'd see if John was aboard his boat."

Sipu sent a plume of smoke into the air and nodded. His eyes focused on nothing and everything. "It's a sign that the fishing will be good."

Sipu pointed his pipe at an osprey that had just landed on the yardarm. "He's been watching us with his wings spread," Sipu said.

Sullivan cupped his hand over his eyes and watched the bird. "I've heard they're supposed to be good hunters."

"They are."

It was Sullivan's turn to nod. "Well, I guess I'll be on my way. I'll see you tomorrow morning."

"Seven o'clock sharp," Sipu said.

Sullivan started to climb back to the dock.

"One more thing," Sipu said. "I have something for you."

Sullivan paused.

Sipu reached in his pocket and pulled out a brown powdery substance in a plastic Ziploc. He handed it to Sullivan. "It's a mixture of American ginseng, dandelion, primrose and milk thistle," Sipu said.

Sullivan turned the object around in his hand.

Sipu said, "Steep it in boiling water and then drink it like tea. It will bring you healing."

Sullivan smiled and slipped it in his pocket. "Thanks."

Again the nod.

Sullivan felt Sipu's eyes following him back to the Ford.

Sullivan pulled into Clarence Boudreau's driveway just before nine o'clock.

Streaks of sunlight bled through the leafy oaks that wrapped the grounds in shade. The grass was still wet from morning dew that left the imprints of his shoes on the blue-stone walkway. Dutch stuck his head out of a crack in the window, his eyes following Sullivan.

Boudreau pulled the heavy oak front door open while the dong of the doorbell was still in the air. "Follow me," he said, and Sullivan did, to a study on the first floor.

Boudreau pointed to a chair in front of an old wooden desk whose massive legs were carved in the shape of a lion's claw. Sullivan looked around while Boudreau pulled a pad of legal-size paper and a pen from the top drawer of the desk. The room was wood panelled. A bookcase, which ran the length of the wall behind Boudreau's desk, was crammed full. Boudreau straightened his bow tie while he made notes on the pad. Sullivan imagined that the old attorney tended his gardens and went to bed in a three-piece suit and white dress shirt buttoned to the top.

"Do you have a list of your assets?" Boudreau asked.

Sullivan handed him a piece of wrinkled paper.

Boudreau looked at the paper and narrowed his eyes. "Anything else?"

"All I have is a houseboat, a pickup and twelve hundred dollars in a savings account."

Boudreau's jaw tightened as he waved the paper. "This certainly doesn't represent a man with ambition and pride. What have you done with your life?"

Sullivan thought of Cappy and his daughter. "I could have done more."

"I'm glad that your uncle isn't here to see this, this failure of character."

Sullivan stared at the floor.

"And what about beneficiaries?"

"On the back," Sullivan said.

"And who is Jessica Manning?"

"My daughter."

Boudreau asked, "So you're divorced?"

"In absentia," Sullivan said. "I was a prisoner of war for more than three years. Missing and presumed dead. My wife was remarried to an attorney. Her father was a judge."

"Yes, I remember hearing about your misfortune during the turmoil in Southeast Asia," Boudreau said.

Sullivan moved to the edge of his chair. "It was a war, sir. Almost sixty thousand of my brothers and sisters were killed there. The word turmoil doesn't cover it."

Boudreau opened his mouth to speak but closed it and just nodded.

"What is your daughter's age?"

"She'll be twenty-five in February."

"No longer in the custody of a parent then," Boudreau observed. "And she lives at this address?"

"I don't know. I was never allowed to visit her. I tried hundreds of times, but my wife got a restraining order."

Boudreau shook his head. "I can understand why. But for the record, on what grounds?" The tone of his voice took Sullivan off guard.

"On the grounds that her father was a judge."

"There must have been a hearing," Boudreau said.

"Yes, there was. My wife had an army of professional witnesses ranging from psychiatrists to social workers. I think the local baker might have even taken the stand. Every one of them swore on the Bible that I was threat to my daughter's well-being. My attorney never called a single witness except me. And when I was cross-examined, I was made out to be a deranged casualty of war, permanently scarred, who could lapse into a psychosis at any moment and go on a killing spree. I think they added that I could never be fully integrated into society."

"I imagine there was evidence to support this?" Boudreau asked.

"None."

"Were there any attempts at reconciliation?"

"I tried calling her when I returned to the States after my release. She got an unlisted number. I did receive a letter from her – it was cordial and apologetic, but she stated in no uncertain terms that she would never reconcile. As for my daughter, my wife basically said that if I had any feelings for her I should stay out of her life. My wife's new husband adopted Jessica, and along with that came rights. It was made clear that my existence would upset the balance of all of their lives and that I'd be selfish if I didn't agree."

Boudreau sat back into his chair and shook his head.

A few questions later, Boudreau said he was done and told Sullivan to return that afternoon to execute the will. Sullivan made one additional request of Boudreau . Sitting in his trunk in Little Creek was a stack of returned letters that Sullivan had tried sending to his daughter. Boudreau promised they would be delivered in the event that the unthinkable would happen.

Sullivan returned to the house. D had left a note saying that she had gone to practise with the band and would be back at five. Sullivan was tired and went to put on water for coffee. Then he remembered the herbs that Todd Sipu had given him. Tossing the powder in the teakettle, Sullivan let it boil for ten minutes and then poured some of the liquid in a cup. It was the colour of cinnamon and it had a taste that was palatable, although not something he would recommend. He mixed some sugar in the potion and drank it down. He put the remainder of the brew in a plastic container that went into the refrigerator. The herbal drink made him sweat almost immediately. He laid down, and when he woke up an hour later drenched in perspiration he felt like the poison of ten thousand Coronas had been washed out of his system.

Boudreau had given Sullivan another thousand in cash in recognition of his progress in meeting the stipulations of his uncle's will. Sullivan would have liked to have spent it all on a binge at the Celtic Pub. Instead he went to a fish market in Ingonish, where he purchased two jumbo lobsters, steamer clams and corn on the cob that came from the Annapolis Valley. On the way home he purchased cut flowers, a Celtic music CD for D and a rubber ball that squeaked for Dutch. And he bought himself a duffel bag to pack his gear for his final journey along with waterproof coveralls, work socks, jeans, rain gear and rubber workboots.

When D arrived home, the kitchen was full of steam from boiling pots that carried the aroma of the tide. It had been this way every Saturday night during the summers of Sullivan's youth on the Island. His uncle had brought home lobster fresh from the traps he had pulled. Nick and Richie dug clams at low tide at the mouth of the Aspy River, and his aunt prepared vegetables from the garden that she planted every spring behind the barn. There had been laughter and celebration and a sense of belonging. And in the kitchen fog that drifted from the boiling pots, the memories clung to him.

"Will wonders never cease."

Sullivan turned to see D in the doorway.

"There's more," Sullivan said. He handed her the CD. "Sorry about the wrapping," he said. The gift was wrapped in newspaper and held together with Scotch tape.

D tore the paper off, examined her gift and looked deeply into Sullivan's eyes. Then she walked over and hugged him. "Just a minute," she said. She left the room and returned a moment later.

She said, "Great minds think alike," and handed him a small decorative blue box.

Sullivan lifted the lid.

"It's Hemingway's The Old Man and the Sea and a book of his short stories," D said. "I thought that you might like something to read when you're out fishing."

D got a hug too. It was hard and needy and long, and when it was over Sullivan looked away.

After dinner, after the pots and pans were scoured and shelved, Sullivan played ball with Dutch until there was no more light. He drank some more of Todd Sipu's herbal tea and went to his room. The evening breeze lifted the window shades and made the curtains dance. He lay in his bed and listened to the surf beat heavily on the shore. Soon, Sullivan thought, he would be a part of it.

The old wind-up alarm with its black steel face and external bell rattled Sullivan from his sleep. The wind howled around the eves and the surf hammered the beach, sending echoes thundering across the bay.

Sullivan lifted the shades on a gun-steel sky. He was chasing the clock. His appetite was lost somewhere in the singular thought that these were his last moments in the old house. He took a moment to pour a cup of coffee and look through an open door at Aspy Bay and the ocean beyond. The view seemed distorted as if he were looking through the wrong end of a telescope.

He went about last minute tasks mechanically. Dutch followed him from the bathroom to the kitchen and upstairs again, where Sullivan went to fetch his duffel bag. Dutch whined and pulled at the hem of Sullivan's jeans.

D drove Sullivan down to Lochinver Harbour and parked next to the docks.

Sullivan tossed an envelope on the dashboard. "There's some cash in there that should keep you and Dutch in groceries for a while."

Sullivan stepped out of the truck with his duffel bag and took a deep breath that the wind tried to take back out of his lungs. The air was warm and transparent. A plastic bottle bounced across the parking lot carried by the invisible gusts of a warm front. He wiped the sweaty palms of his hands down the sides his Levi's. As he walked down the dock, Dutch tugged at his pantleg one final time, begging him to stay. D put a leash on Dutch and followed Sullivan down the dock to the *Aspy Lady*. The boat was tied up broadside to the wharf with a clear shot at the harbour inlet.

Sullivan said, "You two take care of each other." He gave D a hug and then knelt down and gave Dutch one too. D decided to stay to watch Father O'Malley bless the boat.

Sullivan tossed his duffel bag onto the deck of the *Aspy Lady* and climbed down the ladder to the deck. John Sylliboy came out of the wheelhouse, gave D a wave and showed Sullivan where he would be berthing. They re-emerged from the bowels of the boat just as Father O'Malley arrived.

The cleric was dressed in his priestly garb: a black short-sleeved shirt, black trousers and white collar. Sylliboy gave a shout and the crew assembled at the boat's stern. From the edge of the wharf, Father O'Malley read the passage from Matthew that told the story of the storm on the lake and the power of faith. The open pages of the holy book fluttered. The words were wind torn and lost. Afterward, O'Malley sprinkled holy water on the crew and the boat and wished them good fishing and a safe return.

The *Aspy Lady*'s diesel came alive with a roar. D gave Sullivan a final wave and lifted Dutch's paw in a canine salute. She watched with Father O'Malley as the Lady cleared the breakwater and then walked with the priest to the parking lot. Sullivan watched, too, as Lochinver Harbour melted into the horizon. He felt numb and weightless.

John Sylliboy asked his cousin Todd Sipu, the first mate, to introduce Sullivan to the rest of the crew. It didn't take long for Sullivan to learn the theocracy of the boat. John Sylliboy was always addressed as skipper or captain and his second-in-command was referred to as mate or number one.

They found Antonio Perez stowing docking lines in a walk-in locker on deck below the wheelhouse. Saccharine smoke drifted from the ebony briarwood of his pipe.

Antonio was about forty with dark hair and eyes that spoke of his Basque heritage. He wore tan work pants and a blue cotton work shirt that had been fully depreciated. Strong muscles rippled underneath his clothes as he manhandled the line. Antonio had a handsome dimpled face, and when he smiled his perfect white teeth flashed an aura that lit up his space .

Anotonio spoke with an accent that was tonal and crisp like the bells of a church in Seville. He hailed from St. John's. During the winter months, when he wasn't fishing, Antonio would guide hunters into the Newfoundland wilderness in pursuit of moose. In the spring he would earn handsome tips from anglers who tossed flies at hungry salmon. He loved his life and he loved to go after big fish on the *Aspy Lady*.

Sipu led Sullivan along the starboard side of the work deck and up a set of stairs to the bow, which stood stunted and lofty. Gale winds churned the sea into a thousand frothy white peaks that hissed a warning as the boat's bow bulldozed through them. Sullivan held onto the boat's railing as the deck pitched and yawed.

At the bow, a young man with spiked red hair was laying on the deck in the lee of the wind behind a rope locker. His frame was thin and his face narrowed to a pointed chin that was covered with sparse threads of facial hair. He had on a pair of silver-rimmed sunglasses that rested on the fair-skinned, sun burnt nose of his pubescent face. He was dressed in dungarees and a T-shirt with the name of a rock band emblazoned on the front. A pair of empty rubber boots and work socks were strewn next to his bare feet that tapped in rhythm to the music from a CD player that was resting on his stomach. Sipu walked up behind him and lifted the earphones from his head.

"This is young Willie McNeil," Sipu said. "Young Willie here likes rap music and girls more than he likes fishing."

"You got that right," Willie said. "The fishing keeps me and my lady in concert tickets, and it beats working at some fast food restaurant in Sydney. Besides, it's rewarding helping old people around the deck so they don't go tripping and falling in the ocean. It's kind of like being one of them Boy Scouts."

Sipu nodded his head and looked out at the horizon. "Yup, young Willie's spent too much time with that trash music running between his ears. Now everything in between has turned to shit. Every now and then, like now, it ends up dribbling out of his mouth. But we keep him here anyway, one step ahead of the RCMP."

"Funny, real funny," Willie said. "Just wait until we get the fish on. Then we'll see who the real fishermen are."

"Go back to sleep, Willie," Sipu said. "Come on," he said to Sullivan. "I'll take you to meet Paddy."

They traced their way back to the hatch door that led to the crew's quarters and galley below to meet Paddy Gallagher.

At the door, Sipu said in a whisper, "Paddy is going through a tough divorce. He's been—," he paused. "He's been spending too much time at the pub. I'd give him some latitude. He's a big man with a big heart. He just comes across a bit rough around the edges sometimes."

The crew's quarters housed three sets of bunk beds that were tucked against three sides of the bulkheads. Along the starboard bulkhead there was a TV, CD player and a washer and dryer. Through a doorway, immediately forward of the crew's quarters, was the galley. Paddy was asleep in the upper berth on the boat's port side directly across from the galley. Sullivan's berth was directly below Paddy's.

Sipu looked at his watch and said, "Maybe you want to start preparing lunch. Soup and sandwiches would do well on a day like this," he said. "I'll be in the wheelhouse with the skipper if you need me."

He started to leave, but Sullivan stopped him. In a whisper he said," I brewed that remedy you gave me like you told me. I'd be grateful if you could spare some more."

Sipu smiled. He reached into the pocket of his denim coveralls and pulled out a small plastic bag. "Mix it with tea and offer some to Paddy too, when he wakes up."

Sipu went to the bridge, leaving Sullivan alone in the galley. The galley, as with all cabins in the boat, was fitted with a water-tight door. Sullivan had to step over the door's combing to enter the room. A large stainless steel stove complete with a griddle and oven stood against the port bulkhead. An oversized sink with a dishwasher below it was squeezed into a space next to the stove. Cabinets full of dishes and pots were built in over the appliances. Directly across from the stove a refrigerator, freezer chest and a small table were located. A plastic garbage can and stool were tucked under the table. Bags of potatoes, onions, fresh vegetables and bread were piled into any space that remained.

There was a brown paper bag on the table. Sullivan looked inside and pulled out a strawberry-rhubarb pie with a note attached. It read, "Nick – Sorry I didn't see the Lady off this morning. I thought I would save you from worrying about making a dessert on your first night out. I hope the fishing is good. See you when you get back. Caitlin."

Sullivan read the note a second time. He crumpled it into a ball and cocked his arm toward the garbage pail, but something stopped him. He unknotted the paper, smoothed it on the table, folded it and slid it into his pocket.

Sullivan made an inspection of the food in the refrigerator. Then he found a pad of paper in the crew's quarters, prepared a menu for the next two days and taped it to the door. He spent the next half-hour preparing ham sandwiches on Kaiser rolls. A pot of fish chowder had already been prepared and only needed reheating.

After Sullivan put the finishing touches on lunch, he brewed Todd Sipu's herbal tea and leaned against the bulkhead holding a mug in both hands. He braced his feet against the battleship grey deck as the boat pitched and rolled in the heavy seas. Sullivan's eyes shifted as Paddy stirred and wiped sleep from his eyes with a callused hand and ragged fingernails.

"I hope I didn't wake you," Sullivan said.

Paddy sat on the edge of his bunk. His legs, dangling from a pair of blue sweatpants, were connected to size twelve feet that nearly touched the lower bunk. Sullivan thought that Paddy was more brawn than fat, but either way his torso stretched the brown plaid flannel shirt that hung over his waist. Paddy yawned and scratched at the bald spot on his head that sprouted meager stalks of black curly hair.

"No, the engine noise blocks out everything," Paddy said.

Sullivan walked over and offered his hand. It was dwarfed in Paddy's grip. Sullivan smiled. "Nick Sullivan."

"Paddy Gallagher," he replied without an expression.

Paddy nodded toward the galley. "What ya got in there?"

"I just made some herbal tea," Sullivan said. "And there are ham sandwiches and chowder that I can heat up."

"The sandwich and tea," Paddy said.

Sullivan nodded. He brought Paddy a sandwich on a dinner plate and a cup of tea. Paddy sat on the edge of the bed and took large bites out of the sandwich and gulped the tea. Sullivan guessed Paddy hadn't had breakfast and probably hadn't slept much recently either.

When Paddy had finished, Sullivan collected the empty dishes, took them to the galley and put them in the dishwasher. He started a pot of coffee. Then he took a chair from the crew's mess table, leaned it against the bulkhead so it wouldn't pitch over and finished his tea.

Paddy lay down on the olive green wool blanket covering his bunk and stared at the overhead.

Sullivan said, "I'm going up to the bridge. Coffee is ready if you want some."

Paddy didn't answer.

John Sylliboy was sitting in front of the helm in a plush captain's chair. The chair's black vinyl upholstery had several tears exposing its beige foam insides. The wheel was on autopilot and it moved lazily, correcting the boat's course as it was tossed around by the sea. The windshield wipers fought to clear cascades of windswept water that rose from the bow each time it bit into a wave.

Willie stood up from his protected niche on the bow. Sylliboy swung the wheel slightly and Willie was drenched by a wave. He gave Sylliboy a salute with his middle finger and moved off the bow. Sylliboy smiled.

Todd Sipu was sitting at the chart table that was facing the aft bulkhead of the bridge. He was studying a report that he had just torn off the weather fax machine.

Sullivan held on to a stainless steel pipe railing that ran along the circumference of the bridge. "Kind of rough sailing, skipper," Sullivan said.

Sylliboy smiled. "We'll be out of the weather in another twenty-four hours. You'll get used to it, maybe."

Sullivan's stomach pitched and rolled. "I think maybe I'll lay down for a bit, if that's okay."

Sylliboy smiled. "There's Dramamine in the medical locker."

Sullivan went below quickly to find it.

Chapter 12

The *Aspy Lady*'s crew had finished lunch. John Sylliboy was taking a break in his quarters while Antonio and Willie relieved him on the bridge. Sullivan cleaned the galley and then went out on deck for fresh air and to regain his equilibrium.

Paddy was leaning against the bulkhead under the aft bridge wing staring at the boat wake.

"Hi," Sullivan said.

Paddy nodded.

"I don't mean to invade your space," Sullivan said, "but bouncing around below isn't what my stomach needs at the moment."

"Don't matter to me."

"John says we're headed for calmer weather."

"You'll get used to it," Paddy said. "The stern pitches less than the rest of the boat. Just keep your eyes on the horizon and you'll feel better."

"Thanks," Sullivan said.

The *Aspy Lady*'s bow sliced open the waves that the boat's wide stern and propeller wash smoothed into a white carpet of water.

"You married?" Paddy asked.

"Once. Long time ago," Sullivan answered.

"What happened?"

Sullivan told him.

When Sullivan finished Paddy said, "They can be perfect bitches can't they?"

Sullivan shook his head. "I never had a bad thought for my wife. I guess after a while there was enough time and space that it hurt less."

Paddy folded his arms and looked hard at Sullivan. "After the way she screwed you?"

Sullivan nodded.

Paddy blinked his eyes. "I miss my kid. Miss her too."

"Maybe you can work things out?"

"It's complicated," Paddy said.

Sullivan nodded.

He went below and pulled two plump chickens from the refrigerator, cut them in pieces, rolled them in seasoned breadcrumbs and placed them in a broiling pan. He spent the next half-hour peeling spuds, cleaning green beans and preparing a garden salad. The lettuce, cucumbers, tomatoes and radishes had to be used before they wilted.

He was glad to find a stock of rolls – the type that come in an aluminum-lined cardboard cylinder and bake in ten minutes. Gravy was of the variety that was freeze-dried in a foil pouch.

Sullivan ate his dinner hastily in the galley before the crew arrived. The boat continued to pitch and roll. Sullivan had mastered the rhythm and managed to ferry plates of food out to the rectangular table built of heavy, urethane coated, solid wood with a steel base welded to the deck. It could accommodate the entire crew with room to spare. Normally, food would be placed in the centre of the table on slip resistant rubber mats, but the sea was rough. Instead, Sullivan served dinner individually to each of the crew.

Willie and Antonio were the first to finish dinner and relieved Todd Sipu and John Sylliboy on the bridge. Sullivan was in his shirtsleeves scouring the last of the pots and pans when Sylliboy stuck his head through the galley door.

"Nice job," Sylliboy said. "The crew says you're a keeper."

Sullivan smiled. "Those boys know how to eat."

"Wait until we start fishing and they work up an appetite," Sylliboy replied. "When you catch up on things here, come up to the bridge. I want to start your watch early to go over the operation of the electronics."

When he finished in the galley, Sullivan pulled on a sweatshirt and stepped carefully through the crew's quarters and up a stairway into the bridge. The bridge was dark except for the glow of the electronics. Sullivan stood next to Sylliboy, who was nestled in the captain's chair at the helm. They were alone. Through the window that spanned the breadth of the bridge, Sullivan could see waves breaking over the bow, scattering black water and sending it into the twilight.

Sylliboy explained the operation of the Raytheon radar that sent beams out forty-five kilometres searching for ships that plied the same lonely waters. It took some practice learning to adjust the radar to reduce wave scatter and to interpret false signals from a blip on the screen that could kill them. The GPS navigation system was more difficult to operate, but manipulating the sideband radio and bottom recorder came easy.

Sullivan's eyes shifted between the green radar screen and the ocean abyss, watching for the lights of ships. Somewhere in the monotony the radio cracked.

"Whisky, Papa, Tango, one, eight, seven, this is X-ray, Romeo, Sierra, two, six, three, come back *Aspy Lady*."

"Nick, you want to grab that?" Sylliboy asked.

Sullivan lifted the microphone from its cradle on the sideband. "*Aspy Lady*, go."

"Calum here. Nick, that you?"

"In the flesh," Sullivan said.

"Doing your watch, hey. Who's got the helm?"

"The skipper is here making sure I don't do anything that will put us on the bottom."

Calum laughed and then coughed. Although the radio signal was strong, Sullivan thought Calum's voice sounded distant.

"I'm sorry I didn't get to see you off this morning. Feeling kind of tired, I was, so I slept late. Haven't been at the top of the game lately. Anybody on board that wants to pass traffic?"

Sullivan looked at Sylliboy who shook his head. "I guess not, Calum."

"Well then, I'll be signing off to check in with the *Wahoo*. She's out there somewhere with you lads. You want to give me your position and a weather report?"

Sullivan looked at the GPS screen and gave Calum their latitude and longitude. Sylliboy said the seas were two to three metres with nine-second intervals. Sullivan repeated the information to Calum and then signed off.

The feel of the microphone in Sullivan's hand lingered after he replaced it in its cradle. It was an instrument that he once used to call death from the sky. He wiped his hand on his jeans, but the anamnesis of the jungle, burnt flesh and screams were indelible. That was the splendour of death, he thought. It cleansed all the stains from the rifts of the mind.

Sullivan was relieved of his watch at eight, and he returned to the galley. He put a pot of Todd Sipu's herbal tea to brew on the stove while he scrambled a bowl of eggs in preparation for breakfast.

Then he took a shower. The shower was crammed into the head. It was stainless steel, as were the sink and commode. There was a rotating crew's list for the daily maintenance of the head, but each of the crew was responsible for cleaning up each time he used the facility. Sullivan found a spray bottle of disinfectant and a sponge and dutifully put them to use.

When he returned to the crew's quarters most of the men were finishing up a game of cards. Fishing would start tomorrow if the weather improved, and this would be one of the few opportunities to find time to do anything but fish, eat or sleep.

Lights were out at nine. Sullivan stripped down to his underwear and lay in his bunk. Sleep had come easily when he was drinking. Now he was sober and plugged into a world that he didn't want to be a part of. Insomnia crept in.

He remembered the books D had given him. Retrieving one from the duffel bag at the foot of his bed, he adjusted the reading lamp mounted on the bulkhead next to his berth and read the opening pages of one of Hemmingway's short stories.

After a few chapters, Sullivan closed his eyes. The rocking of the *Aspy Lady* and the dull roar of her big diesel reminded Sullivan why he was there. Every revolution of the boat's engine was bringing him closer to the moment that would free him. It was only when the boat's propellers spoke in a hushed monotone with each revolution, "death, death, death," that Sullivan finally fell asleep.

Later that night, he was ripped from the grasp of a nightmare by strong hands.

"What?" Sullivan mumbled, his mind still in the jungle. He blinked his eyes and saw Paddy knelling beside him with his hands on Sullivan's shoulders.

"You okay, Nick?"

"What?" Sullivan asked.

"You were talking in your sleep. The way you sounded, I thought you needed help."

"Sorry, just a bad dream, I guess," Sullivan said.

"I get them too sometimes," Paddy said. "Warm milk helps me get back to sleep."

"I'll be alright now, Paddy. Thanks."

Paddy nodded. "I'm going on watch now. I'll wake you at five."

When Paddy gently shook Sullivan's shoulder again at five, the nightmare was still playing. Paddy climbed into the bunk above Sullivan's and almost immediately began to snore. Sullivan pulled out the clean clothes that he had tucked under his pillow the night before and slid into them. The boat had ceased the wild gyrations of the day before and now crawled up widely-spaced swells and slid down the other side.

Sullivan left the darkness of the crew's quarters and stepped into the galley, closing the door behind him. Turning on the exhaust fan, he lit the oven. Soon the aroma of coffee and fresh baked breakfast rolls mixed with air scented with diesel fuel and stale bodies. He brewed a pot of Todd Sipu's herbal tea and sat on his stool.

The galley door swung open and Willie stepped in. He rubbed his hands together and looked around the galley.

"Am I too early?" Willie asked.

Sullivan stood up and put his cup on the table. "Coffee is on and the breakfast rolls are ready. I can have scrambled eggs and bacon ready in no time. You can take over my stool while I fire up the griddle."

Willie did and Sullivan peeled several pounds of bacon from its plastic wrap and placed them on the grill. The bacon sizzled and sent smoke into the exhaust fan.

Willie said, "So, I guess we start fishing today. I hope we make it big. I need some cash."

Sullivan pushed the bacon around the griddle with a spatula. "For concert tickets?"

Willie sniffled and rubbed is nose with a close fist. "Well, yeah, and for other stuff."

Sullivan turned and gave Willie a stare.

"No, it ain't like that, not that I haven't taken advantage of experiencing all that there is to experience. Besides," Willie continued, "I've got other, uh, things to consider."

Sullivan heaped breakfast on Willie's plate and young Willie ferried it to the crew's mess table.

After breakfast Sullivan went out on deck to dump the biodegradable garbage overboard. A light breeze swept the hair off Sullivan's forehead. The air was heavy with the presence of wet cordage and diesel fumes. Willie was lying on the bow, staring at a sky still and grey. Sullivan wondered what "other things" Willie had to consider.

When he was finished in the galley, Sullivan went to the bridge. The rest of the crew was there, crowded around the screen of the sonar machine as if it was broadcasting the lottery results. John Sylliboy had the helm and Todd Sipu was recording water temperatures in a small notebook. The skipper turned to his mate, who gave him a nod. Sylliboy pulled back at the throttle until the big diesel rumbled and wheezed like the snore of a giant.

Sipu left the bridge and the crew followed, leaving only Sullivan and Sylliboy in the wheelhouse. Moments later the crew emerged on the bow of the boat. Paddy and Antonio stood while Willie propped himself up on his elbows to watch as Sipu knelt on the deck and unfolded a small white cloth. Raising something over his head, Sipu chanted words that Sullivan could not hear.

Sylliboy looked at Sullivan's face and then focused his eyes on Sipu. "The Mi'kmaw people believe that all living things possess a spirit. The taking of another living thing is a sacred act. Todd is asking permission of the fish to hunt them. He is giving thanks and offering gifts of tobacco and sweet root in honour of their spirits. It has been so from the time our people recorded such events on ancient petroglyph stone carvings ten thousand years ago."

Sullivan watched as the wind lifted the offerings over the windward side of the bow and scattered them into the sea. Sipu folded his cloth and tucked it into his shirt. Sylliboy flicked a switch on the instrument panel and the boat's air horn blared. It was time to go fishing.

Chapter 13

Sullivan spent the next hour lifting frozen bait from the fish hold into waiting hands on deck. The smell of thawing bait stained his clothes and flesh until it became part of him.

After the hour of perdition in the bowels of the Lady, he was resurrected to the purgatory of the deck where the sun turned sweat into salt that festered in cracks in his skin. Sullivan learned to bait hooks on seemingly endless spools of line that loitered off buoys and drifted captive in the currents.

Sullivan was grateful when he was granted a reprieve to prepare lunch. He tried to wash the smell of bait from his hands and then tore off his shirt and wiped the dried salt from his arms and chest with a wet towel. After running tap water over his head, he put on a fresh shirt and prepared lunch that the crew ate on deck. Mid-afternoon, Sullivan made iced tea.

Lines were baited and set until the sun was down. Then the crew bathed, ate and rested. Sullivan took his watch after dinner with Todd Sipu. The sky was clear and beginning to show stars, but the heat of the day lingered.

Calum checked in. Near the end of Sullivan's tour in the wheelhouse the radio crackled again. Sullivan answered with the boat's call sign.

"Hi, Uncle Nick?"

"D, where are you?"

"I'm at Caitlin's. The band is going on tour for a week and Caitlin has offered to watch Dutch."

"Thank her for me."

A bronchial static crackled from the ship to shore. Sullivan waited for a reply and, when it came, it was from Caitlin. Her voice was satiny and had the colour of a woodwind.

"Hi, Nick, how's the fishing?"

Sullivan almost smiled.

"We just finished putting out sets this morning."

"That's good to hear. Nick, I'd love to watch Dutch while D is away."

"Well, if you're sure it's okay?"

"I'm sure."

Sullivan's mind foundered. A brain cell sparked and he said, "By the way, thanks for the pie. The crew enjoyed it."

"I'll bake one for you when you get back." Her voice was full of promise.

"That's sweet of you," Sullivan said.

"I've got to go," Caitlin said. "I'm bringing a pot of chowder over to Calum."

Sullivan signed off.

Todd Sipu examined him with his numinous dark eyes and then looked away through the darkened window of the wheel-house.

"Nice lady, Caitlin," Sipu said.

"Yes, she is."

"A woman like that would make the aura of most men glow, but yours is dull, same as it was the first day I met you."

"My what?"

"Your spirit. It's troubled. Sometimes we get lost and think there is no way home, but there is."

Neither Sullivan nor Sipu spoke another word. The balance of Sullivan's watch seemed endless. It reminded Sullivan of the bad dream where you wander naked in a public place with no place to hide.

When his watch was over, Sullivan climbed to the lookout above the wheelhouse to be alone, to get a grip on his emotions stirred by the pangs of withdrawal. The boat's gentle rocking was more pronounced there. Off the stern he could see the boat's wake churning the water into a phosphorescence of twinkling stars. In the distance the strobes of the marker buoys the *Aspy Lady* had put over the side punctured the twilight with millions of pixels. And in the wind's wisp, he could hear whispers.

Sullivan considered what Sipu had said. He didn't know. He couldn't know. Aboriginal hype, Sullivan thought. And damn his meddling. And as for D, she would have to fend for herself. Damn her too. And damn Caitlin for giving him false hope.

A voice called to him, *Nick*.

Sullivan looked below and made out a shadowy figure on the deck.

Then voices, silky then sonorous, whispered on the breeze, *Nick, why wait?*

Sullivan gritted his teeth and gripped the railing of the crow's nest wanting to rip it off. Damn his commitment, damn everyone. He swung his head around like a trapped animal looking for a way to escape. He raced down the ladder from the crow's nest to the aft deck and made for the chain in the utility locker. But he stopped short, bouncing on his heels.

"Nick." It was Willie. He was leaning against the locker with his knee bent and the sole of one shoe against the locker door. A cigarette hung pensively between the fingers of his right hand.

Sullivan wanted to scream.

"Hey man, what's up?" Willie asked.

"What?"

"The way you were coming out of the crow's nest, I thought the boat was on fire." Willie smiled.

Sullivan took a step back. His eyes darted. Sweat dripped from his forehead. He shifted his weight from one foot to the other.

"No, no hurry. Just need to take care of some things," Sullivan said, turning away. "I've got some things to do."

Glancing back over his shoulder, he thought he could see Capello leaning against the locker, arms crossed, a lollipop stick tucked between his teeth.

Sullivan made his way below deck and into the fish hold where some of the frozen food was stored in ice. He cupped ice chips in his hand and pressed them against his face. His entire body trembled. He might have been free by now if he hadn't run into Willie. Sullivan was riding on a detox high. His mind raced. A laugh seeped from his mouth – he muted it in his hand. Then he closed his eyes until his chest stopped heaving.

Sullivan's muscles throbbed, and his skin felt prickly and sun-baked as he made his way to the galley to make breakfast preparations and to try to gain control. The astringent tincture of sliced onion and the homey aroma of raw dough helped to ground his demons. Eggs that once carried the promise of life were broken and beaten for the breakfast ritual.

Later, Sullivan stripped out of his clothes and walked to the head in his shorts and rubber sandals. He winced as hot water shot from the showerhead and bounced off his sun-burnt skin. He embraced the pain.

Sullivan slid into his bunk. The pulse of the boat's engine and the throb of the propeller repeated the word that brought him comfort and sleep.

Paddy woke Sullivan at five. After breakfast Sullivan went up on deck. The sky was threaded with pink stripes woven against a dull white overcast. The sea was oily and still. The *Aspy Lady* was just coming up on the first set of lines that the crew had released the day before.

Todd Sipu removed the safety gate amidships on the starboard side where an opening was constructed in the superstructure to haul in fish. Antonio stood next to him, with the business end of a gaff resting on his black rubber boot.

Willie, shirtless with a baseball bat resting across the strap of his waterproof coveralls, stood back. Paddy was cutting chunks from a half-frozen block of bait to impale on the empty hooks as they were hauled aboard. Sipu told Sullivan to step back and watch before he took his turn packing gutted swordfish with ice in the hold.

Antonio pulled empty hooks from the water for three quarters of an hour before he yelled, "Fish on." Antonio pulled on the wire leader with his heavy gloves until a thrashing head attached to a sharp blade broke the surface. The sea was transformed from sapphire to frothy white that turned pink when Sipu hooked the fish with the gaff.

Sullivan stepped closer as the fish was hauled on deck spurting blood. An eye, black as Cape Breton coal, stared at Sullivan resolute and brave as Willie heaved the bat over his head and stopped the fish from thrashing. Then Willie sawed the fish's head from its body and tossed it into the sea. Sullivan wondered what the fish saw in those brief moments, and his mind fast reversed to that day in Cambodia when he watched the eyes of that young boy follow him as life pumped through his wound.

The fish was small, about ninety pounds, Sipu guessed. Before the afternoon was over, the scene repeated itself eleven times. The biggest fish was about one hundred fifty pounds. It was an average day.

That evening, as Sullivan was hauling garbage on deck to toss into the sea, the sounds of a fiddle washed over the boat. Sullivan washed out the garbage pail over the side with seawater before following the music to the bow.

Antonio was sitting on the rope locker. His cheek was nestled against a fiddle and his head swayed in time with invisible notes drawn on the lines and spaces of some distant thought. Sullivan went unnoticed until the last note faded. Antonio looked up at Sullivan with his sparkling white smile.

"It sounds as if you've been playing all of your life," Sullivan said.

"Since I was a young boy," Antonio replied. He gently placed the fiddle and bow in a scarred black case and closed the lid.

"My grandfather crafted this fiddle. He was a carpenter and shipbuilder by trade. But his passion was playing the fiddle, and when he didn't have woodworking tools in his hands he'd have his fiddle. It would take him two years to craft a fiddle like this one," he said, resting his hand on the case.

Antonio packed and lit his pipe. "I feel like playing one more piece before I turn in. Do you mind?" Antonio asked.

"Please do."

Antonio played what Sullivan guessed was a lively Spanish dance.

When he was done, Sullivan asked, "Is it a difficult instrument to play?"

"The fiddle? It requires a special hand and lots of time and patience."

Sullivan swallowed hard. "I, um, I don't have a lot of time. I was just curious."

Antonio flashed his smile.

"Wait here. I have just the thing."

He disappeared below deck and re-emerged a moment later with a small wooden case in his hand. He opened the lid and Sullivan looked in.

"It's an Irish flute, made in London over a hundred years ago," Antonio said.

Sullivan stared at the flute crafted from African blackwood that lay cradled in the jungle-green, felt-lined case. A memory coursed through him, dragging him back.

—

The open slit in the grey concrete wall of his prison cell in Hanoi had been the only source of light. It was an orifice in the eight-foot-square box that allowed insects, mice and an occasional bird to visit and then leave. More importantly it was a portal of hope.

There was a light bulb too, dangling from the ceiling of his cell, dangling high enough that he could not reach it to wrap the electrical wire around his neck. The light had been turned on for special occasions: random beatings, bed checks and for ten minutes during his evening meal. Those meals had been a prescription for diarrhea and nausea, and one quickly learned to navigate the darkness so as to quickly find the sheet of wood covering the hole in the floor that served as a toilet.

If there had been a bright moment during Sullivan's internment, it would have been the day that Ducky arrived. His name was Duong Duc – Ducky for short. He was tall for a Vietnamese, just about Sullivan's height, and he had an adolescent mustache of fine hair. Ducky was a walking anatomy lesson. His body was foil thin, and his flesh wrapped tight around his bones so that you could make out joints and eye sockets and collar bones. Ducky wore Coke-bottle lenses so thick his eyes appeared to be giant eight-balls.

The first night Ducky was on duty, the light came on. It was after dinner and after bed check, so Sullivan braced himself for a beating. The steel over wood laminate door to his cell had a sliding steel plate opening that was used to pass bowls of rancid rice and fish heads back and forth and for the guards to call you to the door so they could spit on you. The steel plate slid open and the light in the corridor backlit a head and pair of eyes that swept the cell.

"Come to the door," a voice demanded.

Sullivan took a deep breath. He hoped he would receive just a shower of spittle. If he looked tormented enough, perhaps there would be no whipping with a bamboo stick that would rupture his flesh into raw meat that would be marinated when the guards urinated on him. He put on his tormented face.

"What is your name?"

"Sullivan, Nicholas, Staff Sergeant, AF21034066."

"Well, Nicholas Sullivan, what's a nice Irish boy like you doing in a place like this?"

Sullivan said nothing. He studied the face out of the corner of his eye. It was as Vietnamese as Ho Chi Mihn's. But the voice, the voice had been straight from an upscale foggy London neighborhood.

"Do you want a smoke?" Ducky asked.

Sullivan said, "No, thank you."

"Where are you from, Sullivan?"

Sullivan fixed his eyes on the cement floor of his cell. He had learned never to look his captors in the eye.

"Connecticut – a small state in the northeast."

"Well, I'll be. I spent a semester at Yale, part of an exchange program they had with Oxford. It was one of the best times of my life. It didn't take much for those liberal Yale co-eds to take their clothes off." To which Ducky had emitted a sophomoric giggle.

Ducky took a drag from his cigarette and looked at it. "What I wouldn't give for an American smoke. Someday, when this thing is all over, I'd like to go back."

Ducky examined Sullivan and then said, "Look Sullivan, you can relax. I don't have anything against you personally. Don't get me wrong, your government has no right to be here and I hope we kick your ass all the way back to Duluth, but I have no personal grudge. You behave, I don't get hassled, and things will be fine, okay?"

"Yes," Sullivan said.

Ducky explained that after graduating from Oxford with a degree in business and economics, he had secured a scholarship for graduate school at his alma mater. But when he returned home for the summer, he was not allowed to leave. And there wasn't much need for economists in the Hanoi government.

"So," Ducky said, "I got drafted. If I were an American, I'd be in Canada."

Sullivan's cell block held seven other prisoners. Ducky had responsibility for six other cell blocks during his twelve-hour shift. Most of Sullivan's prison mates were Navy or Air Force aviators, and most were officers except for a few enlisted personnel that had been part of B-52 crews that discovered too late the range of Russian surface to air missiles.

And Ducky had favourites, especially among the enlisted prisoners, and Sullivan was one of them. An extra piece of bread or a piece of fruit appeared in Sullivan's bowl at dinner from time to time.

Ducky spent idle time patrolling his cell blocks by blowing on an Irish tin whistle that he had picked up in London. And Ducky was accomplished. Sullivan put his ear against his cell door whenever Ducky played. It reminded Sullivan of Cape Breton, when the soft tone of a fiddle or flute wafted across the Aspy River and settled in his head.

"What do you think, Sullivan?" Ducky asked after a performance, as if Sullivan's heritage had eminently qualified him to render an opinion.

When Sullivan didn't answer, Ducky slid the steel plate in the door open and looked in. Sullivan was sitting against the wall of his cell, crying. When Ducky asked why, Sullivan told him about his wife and daughter and Capello. A week later Ducky beckoned Sullivan to the cell door. Through the narrow opening, Ducky passed a primitive bamboo flute to Sullivan. During the next two years, Sullivan learned to play it.

Just months before Sullivan had been released, Ducky revealed that someone decided that he should have a chance at becoming a national hero and that he had been assigned to an infantry unit. Ducky shook Sullivan's hand and wished him well. Sullivan gave Ducky his address and they had exchanged promises.

———

Now, Sullivan wondered what had become of Ducky. Had he written and his letters were discarded by Sheila, or was his body decaying somewhere under the green tropical canopy of the jungle? He would like to see Ducky again, to embrace him, to thank him for what he did. Perhaps he would have that chance someday on the other side of the tunnel of light.

Antonio assembled the instrument and played a few notes. "Here, now you try it." Antonio wiped the mouthpiece in his sleeve and handed it to Sullivan. Sullivan managed a few notes.

"Not bad, not bad at all. It sounds as if you've played before. We'll practice a little before your watch each night and by the time we make landfall we'll be able to play a tune together."

Sullivan wasn't sure why, but he said, yes. Maybe it was for Ducky to hear.

Sullivan stood watch with Todd Sipu again that night. He asked Sipu about his home and heritage.

Unlike the night before, Sipu was talkative. He told Sullivan about his home in Bear River, Nova Scotia, where both his grandfather and father were tribal chiefs. He shared stories of his childhood when he would canoe the waters of Kejimkujik and camp on wilderness shores with members of his tribal youth group. Tribal elders would tell stories that could be traced back thousands of years. One year, when the waters of the lake were low, Sipu guided archeologists into the lake area. He was only seventeen at the time.

"What did you see?" Sullivan asked.

Sipu's eyes became distant and he answered in a soft voice. "The topsoil was stripped away exposing the land as it was a millennia ago. I sensed that I had gone back in time. I found ancient stone carvings, arrowheads and eel pits just as my ancestors left them. After that I spent a great deal of time wandering the lake area, looking for a sign that would show me the direction I should take in my adult life. As I was asking guidance from the spirits of my ancestors, I remember looking down and seeing an ancient stone spearhead. At that moment I was thinking that I should live my life on the reserve and work with the youth, passing down the heritage of my people to them. I asked the spirits to show me another sign, if this was the path I should follow. At that exact moment I saw a bear standing motionless and watching me. The bear is a powerful sign in our culture. The bear watched me for a long time, and when I blinked my eye, it disappeared."

"But you became a fisherman," Sullivan said.

"Only to earn money during the fishing season," Sipu said. "The remainder of the year I spend on the reservation teaching youth our ancient traditions and art forms. I have a degree in education, not that I've ever used it to turn a loonie. And I wouldn't have it any other way."

As Sullivan's watch grew older, the dull tones of dusk bent over the horizon. The boat's searchlight cut a path through the twilight. Sullivan watched dots move across the radar screen and called out their distances and headings to Sipu. Then around 9:30 the radio crackled with the boat's call sign.

"Whisky papa tango one eight seven, this is X-ray Romeo Sierra two, six, three, come back *Aspy Lady*."

"X-ray Romeo Sierra two, six, three, this is the *Aspy Lady*."

"I see you haven't been tossed over the side or mutinied, Nick," Calum said.

"Not yet," Sullivan said. "I'm doing my watch with Todd."

Calum expelled a raspy laugh from deep in his chest. "Yeah, that's a tough bunch of pirates you sail with, especially that Sipu."

Sipu motioned Sullivan for the mic. "They don't make sailors like you any more, Calum," Sipu said.

"Just wanted to make sure you were listening," Calum said. "Now give the mic back to Nick, I got some good news."

"Nick," Calum said. "What a day it was, lad. The yard installed the new engine in the ketch and balanced the shaft. That motor purrs like a kitten. I was talking about the ketch at the pub last night to a few of the lads waiting for their boats to turn around, and a bunch of them come down to the yard today to watch. The next thing you know, they're helping out putting on fittings, and we even got the mast stepped. Nick, you should have been there to see it. But because you weren't, Caitlin took pictures. It was a sight, Nick, I want to tell you."

"I owe you in a big way, Calum," Sullivan said.

"No need to be thanking me, Nick. You know you'll be needing to name her soon. Have you thought about that?"

Sullivan hadn't. But he didn't need to. "The *Jessica Elaine*," Sullivan said.

"That's a right pretty name for a beautiful boat, it is, Nick."

There was no traffic to pass and Calum disappeared into the static.

Sullivan could see Sipu's face reflected in the glass of the cabin window as Sipu studied the waters in front of the *Aspy Lady*.

"You know you brought some happiness into that man's life," Sipu said. "He gets up in the morning with something to look forward to. It's hard to grow old alone."

Sullivan nodded.

Sullivan prepared the galley for breakfast when his watch was over. Paddy poked his head into the galley.

"Time for a game?" Paddy asked.

There was something affable about ritual, Sullivan thought. He looked forward to a game of checkers with Paddy when the bulk of the day had ended. A familiarity had grown between them.

"Sure," Sullivan said. He lit the stove and put a kettle of water on for tea.

Paddy opened a cardboard box and set the checkerboard and pieces on the galley table. Pieces moved across the board. Paddy was not on the top of his game.

Sullivan carried two mugs of tea over to the table. "If I didn't know better, I'd think you're letting me win."

"My mind's not on it, I guess," Paddy said.

"Oh?" Sullivan waited.

"I was thinking that you're a pretty smart guy that might have some ideas, you know … some ideas on how I might be able to get back with my wife and kid."

"I'm not sure I can help you, Paddy," Sullivan said, "but I'd be glad to listen. Sometimes when you talk about a problem you get some new ideas."

Paddy rubbed his hand over the heavy black stubble on his face. "That's what I was thinking." Paddy leaned forward on the stool. "It all started about two years ago. I knew this guy out of Sydney that would come around to the pub now and then. Word was that he had connections." Paddy paused and looked over his shoulder. "You know what I mean?"

"Not really," Sullivan said.

Paddy shook his head and let out a puff of air. "I'm trusting you now," Paddy said in a tone of caution.

"Go ahead," Sullivan urged.

"Okay. This guy was looking for someone who could take a boat from Cape Breton to the east coast of the States and back."

Sullivan's eye narrowed. "Drugs?"

"No! I'd never do anything like that. Mostly just cigarettes and booze to avoid having to pay the heavy tax we got up here. Anyway, the money this guy was paying was good and seeing that we only fish six months out of the year, well—"

"So you took the guy up on his offer."

"Right. But there's more to it. See, I needed a boat. So, I took out a loan and got me a used forty-footer with a decent sized hold and plenty of room in the cabin. They had the stuff warehoused in Portland, Maine. So, I'd wait for a forecast with a couple days of heavy fog and sneak down the coast. Then I'd load up and follow the ferry on the run between Portland and Yarmouth. I'd stick my bow so close behind the Portland ferry that the Coast Guard's radar would only show one radar signature, and I'd be too low and too close for the ferry to pick me up on their screen.

"So, everything is going just fine. I'm bringing in a bundle and even got enough to get a mortgage on a small place in town. Then one night last September, I pull the boat up to the dock in Portland where I normally loaded up. This guy meets me and tells me that there is someone who needs to talk to me. Well, I follow this guy into an old brick building right on the waterfront. There was the faded name of some molasses company painted on the side of the building and a date of eighteen hundred and something."

Paddy wet his lips. The dull rumble of the *Aspy Lady*'s engine and pulse of the propeller filled the small galley.

"When I stepped inside, it smelled like the building had been closed up for two hundred years – you know, all musty and damp. He takes me up two flights of stairs to an office without any windows. There's a guy there that must have been the boss. He was Irish – I mean Irish like from downtown Belfast. He wasn't a big man, but he had a cold look to him that made me think this guy could cut your heart out without blinking an eye. I was thinking that he might be connected, you know, to the movement.

"He tells me that he needed someone to make a onetime run – no middle man, just him and me. There was five thousand U.S. in it for me and all I had to do is take some inventory up the coast to Newfoundland. He asks me if I can do it, and I said sure for five thousand I'd take it all the way to Ireland. It was a joke, but this guy thought about it for a minute and then he smiled and told me that he'll give me a call when I should come and pick up his stuff.

"On the trip back, I'm wondering what kind of cargo would be worth five thousand to haul up the coast. And then, on my way back home, it comes to me."

"What did you think it was?" Sullivan asked.

Paddy hung his head. "I was thinking it must be guns and that I didn't want no part in any killing of people like they have going on in Northern Ireland."

"I thought that was all over," Sullivan said.

"Yeah, right, until it starts again. And it will."

Sullivan nodded. "What happened next?"

"I got a call three weeks later. My wife takes a message to dial a number in the States, but I don't call back. I figure if I don't call back maybe this guy will go away, except he doesn't. Then one morning my kid goes outside and finds his puppy hanging from a tree in the front yard. Now I'm scared. Not for me, but for the wife and kid. So, I call the number and tell them I can't do it – that the motor in the boat is shot and I can't afford a new one. Two days later, I get a call in the middle of the night from the RMCP saying that my boat was burning. I thought that might be a good thing until I find out the insurance company won't pay out 'cause the fire was arson. The bank calls in the loan, and they take the house, which was listed as collateral. The wife moves to her mother's and takes the kid with her."

Paddy blinked his eyes. The words came softly. "Can't blame her."

"Did you try talking to her?" Sullivan asked.

Paddy nodded. "Until I was blue in the face."

"Maybe if you could turn things around and get the house back?"

"On what I make fishing? It won't happen."

"What about the rest of the year?" Sullivan asked.

"All I know how to do is fish. I collect unemployment for the rest of the year."

"Paddy, it sounds to me like you need to start thinking outside the box. Why, you probably have skills that you haven't even thought about that you could turn a buck with. In fact I'm sure of it. I'll think about it too. Okay?"

"So, you'll help me?"

"We'll work on it together," Sullivan said. "But right I've got to finish getting things set up for breakfast."

Paddy stood up. He started to say something, but the words were lost. He nodded and left the galley. A moment later Sullivan heard the television switch on. Maybe Paddy searched for a revelation on the news or in a beer commercial, or maybe Paddy just wanted to lose himself in the millions of coloured dots on the pixel glass.

The crew of the *Aspy Lady* were roused from their bunks early. The captain said the seas would be building and that they needed to get on deck while they still could work.

And work they did. Fish were packed in the hold and the crew went below to rest. Now it was early evening. John Sylliboy was alone at the helm. Sullivan got a head start on dinner, and while the oven was warming, he brought a mug of black coffee to the bridge.

"Thanks, Nick," Sylliboy said as he took the cup and placed it in a cup holder attached to the helmsman's chair.

The sea had been building all day and the deck of the *Aspy Lady* pitched and rolled.

"I expect the crew is spent and catching a nap," Sylliboy said.

"They had all crawled into their bunks when I left the galley," Sullivan replied.

"I worked them pretty hard today. It's hard work on a good day, but with the sea like it's been it's twice the job."

Sullivan looked out at the bow as it dug into breaking waves, shuddered and rose again.

"Is that Willie out on deck?" Sullivan asked.

Sylliboy nodded. "He headed out to the bow as soon as we finished baiting the last set. Seems he's been trying to reach his girlfriend on his cell phone but we're way out of range of any towers. I offered him the use of the marine radio-telephone but he declined, said it was personal."

"Maybe I'll go down and see if wants a cup of coffee or tea," Sullivan said.

Sylliboy shrugged his shoulders.

Sullivan rock and rolled his way to the bow, gripping the handrail, and sat next to Willie under the bridge wing.

"I just brought the skipper a mug. You want coffee or tea?"

"No, thanks anyway."

"I'll leave you be then," Sullivan said. He started to get up.

"It's okay if you stay," Willie said.

"Thanks. The crew's quarters get a bit stuffy after a while."

Both Sullivan and Willie stared out at the bow, seeing grey seas one moment and grey skies the next as the *Aspy Lady* rode the waves.

"I guess you'll do pretty well when the Lady gets back to port and sells her catch," Sullivan said. "You said you could use the cash. A young fellow starting out ought to start putting something away for the future. Someday you'll have a wife and kids depending on you."

Willie leaned forward and dropped his head on his chest. "Responsibility."

Sullivan gave him a glance and then turned his attention back to the horizon. "It's what becoming a man is all about."

"Well, that's what I was saying before. I could use the cash all of a sudden," Willie said with his eyes still fixed on the deck.

Sullivan turned and faced Willie. "Sounds like life caught you off guard."

"It's kind of personal," Willie said.

"Well I'm probably not full of wisdom," Sullivan said. "But I remember my mom saying two things. She said that I should that I should try to do my best at everything I did. If I did that, no one could fault me, especially myself."

"What was the second thing?" Willie asked.

"She said to always do the right thing."

"You mean good and evil like in the Bible"?

Sullivan nodded. "Yeah, like in the Bible, Willie."

Sullivan stood up and grabbed the railing. Then he turned back toward Willie.

"I'll leave you in peace . It sounds like you've got some thinking to do," Sullivan said.

Somewhere in the night, the throb of the boat's engine was silenced – the whispering chant of Jackie D's friends stopped. Paddy carried the odour of engine oil and grease when he shook Sullivan awake the next morning. The turn of the propeller was present once again, carrying Sullivan closer to the netherworld.

Sullivan could hear accolades bearing Paddy's name carry into the galley. Later, when Paddy ferried his empty breakfast dishes into the galley sink, Paddy's face was lit with a smile.

"Rumour has it that you repaired the engine last night and saved the day. That right?" Sullivan asked.

"Saved the skipper a bunch of money not having to return to port. And those diesel mechanics don't come cheap either," Paddy said. "You know when you said there might be other things I can do to earn a loonie?"

"I remember."

"Maybe I could become a diesel mechanic. I don't have any formal training, but I've been around engines all of my life."

Sullivan said, "I bet with the skipper's endorsement, a boatyard or trucking firm would sign you up in a minute."

"You think?"

Sullivan nodded.

"You're okay," Paddy said.

"Back at you."

Paddy left the galley taking his smile with him.

Sullivan wondered what Paddy would say about him at his funeral, if his body surfaced, or at his memorial service if didn't.

Chapter 14

Days spun into a week, then two. The fish holds were almost full and the crew started talking about returning home. Sullivan felt at peace with himself and almost happy at times. Willie had announced that he was going to propose to his girl. Sullivan noticed maturity in his demeanour that hadn't been there when they sailed. Maybe he just knew him better. Paddy talked about the prospect of working as a mechanic.

Each night like clockwork Calum reported the latest news from shore. Caitlin called occasionally on the sideband radio so Dutch could listen to Sullivan's voice. Sullivan missed the dog in ways he did not understand. D spoke to Sullivan about her music and the people and scenery she chanced upon while travelling with the band. Someone had begun to cross off days on the calendar. Sullivan wanted to thank whoever it was.

Passing her third week at sea, the *Aspy Lady* was in ballast with her hold nearly full. The ocean was windless, and they sat dry dock still. Lines had been pulled and baited, the crew had been fed and the galley readied for breakfast. Sullivan followed the sound of rosined bow and strings to the bow of the Lady where Antonio was playing, his eyes closed. Waiting for a pause in cut time, Sullivan blew across the lip plate a triad above the strings. At the final bar line Antonio opened his eyes and smiled.

"You've come a long way, Nick," Antonio said.

"Good teacher," Sullivan replied.

Antonio took a cloth and wiped perspiration lovingly from his fiddle.

"Playing reminds you of your grandfather, doesn't it?" Sullivan asked.

Antonio grew silent. A bronze sky melted into the horizon and washed the sea in gold leaf. He pulled his pipe from his shirt pocket and flicked a match that he curled in the palm of his hand. His ebony eyes glistened in the blue smoke that swirled around his head.

"Yes. Sometimes I wake up from a dream with the smell of new wood and lacquer in my nose. It's as if that dream took me back to his shop, as if through some magic I actually went to visit him, although he's been dead for nearly twenty years. You ever have something like that happen?"

Sullivan nodded, but when his dreams became alive they brought along the smell of cordite, bug dope and dried blood.

After breakfast Sullivan reported to the bridge, as he did each morning when his duties in the galley were complete, so that John Sylliboy could put him to work where he was most needed. Sullivan could perform most of the tasks on the boat now and was even allowed to man the helm alone during daylight hours. When Sullivan arrived in the wheelhouse, their skipper was at the helm. Sullivan stood beside him and looked out over the bow. He could see Todd Sipu kneeling at the edge of the boat's stem with his hands lifted toward a clouded sky. White caps were beginning to build, and Sipu's black hair fluttered in a building wind.

"We're heading back in tomorrow after we pick up our last set," Sylliboy said. "We've done pretty well and there might be a few more loonies in our pockets then we expected." Sylliboy turned and looked at Sullivan. "You've done well too, better than I expected. You should be feeling good for a lot of reasons."

Sylliboy noticed Sullivan look down at the deck just as he turned his gaze back to the horizon.

Sullivan swallowed hard, trying to find words that he couldn't find. He felt he had to say something, so he asked, "Is the mate giving thanks again for our success?"

Sylliboy shook his head. "He is praying for someone's soul."

"Is someone sick?"

"Worse," Sylliboy said. "Someone is dying. It's the Mi'kmaw version of the last rites. It came to him in a dream, but he could not see the face."

Sullivan shuddered in a windstorm of realization. He gasped audibly, causing Sylliboy to study him.

"Well, we've got reason to celebrate even if someone out there doesn't," Sylliboy said. "How about cooking up something special for tomorrow night, kind of the last supper of our voyage."

Sullivan was glad that Sylliboy's gaze was fixed straight ahead. Sullivan's right eye began to twitch.

"Sure," he managed to say.

"Good deal," Sylliboy said. "Nothing doing on deck, so you've got some free time."

Sullivan left the bridge and passed through the crew's quarters and into the galley. Paddy, Willie and Antonio were talking in an animated tone but stopped when Sullivan entered.

Willie broke the silence. "Did you hear the good news? We're heading in."

"I heard," Sullivan said. He managed a smile. "Maybe then you guys can get a decent meal."

Sullivan turned his back on the laughter and went into the galley and closed the door behind him. He sat down on the stool and propped his elbows on his knees. He held his head in his hands. He was shaking and he couldn't think straight. He hadn't thought much about drinking since he came aboard, but now he had a craving. He needed just enough to calm down and clear his head. Instead he brewed the last of Todd Sipu's tea and sorted out what he was feeling.

He thought about those few moments of terror as his physical body would fight to stay alive. The suffering would be his penance. He focused on the passion of that moment when his worthless life would be over. He wished he could spend the last moments before going over the side with his old buddy Jackie D. Jackie could have seen him through. But Jack didn't even have a casual acquaintance on board – John Sylliboy had seen to that.

There were some antihistamine tablets and cough syrup in the dispensary – a cabinet mounted on the wall of the bridge. And maybe the flute would put him in the right frame of mind and keep him company in those final hours. The rest would be easy.

He kept to himself the rest of the day, either working in the galley or reading the last few chapters of Hemingway's *The Old Man and the Sea*.

Sullivan prepared one of his favourites for dinner: meatloaf, mashed potatoes, corn, gravy and biscuits. And for dessert, he served one of those frozen apple pies that promised to taste just like it came out of your grandmother's oven.

Afterward, the crew not on watch settled in for a game of cards. Sullivan went on deck to empty the garbage. The wind was stiff, and through the searchlights he could see the ocean as it hissed and thrust its white fangs at the boat's hull.

He walked to the locker where the chain was stored and looked inside. The rusted coil of steel was waiting for him. Sullivan choreographed the steps that he would use to waltz out of his life in just a few hours.

After rehearsing the steps, he walked to the opening in the port railing and removed the safety chain. He heaved the contents of the thirty-litre garbage can into the water and watched as the sea devoured it. Wrapping the loop of the nylon cord attached to the can's handle around his hand, he lowered it just enough to gather sufficient water to rinse it. Just then, the boat pitched and the can went under – pulling Sullivan into the ocean with it.

There was a vacuum, a place barren of consciousness and time that sucked Sullivan into its womb. It was the icy slivers of cold that ripped him back into the intersection of the incarnate and the immortal. Sullivan was spun into a brilliant spectacle of light as the *Aspy Lady*'s propeller wash awakened billions of bioluminescent microbes. The sound of the boat's engine grew dimmer as he was dragged downward toward a place of darkness. The pressure in his ears exploded with pain, and firecrackers and party balloons popped inside his head.

Sullivan tore at the rope that imprisoned his hand. He crawled and kicked and finally thrashed in uncurbed panic, ripping tendon and muscle from bone. A flood of pain, which was white and hot like burning magnesium, boiled air from his lungs and spewed blood through clenched jaws.

Suddenly, it all stopped. The frigid downward spiral into the abyss, the searing pain, the hysteria of survival, the beating of his heart. Instead, there was warmth and peace and a lucidity that he had never experienced before.

"I can see so clearly," Sullivan thought. He was surprised that he could hear his own voice. And he could see: the barrel that was still knotted to his hand, a distant school of fish, particulates of detritus as they sailed past in the current. But there was something else, an incongruity of something both near and distant.

He floated over the floor of the valley and into the mountains that stood snow-capped and touched the stars. Somewhere a cosmos away, he heard the sounds of laughter. He looked with his soul to a time and place eyes could not see. It was Christmas morning, the third of his life, and there he was, a toddler, opening presents tucked under the tree that he had helped decorate. There was a rabbit mounted on a carriage, whose feet and arms would move when the wheels turned. His mom and dad looked on as he mounted the locomotive that had pedals that could carry him halfway around the world if he had the mind.

The scene changed to a sandlot baseball game where the neighbour kids ran mud-puddle bases and skidded into a home plate of dandelions and clover. And when the game was over, he would ride his royal purple bike into the alien landscape that lay beyond the map of his neighbourhood, waiting to be discovered. And the scenes changed again, and again, painting portraits of his life: the death of his dog, his first school dance and fishing with his dad, uncle and cousin in the Aspy River.

He could sense it before he could see it. It felt like love and warmth and peace, and it was beautiful, so very beautiful.

An apparition, cosmic and brilliant appeared. Cappy was dressed, as always when he made an appearance in Sullivan's dreams or drunken stupors, in his camouflage tiger suit. His youthful face bore a smile and he wrinkled his nose before he spoke.

Soon, Cappy promised.

In that instant Sullivan realized he was truly free. Sullivan was pulled from his watery grave and into a kaleidoscopic field of flowers with shades of colour he had never seen before. His movements were hair-triggered and void of a sense of time in this place where time did not exist.

—

A grenade launched from Caputo's M-16 exploded on a vehicle. As Sullivan swung the barrel of his weapon to acquire another target, he could see the muzzle flash of Capello's rifle opening up on full auto from the centre of the camp. The NVA returned Capello's fire so that their comrades were caught in their own crossfire.

The explosives that Sullivan had set underneath the truck triggered a spectacular arc of light – a diversion that would allow Sullivan and Capello to slip out of the encampment to their rendezvous point.

Sullivan stopped to radio the rescue chopper. The voice that crackled from his radio told him that salvation was just minutes away. Behind him he could hear the thunder of the two claymores he had set out earlier.

Sullivan finally reached the clearing. He readied a flare to light when Capello arrived. He could hear the whomph of the Jolly Green's blades beating the air in the distance. But there was another sound. It was the unmistakable report of an M-16 rifle echoing among the chatter of the enemy's AK-47s. The steady discharge of Capello's weapon seemed desperate and stationary.

Sullivan sprinted toward the sound. He nearly tripped on Capello's body before he saw it. Sullivan helped him to his feet. Capello stumbled and fell. Fuelled by fear, love and duty, Sullivan hoisted Capello over his shoulder.

Then the world stopped. Jet engines screamed so close overhead that Sullivan ducked. He could actually feel the searing engine exhaust from the flight of four F-105s as they exploded through the sky. Blinding light ignited the jungle. Seconds later a shock wave lifted Sullivan off the ground. He stumbled, and the weight of Capello's body knocked the wind out of him.

Sullivan could see the Jolly Green land hard, its turbines screaming, ready to leap from the hail of small arms fire ripping through its olive drab metal skin. The faces of the chopper's crew were vivid as he dragged Capello the final fifty yards. The door gunner was raking their flank when a dozen bullets shredded his torso in a puff of blood and tissue. Then a torrent of white light whisked past Sullivan and arced into brilliant sunlight. He fell on top of Capello as the explosion swept their hopes into a cloud of machinery fragments, body parts and bits of jungle.

He could not hear the words that the ragged black-robed soldiers spat at them. Even the scourge from rifle butts and feet were numbed by shock. Sullivan's hands were bound behind his back. A young NVA regular smiled, and through rotten teeth hurled spittle that hung on Sullivan's face. Someone tightened a coarse rope around his neck, and another cord fettered his hands.

Capello was dragged to his feet, but he stumbled and fell. Sullivan could see where small arms had torn holes in Capello's tiger suit at an eleven o'clock point in his torso and his upper arm and, at seven o'clock, inside his thigh, wounds that he could survive if he got medical attention. No amount of beating could compel Capello to move. An authoritative voice brought an end to Capello's torment. He was placed on a stretcher and together they were led away.

They travelled back through the aftermath of burning jungle, past the charcoal scraps of what were once human beings and things of war. They were made to look closely at what napalm did so well.

In the tunnels below the scorched earth, the air was filled with the smell of burned flesh and the screams of the dying. Sullivan fell, butt-stroked to the ground next to Capello. His ribs were kicked until they broke. Then he was made to stand and was interrogated.

A cloud overshadowed the valley, turning all colours into a single shade of grey before the next images appeared. This prelude to his adult life, with the whirl of helicopter blades, blood-curdling screams and body parts, was followed by drunken orgies and scenes of hell that had become his life.

He watched as his life unfolded, chapter by chapter. The villain appeared in each scene, piling misery upon misery. And when he looked closely, he could see that this perpetrator of torment was no other than Nick Sullivan. Self-pity and self-righteousness, the sisters of the unpardonable sin, had undone Nick Sullivan, and for a brief second he asked for forgiveness. It was in that moment that he was swept back into the cold depths of the Atlantic.

The gleaming carbon steel blade of Cappy's fighting knife appeared from thin air and sliced the line that ushered Sullivan into eternity. Cappy held his ebony eyes on Sullivan. *But not now, Sulli, not now*, the spectre said.

And then it was gone. In its place came oblivion and timelessness. Arcs of stabbing orange neon splashed across a black milieu. Neurons sparked and sputtered against an incessant hum. Everything was fragmented and adrift.

Then came a sound. It was something recognizable that caused a flutter of certainty. It was loud and it hurt and it came from something moist and warm and full of love. Sullivan looked up and blinked at the sterile light that hurt his eyes.

—

"Mr. Sullivan?"

Sullivan tried to speak, but his tongue was bonded to the desiccated membrane of his mouth.

"It's okay, Mr. Sullivan. Blink your eyes if you can understand me."

Sullivan's eyes focused on Dutch who stood on his hind legs and licked his face.

"Over here, Mr. Sullivan," said a man dressed in surgical garb.

Sullivan tried to lift his head, but it fell back onto his pillow.

"Do you know where you are?"

Sullivan nodded his head. "Hospital?"

"Yes. Do know what happened to you?"

Sullivan opened his mouth and spoke in a ghostly tone. "Drowned."

"Well, almost, Mr. Sullivan. But you're alright now."

"Drowned."

The green garbed man whispered something to a nurse and then stabbed a light into Sullivan's eyes. He scribbled notes. Then the man turned and said, "Just a short visit please. We don't want to overwhelm him."

D, Caitlin and John Sylliboy were standing around Sullivan's bed nervously.

"Welcome back," Sylliboy said.

"I don't remember," Sullivan said.

Sylliboy looked at the doctor, who nodded. Sylliboy forced a smile. "I was on the bridge with Todd. He saw you go out on deck to empty the garbage. He looked away for a second and when he looked back you were gone. The next thing I know he was leaning on the air horn and yelling, 'Man overboard!' The crew was out on deck in just seconds and threw out a life buoy. I turned the helm in a Williamson figure eight and came about. Willie ran up to the crow's nest and spotted you. Paddy went into the water and hauled you out."

Sylliboy took in a breath of air, looked down at the floor. He picked nervously at a hangnail on his thumb and exhaled. "When we got you on deck, the broken line from the garbage can was still attached to your wrist. We couldn't detect a heartbeat and you weren't breathing. The crew took turns doing CPR on you. Todd got out the oxygen bottle and we got a tube down your throat. By the time the Coast Guard helicopter arrived over an hour later, you had a heartbeat and your breathing was laboured. That's about all there is to tell."

Caitlin pulled a chair from a corner and sat down. "We've been coming in shifts. There's been someone with you for the last two days. The doctors said you were in a coma, and that—"

"Father O' Malley came too and...." D looked down at her hands that were folded as if prayers had been answered.

Sylliboy said, "The crew was here too – all of them. Paddy was camped out here until I made him go home."

A nurse appeared and announced it was time for Sullivan to rest without visitors for the next twenty-four hours.

"We'll be back tomorrow night," D said.

Sylliboy patted Sullivan's leg. "Later, partner."

A moment later, the room was empty and he fell asleep.

When Sullivan awoke, sun streamed through the window of his hospital room on the first day of the rest of his life. He found his Timex in a plastic bag in the top drawer of the stand next to his bed. It was filled with cloudy saltwater, and rusted hands marked the time of his death.

For the remainder of that day, Sullivan lived in a world of Jell-O, beef bouillon and wheelchair excursions down disinfected halls redolent with citrus groves and strawberry fields. He was wired, scanned, probed and made to inhale canned air through a plastic mask.

Afterward, he lay in his bed and studied a wall-mounted impressionist print of a boy and girl sitting barefoot and lazy on a lakeside dock. When would the world betray them? How would their innocence be lost?

A nurse came in to remove his catheter and bedpan and then helped him to the bathroom to see if his internal plumbing could be restored. Sullivan braced himself on the sink and looked into the mirror hanging above it. There were bags under his eyes. His hair was in a tangle and he needed a shave. But what he noticed most was that nothing had changed at all. He was still a captive in the world of the living.

That weekend, Sullivan's phone was busy with calls from the crew of the *Aspy Lady*. D and Caitlin visited once. Calum kept in touch too. Surgery was scheduled for Wednesday to repair the torn ligament in his shoulder, and respiratory therapy would be ongoing.

A week later, Sylliboy settled Sullivan's bill and drove him home. The drive from the hospital in Sydney to Dingwall took more than an hour. Sylliboy brought Sullivan up to date on dockside and barstool gossip, but the incident aboard the *Aspy Lady* was never broached.

Sylliboy's truck pulled in front of Sullivan's house and stopped.

Sullivan got out of the truck and looked at the house before stepping onto the porch. His left arm was in a sling, so Sylliboy put the key in the lock and opened the door. The inside of the house looked the same except the kitchen. The kitchen table was covered with dishes filled with pastry and pies and bags of fruit and vegetables from local gardens. A note from D taped to the refrigerator door said that she was playing with the band and would be home the next day. Sullivan opened the refrigerator door to get Sylliboy a beer and one for himself. The shelves were packed with bowls and pans filled with enough food for a week.

"It's kind of warm in here. Want me to crack open the windows?" Sylliboy asked.

"I'd be obliged," Sullivan said

Sullivan handed Sylliboy a bottle of beer and took a long pull from his own, nearly emptying the bottle. Nothing tasted so good.

"Did your doctor say it was okay to start on booze?" Sylliboy asked.

"I don't recall the topic coming up in conversation and if it did, it's only a beer, John."

Sylliboy stared at the worn linoleum floor of the kitchen and took a deep breath before he locked his eyes on Sullivan. "Look, Nick, I don't know how to say it, but I think it's important enough to risk offending you. I know it was a struggle for you to get handle on your drinking out there fishing on the Lady – we all knew it. Personally, I didn't think you could get your head around it, but you did."

"What are you saying, John?"

"Shit, you've been dry for nearly a month. "You beat the beast. Why invite it back into your life?"

"Thanks, John, but I have it under control."

Sullivan nodded his head away from the conversation in the direction of the food laden table. "This happen often?"

"Usually when someone doesn't come home, but in your case it was close enough. Besides, that's the way things are here. Locals take care of their own. So I'm guessing you must be part of the family now. Nick, I don't know much about your past and I don't really care. But you've been given another chance at things. Don't turn your back on it."

Sylliboy placed his drink on the table and reached into the side pocket of his pants. His hand came out with a thick envelope. "Hope you don't mind cash. Figured I'd save you a trip to the bank and also give a blind eye to Immigration and Canada Revenue."

Sullivan held the envelope in the fingers of his bandaged arm and lifted the flap with the hand of his good arm. It was filled with hundred dollar bills.

"Look, Nick," Sylliboy said. "The boys would love to fish with you again, once that arm heals that is. And I know going fishing again is probably the last thing you're thinking about. But you did well and there's a place for you on the crew roster if you want it. Besides, I think it would be good for you."

"I'll think on it," Sullivan said.

"Good enough," Sylliboy said. "If you need something, just pick up the phone and call the house. If I'm not home, the wife will find me."

"Thanks, John. You're a good friend."

"You take care of that arm. Think about what I said. I'll check in on you soon."

Sullivan saw Sylliboy to the door and watched him drive away.

The sun was summer hot and the wind was off the ocean. Sullivan opened another beer, went to the back porch and sat in one of the white-washed slat chairs that his uncle had built when Sullivan was still a boy. His eyes followed the Aspy River to where its waters flowed into the sea. The golden sunlight that reflected off the water made him squint. The sand was white and sugar fine.

Through the shimmering mirage of heat that rose from the shore, Sullivan watched the emerald highlands rise vertically from the shore in a way that reminded Sullivan of the island of Maui. He had visited when he had R&R from 'Nam.

Sullivan rolled the cold bottle of beer across his forehead and cheeks and remembered what it was like when a Corona Light kept him company until Jackie D took over. He closed his eyes. He could hear the sounds of the surf and a faint cry of delight from a child at the water's edge. And when he listened carefully, the tones of an Irish flute drifted from somewhere far in the distance.

———

The wiry grey-haired officer spoke softly and his English was polished. The warm dark eyes behind the wire-rimmed glasses forgiving, at first.

Later, when Sullivan's face was a bloody pulp, he told them lies. When they prodded Capello's wounds with a bamboo pole, he begged. After that he traded his secrets in exchange for Capello's medical care. But there would be no care. The questions stopped, blood coagulated and they were left alone.

Sullivan lay next to Capello on the dirt floor. He rolled over on his side and examined Capello's wounds. Frothy blood seeped from Capello's mouth and Sullivan tore a piece of scrap from his tiger suit and stuffed it into Capello's chest wound.

"Shit," Capello said. His face was twisted in pain.

Sullivan grabbed Capello's hand and held it firmly. "One of their medics will be by to patch you up. You hang in there and you'll be fine. You hear me?"

Capello's eyes blinked and opened wide. His lips moved, "I don't want to die here, Sulli."

"You won't. I promise."

Sullivan told him that he loved him and watched him take his last breath. He lay next to his friend's body, staring at it for a long time.

Somewhere in the darkness the F-105s returned, collapsing tunnels and raining hot steel and death. Sullivan thought of Sheila and their unborn child. He thought of Capello. He thought about wanting to die.

Later he was confined to starvation, disease and daily torture. Then one day he was scoured, deloused, dressed in clean clothes and delivered back to a world where he discovered his nightmares had just begun.

—

A touch as soft as angel wings awoke Sullivan. His eyes opened on a sun being pulled toward the horizon that left scorched air in its wake.

"Hey, sleepyhead."

Sullivan blinked and Caitlin's face came into focus.

"Hey," Sullivan whispered.

"I called and there was no answer, so I thought I'd stop by and see how you were doing," Caitlin said.

Sullivan smiled. "Better, now."

"And I brought a friend," Caitlin said.

Sullivan turned around in his chair. Dutch stood wagging his tail, and when he saw Sullivan's face he covered it with canine kisses.

"He missed you, Nick," Caitlin said.

Sullivan rubbed Dutch's head and ears.

"Did you eat?" Caitlin asked.

Sullivan shook his head. "There's a ton of food in the fridge. How about being my dinner guest?"

Caitlin smiled. "You're on, sailor."

They walked into the kitchen. Caitlin took inventory of the food in the refrigerator and verbalized the possibilities. Sullivan prepared place settings for two with his good arm and Caitlin dished out dinner. They talked about Caitlin's day at the chandlery, D's budding career as a musician, the weather and Calum's seemingly failing health.

After the dishes were stacked to dry, they retired to the back porch. The sun was almost down and the beach was quiet and still. Caitlin saw Sullivan staring at the horizon.

"Feel like a walk?" Caitlin asked.

Sullivan turned and smiled. "Sure," he said.

They walked along the edge of the surf.

"Come on," Caitlin said taking his hand and leading him to a spot above the rise of the tide where the sand was still warm. She stopped next to a beached tree trunk deposited long ago by a storm and laid on her back in the sand with her hands behind her head. Sullivan sat next to her, resting his back against the bleached wood, cradling his injured appendage across his chest. Dutch scampered along the water's edge chasing sandpipers.

There was a long moment of pregnant silence.

"How are you feeling, Nick?" Caitlin asked.

Sullivan looked down as if the answer was scrawled in the sand. "I don't know," he said. "I've never died and returned to life. I don't know what I'm supposed to feel. Numb, I guess. Kind of like being stuck in neutral. And I'm more tired than when I was working sixteen-hour days on John's boat."

"I can't imagine," Caitlin said. "I mean you hear stories, but...."

A full minute passed before Sullivan said, "The experience of drowning was terrifying, but what came after was beautiful." He looked at Caitlin. "I'll never be afraid of dying."

Caitlin stared at the night sky. It was clear and the stars were coming out. "When I was young my mother told me that if you made a wish on the first star that appeared in the sky, and if you are worthy, it would come true," Caitlin said.

Sullivan looked over at her. "Did your wishes come true?"

Caitlin took a deep breath and sighed. "Still waiting, I guess."

"Did you ever play 'what if'?" Sullivan asked. "I mean, if there was enough magic in those stars and you could be anything in the world, what would it be?"

Caitlin was quick to answer. "A mother and a wife to a loving man who is my best friend and a house with a warm kitchen and a white picket fence. A place filled with children and happiness and things that you'd want to remember over and over when you grew old. And you?"

"That was my dream a long time ago. I'm not much of a dreamer anymore."

"That's sad," she said.

"Not if you don't think about it."

Caitlin looked at her watch. "Hey, you've had a long day, and I've got to open the shop at seven tomorrow morning," Caitlin said.

Sullivan said, "Maybe I'll see Calum tomorrow and drop by the shop to say hi afterwards."

"You know where to find me."

They walked back to house and Caitlin gathered up her shoes and purse. At her car door, Sullivan put a hand on her shoulder. She turned and kissed him on the cheek.

"See you soon," she said.

That night Dutch jumped into bed alongside of Sullivan and no amount of coaxing would get him to leave.

—

D was in the kitchen working the business end of a spatula. She gave Sullivan a hug. "Hey, good morning. I hope I didn't wake you last night. I got in kind of late."

"I don't remember a thing," Sullivan said as he opened the door for Dutch to go out.

"I looked in on you before I went to bed. You weren't alone, but it's not quite what I expected," she said looking at Dutch. D pointed the spatula at Sullivan in a way that reminded him of a parochial school nun. "I found two sets of dinner dishes in the drying rack this morning. Did we have company last night?" Her grin would have been the envy of Cheshire cats everywhere.

"Caitlin stopped by and helped me with dinner." Sullivan raised his sling.

"And?"

"And she visited for awhile."

"And?" D folded her arms, spatula still in hand.

"Can't you begin a sentence without the use of a coordinating conjunction?"

"Impressive, professor, but don't change the subject."

"And I think we've exhausted the topic," Sullivan said. He waved the hand of his good arm in the direction of the kitchen table. "Do you have any idea who I need to thank for all this food?"

"Yup, made a list and picked up some thank you cards when I was in Pictou for our gig yesterday. I'll help you with them after dinner."

Sullivan nodded. "Okay."

"Unless you have other plans," D said. The smile again.

Sullivan rolled his eyes.

D lifted two eggs, sunny side up, and placed them next to buttered toast on a plate for Sullivan. She poured them each a cup of coffee. At the table she asked, "What's doin' today?"

"I thought I'd get my uncle's old Chevy started, it's got an automatic transmission," he said, looking at his arm, "and maybe look in on Calum. And you?"

D shrugged. "Pick up some groceries, work on my tan maybe. I've been helping Caitlin in the shop when I get bored, so maybe I'll head over there."

Sullivan nodded. "You can take the Ford. Need money for groceries?"

"Nope, we're cool," D said. Then. "Ahh ... got something to tell you. You're not Uncle Nick anymore."

Sullivan took a deep breath and exhaled. "And why is that?"

D clicked her tongue and put on a cute face. "Cause I was tired of lying to my friends and I told them the truth."

Sullivan winced. "Who exactly?"

"Um, Caitlin and Calum know. And Father O'Malley. I think John Sylliboy knows and maybe some of the *Aspy Lady*'s crew. I didn't make it a secret."

Sullivan sighed. "What did you tell them?"

"Just that we're not really related. That I met you hitchhiking on the highway and that you're a good man who took the time to help me when I needed help. Now there's one less ghost in my closet."

Ghosts, Sullivan thought – his pantry was full. "The truth will set us free. I guess you did the right thing, but wait until the local gossip twists the truth around – we'll both have scarlet letters pinned on our shirts.

D giggled. "Cool!"

Sullivan shook his head and went out to jump-start the Chev. Then he took Dutch for a walk on the beach while the truck's battery charged.

The shoreline was spotted with blankets and umbrellas. Children played at the water's edge with plastic shovels and pails that dotted the sand with brilliant reds and yellows and blues.

He watched a little girl with a ponytail and golden locks sitting in the sand, talking to a seagull. Sullivan gave her a smile. He thought of his own daughter and flinched at the ache where a piece of his soul had been cut out.

He and Dutch walked further to where the Aspy River spilled into the sea. The tide was low and the river was ankle deep when they crossed to the other side. Sullivan found a weathered piece of driftwood the right size for a game of toss with Dutch.

Afterward, Sullivan found a patch of dry sand above the high-water mark. He sat down and stroked Dutch's head. The wind was light, and coddled waves struggled to break against the shore.

"I guess we're a team, you and me."

Dutch's brown eyes painted Sullivan with love.

"So, what are we going to do? We could go back to Virginia. If we sell the house here in Dingwall, we can get us a new truck and a nice travel trailer that we could haul from place to place – warm in the winter, cool in the summer. It doesn't have to be the same place or even the same coast. But we don't own the house yet; there are conditions."

Dutch listened and then tilted his head to one side.

"Adoption by a Canadian canine doesn't qualify me for immigration status. Nobody really needs us. I even managed to get kicked out of ... well, I'm not sure it was heaven. It was more like the waiting room where they decide if you take the up or down escalator."

Dutch lay in the sand and looked up at Sullivan.

"I guess we'll think on it."

Sullivan grabbed a fist full of sand and let it run through his fingers. "The thing is, nothing's changed. I died and came back to the same damn life. And it's probably out there thinking up new ways to tear me up. But I'm not going to give it a second chance. "

His mouth was dry just like it used to get before he tempered his fiends with a Corona before Jackie D came along to drown the sons of a bitches. Sullivan walked back to the house to quench his thirst.

Chapter 15

The next morning Sullivan arrived at the hospital in Sydney at nine, went through hospital admissions and directly to radiology. The orthopedic surgeon who had repaired his tendon told him he was doing just fine and sent him for physical therapy for an hour to practice the exercises he was to perform daily at home.

Then he sat in the waiting room for about an hour before Doctor Bonadies, his attending physician, called him into his office. They shook hands and the doctor settled back in his chair. The physician was about his age, Sullivan thought, as he watched the man examine his medical charts through a pair of reading glasses. He thought too that the doctor took good care of himself, probably playing racquetball or running. And he was well styled, from his salt and pepper hair down to his manicured fingernails.

The doctor took off his glasses and set them on the desk. "How's the shoulder?"

"Just a bit stiff," Sullivan said. "It didn't hurt until I went a few rounds with the folks in your physical therapy department."

The doctor smiled. "You're going to be on light duty for the next sixteen weeks or so. I'm going to put you in touch with someone in your area for weekly physio, but again, no lifting of anything over ten pounds for the time being and no repetitive movement of your arm other than the exercises that have been prescribed. Any problems breathing – congestion, coughing, shortness of breath?"

"No, I just seem to be more tired than normal."

"I wouldn't be too concerned about that. Your body was traumatized both by the accident and by your surgery."

Doctor Bonadies paused for a moment looking at Sullivan and asked, "Do you have any problem sleeping?"

Sullivan shook his head.

"How about nervousness or melancholia?"

Sullivan shrugged his shoulders.

Sullivan could see the physician thinking. "I'd like you to see one of our specialists before you leave. Just to discuss a few things about what you might expect as a result of your accident."

Sullivan shifted in his chair.

"I think you may be just fine in all regards, but I think we need to cover all the bases."

Sullivan opened his mouth to speak, but before he could the doctor was on the phone. After he hung up, Bonadies walked Sullivan to an elevator, took him up two floors and then escorted him to an office that purported in bold black lettering to belong to Donald Esherick, doctor of psychiatry.

The wait in Doctor Esherick's office was short. An animated man, not a day over thirty, came into the waiting room, shook

Sullivan's hand and motioned him into an inner office. He was dressed casually in oxblood loafers, tan pants and a blue shirt , with the top button loose, along with a gold and blue striped tie.

"Please have a seat, Mr. Sullivan," Esherick said, pointing to an upholstered velour lounge chair. Esherick sat in a chair directly across from Sullivan. He had a spiral notebook in his hand with a pen clipped to the cover. "May I call you Nicholas?"

"No, but you can call me Nick."

Esherick smiled and unclipped the pen.

Sullivan looked around the room for a couch but couldn't find one. And the doctor didn't have a beard or goatee or some other type of facial hair that would pronounce him as one capable of tapping into his inner thoughts.

"How are you?" Esherick asked with a smile. He crossed his legs, slouched a bit in his chair and waited for an answer.

"Just fine, and you?"

Esherick nodded. "Couldn't be better. Did Doctor Bonadies tell you why he referred you here?"

"In a roundabout way. I'm guessing he's concerned that I may be experiencing PTSD as a result of my near-death experience. Actually, I was clinically dead so near death is a misnomer."

"You know about post traumatic stress disorder?"

"Yup."

The doctor leaned forward in his chair. "Tell me about it."

Sullivan did and added that the experience of having your heart stop is anticlimactic in comparison to spending three years, seven months and eleven days in a prison where they tortured you twenty-four/seven. And discovering that your wife and daughter had deserted you ties for first place. Drowning was a weak third at best.

"You mentioned your friend, Tony Capello, a number of times. I take it you grew to be close friends, during your time in the military."

"I loved him like the brother he was. He risked his life more than once to keep me alive. You'd have to have been a combat veteran to understand what I mean."

The doctor lowered his eyes and when his gaze returned it was faded. "Oh, I think I may have a fairly good idea, Nick. I don't talk about it much, but I was on active duty in the Canadian Forces from 2008 to 2011 and now I'm in a reserve unit. While I was in Kandahar I saw things that I was never prepared to see either as a physician or a member of the human race. While my specialty is diseases of the brain, I trained as a generalist like all medical students. And on a few occasions I had to help out in the surgical unit. It's not easy seeing what's left of someone who came in contact with an IED. Many members of the Forces that returned home had severe psychological impairments. Some even took their own lives. Most realized they needed help and got it."

Esherick tried to manage a smile. "Including me, Nick. So, no one gets a free pass. You came back from Vietnam alive – Tony and a lot of others didn't. It's what we call survivor's guilt, sometimes referred to as KZ or Konzentrationslager syndrome, named after the survivors of the holocaust. It's a symptom of PTSD.

"Have you ever talked with a medical professional before about your war experiences?" Esherick asked.

Sullivan said he had during his recuperation after leaving Vietnam and for several months after. And again when the Air Force took a way his pilot's wings.

Esherick scribbled in his notebook and nodded his head. "The past and present are separated by a pencil-thin line. There's a lot that has happened in this field of medicine in the last several decades. We now know that a single traumatic event can cause permanent epigenetic changes in the physiology of the brain. The results are what we commonly call depression, which is associated with PTSD. I'm guessing that you have experienced some of the symptoms." He read them off like the answers to an exam question in medical school.

Esherick said, "The good news is that there is effective treatment available."

Sullivan said, "Sometimes it just rains on your picnic. But thanks for the history lesson."

"I'd like to talk to you more about this," Esherick said.

"I'm not planning to be in town long," Sullivan said, "but thanks for the offer."

Sullivan stood up and put out his hand.

Esherick took it. "Think about it. If not here with me, with another professional when you reach your destination."

If I had one, Sullivan thought.

Sullivan turned to leave but paused and asked, "What happened to your couch?"

Esherick just smiled. "You're good at masking your feelings."

"Thanks for your time, Doc."

Sullivan checked the oil in the Chevy before he left the hospital parking lot and made his way back to Dingwall. The windows were cranked down, letting in the amalgam of ocean with a hint of exhaust. His thoughts shifted to Caitlin. And as he conjured up her image, he felt a sense of promise. Maybe Doc Esherick was right. Maybe not.

The house was quiet when he returned home. D was staying overnight on Prince Edward Island with the band. Every window was open, letting in a pure, sun-bleached sea breeze and ocean sounds. Sullivan lay down on the living room couch and dissected the sounds drifting up from Aspy Bay: the distant motor of a fishing boat, a carpenter's hammer driving steel into wood, a mother calling her child, the call of a lone gull and the windchime arpeggio performing on the back porch – all sounds of a world that he still didn't feel connected with.

The rhythm of the tones beckoned sleep. His dreams played softly and tonal and were accented Caitlin's freckles and blue eyes. Muddled as dreams often are, the crew of the *Aspy Lady* appeared too.

When he awoke Sullivan recognized neither place nor day for a moment. He kept his eyes closed until the glow of his dreams faded. He thought about Paddy who had risked his life to drag him from the ocean and who then stood vigil in his hospital room.

And he thought about Capello who had saved him so long ago in a war still so present.

Sullivan made a telephone call. The voice at the other end said that he had heard of Sullivan's ordeal on the *Aspy Lady* and hoped Sullivan was doing well. Sullivan thanked Leonard Boudreau and told him that he was in need of legal services. When asked how he might be of help, Sullivan explained how Paddy Gallagher's home was repossessed and asked how much it would cost to get it back from the bank.

Two hours later Boudreau informed Sullivan that five thousand plus interest was all that the bank wanted to reinstate the mortgage. Sullivan told Boudreau to set the wheels in motion. It would be tight, but the money he received from Sylliboy plus the progress payment due for work on the ketch would cover Paddy's refinancing costs. And Sullivan was sure that Paddy would eventually repay the loan.

Sullivan loaded Dutch in his uncle's Chevy and pointed it in the direction of Lochinver Harbour. He could see movement on the *Aspy Lady* when he stopped in the harbour parking lot. He hadn't been aboard the boat since he left it unexpectedly. He jumped aboard and lifted Dutch from the wharf to the deck. Paddy stuck his head out of the companionway between the crew's quarters and the deck. He wore the same clothes that he fished in.

Paddy smiled and walked over to greet Sullivan. "Good to see you, Nick."

"Good to see you too, Paddy. And thank you for pulling my butt out of the ocean. I was almost a goner."

"No big deal," Paddy said.

"Yes, it was."

Dutch went over to Paddy and lifted his paw. Paddy shook it and smiled.

"You can't get enough of this old tub can you?" Sullivan asked.

Paddy shrugged his shoulders. "I was renting a room in town, but I can save some if I stay on the Lady."

Sullivan nodded. "I think I might have a solution to that."

Paddy's eyes narrowed at Sullivan for an explanation.

"I had a talk with old man Boudreau's son, the lawyer that handled my uncle's estate, and he talked to the bank that foreclosed on your house."

It seemed as if Paddy stopped breathing.

"The bank needs five thousand to reinstate the mortgage."

Paddy's voice crept up a notch. "You know I don't have that kind of cash."

Sullivan held his hands up and Paddy grew silent. "I'll advanced the cash for you."

Paddy's jaw dropped and his eyes danced over Sullivan.

"It's just a loan mind you. There's no interest and you can pay it back whenever you're able."

Paddy shook his head and began to speak, but Sullivan said, "It's a done deal Paddy, so there's nothing to talk about. Why don't you speak with your wife? You can probably move back in a week or so when the paperwork clears. The bank will be in touch."

"Why?" Paddy asked

"Why not?" Sullivan said.

There was a bounce in Sullivan's step as he walked down the wharf to the chandlery. Dutch noticed it and nipped playfully at Sullivan's heels.

Caitlin was on the phone; she raised her index finger.

"So, what have you been up to?" she asked when she finished the call.

Sullivan told her about Paddy, and then out of nowhere, he asked her out to dinner that evening.

Caitlin insisted that they drive her car, a pearl-white Jeep wagon, to a restaurant in Baddeck.

Sullivan was spit-shined when Caitlin knocked on his door. Her dressy, black slacks hugged her at the waist, contrasting with a loose-fitting, pearl-coloured blouse.

They sat in a corner of a century-old inn. The room was filled with whispers that were intimate and furtive. There was small talk over drinks – wine for Caitlin, beer for Sullivan. Caitlin mentioned D, and Sullivan took the opportunity to apologize for the deceptive explanation of their kinship, although Sullivan admitted she did seem almost like kin to him. The waiter took their orders: Caitlin chose the salmon and Sullivan prime rib.

After dessert they sipped coffee.

"What are your plans, Nick?" Caitlin asked. "I mean, will you be staying for a while?"

"I just had that conversation with Dutch," he replied. "My doctor says that I won't be using my right arm for sixteen weeks. I can't drive the Ford and I don't trust my uncle's Chevy to make it out the driveway. The Ford is my only way back to Virginia."

"So, what did Dutch say?"

Sullivan smiled. "He's indecisive. Like me."

"Cape Breton is good place to stay while you're making up your mind."

"How so?" Sullivan asked.

"The people," she said. "They're like family. It's quiet here too, and it's comfortable in its predictability. You don't have the problems like you have in the city. And I like being near the ocean. But nothing is perfect. Sometimes I think I'm missing something. I mean, I miss Montreal. It has a personality and a diversity that's refreshing. And there's always something going on. It's an old city with something new happening every day."

"What about your business? You seem to enjoy your work."

"I don't know, Nick. I mean it keeps me busy, but I don't really feel challenged. It was there when— when I lost my husband. The shop was convenient and kept me occupied and I needed something to immerse myself in."

"I'm sorry." Sullivan said. He watched the reflection of the candle flame flicker in her eyes.

Caitlin looked at the drink in her hand. "There's still a lot of hurt. But I do have hope."

"Calum says hope gives you a reason to stick around and see how things turn out."

Caitlin smiled. "I've never heard it put that way, but yes, Calum is right."

On the road back to Dingwall, Sullivan had the wheel. Caitlin surfed the channels on the radio and, finding nothing but rock, slipped a CD into the player on the dash. Sullivan hadn't heard of the artist, Mary Chapin Carpenter, but he liked what he heard.

Caitlin slipped off her shoes and curled her legs underneath her. "Why didn't you remarry, Nick?" she asked.

Sullivan kept his eyes on the two lane road. "Who'd want a worn out old flyer like me?"

"But you've thought about it?"

"Sometimes. And you?"

"Sometimes," Caitlin replied.

Sullivan sensed Caitlin watching him and wondered what she saw. She turned the music lower and they talked about people and places and things they wanted to do before the summer was over.

When they reached Caitlin's house, she was asleep with her head nestled against Sullivan's shoulder. Her eyes flickered when he stopped the Jeep. Sullivan opened the car door for her and walked her to the front step. "I had a great time. Thank you."

"Me too," Caitlin said.

Sullivan put his hand on her waist and kissed her on the lips. She kissed him back, but then pressed her hands against his chest.

"It's late," she said. "Thanks again." And then she disappeared through the door of her house.

Sullivan packed Dutch into the Chevy and drove to the café at Lochinver Harbour for breakfast the next day. Sullivan could see Paddy's pickup in the parking lot and Caitlin's Jeep in front of her shop. As he sipped his coffee waiting for his order, he dissected his evening with Caitlin. Their conversation over dinner was easy and familiar. And she had kissed him back at the door but then abruptly terminated the encounter. What was that: a sign to take things slowly, a discretion she regretted?

Sullivan relived the kiss. He missed that moment of intimacy and wrapped his mind around it.

Chapter 16

Warm days and cool nights – it was mild for late September. Sullivan looked forward to Sundays when D wasn't playing with the band. After church she flaunted her culinary skills. The aromas of brunch filled the kitchen. Sometimes it was rappie pie, seared scallops with marmalade or Acadian stew.

"It seems like yesterday when I picked you up on the highway and now it's autumn. Time flies."

Inland, Sullivan could see the hardwoods bleeding colour. But where the ocean kissed the shore, where evergreens reigned supreme, the only hint of the equinox was the measured conquest of cold over warmth.

D said, "Time is a contradiction."

Sullivan rubbed his shoulder and arm, trying to abate the pain that came less frequently now. "How so?" Sullivan asked.

"Like, look at the light that comes from a star. The star may have burned out a thousand years ago, but it stills twinkles at night. So what you're seeing is something that exists both in the past and present. And that's a contradiction, right? And anything that is a contradiction is meaningless. Ergo, time is a contradiction and therefore meaningless."

Sullivan stared at her. "What have you been reading?"

"My philosophy text. Cool, huh?"

D was commuting to take music and liberal arts classes once a week at the Cape Breton University campus near Sydney; with Leonard Boudreau's help, she'd obtained a student visa.

"Speaking of heavy reading," D said, "I saw a book in your room while I was house cleaning. I think the title was Shook Over Hell or something like that, about veterans of the American Civil War and Vietnam. Any good?"

The book by Eric Deane, Jr. showed up in Sullivan's mailbox one day with a letter shoved into the inside flap of the cover. Accolades printed on the back panel of the dust cover praised the author for his scholarly efforts in paralleling post-traumatic stress in veterans of the US Civil War and Vietnam.

The penned note said, "'It's a good read, Nick. Thought I would share, Don Esherick." Below Esherick's name he had printed out a poem by Robert Frost.

"The Armful"
For every parcel I stoop down to seize
I lose some other off my arms and knees,
And the whole pile is slipping, bottles, buns –
Extremes too hard to comprehend at once,
Yet nothing I should care to leave behind.
With all I have to hold with – hand and mind
And heart, if need be, I will do my best
To keep their building balanced at my breast.
I crouch down to prevent them as they fall;
Then sit down in the middle of them all.
I had to drop the armful in the road
And try to stack them in a better load.

"I'm still reading it," Sullivan replied.

He was still undergoing weekly physiotherapy. And while his physical wounds healed, old familiar demons began to visit again. A war was still waging for his soul. Ramparts were built: there was no hard alcohol in the house. The battlefield was limited to evenings, when Sullivan warred with eighty-proof ghosts and five percent Alexander Keith's.

That evening, like most, he drove to the ketch and climbed aboard when Caitlin had left the store and the docks were quiet. Sometimes he'd take Dutch along, but not today. He parked next to the ketch to feign some work on the old boat that had been left untouched since his accident.

He climbed the wooden ladder to the cockpit, looked around and slithered down the hatchway to the cabin, pulling the splash boards closed behind him. Curtains were pulled over the port holes for anonymity.

Sullivan unlatched a cabinet above the galley table and pulled out a 375ml bottle of Havana Club Reserve rum – something new he imbibed with a clandestine aroma forbidden south of the border. And the demitasse bottle gave him the false impression that his addiction had limits.

The infusion of warmth increased with each sip he took from a brandy snifter, which seemed to add an ambiance of style to his addiction. He settled into the corner of the galley bench cushion. His head spun when he closed his eyes and when he opened them, Capello was lying on the settee on the opposite side of the galley. The ghost had his hands behind his head and his boots were hanging politely over the edge of the cushions.

Sullivan took another sip from his glass. Then he stared at a sliver of melting daylight, escaping through a porthole that the curtain didn't cover. Capello followed Sullivan's gaze toward the chandlery.

"No sparks coming from there, buddy," Sullivan said. "We go out to a movie or dinner every couple of weeks. I walk her to the door and get a hug and quick kiss on the lips – not exactly thunder and lightning."

You're old and washed up, Nick, a voice hissed.

Sullivan turned his head. "Fuck off."

In reply he received a menacing cackle from his demons, then silence.

Sullivan leaned his head back on the soft cushion of the galley bench and closed his eyes. When he blinked awake, he rose and pushed the splash boards open. Inhaling brine and creosote, he made his way down the ladder. He walked around the docks until he was sober enough to drive and to hide his dependency from D.

The melody of Sullivan's life consisted of mostly empty measures with an occasional note that dotted a line or space. There was Canadian Thanksgiving in October. D and Sullivan baked and boiled and whipped a traditional feast that was shared with Calum and Caitlin.

Halloween arrived with a hunter's moon. Almond Joy and Snickers bars were traded for youthful smiles. And there was Remembrance Day in November when Flanders poppies and French rondeaux of recollection cursed the dreams of survivors.

It was during those dark November days that Sullivan would curl up fetal in the ketch and drink himself numb; an electric heater kept the cabin cozy. And then came December.

The first weekend of December it was D that pulled him from his funk. It was her idea to drive the Ford to Halifax. It took most of daylight to drive to the outskirts of the city. The pet-friendly motel room that they shared was clean and simple.

They freshened up and dressed, D in the bathroom and Sullivan in bedroom, with Dutch watching with canine enthusiasm, and then they drove off to the mall. Cards at Carlton and Hallmark, a Windwall jacket for D from American Eagle and a wool sweater from the International for Sullivan were hidden in shopping bags to be unveiled Christmas day.

Sullivan smiled as D skipped down sugar-plummed aisles at Walmart and the Christmas Shoppe, loading carts with lights and tree decorations and a manger with ceramic figurines. Luckily, old man Boudreau had advanced a progress payment given the fact any sort of work on the ketch was contraindicated by his injuries.

They freed Dutch from the cab of the Ford and walked him to the city's Christmas tree on Grand Parade. LED lights cut the night in purple, red, green and white. A white picket-style fence kept peepers at distance. The cold air carried children's exclamations, a dog's bark and traffic sounds.

"It's magical," D said.

Sullivan looked at her and could see the reflection of the lights in her eyes. She'd make a wonderful wife and mother someday, he thought.

"I wish I could box and wrap it up and keep it fresh all year – the wonder, I mean," D said.

She took his hand. "Come on, I'm hungry."

Dutch was returned to the Ford, happy with some Old Mrs. Hubbards oven-baked dog biscuits.

They walked to Stories Restaurant, D stopping to window-shop, dreaming herself into the Christmas displays.

Inside the Morris Street restaurant their waiter took their order for drinks and starters: Jackie D straight up and white wine, scallops wrapped in rice paper for D and spice braised boar shoulder for Sullivan. For dinner, Barbary duck breast, bourbon mashed potatoes, blueberry port jus and grilled swordfish, a carafe each of red and white.

"This is the most delicious food I've ever had, anywhere," D said, sipping her coffee.

Back at motel anonymous under the cover of blankets and night, D whispered, "This was the best day I've had maybe in my entire adult life. And I love you for it, Nick."

"Goodnight, Raindrop," Sullivan said.

The next day, once they were caffeinated and fed at a Circle K and on the road by nine, the Ford pointed its nose toward Dingwall. They included some alternate routes on the return – Glendale, Blue Mills, Scotsville to Route 19, Margaree Forks. A light snow began to paint the hills and fields with winter.

D was driving and Sullivan leaned against the passenger door, eyes closed with Dutch laying across his lap. The Ford took a sharp turn, wheels hitting ruts and rattling worn shock absorbers.

Sullivan blinked his eyes awake.

"What?"

"This is going to be so cool," D said, pointing to a sign that advertised a Christmas tree farm and hay wagon rides and sleigh bells if the snow was deep enough.

They stopped at a farmhouse next to what must have been fifty hectares of blue spruce, Douglas fir and pine. Smoke drifted from black pipe raised above a shop that was once a small barn. Inside a fiftyish man in suspenders and plaid stoked the stove while a woman and a preadolescent boy decorated wreaths.

D and Sullivan left for the hinterlands of the tree farm, Sullivan with a borrowed saw in hand and Dutch running in circles and pulling at the hems of D's jeans.

"Remember the house only has an eight-foot ceiling," Sullivan said.

After forty-five minutes and a kilometre of footprints tracked in the snow, D announced she'd found the perfect one. A few minutes of sawing and the Douglas fir was free of its earthly bounds and ready to be transformed in D's mind's eye.

Already sweating from his efforts, Sullivan grabbed hold of a branch and began the trip back to the farmhouse. Dutch grabbed a branch too, tugging with enthusiasm to Sullivan and D's praise.

"I wish I had gloves," Sullivan said at about the same moment Dutch lifted his ears. Sullivan could hear it too – the rattle of a diesel engine coming over a rise, hay wagon in tow. Sullivan waved and the farmer gave a wave back and drove down a dirt track toward them after dropping off a family of four to wander the artificial forest for their perfect boughs.

"You and the Misses picked yourself a nice one," the farmer said.

"Yes, we did, didn't we, dear?" D said.

Sullivan's face lit up Rudolf red and he let out a puff of air. D giggled.

They climbed aboard the wagon, Dutch perched on the tree in canine triumph, smiling, on top of his world.

While the farmer wrapped the tree in netting, D and Sullivan helped themselves to a complimentary cup of hot spiced cider and milled about the shop with a half dozen others. With an undecorated wreath and a small brown bag of bows in hand, they waved goodbye to the farm family and were back on the road, the snow light and fading, slipping beneath balding tires.

"I should have stopped in Sydney for some retreads," Sullivan said. "These would probably get me through another season in Virginia, but I never expected this," he said, waving his free hand at the road and gripping the steering wheel in the other.

"Have you thought about going back?" D asked.

"I'll have to sooner or later. My arm has healed as good as it's going to get."

"But you're coming back, right?"

"I haven't thought it through." Looking at D, he could see the apprehension. "You can stay as long as you want. It will be some time for the estate to be probated, and then who knows."

D grew quiet, rubbed Dutch's ears and stared ahead at twist and turns in the road ahead.

They stopped at a hardware store just before closing and purchased a tree stand and then headed home. D was fixing a late dinner when Dutch barked at approaching headlights. A moment later John Sylliboy was stomping snow from his boots and grabbing a seat next to the woodstove that crackled and clinked as the stovepipe expanded.

Sylliboy rubbed his hands.

"All done for the season, John?" Sullivan asked.

"We're finished. I scheduled the boat to be pulled for maintenance and painting in the spring, then we do it all over again. I hope you'll fish with us again?"

"We'll have to see about that."

"There's nothing wrong with a maybe," Sylliboy said. "Are you going to hold out here for the winter?"

"Leonard Boudreau mentioned I could only stay six months. He said I could apply for an extension. But I should make my way back to Little Creek anyway."

"Well, best I make my way home. I'm having an open house the Saturday before Christmas – noon until whenever. I hope you can stop by?" Sylliboy asked.

"What can we bring?" D asked.

"Your guitar and voice. I've got a handle on everything else," Sylliboy said. "Well, I'm off." He walked to the door and slipped his feet into his boots. "Oh, and here's one for you. Our very own Willie is getting married." Sylliboy shook his head. "Word is that his wife to be is expecting."

Sullivan nodded, remembering the conversation he'd had with Willie. Good to know the lad had done the right thing.

After Sylliboy left, the room seemed empty. Sullivan sat down and looked at the fire through the glass door of the woodstove.

"Hey, what are you, the Grinch? How about a little Christmas spirit here?"

Sullivan smiled for D's sake.

"How about I invite Calum and Caitlin over to decorate?"

"Okay."

"And we can send out some Christmas cards. I bought enough for you too. We could make some Christmas cookies together," D added. "Get you out of de funk you in."

Sullivan laughed. "What's with the rap?"

"Got you to laugh, didn't I?"

Sullivan managed a smile.

Decorating day arrived. After breakfast D sprinted out to the mailbox and dropped the contents on the kitchen table. "Here's one for you, Nick."

She handed Sullivan a Canada Post cardboard mailer.

Sullivan ripped the "pull here" tab and shook out the contents. Dutch finished his morning meal and sat watching as his master's eyes narrowed.

"A Dr. Seuss book, cool," D said.

The cover proclaimed the title – Oh, the Places You'll Go!

D looked over Sullivan's shoulder. "It's about choices," D said, "and life's ups and downs. I read it when I was um— getting some help, before I came here."

Sullivan wasn't surprised at the blue ink greeting on the inside cover: "Merry Christmas, Nick. Don Esherick."

The book was a quick read. It had been a long time since D heard Sullivan really laugh.

"Do you have any writing paper?" Sullivan asked.

"How about a Christmas card?" D replied. Sullivan nodded and began writing a thank you to Doctor Esherick.

Late morning into afternoon, D and Sullivan spilled milk, flour, sugar, eggs and spices into bowls. The Mixmaster mixed, cookie presses were loaded that turned raw dough into green wreaths with red candied bows. That night was starlit and December cold. Eggnog married with hundred-proof Southern Comfort set the mood.

They worked their way down from the treetop where an angel glowed in adoration. White lights were spun around the breadth of the evergreen, a Madonna ornament was nestled in the heart of the tree, decorations were colour-coded and arranged by size. Calum watched, rubbing Dutch's mane.

After dinner, D wrapped garland silver on evergreen while Caitlin and Sullivan did the dishes.

"Thanks for the flowers, Nick . They were beautiful."

"Then they were fitting," Sullivan said.

"And maybe you've had too much eggnog."

Caitlin wiped her hands on a dishtowel. "I didn't know what to get for you. I, ah, I didn't want it to be too ... I mean we're, you know...."

Sullivan nodded.

"So it's just a little something for the boat that I hope you like. I put it under the tree."

Sullivan forced a smile. "If it's from you, I'm sure it will be perfect."

He finished drying the last of the pots and pans and helped Caitlin put the dishes away.

"I'm going to Montreal for Christmas to be with my family. I'm kind of excited."

"Good for you."

"My parents are getting older and so are my nieces and nephews. I don't see enough of them."

"John is having an open house. Will I see you there ?" Sullivan asked.

"No, I thanked John for the invitation, but I'll be leaving for Montreal that day. So, I guess I probably won't see you before I go. Merry Christmas, Nick."

Sullivan opened his arms and Caitlin slipped into a hug. "Merry Christmas," he said.

He wanted to hold her long and hard, but she broke the embrace.

Later, when D was asleep and deceit was free to roam, Sullivan sucked hope from the spoils of the party and sat in the darkened living room in front of the tree. In the dazzling light, which bounced off ornaments and angel wings, he remembered . Dutch, leaving contentment next to the woodstove, walked over to him and rested his head on Sullivan's lap. Sullivan rubbed his ears.

Christmas. So very long ago it had been his favourite time of the year. Now it was just another day. Sullivan made his way to the kitchen and rummaged through open bottles of liquor and wine and chose a dry red from the Bear River Vineyard that would take the edge off with style.

He lifted a cork screw from the kitchen table and noticed a pile of outgoing and incoming Christmas cards. Sullivan wasn't much for marking occasions or old acquaintances with paper and ink; he had only penned a few Christmas cards to the Little Creek crowd. But D had purchased an assortment of cards. Sullivan uncorked the wine and began to look through them. Sorting through Santas and snowmen and stocking-hung hearths, he stopped. Christmas morning: A young girl's delight, ribbon and paper and a puppy attired with a red bow – all wrapped in Hallmark glitter.

Sullivan's hand shook as he drank from the bottle of Bear River. It had been, what, nine, ten years since he last wrote to her, only to receive the mail back marked undeliverable. He was drunk now and in his element – he picked up a pen and began to write.

Chapter 17

Christmas Eve came on the wings of a nor'easter. Cape Breton Island was brushed in soft and faultless white. There was an eight o'clock Mass at St. Joseph's. Headlights like stage cycloramas backlit the snowflakes. Neither the heater nor wipers in the Ford could rout the scheme of things. Inside St. Joseph's, warmth and light and the children's choir sang of peace and promise.

At the house, the Christmas tree glimmered through the night, and in the morning presents were unveiled. Sullivan opened the gift from Caitlin – a brass ship's bell engraved with the name of the ketch.

D, dressed in slippers, pajamas, robe and smiles, and Sullivan, in denim and flannel, lingered over breakfast. While D showered and dressed, Sullivan plodded through the eighteen centimetres of snow to warm up the Ford parked in the barn and then to the foot of the driveway where the snowplow had left behind a veritable mountain.

An unsteady barometer threatened flurries and grey sky. Sullivan parked the Ford off the edge of the road and he and D walked up John Sylliboy's long drive. Freshly plowed snow crunched beneath their shoes and somewhere off in the distance they could hear the sounds of a labouring snowplow. As they grew closer, they could see smoke spilling from stovepipe and from inside came the sounds of music and step dancing.

D quickly integrated her voice into the music while Sullivan indulged in food and drink and the company of locals and some of the crew from the *Aspy Lady*. Then, like a thief in the night, Christmas was gone.

Just after New Year's, at breakfast, Sullivan took a sip of coffee and wrapped his hands around the warm cup.

"As soon as I get a clear shot at the weather, I'm heading to Virginia," Sullivan said.

D was sitting across the kitchen table, her feet propped up on an adjoining chair.

"Is Dutch going with you?"

Dutch looked up from his perch nearby one of the old cast iron radiators that hissed and clanked in every room.

"What do you say, Dutch? Do you want to go on a road trip in the truck?"

Dutch bristled at the invitation.

"I guess he's coming with me."

"He'd want to go with you into a burning building," D said. "Anyone who says dogs can't experience human love are correct; canine love exists on a higher plane."

"I'll get my uncle's Chevy running so you'll have transportation to school. It seemed to run okay last summer."

"How long will you be gone?"

"Until spring, to be legal with Immigration. Are you going to be okay by yourself for awhile?"

D looked into her coffee cup. "I'll miss you and Dutch."

"And we'll miss you too."

"But you promise you will come back?"

"Things aren't finished here," Sullivan said. "After that?" He shrugged his shoulders.

It took a week and a day to get the Ford and Chevy fit and have Dutch examined by a vet to ensure his vaccinations were up-to-date so that a certificate of health could be presented at the border crossing.

Travel day came. D heard the shower running at three o'clock and had breakfast ready when Sullivan came down the stairs lugging a suitcase with Dutch running in front of him.

"Do you have your passport and Dutch's papers?"

Sullivan nodded.

"And your friends in Virginia know to expect you?"

"They've been warned."

"You have your auto club card?"

"Just renewed it."

"Do you want to take my iPod?"

Sullivan shook his head.

"You'll drive carefully and call me tonight?"

"What are we, married? We'll be fine."

D sat across the table with her arms crossed.

"The battery charger is connected to the Chevy and is set on trickle charge. Remember to add a can of additive with every fill-up so the gas line doesn't freeze."

D pouted. "Humph."

Sullivan bused his dishes to the kitchen sink and when he turned around D had tears in her eyes.

Sullivan rolled his eyes. He gave her a hug and Dutch leaned up against her leg.

"It's just, well, it's like we're a family," D sobbed. "And I feel like I won't see you again."

Sullivan held her as she sobbed then put her at arm's length.

"Like a really bad fungus, we're hard to get rid of."

"Well, I'm glad you're so honest about it."

They both laughed, and before smiles faded Sullivan and Dutch were out the door.

Sullivan stopped for gas at a Circle K in Sydney. Dutch sat in the passenger seat watching the herd of humans come and go. Sullivan's hands were stuffed in his coat pockets, the pump nozzle locked open, his eyes lazy and wandering. Then, "Doc, is that you?"

A head appeared from behind a gas pump on the other side of the pump island. "Nick Sullivan," Esherick said. "The world is full of small wonders. What brings you down this way?"

"Heading back to the States one step ahead of Immigration."

Esherick laughed. "Got time for a cup of coffee?"

"Sure, why not," Sullivan replied.

Esherick was sitting in a booth when Sullivan finished filling the big tank of the Ford. Sullivan sat across from him and shook his hand. "Belated Happy New Year, Doc."

"Same to you, Nick. How were the holidays?"

"They were okay. And thanks for the books."

"You already thanked me. I got your Christmas card," Esherick said.

"Well, thanks again."

Esherick ordered coffee for both of them and the waitress returned like a genie with a coffee urn.

"Dr. Suess," Sullivan laughed.

"The good doctor had a lot of wisdom," Esherick said. "His books weren't written just for kids. In fact the book I sent you has probably been purchased for more adults than children."

Sullivan sipped his coffee.

"A new year," Esherick said. "Any New Year's resolutions?"

"It's a day at a time, Doc. How about you?"

"Nothing wrong with the day at time approach. Me? Yes, I made a few promises. One is that I'm going to try to take five strokes off my golf score. I'm also going to make it a point to be home for dinner with my wife and children. I may have to get up an hour earlier, but you know what they say about the early bird. And a third, well, the third I just don't feel like sharing."

"Well I hope it's good, because you deserve it, Doc."

"Thanks, Nick. Well, I'm off to office. What's happening after your visit to the States?"

Sullivan shrugged his shoulders. "A day at a time, Doc. But I'll probably head back to Cape Breton."

"Hey, why not give me a shout on your way back through Sydney. We'll do lunch, my treat." Esherick scribbled his cell phone number on his business card, which did not indicate his medical specialty.

"Sounds like a plan, Doc. Stay well."

"And you, Nick. Stay well too."

Familiarity was lost in the blue exhaust fumes of the Ford. And when Sullivan crossed the bridge to the Nova Scotia mainland, he had a sense of departure, rather than being on the advent of arrival. Cape Bretoners regard this bridge and causeway that connect it with the mainland as a gateway; celebrated in story and song, the causeway evokes homesickness on one side, warmth of home on the other. Dutch stared out the window, memorizing sights, sounds and scents so as to find their way back.

The Ford pointed its hood ornament east toward Saint John, New Brunswick. The Yarmouth boat was mothballed for the winter and the Digby ferry would have added hours to their journey.

They spent the night at a pet friendly motel in Saint John. Awake at four o'clock, they crossed the border from St. Stephen to Calais, Maine, a couple of hours later. The customs officer checked Sullivan's passport and Dutch's papers, examined the pickup bed, asked a few questions and waved them through.

Sullivan set his new Timex an hour back to Eastern Time and stopped for cheap gas in Calais and again in Portland.

It was four in the afternoon, driving down Interstate 91 in Connecticut, that it happened. Sullivan believed that home was where you slept at night, but that wasn't always the case. He'd had a childhood and parents. He attended kindergarten through high school in the Farmington River Valley. He rode tricycles and bicycles and motorcycles there, and it was there that the sum of his learned child and adolescent being was forged. The last time Sullivan had visited Connecticut was when he buried his mother next to his father, so it was prophetic that the alternator on the Ford decided to die there too.

A state trooper soon pulled up behind him, checked his licence and registration and called an auto club tow truck to haul the Ford into a repair shop. The good news was the alternator for the Ford was available, but the bad news was that the part couldn't be delivered before the shop's five o'clock closing time. As luck would have it, the shop was also a Rent-a-Wreck franchise. Sullivan put his credit card down and drove out with a minivan with his suitcase and Dutch's food bag and dishes in the back and directions to an inexpensive Motel Six thirty kilometres away.

As Sullivan drove to pick up the Interstate, he noticed an American Legion Post and pulled in. He wasn't a member, but the Legion was open to the public and had good chow at a reasonable price.

Sullivan told Dutch to stay and that he'd back soon. Inside, the Legion was warm and nearly empty save the bartender and three guests. Sullivan took a stool at the bar and ordered a draft while he looked at the menu.

Two stools down, a man hunched over a glass of amber and ice cubes.

"You can't go wrong with the meatloaf," the man said.

Sullivan turned his head. The voice belonged to a buzz-cut head that was as silver as a new quarter. He seemed more husky than overweight and wore a grey hoodie and denim pants. A meaty hand was wrapped around his drink as if someone might try to steal it.

"Thanks for the heads-up," Sullivan said and ordered the meatloaf.

"New member or passing through?" buzz-cut asked.

"I was heading to Virginia when my truck broke down," Sullivan said. "It won't be fixed until tomorrow. I saw the Legion hall and decided to stop in."

Buzz-cut nodded. There was a look about buzz-cut that Sullivan was familiar with. It was the look and demeanour of men that marked time in veterans' society and legion halls and bars like the Barbecue Pit. Sullivan knew that war cut a piece out of you, a hole that could never be patched, and men like buzz-cut wandered places like this where vets gathered, trying to find those lost pieces among other war crippled bodies and minds. And when they discovered they couldn't, they'd infuse their bodies with eighty-proof like a hit of battlefield morphine.

Sullivan took his beer and walked over to the post roster, listing members and when they served. Buzz-cut watched him.

"Over the last thirty-five years there have been a lot of names taken off and some new ones added. I guess there will always be a war going on," buzz-cut said.

"You up here?" Sullivan asked.

"Vietnam, third from the top."

"Vincent Meilo, USMC, 1966–69."

"Vinnie. Wounded twice. The second time in early '68 put me out of the game. The remainder of time served was in a VA hospital."

"Bad time to be there," Sullivan said.

"There was no good time," Vinnie replied. "You there then?"

"Later," Sullivan said. "Nine months in my boots and three plus years in the Hilton."

"Pilot?"

"Not then. Got my wings after the smoke cleared."

"What did you do in your black cadillacs?" Vinnie asked, referring to the jarhead jargon for combat boots.

"First Air Commandos."

Vinnie turned in his stool. His mouth opened slightly and his eyes became distant. "Air Force PJs."

"Same school, different class. The PJs, para-jumpers, specialized in search and rescue and combat medicine. We specialized in the other end of things." Sullivan walked back to his stool.

Vinnie rubbed his hand over the grey stubble on his face and Sullivan noticed his hands tremble. He drained his drink and pointed out the empty glass to the bartender and motioned toward Sullivan's chair for a refill of beer along with a shot. Sullivan nodded and raised his glass in recognition.

"Reason I asked," Vinnie said, "was one of your guys, a PJ, pulled my ass out of the fire."

Sullivan turned in his chair toward Vinnie. There was an endless loop of audio and video that played through the minds of war vets, and sometimes the lines of their screenplays slipped from their lips like a pressure relief valve.

"When was that?" Sullivan asked.

Vinnie sniffed and cleared his throat. "December '67. Learned later that the PJ was killed, taking bullets meant for me. When I was back at Bethesda Naval hospital, someone translated the Latin words on the patch the PJs wore – 'so that others may live.'"

Vinnie bit his lip and slugged down his drink. Then he ordered another.

Sullivan's meatloaf came. While Sullivan ate, Vinnie stared into his glass, trying to get his head above the morass of memories that wanted to drown him.

"Hey, Vinnie," Sullivan said. "You're right about the meatloaf."

Vinnie nodded. "The turkey dinner ain't bad either."

Vinnie left his stool and went to the head.

"Does he have family?" Sullivan asked the bartender when Vinnie was out of earshot.

The bartender bused Sullivan's dishes to the dishwasher and wiped down the bar top as he answered.

"Vinnie? He's got a son lives out of state. Got divorced a long time ago. Retired from his job as a prison guard a few years ago and worked for a while as a marshal for the courts, but—" The bartender pointed to Vinnie's drink.

Vinnie staggered from the bathroom and regained his stool and his drink. Sullivan thought he looked pathetic.

Sullivan got the bartender's attention and motioned to the widescreen over the bar. The bartender turned it on. Sullivan hoped the early evening local news would pause the movie playing in Vinnie's head.

Sullivan finished the shot and washed it down with the remainder of his beer. The alchemy that came from the bottles behind the bar bathed him in warmth, slowed down his world. He was about to ask Vinnie if he wanted another jag when Sullivan caught his image, along with Vinnie's, in the mirror behind the bar. Their reflections were indiscernible – empty as an echo. Sullivan looked past the inebriated smile of his reflection into his own dull eyes and saw that, like Vinnie's, they belonged to a living corpse whose mind clawed its way day by day over the terrain of an endless war until that day when it just gave up.

Sullivan ordered coffee for both of them with a hit of Kahlua mixed in and an order of potato skins for Vinnie. Nothing more was said. Sullivan wanted to ask Vinnie if he saw ghosts too, if he heard the voices of demons, and taps playing and final roll calls where their names were called three times for which there would never come a reply.

After the coffee and food knocked the booze down a notch, Sullivan left his stool and put his hand on Vinnie's shoulder. Then he raised his hand in a salute.

"Semper fi, Marine."

"Semper fi, brother," Vinnie said.

Sullivan stepped out into winter and walked Dutch before he drove to the Motel Six off the Interstate.

Breakfast at Denny's. After griddle cakes and coffee, Sullivan had time to kill before the Ford was fixed. He stopped by a discount liquor store for some Jackie D.

They picked up the Ford just after ten. With any luck, they'd arrive in Little Creek within twelve hours. Each time Sullivan looked in the rearview mirror he saw the same pathetic image that had stared back at him from the mirror at the American Legion post.

Chapter 18

Sullivan and Dutch arrived at the Pit's parking lot just after ten. It took three trips to ferry a suitcase, Dutch's dog food bag, dishes and bed, a cooler and sleeping bag to Sullivan's floating shack. Someone had turned on the electric baseboard heat and removed the window fan. Dutch sniffed around the shack and looked up at Sullivan in approval.

Sullivan crawled into his sleeping bag and Dutch sprawled on his dog bed. On the makeshift nightstand, Jackie D rested in his notch.

Night bled out to morning. Sullivan lifted his eyelids not knowing where he was. Then he felt his floating shack rock in the wind. He looked at his Timex: six o'clock. His body was still on Atlantic Standard Time.

Pulling on a heavy sweatshirt and pants, Sullivan stuffed his feet in his shoes and walked Dutch on the banks of the Intracoastal Waterway. Dutch ate his morning bowl of Science Diet while Sullivan shaved and showered. The temperature was typical for a Virginia winter that called for a sweater and windbreaker. They walked to the parking lot at the Pit and retrieved the Ford to run errands. The Pit was quiet: Ma, Joe and Rocko wouldn't arrive until almost noon.

Sullivan stopped for a coffee and muffin at the local donut franchise and then grabbed some cash from an ATM before heading for the grocery and the pet supply shop for canine food and cookies.

Sullivan had just put the groceries away and plugged in the refrigerator when the sky turned a storm patina. The Timex declared it was only 9:15 when a windswept rain tore down the Intracoastal. Sullivan was tired from his trip but not tired enough to sleep. So he looked to Jackie D for some help and slept until almost noon.

Sullivan pawed through his duffle bag and came out with a raincoat and a towel and, after splashing cold water on his face, walked over to the Pit with Dutch. A wind-driven drizzle swept the canal. The back door to the Pit was open and Sullivan ushered Dutch inside and wiped him down with the towel. Downstairs Ma was sitting behind her desk just as she'd done each day since Sullivan first met her.

Ma stood up and hugged him.

"It's so good to see you, honey," she said. And then, "Who is this handsome boy?" she asked, looking at Dutch.

"That would be Dutch," Sullivan said. "He was part of my inheritance and we ended up adopting each other."

Dutch sat with a wide smile on his face, knowing that he was the topic of conversation. Ma bent over Dutch and oohed and aahed over him, getting a canine kiss in return.

"I'm sure we have something in the kitchen for you, Dutch," Ma said.

Dutch barked, understanding that a kitchen was where food was kept.

They walked upstairs and Ma found Dutch a piece of roast beef in the refrigerator.

Ma poured coffee from the Bunn coffee machine behind the bar into two cups and sat next to Sullivan on the stool.

"How was your trip home?"

Sullivan struggled for a moment to assimilate the word "home."

"I had the alternator go on me in Connecticut and had to stay over, but otherwise it went okay. I'm just not use to the traffic compared to Nova Scotia."

"And you've fully recovered from your accident?"

Sullivan had only told Ma that he fell overboard and hurt his arm and shoulder.

"On the mend," Sullivan said. "And how about you, Ma? Everything okay?"

Ma let out a sigh. "Well, I'd thought I'd wait to tell you in person."

Sullivan held his breath.

"I'm okay, Nick, just growing old and starting to feel it more every day. But Suzie has had a relapse and there's not much more they can do for her."

"Where is she?" he asked.

"Right now in the hospital, but her family wants to move her to a hospice when she's released."

Sullivan shook his head. "Shit." He felt himself tear up and swallowed some coffee. "What hospital?" he asked.

"Sentara General," Ma said.

"This is going to be a tough one, Ma."

"I know, dear," Ma said, patting his arm.

"And there's some sweet and sour news as well," Ma said. "You know I turned seventy in September. And thank you again for sending the flowers and the Nova Scotia tourmaline brooch. I've received so many nice comments about the brooch. But, Nick, I'm tired. You know I have a small place on Sanibel Island in Florida, and it's time for me to go rest my bones. So, I've put the Pit up for sale."

"What about Joe and Rocko?"

"They're getting tired of working seven days a week too. Joe has his retirement income and Rocko has done well by his real estate investments. They'll continue to run the place until it's sold."

"Well, it's about time you enjoyed life a little," Sullivan said, "although it won't be the same without you here."

"You can always come and visit me in Florida," Ma said. "And I'd be very disappointed if you didn't. And of course I'll be coming back here to visit too. Both Joe and Rocko plan to stay in the area – for the near future, at least."

Sullivan felt numb and lost. The Pit was his home and Ma was family, and he was about to lose both.

"In the meantime," Ma said, "I'm short on help and will be working harder than ever."

"I'm here every night," Sullivan said." I can mix any drink that has a name and I've fed the cash register so many times I can operate that too. So why not let me work the other side of bar and take some of the pressure off?"

"I'd pay you, of course," Ma said.

"You already have – in more ways than one," Sullivan said.

Sullivan looked down at Dutch. "Now if I could only teach you to wash dishes."

Ma gave Sullivan a refresher in the operation of the register. He'd be helping out the cook, Paulie, too.

"I'll be in at five for the night shift," Sullivan said, "unless you need me earlier."

"That would be wonderful, honey," Ma said.

Sullivan turned to leave and remembered something. "Um, Ma, could I use the phone for a long-distance call?"

"Of course," Ma said. Her eyebrows bowed like a question mark. "Someone special?"

Sullivan stumbled at the question. He's never been asked to define the relationship he had with D.

"Hard to explain. I'm not sure if Dutch and I adopted her or she us."

Sullivan told the story of how they met. And as for their affiliation, he described it with a fatherly affection.

Sullivan went downstairs to the office and called D. The answering machine kicked in and he left the message that he and Dutch had arrived safely.

That night, as Sullivan worked the bar and worked the patrons – obviating inebriated attitudes, filling prescriptions for broken hearts and providing a momentary harbour for lost souls – he saw himself.

—

Sullivan and Dutch became a part of the Pit like the smoke-stained ceiling tiles and worn furniture. He had taught Dutch to follow the waitresses with a baseball cap clenched in his mouth for tips, which Sullivan learned had nearly doubled. And when the gratuities were divided, a small share went to Dutch for the pet insurance Sullivan had obtained. And with free meals and free booze, which he consumed judicially each shift, he had money to spare to feed his bank account. He even purchased a no contract cell phone, which he used to call D weekly and Calum and Caitlin from time to time.

Suzie died the third week of March. Sullivan had gone to the hospice each day she was able to have company. The Pit was closed to the public and reserved for her family and friends to gather after graveside services. Sullivan stayed drunk for two days. Jackie D and friends resumed their whispers and cackles from the other side.

It was nine o'clock one night when Ma knocked on the door of Sullivan's shack. Dutch growled a warning. She cracked open the door and Dutch nosed his way into the opening. Seeing it was a friend he let her in and then ran to the banks of the canal to empty his bladder. Ma could see Sullivan, eyes closed, on his bed. Half eaten food coagulated on dishes and a funky aroma of garbage and body odour filled the shack. Beer cans and empty bottles had free reign of the floor.

Ma let out a heavy sigh. "Nick. Nick, wake up!" She gently shook his arm.

Sullivan mumbled something unintelligible and partially opened his swollen eyelids and then closed them again. Ma found a washcloth in the bathroom, soaked it in cool water and placed it on Sullivan's forehead. A groan escaped Sullivan's lips and his eyelids fluttered.

"God, what have you done to yourself, Nick?"

Dutch returned through the open door, barked and lifted his food dish in his mouth.

Ma dabbed Sullivan's cheeks with the damp cloth. "Here, hold this on your head," she told Sullivan, then she went to fill Dutch's water and food bowl.

She washed dirty dishes and straightened up the shack while Sullivan tried to regain some dignity. She gathered up all the liquor and beer she could find and poured it down the sink.

"When did you eat last?" Ma asked.

Sullivan shook his head.

Ma pulled back Sullivan's lower lip and touched it with her forefinger. "You're dehydrated," she said.

Ma got Sullivan to drink some tap water and then put a pot of canned soup on the stove.

"What day is it?" Sullivan asked.

"It's Thursday night. You didn't show up for the evening shift."

"Sorry," he said, his voice slurred and raspy.

"Nick. I want you to listen to me. We all were torn by Suzie's passing. People deal with grief in different ways: faith and prayer, engaging life in some positive way or just focusing on fond memories of those we've lost. But you, Nick, you use it as an excuse. You're an alcoholic. It's a disease. It's nothing to be ashamed about unless you choose to do nothing about it. It's treatable. I'll make an appointment for you with the VA hospital. I'll even take you to an AA meeting and try to find you a sponsor. But Nick, you have to want to get well, otherwise it's a waste of time."

"I've got it under control," Sullivan said. "Really, Ma, I do."

Sullivan swung his feet over the edge of the bed and steadied himself with both hands on the mattress. "I just got carried away. I loved Suzie. She was a saint. I just went over the edge, I guess."

"Nick, if you really want to honour Suzie get yourself straightened out. That's what would make her soul happy."

Sullivan raised both hands in surrender. "Ma, just leave it alone. I'll be fine – I promise."

"Nick, stop lying to yourself and your friends."

Ma helped Sullivan to the kitchen table and watched as he tried to spoon soup in his mouth with a shaking hand.

"I've got to get back to the Pit. I'll check in on you before we close for the night."

Sullivan knew enough not to argue.

He didn't visit the VA. He kept a loose cap on his drinking, but at least it was a cap, his friends thought. Eleven weeks later the Pit was sold. There was no last supper. Ma flew out to Colorado to visit her sister, which was to be followed by a cruise to Alaska later that summer to escape the crock-pot heat of Florida. The important people in Sullivan's life had disappeared as if they'd never existed. The new owners shut down the Pit for renovations, and like an obituary the tavern's name was torn off the building.

Sullivan had managed to save sixteen thousand dollars in under-the-table compensation and tips. The Ford was resting in the tall grass on the edge of the Pit's parking lot. Even before the sale of the Pit was consummated the then potential new owners stated they wanted the relic removed. Sullivan advertised the Ford in the local paper and sold it for two hundred dollars.

Perusing the classifieds and debating the merits of another pickup truck versus an SUV, and deciding that given the transiency of their future a pickup would provide the most utility, Sullivan purchased a 2003 Dodge pickup. The garnet red, three-quarter ton, quad cab truck came complete with a camper top and diesel engine, and to Dutch's liking, a fold-down rear seat that became his bed.

Upon returning to their floating palace, they were greeted with a yellow sign with black lettering, which declared the shack to be condemned. Stapled to the door was a letter that informed "whom it may concern" (the shack was never listed on the town's property records and there was no record of ownership) that he had fourteen days to remove the shack or it would be removed and/or dismantled by the city – at his expense.

Sullivan moved all of his personal belongings into the Dodge, called D to say he'd be arriving in two days and the next morning left Little Creek. He was orphaned from things precious: Ma, the Pit and Suzie, the serenity of the canal. Any sense of belonging was lost in the rearview mirror of the Dodge.

Chapter 19

The newer Dodge drove like a dream compared to the old Ford, and the landscapes of the eastern seaboard and New England states passed by quickly. As on the trip down, Nick opted to continue on the highways through Maine and New Brunswick rather than the ferry from Maine to Nova Scotia.

They stayed overnight in Moncton, New Brunswick, and were on the road at six the next morning. A blinding June sun rose in front of them, guiding them east like an Advent star. Dutch sat in the back seat, staring out the right window: a coastal fog, the sky shifting blue to grey, the causeway and bridge once again separating what was left behind and what lay ahead. Dutch turned to Sullivan and smiled at the sensory prompts that told him where he was and where he was going. On the other side, the sun found them again, lighting the way: Judique, Port Hood, Inverness, passing through Chéticamp and the Cape Breton Highlands, turning now at Pleasant Bay and down the far side.

It was mid-afternoon on Thursday when they turned into the gravel driveway, Dutch barking and scampering from one side of the truck to the other. The rear door opened, he raced to the front door of the house, ran in circles and left a message on the lawn saying that he was back.

Inside, a banner hung over the stairway that said "welcome home," and helium balloons pulled at the banister. A note taped to one of the balloons said that there were sandwiches in the fridge and that D could be found at the chandlery. Dutch ran from room to room, looking for D and inhaling things thought lost but found again.

Sullivan took bites from a sandwich as he moved the contents of the truck into his uncle's house. Afterward, he stepped outside to the surf spilling on the sand, the call of gulls and from somewhere the faint sounds of a fiddle.

Sullivan asked Dutch if he wanted to see D and Calum and Caitlin. Dutch whimpered please, and Sullivan packed him into their new ride and drove off to Lochinver Harbour.

Pulling into the harbour parking lot, he saw his uncle's old Chevy parked in front of the chandlery. Sullivan was preparing to park in front of the shop when he pulled up short and jumped out of the truck, looking in disbelief at what was both there and not there.

As he walked closer, he shaded his eyes, unsure of what he was seeing. It was a sailboat, alright, but hardly the one he remembered being there, not his uncle's boat, but it was. Sullivan walked around the ketch as if he were lost.

He ran his fingers across the flawless finish of the ketch's blue hull. His mirror image stared at him like the ghost he'd left behind in the dark blue abyss the summer before.

A ladder leaned against the boat's stern where the words "*Jessica Elaine*" were painted in gold old English script. The new inflatable boat his uncle had left boxed in the chandlery hung over the stern from davits.

Sullivan tested the first rung and then climbed into the cockpit. The brightwork shone like glass under layers of spar varnish. The teak deck had been sanded and oiled to a honey tone. And the brass binnacle and deck hardware posed as gold statuary. Down in the cabin it seemed as if a dozen carpenters and painters must have toiled to bring back the luster and grandeur that spoke of another age, when railroad tycoons and rich industrialists built palatial mansions and wallowed in the pornography of their wealth.

Dutch was waiting for him at the bottom of the ladder and tugged at his pantleg, pulling him toward the chandlery.

Calum was parked just inside the door. "Ceud mile failte, Nick. It's good to see you, lad."

D hugged Sullivan like a lost teddy bear, saying nothing. She wiped her eyes and hugged and kissed Dutch.

"Nick, we missed you," Caitlin said.

Caitlin gave him a hug. Sullivan inhaled her aroma: perfume and herbal shampoo and something that was sweet and pure and worthy.

"Dutch and I missed you all too."

"I have a cookie for you, handsome boy," she said to Dutch who followed her behind the counter.

"And I have something for you too, baby," D said after Dutch devoured his treat. D reached into a plastic bag and took out a stuffed toy duck that quacked when you squeezed it. Quacks resounded in the chandlery.

Calum said, "So, what do you think of the boat, Nick?" He exhaled a plum of fragrant Cavendish smoke from his pipe.

Sullivan shook his head and ran his fingers through his hair. "Someone worked a miracle on that thing. I have a strong suspicion that you were heavily involved."

Calum's eyes twinkled and a smile spread across his face. "Might be so." He shrugged his shoulders.

"I thought so," Sullivan said. "Who were your accomplices?"

"I wouldn't be saying." Calum took his pipe from his mouth and folded his arms across his chest.

"I'm guessing John Sylliboy is mixed up in this too," Sullivan said.

"You'd be surprised."

Sullivan looked over at Caitlin. She was bent over the counter, writing out a sales order and grinning.

"Why would people do all that work – for nothing?" Sullivan asked.

Calum's smile shrunk and his eyes narrowed. He pointed the stem of his pipe in Sullivan's direction. "It wasn't for nothing, it was for something and not wanting anything in return. The something is what needs figuring out, and no one here can help you with that!" Calum swung his pipe hand around the room.

Sullivan raised his hands in surrender. "I just wanted to know who to thank."

Calum shook his head and wheeled himself to the coffee pot behind the counter.

D said, "Hey, Nick, they did an awesome job on the boat, huh. We should have a christening."

"Now that would be a right fine idea," Calum said. "When's it going to be?"

The bell over the door to the chandlery chimed. Sullivan turned to see John Sylliboy, Todd Sipu and Paddy Gallagher.

"Welcome back, brother," Sylliboy said.

Sullivan shook the hands of his former crew members.

"Paddy said he saw you and Dutch in a red pickup," Sylliboy said.

"Made a few loonies back in the States so I retired the Ford," Sullivan said.

"We were just talking about having a ceilidh, kind of a combination welcome back for the prodigal son here and a boat christening," D said.

Calum smiled. Everyone looked at D. "You know. A ceilidh. A party," D said .

"We're leaving next week for a trip out to the banks," Sylliboy said. "Should be back in about two and a half weeks."

Sylliboy put his arm around Sullivan's shoulder. "And the crew is getting pretty damn tired of making each other sick."

"It's the newest thing in weight loss – crew slop," grinned Paddy.

"So, we were kind of hoping we could get you back on board to help us out," Todd said.

"I just got back," Sullivan said. "Maybe next trip."

Sylliboy released his grip on Sullivan and let out a sigh. "I guess we better go tell Antonio and Willie the bad news."

The christening date was set four weeks from Sunday after the ten o'clock Mass at St. Joseph's. D was sure her band would attend in exchange for a good meal. The *Aspy Lady* would be back in port and, being Sunday, the chandlery would be closed so Caitlin could come.

When Sullivan asked who else should be invited, Calum gave Sullivan a puzzled look and replied, "Why, everyone, of course."

The party idea snowballed and by the end of the afternoon, everything was in place. Details were decided with little input from Sullivan, the host. There were to be no formal invitations. Notices would be posted about town and a sign-up sheet would be available at the Celtic Pub. Those attending would be asked to bring a small donation for the families of a crewman recently lost at sea. The donation was Calum's idea, and Sullivan was sorry he hadn't thought of it first.

Sullivan was to provide a pig (Todd Sipu had a trailer-mounted barbecue), and folks could sign up to bring a vegetable dish, dessert or side dish to keep the menu in balance. Sullivan called Don Esherick who said he'd be there. Sullivan had spoken with the doc on his cell when he passed through Sydney on his return, but their schedules hadn't aligned for a meeting.

That night, cloudless, still and moonlit, the Aspy River flowed like liquid silver. D made seared scallop with marmalade for dinner. Their conversation seemed like a book report: freeze-dried accounts and mundane events that filled the time of their mutual absence.

After dinner, Sullivan lifted the cap off his fourth beer of the night and settled in his favourite living room chair. It was summer warm. Drapes frolicked in the offshore breeze that carried a bouquet of sea grass, wild rose and the hiss of sand and surf colliding. D was curled up on the sofa with a glass of wine within reach on the coffee table.

D said, "I really missed you guys."

"We missed you too, Raindrop."

"Sometimes after you called, I cried," D said. "It was like I had nobody."

Dutch rested his head on the sofa so D could rub his ears.

Sullivan had missed D, Caitlin, Calum and his friends – that realization sharper now that he'd been reunited.

"It was sad for you there, wasn't it Nick."

"Virginia? The world lost a special person – Suzie. And then Ma left and sold the Pit to strangers and I had the roof over my head taken from me. So, yeah, my life changed and I was sad."

"But you're not sad now that you're back here, right?"

Sullivan finished his beer and thought about inviting Jackie D into the conversation.

"I'm less sad than I was. Virginia seems distant now, like so many other places I've left behind."

"I feel like that too sometimes. There are lots of things I'd like to forget."

"We can't always do that," Sullivan said. "Sometimes it good not to forget but to put things on a back shelf. We don't see them all the time, but we know they're there."

D nodded. "That's almost poetic, Nick."

Sullivan had another beer and they talked for a while. Then Sullivan went upstairs to crawl under the covers and spend some time with Jackie D. Dutch was sprawled out next to Sullivan on his doggie bed, snoring.

Sullivan closed his eyes and when he opened them again Capello was sitting on the only chair in the room.

"You're looking good, Cappy. I guess over on your side you never age."

Capello leaned back in the chair and folded his leg across his knee.

Sullivan lifted Jackie D in a salute, took a swallow and smacked his lips. He held the bottle up to the table lamp and examined it.

"Did you know that the liquor commission here charges three times as much for this as I pay in the States? But Cappy, worse is that Alex Keith sells for forty dollars a case here, and only twenty in Virginia – and it's brewed and bottled in Nova Scotia. But I'd better get used to it because right now I've no place else to go."

Sullivan closed his eyes. "You know I almost jumped without a chute back there when Suzie died. I heard voices, really sweet voices calling for me to take the ride."

When Sullivan opened his eyes, Capello was gone. Sullivan took a last sip from the bottle and switched off the light.

—

The next day Sullivan drove to the grocery store to order the guest of honour for the pig roast. D gave him a short list of household items she needed. As he turned into a grocery aisle in search of brown sugar, he stopped in his tracks. At that same instant, Elizabeth noticed him too. She dropped the plastic bottle of garlic powder that was in her hand and her husband bent down to retrieve it. She wavered, looking for an escape, and shook her head ever so slightly.

Sullivan eyeballed the shelves and walked to within several steps of her and said, "Good morning."

Her husband nodded. Sullivan could see Elizabeth tremble.

Sullivan finished his shopping. When he stepped outside, he saw a big BMW sedan parked away from the dented pickup trucks and rusted sedans. Right choice, Sullivan thought.

Putting away the spoils of his sortie, he sat down at the kitchen table with the newspaper and a second cup of coffee. Enlightened by the news and caffeinated, he gathered up Dutch and drove his uncle's Chevy to take another look at the ketch. D was off to band practice in St. Joseph de Moine, driving the new Dodge.

Sullivan stopped in the chandlery to see if Calum was there but more so to rest his eyes on Caitlin and feel the caress of her voice. Caitlin was busy with a customer and said that Calum was having breakfast at the café. Sullivan was walking across the lot to the café when old man Boudreau's Mercedes pulled up next to the *Jessica Elaine* and stopped. By the time Sullivan reached the ketch, Boudreau was examining it like a marine surveyor.

"Hello, Mr. Boudreau," Sullivan said.

"I heard you were back," Boudreau said grudgingly, still looking at the ketch.

"It looks as good as it did when it came out of the shipyard," Sullivan said.

"They had real craftsmen then. Now all you see is that plastic garbage," Boudreau said, pointing his cane in the direction of the fiberglass hulls floating in the harbour. He started up the ladder to the cockpit.

"Do you need a hand?" Sullivan asked.

Boudreau paused on the ladder. "I didn't ask for help, did I?"

He climbed into the cockpit, looked around for moment and ducked into the cabin with Sullivan in tow. Boudreau took a seat on a settee. Sullivan sat across from him at the galley table.

Boudreau looked around nodding his head. "I think Sean would have liked to have seen this, although, he'd be disappointed in you. You have no ambition or direction, do you? I thought you showed some promise by going to work for John Sylliboy. But no, you take a little spill and quit."

"I think we had this conversation before, Mr. Boudreau." Sullivan stood up to leave.

"I'm not finished," Boudreau said. He shook his head and ran his hand over the varnished mahogany bulkhead. "Splendid work. Not that you had a part in it."

He glanced out the porthole for a long moment, and when his eyes fixed again on Sullivan his demeanour had softened. "It will need some outfitting, electronics and the like. I'll release funds for that." Boudreau put both hands around the handle of his cane. "The condition remains, however, that you sail the boat to the destination specified in your uncle's will."

"You were my uncle's attorney and friend. Why would he have me sail to some remote island? What purpose could it possibly serve?"

"There was a reason. Why don't you make an effort and find out? And mind that if you don't fulfill that stipulation, the house and the remainder of his assets go to charity."

"You've made that clear, Mr. Boudreau."

"So, what are your intentions?"

"I don't know. I really don't have any plans. I mean, I can only stay here six months of the year anyway. It's possible to sail her south, I suppose. I've got nowhere to go, and I can't stay here indefinitely. Maybe I could live aboard for awhile – somewhere on east coast of the States."

Boudreau stood up to leave. "In the meantime, I suggest you hone your sailing skills."

Sullivan watched him descend the ladder and leave.

He was still standing in the cockpit when John Sylliboy drove into the lot. Sullivan waved and Sylliboy climbed aboard.

"Old man Boudreau was just here."

"I know. He almost ran me off the road," Sylliboy said, looking at the lingering cloud of dust left in the wake of Boudreau's sedan. "What's up with him?"

"He wanted to check on the progress of the ketch and whittle on my self-esteem."

"Then he must have been impressed."

"With the ketch, anyway."

"You know, all this blow boat needs is some ice for the ice box and some Molson," Sylliboy remarked.

"And some electronics," Sullivan added.

Sylliboy said, "I can help with that. In fact Caitlin can order just about anything you want. Why don't we swing by her shop around nine tomorrow morning and I'll help you get an order together."

Sylliboy could see Sullivan looking toward the chandlery. "You know, when you go fishing with a man and share the same space with him for a few weeks you get to read him pretty well."

Sullivan turned toward Sylliboy. "How does the headline read?"

"None of my business, but you asked. I think there's something brewing here besides friendship."

"I thought so too, but I'm not so sure. We dated before I left for the States, and I got mixed vibes," Sullivan said.

"Maybe you need some more time together before you make a call on whether or not the puck is in the net."

Sullivan looked back at the chandlery for a long moment. "Maybe."

"You know, Paddy has been back in his house with his wife and boy since last autumn," Sylliboy said. "That's a mighty nice thing you did."

Sullivan looked over at the *Aspy Lady*. "He only jumped in the ocean and pulled my dumb ass out of the water."

"I put a little extra in his last pay and hired him off-season to do some work on the Lady. And he's working as an engine mechanic's assistant part-time. I think he will be able to swing the mortgage now. He and his wife are trying to make a go of it," Sylliboy said.

"There's way too much misery in this world. It's nice to see a dream come true every once in awhile," Sullivan said.

Sullivan had a coffee with Calum and then drove into town and purchased an assortment of cleaning supplies. He dropped Dutch off at his uncle's house so he could share a walk with D when she arrived later that afternoon. Returning to the boat, he borrowed a shop-vac from the *Aspy Lady* and spent the remainder of the morning and most of the afternoon making the cabin habitable. Sylliboy had promised to contact someone he knew that did upholstery work so that the mattresses and settee cushions could be replaced. Other than needing sails and new roller furlings for main, mizzen and jib, the ketch was ready for sea trials.

Sullivan stood on the steps leading from the cabin to the cockpit and looked toward the chandlery. He hoped Caitlin would see his uncle's truck parked next to the ketch and stop by – she didn't.

Sullivan found a half empty bottle of Havana rum he had squirrelled away the previous autumn and lay down on the forward berth. The ketch's open hatch caught a breeze. The ocean exhaled a briny halitosis of fish, creosote and diesel fuel that drifted through the cabin. When the wind shifted, he could taste the sweetness of a salt marsh that reminded him of Little Creek.

———

Sullivan awoke with dull veins of sunlight dancing across his face through a porthole. He would need curtains for the boat too, he thought. Through the porthole he could see that Caitlin's Jeep was gone.

It was an hour past dinnertime when Sullivan sobered and arrived home. The Dodge was parked next to the house and he found D on the back porch sitting motionless in one of the large wooden-slat chairs next to Dutch. She looked like a barefoot mannequin modelling hot-pink shorts and a sporty print blouse tied above the waist. A pair of sunglasses hid her eyes. On the deck Dutch was resting his head between his paws with a worried look.

"D, you awake?" He waited for an answer.

"I guess." Her voice was sandbar shallow – raspy and barely showing. At her feet an empty tall glass with a lime slice floating on melting ice cubes exuded a gin tang that Sullivan inhaled and held for a moment.

"You hungry?"

"No."

"I think there's a steak somewhere in the fridge. Maybe I'll fire up the grill?"

"Whatever," D replied.

Sullivan poured charcoal briquettes in the rusty barbeque grill, doused them with lighter fluid and tossed in a flickering match. Twenty minutes later, when he tossed the steak and foil wrapped sliced potatoes on the grill, D still hadn't moved. Sullivan stood with a cooking fork in hand.

"You feeling okay?" Sullivan asked.

"I'll feel better after I make myself another one of these," she said struggling out of the chair and picking her glass off the deck. A few minutes later she walked past Sullivan toward the beach, a gin-flavoured cloud in her wake.

The sky was almost drained of daylight when he finished his meal. Sullivan cleaned his dinner plate in the company of an open bottle of gin that he fondled and would have gone further with if D hadn't used the last of the tonic water.

Sullivan walked to the beach. D was lying in the sand. An empty glass was broached next to her.

Sullivan sat beside her. "So, let's hear it."

"There's really nothing you can say that will change anything," she said.

"I think I said, 'let's hear it.' Me talking is optional."

D sighed. "I met this guy, this really dreamy, perfect guy on Prince Edward Island where we did our gig a few weeks ago. After our set, I went to the bar for a drink, and there he was, just standing there like fate or something was giving me this golden opportunity. And he was perfect: perfect manners, perfect body, perfect smile, perfect education, perfect job. He sailed in some race from Massachusetts to Yarmouth and decided to spend some time sightseeing before he returned home. Then he's got to return to Nova Scotia and help sail the boat back to Massachusetts next month when we're having the christening of the ketch. He's an attorney from Boston. Did I tell you that?"

"No," Sullivan said.

"Well, he is. The first half-hour or so went well. You know, small talk: where did you grow up, where did you go to school? That's when I started slipping the lies in. I said I took some time off from studying voice at Hartt College, in Connecticut – it's one of the best schools for voice, you know.

"After the first lie, the rest came easy except I told him about your boat. He thought that was cool. Anyway, they weren't big lies just little ones about what I've been doing with my life. What I am supposed to do, tell him about my so-called modelling career? And what if I really fell in love with a guy like that? What do I do – keep my past a deep dark secret? I've ruined my life. No decent guy is going to want someone like me except for this," she said waving her hand over her torso.

Sullivan watched her. She still had her sunglasses on and her speech was slurred, but Sullivan thought she did a fine job of forming cogent sentences.

"Well, what are you going to do, just sit there and say nothing?" she asked.

"I was busy listening."

"You know I'm right."

"No, you're not," Sullivan said, "not even borderline right."

D propped herself up on one elbow.

"Those little lies you mentioned are just you talking about what you want to be. You want to go study voice at college? Go do it, and then it won't be a lie. And as for the bad stuff that happened in your life, I bet your perfect guy from Boston has a few skeletons in his closet too."

"You think?"

"I'm sure of it. I'm also sure that whoever falls in love with you will do so because of who you are, not who you were. You've overcome a lot in your life just since I met you. That's speaks volumes about your character."

"You really think so?"

"I wouldn't lie to you, D. And, I know something else."

"What?"

"I'd invite Mr. Perfect to the christening of the *Jessica Elaine*."

"You would?"

"Yes. And, one more thing."

"What."

"If you don't get out of the sand, you're going to have sand flea bites all over you."

"Eww," D burbled. She stumbled back to the house, made herself some tea and an English muffin then went off to bed. Sullivan took Dutch for a walk around the grounds and went upstairs for a chat with Jackie and his friends.

D was still sleeping the next day when Sullivan left the house. He stopped on the way to Lochinver Harbour for coffee and a muffin. He had an hour to kill before he met John Sylliboy, so he spent it taking measurements of the navigation station aboard the *Jessica Elaine*.

Morning light seeped through polished brass portholes. The cabin still held the odour of fresh varnish. The navigation station, which was nothing more than a small settee and a large slanted chart table with storage underneath, was on the port side next to the cabin stairs. Sullivan traced lines in the bulkhead above the chart table with his finger where a clock and barometer were affixed long ago. Aft of the nav station was a cozy pilot's berth.

On the opposite side of the stairs was a new galley that his uncle had installed. It featured a small propane-fuelled oven and a three-burner stove, a sink and a roomy ice box with a small AC/

DC powered refrigerator beneath it. Cabinetry with ornate hardware provided ample room for foodstuff.

The remainder of the boat, except for the head, was original. The main saloon consisted of a folding galley table crafted of mahogany and surrounded on three sides by a settee. Across from the table was another settee that folded out for use as a berth.

Forward of the main saloon was a closet and shelf space and a head complete with a small shower on one side and on the opposite side, a brass sink with ivory faucet handles. Across from the head was a spacious cabin with bunk beds built into the starboard bulkhead.

Bow forward was the master stateroom. Instead of a traditional V berth, the ketch had a queen-sized single berth with a carved headboard and built-in drawer space. Like the rest of the boat, all of the bulkheads and cabinetry were finely finished in mahogany, and all fixtures were opulent brass or gold finished.

Sullivan made a rough sketch with measurements of the navigation station. When he finished, it was twenty to eight. Caitlin's Jeep was parked in front of the store. He took a deep breath and walked inside. She was on the phone and gave him a wave. A few moments later she finished her call.

"Hey," she said.

"Good morning."

"That was a friend from Montreal on the phone ," she said. "She's trying to talk me into going to our high school reunion."

"Sounds like fun. You should go."

"Well, it would be nice to visit with my family. So I'm thinking I will if I can have someone watch the shop. There's a retired fellow that helps me part-time now and then. I'm going to give him a call sometime today. Have you had coffee yet ?"

"I could use a second cup, thanks." Sullivan walked behind the counter and poured coffee and cream into a Styrofoam cup while Caitlin punched keys on her computer and a printer spewed out forms.

She paused and asked, "What are you up to today?"

"I'm here as a paying customer. Actually, old man Boudreau is doing the paying."

"You need some equipment for the ketch?"

"Electronics. John Sylliboy is going to stop by and give me a hand."

"So you're actually going to sail her south?"

"Maybe, assuming the electronics you sell me don't point me in some other direction."

Caitlin smiled.

"Do you want to come along?" Sullivan asked.

Caitlin spread her arms and glanced about the store.

"Well, what about a day sail somewhere, that is if I learn to make it out of the harbour without causing any fatalities."

"That, I might take to you up on."

This time it was Sullivan who smiled.

The door opened. It was Calum. "Top of the morning."

"Coffee is on," Caitlin said.

"That's right nice of you," Calum said. He rolled his wheelchair over to the coffee machine.

"I'll get some catalogues together for you," Caitlin said.

"What are we looking at?" Calum asked.

"Electronics," Sullivan answered.

"Can't help you much there," Calum said. "In my day we used our charts, a timepiece and a good compass. Never went off course in forty years of being aboard a vessel. Of course they were coming out with Lorans A when I was still crew."

"I'll need to relearn some of the sailing fundamentals my uncle taught me," Sullivan said.

"Not a problem there," Calum said. "I cut my teeth on a fishing schooner out of Lunenburg. That ketch of yours is a lot simpler, hey."

"Sounds like I'm in luck," Sullivan said.

John Sylliboy arrived, and forty minutes later Caitlin wrote up an order for a Raymarine combination radar and chart plotter, a Furuno bottom machine, a Garmin GPS and an Icom single sideband radio. She threw in a free weather fax as a thank you for the order that totalled nearly eight thousand dollars. Caitlin would arrange for a marine electrician to install the equipment.

Sullivan treated Calum to an early lunch and then drove home. D came home just before dinner with a load of groceries and found Sullivan with a beer on the back porch, pouring over the latest edition of Chapman's Piloting and Seamanship that Caitlin had on the shelf of the chandlery.

"Well, I did it," D said.

Sullivan slipped a bookmark in the binding and closed the cover. "Did what?"

"Called Scott and invited him to the commissioning of the *Jessica Elaine*."

"He's coming then?" Sullivan asked.

"Yup." D sat down heavily.

"You nervous about it?"

"Him coming, no. Me squaring things with him, yes."

"Why not wait until you're sure there's a real connection?" Sullivan asked.

"'Cause I don't want him to invest a lot of time in me and then get disappointed when he learns the truth."

"That's noble of you, but you could have done that over the phone."

"I can't work my charm over the phone like I can when I make a personal appearance. And besides, I want him to get to know me better over the weekend before I bare my soul."

"I hope that's all you're going to bare."

D wrinkled her nose and stuck her tongue out. "Speaking of romance, how are things going with Caitlin? I haven't spoken to her since you returned. I can tell you she isn't seeing anyone."

"And I don't want you speaking with her," Sullivan said, "not about that anyway."

"Troubled waters?"

"More like a small craft warning. I did get a smile out of her today though. I ordered about eight grand in electronics for the ketch."

"Nick, are you really going to sail to that place in your uncle's will?"

"I don't seem to have any other plans, and I'm going to have to leave Canada again in six months. And what about you?"

"I contacted the Hartt College of Music today and they are sending an application. Even if I don't get into the School of Music, I can attend the university as a non-matriculated student and take music classes. Mom said she would help me with tuition."

That night, with the moon half full and hope half empty, he walked to the barn with Jackie and his friends and climbed the ladder to the hayloft where he and Richie used to play cards and smoke cigarettes. The assortment of old tools and lobster fishing gear stored there looked to be the same as when he was a boy. Sullivan swung open the loft door once used to move hay into and out of the barn long before his uncle took over the place. Moonbeams caught the white crest of waves like stage lights. And he wondered what it would be like to step over the edge.

Chapter 20

Sullivan tried to keep a lid on his addiction. And when he frequently failed, he did so behind the backs of D and Caitlin and his friends.

What began as a necessity mutated into something quite different . It began when he stubbed a bare foot on a loose screw on the deck of the house. After he refastened the screw, he tightened all the rest and re-stained the deck. As with the *Jessica Elaine*, there came a sense of pride and accomplishment in placing his hands on something and making it better.

D was off playing with the band. The old homestead was still. Sullivan was putting away his tool box and paintbrush in the barn when he looked up. Dust and cobwebs hung in slivers of daylight that slipped through neglected shingles and sheathing, and old timbers that held the barn together had begun to show signs of water damage.

Using an old steel extension ladder his uncle kept in the barn, he scaled the roof and removed a section of loose shingles. The entire barn roof would need to be replaced, and given that he was tapped out of cash and his sole source of income was his meager military disability pension, he couldn't afford to hire a contractor.

Sullivan drove to the hardware store and left with roof staging and a shingle remover. Three days later a rented dumpster was half full of old roof shingles and tarpaper. Dutch had sat at the bottom of the ladder watching Sullivan on the roof and whining at the danger. When a piece of shingle or tarpaper missed the dumpster, Dutch would retrieve it and set next to the dumpster.

Rotted sections of sheathing were marked and cut out with his uncle's old circular saw, and new plywood was nailed in its place. Sullivan's bare skin was caked with sweat and sawdust. His hammer developed a rhythm, three beats per measure.

Sometimes he'd fall asleep on the couch at half past Coronation Street with an assist from a cold beer or a smack or two of whisky after his tools were put away.

The afternoon he finished replacing the decayed sheathing and tacking on new tarpaper, Sullivan sat on the ridge of the roof. He could see boats dragging for groundfish, the Aspy River flowing like mercury, sun worshippers and water gazers. And he wondered what waited beyond the curvature of the earth.

While the metal roofing was on order, Calum tutored Sullivan in seamanship. There wasn't a knot Calum couldn't tie, and Sullivan learned them all. As an Air Force pilot, Sullivan already knew how to plot a running fix, chart a course factoring in the set and drift of the current and wind and use a sextant in a rudimentary way. Sullivan had the international rules of the road down solid, except the lights and day signals of ships, which Calum quizzed him on daily. From his wheelchair below the jack-stand-raised deck of the *Jessica Elaine*, Calum drilled Sullivan on the skills of tending sheets and hoisting sail.

The *Aspy Lady* had returned from chasing fish. Sullivan stopped by the chandlery frequently for odds and ends. Caitlin was affable, and they ate lunch together several times at the café. Sullivan dissected her body language, studied what was said and, more importantly, what wasn't. Boundaries were set, walls constructed and Sullivan stood in the periphery as a close friend with social privileges.

It was the day before the commissioning of the ketch. Sullivan was cleaning up in the aftermath of the workers who had installed the electronics. Even with the hatches open, the cabin air hung heavy and hot. His gray tank top was soaked with sweat as he finished his work. Sullivan grabbed a cold beer from an ice-filled cooler. Condensation from the can leaked through his fingers, and he dried his hands on his shorts.

He hadn't completely explored the storage area underneath the chart table, so he opened the hinged top and rummaged through its contents: a box of sharpened pencils, dividers, a brass ruler, a protractor and several cruising guides and charts in large booklet form.

There were rolled-up charts, too, stored in a rack next to the navigation station. The charts had been purchased by his uncle just before his death, from the dates printed on the legend. They covered the waters from Newfoundland to the Lesser Antilles.

Sullivan sat at the galley table and flipped through the pages of the chart book while sipping his drink. There were circles drawn around ports of call where his uncle had planned to overnight or put in for supplies. Notations in the margins of the charts crossreferenced pages of the cruising guide or served as reminders of maintenance to be performed and places of interest.

The chart detailing Norfolk, Virginia, had a circle drawn around Little Creek and a note in the margin that read, "Talk with Nick." Sullivan poured through the rest of the charts and cruising guides for a clue as to what his uncle had meant, but there was nothing.

About three that afternoon, Todd Sipu stopped his pickup next to the *Jessica Elaine* with the pig-roaster in tow. Sullivan stepped into the cockpit, gave a wave and climbed down the ladder. He walked around the roaster. It was constructed of brushed stainless steel and was mounted on a car axle. An electric motor hung off the side.

"I hope that thing comes with instructions," Sullivan said.

Sipu smiled. "I'll get you started. John and I will stop by about ten tonight to help you put the pig on. Who's going to stand watch?"

"D and her friend will be on from midnight until two thirty, and I'll be on again until five. Antonio will be on after that, until you and John come by around seven thirty."

Sipu nodded. "When is the yard going to put her in the water?" he asked, looking up at the ketch.

Sullivan looked at his Timex. "Anytime now. You haven't seen her since she's been prettied up and had the electronics installed. You want a tour?"

Sipu said he did. He moved the roaster next to the dock and then climbed up the ladder after Sullivan and stepped into the cabin. Sullivan sat at the galley table and Sipu looked at the electronics and walked slowly forward, running his eyes over the cabin interior. Then he took a seat at the opposite end of the table from Sullivan.

Sullivan handed him a beer from the icebox. It was rarely Sipu's nature to look directly into one's eyes. It was not a matter of subordinating himself or expressing a lack of confidence, but rather it was an ability to see the physical and metaphysical world in the same plane and his focus seemed to be everywhere.

"Old things, like old people, have seen a lot," Sipu said.

When Sullivan said nothing, Sipu explained. "The past and present co-exist. Everything we say and do is permanent. Old things harbour the past, like this old boat. It has tales to tell."

Sullivan nodded.

"If you concentrate, you can almost see the men that built this boat, the sailors that sailed her and the fools that owned her. You always have company when you are in the presence of old things, don't you think?"

Sullivan said that he thought he did.

"That's because the dead visit us," Sipu said. He looked at Sullivan and smiled. "I sense that having been in a war and having life and death slip through your hands, you already know that."

Sullivan thought about Capello.

He could see Sipu thinking. Sipu's eyes would sometimes roam before fixing on some thought.

"You have a lot in common with this old boat," Sipu said.

"We're both looking rather handsome in our old age?" Sullivan said.

Sipu smiled again. "I was thinking more that you've both been resurrected: this old boat from the scrap heap and you from a similar fate. And your uncle had a hand in both – caring for this old boat and caring enough for you to bring you home to Cape Breton."

Sipu took a pull on his beer. "You hear stories sometimes, stories of how people die and come back with a gift. When we got you back into the boat last year, I took turns pumping your heart and breathing air into your lungs even though I knew you were dead. I had my hand over your heart when it made its first beat, just like a new born infant. Not many people are given the chance to redo their lives."

Sipu's eyes wandered around the cabin again. "I wonder what tales this boat will tell years from now, after we're long gone?"

"Maybe that two friends once sat here, in the midst of an uncertain world, and found comfort in their friendship," Sullivan said.

"Nothing could be better," Sipu said.

"Or more true," Sullivan replied.

Sipu let the thought linger. He took a last swig of his beer and then stood up to leave.

"Thanks for the beer. See you tonight."

Then he reached into his pocket and handed Sullivan a small turtle carved from burl wood that hung from a leather cord. "It will bring you good luck in your journey," he said.

Sullivan thanked him, and when Sipu left, Sullivan hung the turtle from a brass lamp original to the ketch.

Sullivan had dinner with Calum at the café, and they stopped by the house to pick up his toilet kit and a change of clothes for the next day. Then they picked up the pig and drove back to the *Jessica Elaine*. The ketch was in the water supported by slings attached to the crane that moved her.

"The yard will keep her in the slings a day or so to let the wood swell and to check for leaks, but she's as sound a boat that's ever put in at Lochinver Harbour, and she's the prettiest," Calum said.

Calum rolled his wheelchair to the finger pier next to the boat, and with dexterity that surprised Sullivan, raised himself on his crutches and slid over the gunwhale and into the starboard cockpit bench. The shore power cord was plugged in. Sullivan lit the cabin lights so Calum could peer inside, and he gave him a virtual tour of the interior. Then Sullivan joined him in the cockpit.

The harbour was quiet with only the sounds of the waves washing against the breakwater and a bell buoy clanging lazily in the distance. Lights from the dock spilled over the *Jessica Elaine* and reflected off the asphalt-black water of the harbour.

Sullivan smiled at Calum. He loved the old man. "If it wasn't for you, Calum, we wouldn't be sitting here tonight."

"She's a sight, Nick Sullivan," Calum said. "Your uncle is here watching this as sure as the tide will change, hey."

Calum asked Sullivan to fetch a flask from his wheelchair on the dock. Sullivan did and Calum took a long swallow.

Calum held the flask in Sullivan's direction.

Sullivan nodded and took the flask from Calum's hand. He took a swallow. It was imported Scotch as good as he had ever tasted. Sullivan handed the flask back to Calum, who smiled and took another sip.

"Are we still on for Monday morning after coffee?" Sullivan asked.

"You come by and pick me up at seven and the two of us will put her under sail. You've got your charts aboard?"

Sullivan said he did and went below to gather up the chart that Calum wanted.

"Where are we going to go?" Sullivan asked.

Calum unfurled a chart. "Not far. We'll see what the weather is doing and decide that morning," Calum said, running his finger around an area that showed the coast off Dingwall. "You'll be wanting to be familiar with the bottom around here."

Calum and Sullivan examined the chart for several minutes and then Sullivan said, "Calum, I found a note on one of the charts that indicated my uncle was planning on paying me a visit in Little Creek on his way south. In fact the note said that he wanted to talk with me. Any idea what he wanted to say?"

Calum smoothed his beard. "He never mentioned a thing to me, lad. You know, when you get older like your uncle and me, you begin to think a lot about living on borrowed time. The man might have been wanting to clean the slate, so to speak."

"Maybe it had something to do with Richie?"

"Might be, lad, but a lot of years passed by since then, and you two were a bit disengaged, you might say. Could be he had a lot to catch up on with you."

Sullivan nodded. "It's a mystery, just like the reason why he wanted me to finish restoring the ketch and sail it south."

"Who knows?" Calum said. "Maybe somewhere between here and the Lesser Antilles you'll be finding it out." Calum winked and nodded his head.

When Calum emptied his flask, Sullivan drove him home.

John Sylliboy and Todd Sipu were waiting when Sullivan returned to Lochinver Harbour. Sylliboy raised his hand and Sullivan pulled to a stop. The pig was in the bed of Sullivan's Dodge, wrapped in plastic and covered with a sheet of cardboard.

Sylliboy lifted up the cardboard. "The sooner we put the fire on the better, if we want to eat around one tomorrow afternoon."

Sullivan and Sylliboy pulled the pig to the tailgate, unwrapped it and placed it on a rack in the cavernous roaster. A matching rack was lowered over the pig and latched to the lower one. Sylliboy lit the propane burners and plugged the rotisserie motor into an outlet on the dock while Sipu began brushing a condiment on the pig with a large paint brush.

"Brush some of this on both sides every forty-five minutes or so," he said.

Sullivan sniffed the plastic pail that was filled with several litres of the condiment. "What's in this?"

"An old Mi'kmaw recipe," Sipu said.

"Don't you believe him," Sylliboy said. "The Aboriginals didn't have garlic and olive oil."

Sipu smiled. "Nothing wrong with a little poetic licence."

"If you've got the drill down on the roaster, we're out of here," Sylliboy said.

Sylliboy pulled four folding lawn chairs and a card table from Sipu's pickup and told Sullivan they'd be back in the morning.

Sullivan settled into one of the chairs and looked at his Timex. It was ten forty-five, and D and her friend weren't due to arrive until midnight. Lochinver Harbour seemed asleep. The café closed at ten and the occasional glow of headlights from fishermen checking their boats seemed to have subsided for the night. The sound of a dock line stretching and a hull rubbing against a rubber fender punctuated the stillness. Sullivan could see the muted blush of lights from houses in the distance.

A breeze came off the water, and Sullivan, still dressed in his shorts and tank top, felt a chill. He walked down the dock ramp to the *Jessica Elaine* and slipped into the cabin. He had left a sweatshirt onboard and he pulled it on.

Headlights from a car arced over the ketch and stopped. Sullivan stepped into the cockpit and shielded his eyes from the headlights until they were switched off. It was Caitlin's Jeep.

Caitlin walked toward the ketch. As she grew nearer, Sullivan could see she was dressed about the same as he was: shorts, sandals and a sweatshirt. The white shorts showed a lot of thigh, and she wasn't wearing a bra underneath her sweatshirt. She was cradling a litre-size thermos and a grocery bag in her arms.

"Hey, sailor. I saw the ketch go in this afternoon."

Sullivan smiled and slipped out of the boat. He walked up the dock ramp and took the bag from her. He could sense the aroma of herbal shampoo and a touch of perfume. "What do we have here?" he asked, peeking in the bag.

"Just some butter pecan tarts, crackers and cheese, and cream and sugar for the coffee. I thought the barbecue watchers camped out here might get hungry."

His eyes looked into hers. "I'm really glad you did."

She stared back. "Where should I put the coffee?"

Sullivan pointed. "How about on the card table next to the roaster?"

"Sounds like a plan. Do you want a cup?"

"No thanks," Sullivan said. "I was thinking of cracking open one of the bottles of champagne that I brought along for tomorrow. You interested?"

"Maybe, just a little."

"Come on. You haven't seen the ketch with the new curtains and upholstery."

Caitlin slid into the corner of the U-shaped galley table in the saloon. Sullivan took a bottle of champagne from the refrigerator. He wrapped the neck of the bottle in paper towels, popped the cork and filled two plastic cups half-full of champagne.

Sullivan raised his glass. "Cheers."

"Happy sailing," Caitlin replied.

Sullivan laughed.

"What?" Caitlin asked.

"The guy at the provincial liquor store said this was one of the better bottles of genuine French champagnes that he had. And here we are drinking out of plastic cups."

She took a sip. "It tastes just as good," she said, "not that I'm a connoisseur, but that's the way things are here on Cape Breton. It's the quality of the gifts, not the way they're wrapped."

Sullivan nodded. "That's always been true. If you lose that, you might as well live in Manhattan or Toronto."

"Speaking of cities," she said, "I'm going to my reunion in Montreal."

"That's great!"

"Um, I don't know. I feel a little bit threatened by the whole thing. You know, hearing about how everybody's life is so terrific."

"Hey, you've got bragging rights too."

She shrugged her shoulders. "Not when it comes to important things."

A brass light fixture on the overhead spilled light over her blond hair and freckled face. Sullivan wanted to explore each freckle, to roam the hills and valleys of her landscape.

"I guarantee that you will be the prettiest woman there."

A smile lit her blushed face. "No, I won't."

"I think you're just about the most beautiful woman I've ever met."

Caitlin stared at her glass for the moment it took her to regain her composure. "I think that champagne is affecting your vision."

"My vision is perfect."

The bottle was nearly empty when the sound of a car rolling over the gravel parking lot halted at the top of the dock. Sullivan heard two doors open and close. He stepped up into the cockpit.

"We're down here," he said.

D came down the dock ramp holding the hand of a handsome young man. Sullivan took him to be in his early thirties. He looked Ivy League in the way he was dressed. Sullivan guessed that the watch on his arm was a Rolex. He was several inches taller than Sullivan and his dark wavy hair and features reminded Sullivan of John Kennedy Junior.

"Come aboard," Sullivan said.

They did and Sullivan made introductions. "Champagne?" Sullivan asked.

"That would be great," Scott said.

Sullivan filled two plastic cups.

"D told me about the brilliant restoration you did on the ketch, but this is phenomenal," Scott said as he ran his eyes over the cabin. "Do you mind if I look around?"

Sullivan bade him welcome and Scott walked around inspecting the interior as if it were a priceless antique.

"It's a remarkable restoration. Most of the interior looks original," Scott observed.

"Except for the galley and the head, where the original tub was replaced with a shower. I'm told that there was a small schooner stove installed at one time too. And, of course, the entire boat was rewired, and the through-hull pipes and fittings were replaced," Sullivan replied.

Scott asked Sullivan's permission to go on deck and asked D if she wanted to come along. She declined and Sullivan switched on the cockpit lights and spreader lights on the mast.

When the sounds of his footsteps moved toward the bow, D asked, "Isn't he wonderful?"

Sullivan smiled and imagined for a moment what it would have been like if his own daughter had asked the question.

"He's really handsome," Caitlin said.

D giggled. "He's the best."

Scott finished his tour of the deck and returned to the cabin. "What does she draw?" he asked.

"About one and a half metres," Sullivan answered.

"She'll handle any sea that Mother Nature will throw at her, and she's still shallow enough for gunkholing in the islands," Scott said.

Sullivan didn't know what gunkholing was, but agreed anyway.

D said, "Before we forget, we have something for you." D retrieved a shopping bag that she had brought aboard and produced a gift-wrapped box. Sullivan untied the ribbon and peeled back the wrapping paper. Inside he found a pair of boating shoes that looked like Scott's. Sullivan slipped out of his sandals and tried on the shoes.

"They fit perfectly. Comfortable too," he said, walking a few steps in them. "Thank you." He gave D a hug and shook Scott's hand.

"Hey, it's about time to paint the pig," Sullivan said, hoping to avoid any technical questions about the ketch that he was sure he couldn't answer.

They all vacated the ketch and Sullivan demonstrated his newly acquired knowledge of pig basting. When he was done, he and Caitlin returned to the *Jessica Elaine*.

"There's a little champagne left in the bottle. It would be a shame to let it go to waste," Sullivan said.

"Sure," Caitlin said. She sat with her back against the bulkhead and her legs stretched out on the galley settee. She had taken her sandals off.

"Do you want a pillow?" Sullivan asked.

"No, thank you, I'm fine," Caitlin said.

Sullivan handed Caitlin a cup nearly full with the remnants of the bottle and sat down at the far end of the settee. Her pedicured toes were nearly touching his thigh. "What do you think of Scott?" Sullivan asked.

"He seems nice enough. You can tell he's had a privileged upbringing."

"Sometimes I think D is too naive."

"We all were at that age, don't you remember?"

"Life's a long road with lots of bumps and learning curves, I guess, and learning about love is one of the bumps in the road."

"Young love is precious," Caitlin said.

"Old love too," Sullivan added.

Caitlin took a sip of champagne, leaned her head against the bulkhead and closed her eyes. "Maybe that pillow isn't a bad idea."

"Why don't you lie down in the forward berth?"

"Maybe, just for a minute. I really need to get going."

Sullivan turned on the lights in the berth, leaving Caitlin alone for a minute while he tidied up the cabin. When he looked in on her a few minutes later, she was sound asleep. Sullivan slipped into the pilot's berth behind the navigation station and the next thing he remembered was a rapping on the cabin hatchway. He looked at his watch. It was nearly three in the morning.

"Nick?"

"Yes?" Sullivan swung his feet out of the berth and poked his head into the cockpit.

"We're going to head home and get some sleep," D said. "We just finished basting the pig so it will be fine for awhile. See you in the morning."

Sullivan listened to D drive off and then walked to the galley sink and splashed water on his face. What he needed was coffee. He went in to check on Caitlin before retrieving the thermos of coffee she had left on the table next to the roaster. Sullivan could see her stir and then blink sleep from her eyes.

"My gosh, what time is it?"

Sullivan sat on the edge of the berth. "Almost three."

"I've got to get home," she said. She swung her legs over the side of the berth and rubbed her eyes.

Sullivan stood up. "Why not just sleep here?"

She shook her head and pushed herself off the bed. Sullivan offered her his hand. Her bare feet stepped on Sullivan's and he felt a quiver of warmth surge through his loins. Caitlin felt something too. She looked into Sullivan's eyes and he kissed her. She kissed him back and he wrapped his arms around her and rubbed her back. His caresses moved from her lips to the lobes of her ears. Their tongues wrestled and Sullivan's hand probed the soft bulges under her sweatshirt. He lifted her shirt so that her breasts were exposed and he kissed her nipples. Caitlin moaned and ran her fingers through his hair. He undressed her and then himself. Sullivan picked her up in his arms and laid her on the bed. She guided his sex inside of her. She trembled, and when she grew still, it felt as if Sullivan was holding a lifeless doll. Then Caitlin began to cry. Sullivan held her and kissed the tears from her eyes.

"My God, what have we done," she sobbed. She pushed him away and grabbed her clothes, putting them on as she moved toward the stairs to the cockpit.

"Caitlin, wait," Sullivan pleaded.

Caitlin was running to her Jeep when Sullivan leaped from the cockpit half dressed. He caught up to her just as she was turning the key in the ignition.

"Caitlin, please, let's talk about this."

"No," she said. "No, I can't."

Sullivan watched her drive away. A wave of dread washed over him. He walked up and down the dock for nearly an hour, searching for answers, and in the end he did what he did best.

Sullivan never heard Antonio slip aboard the *Jessica Elaine*. Antonio found the switch for the cabin lights. Sullivan was laid out in the pilot's berth, bare to the waist. An empty champagne bottle was clutched loosely in his hands. Antonio looked around the cabin. A pair of women's underwear lay near the entrance to the forward berth. He picked up the bottle and the underwear and tossed them both in the dockyard trash bin. Then he basted the pig.

—

A firm hand on his shoulder wrestled Sullivan from his sleep. "Cappy!" Sullivan shrieked. He opened his eyes as Capello's image faded from his nightmare. Antonio appeared, standing over him with an anxious look.

"It's almost seven," Antonio said. "I thought you might want to get up and get things straightened out."

Sunlight was streaming through the cabin. Sullivan put his arm over his eyes. A surge of memory eviscerated him and stuck in his gut. He stumbled to the head a step before a wave of nausea. When it was over, he splashed water over his face and sat down on the port settee. His elbows rested on his knees and he held his head in his hands.

"You want me to stay?" Antonio asked.

Sullivan shook his head.

Antonio nodded. "Okay. I'm going to go out to grab some breakfast. You want me to pick up anything for you?"

Sullivan shook his head again.

"Alright. I'll bring something along just in case you change your mind. I won't be long."

Sullivan climbed the first step of the stairs to the cockpit and looked out. The café was open and a handful of cars were parked out front. Sullivan pulled on his shirt, found his sandals and walked to the payphone outside the café. He found change in his pocket and dialed Caitlin's number. The phone rang four times before the answering machine switched on. A cheery voice greeted him.

"Hi. I'm sorry I can't come to the phone right now. Please leave a message and I'll return your call as soon as possible. Bye."

The recorder beeped and Sullivan searched for words that did not come. He hung up the phone and began to walk back to the ketch. In mid-stride he turned around and walked back to the phone. He dialed and waited for the beep.

"Caitlin." He paused, took a deep breath and tried to concentrate through the alcohol haze. "I think I know what's going through your mind. I need to tell you what's going through mine. I've wanted to tell you for a long time about the feelings I have for you. Apparently you don't feel the same way. I'm sorry about the way you feel, but I'm not sorry about what happened. And what happened, happened to both of us, not just you. I think you have a responsibility—"

Sullivan heard a click on the other end of the line. "Nick, I don't know what I feel, except I know what we did last night was wrong. I need some time to sort things out. Will you accept that?"

Sullivan let out a sigh. "Of course. I just wanted you to know that—"

"I know," Caitlin said. "I know what you wanted to tell me. I'm just not ready to hear it, okay?"

"Okay. Will I see you today?"

"I don't know," Caitlin said. "I've got to go now."

Sullivan heard the phone disconnect, and he walked back to the boat.

John Sylliboy and Todd Sipu were driving into the parking lot. Sipu's truck stopped next to Sullivan.

"Everything is going well, I hope?" Sylliboy asked.

The way Sylliboy and Sipu ran their eyes over him, Sullivan thought they must have passed Antonio on the way in. "As well as can be expected," Sullivan said.

"And the pig?" Sipu inquired.

Better than I am, Sullivan thought. "Haven't heard any complaints from him," Sullivan said.

Sylliboy smiled. "We've got coffee. Why don't you freshen up and meet us up here," he said."

Sullivan walked back to the ketch and looked into the mirror in the head. The image in the mirror was like a pointillist painting. The dots were becoming disconnected – serotonin ebbing from his brain cells.

He shaved and took his first shower in the *Jessica Elaine*. The water heater hadn't had time to fully heat the sixty-litre hot water tank, and the tepid water felt sobering. He dressed, popped two Aspirin that he dug out of his toilet kit and walked out into the sunlight. The drumbeat in his head that had started when he awoke was now an entire percussion section of hurt. He found a pair of sunglasses in the Dodge.

Antonio had returned, and Sullivan took a seat in one of the chairs by the pig roaster. He drank some coffee and ate part of a donut that Antonio had brought back. Nobody was saying much and everyone was looking at him.

John Sylliboy said, "You look a bit green around the gills, Nick. Maybe you should lie down for a while. We've got things under control here."

Mass at Saint Joseph's didn't start for another two hours, and he would have skipped out on church if he hadn't promised to pick up Father O'Malley directly after services were over. Besides, his crewmates wanted to talk about him behind his back, not that he cared.

"That might be a good idea," Sullivan said.

Inside the *Jessica Elaine*, reminders of the night before lingered in the air: Caitlin's perfume, the scent of her hair, the sweet odour of spent champagne, the musky odour of their sex. Sullivan remembered what Todd Sipu had said about the timeless nature of life's episodes. Sullivan opened all of the portholes and hatches in the ketch, but the events of the prior night had already set into the woodwork.

Sullivan slept until a gentle hand shook his shoulder.

"Nick. Up and shine, troop."

Blue eyes peeked through swollen eyelids. "Doc?"

"In the flesh. Jeez, you look like shit," Don Esherick said.

Esherick helped Sullivan sit up and brought over a wet washcloth that he made Sullivan hold on his forehead.

"You going to puke?" Esherick asked.

"Don't think so."

Esherick stepped away and came back with a plain donut and weak coffee. "Small bites. You need to get something in your stomach. So, what's the excuse this time?"

"What?" Sullivan asked.

"For this." Esherick held up an empty champagne bottle.

Sullivan told Esherick about the night before.

When Sullivan finished, Esherick said, "So what. Relationships have bumps in the road. Sometimes they lead to a dead end, and I'm sorry if that's the case. But you're using this unfortunate episode with Caitlin as excuse number one-thousand-something to drink yourself unconscious." Esherick examined the label and put the empty champagne bottle on the galley table. "Pretty expense stuff to guzzle.

"But I don't think this is really about Caitlin," he continued, "not at the root of things anyway. Nick, you ever watch a dog chase his tail or a child that tries to keep the high tide from washing away a sandcastle? It folly. It's never going to meet with success. And guess what? Getting drunk isn't going to bring Tony Capello back. It's not going to ease your pain. All it does is feed your depression and pickle your liver. It's folly, Nick. You're a bright guy, and I think a hell of a nice guy. And you had nothing to do with your friend's death. Nothing.

"Here's my professional opinion," Esherick said. "You continue on your present course, the booze is going to kill you with one hundred percent probability."

Sullivan shrugged his shoulder.

"If you get tired of chasing your tail, I can help you. There are medications that will help you stop drinking, others that will treat your depression, and I promise I'll be there every step of the way. But it's not going to happen unless you want it to happen. And I'm not one to chase my tail. Think about it. As for now, let's get cleaned up. I came here for a pig roast and to see your boat float."

Sullivan arrived at church just before Mass began and found a seat in the last pew. D and Scott were sitting in a middle pew – their faces lit with glows that had not yet unravelled love from lust. Sullivan looked around the church for Caitlin, but he couldn't see her, and she rarely missed Mass.

After Mass, as the church emptied, D saw Sullivan and gave him a wave and a smile, but the smile was lost as she ran her eyes over him. Sullivan returned the wave, gave his best imitation of a smile and walked past her at the opposite end of the pew.

He found Father O'Malley on the other side of the sanctuary, already stripped of his vestments down to his white collar and black shirt and pants.

O'Malley looked into Sullivan's eyes and pursed his lips. "So, that's the way it is, Nick Sullivan," the priest said.

Sullivan winced. "Now is probably not the best time to get into it, Father."

O'Malley nodded his head. "Okay, we'll leave it for later. But you'll be hearing me out sooner or later."

Later was in the truck on the way to the Lochinver Harbour. O'Malley said, "You won't be having a long lecture from me, Nick Sullivan. You've been fighting your addiction and God loves you for it, but sometimes a problem like that is bigger than a man can handle. You think you've hidden your drinking from your friends – well, you haven't. There's help available if you'd be wanting it. But you've got to want it, and that means that you got to lose that stubborn-headedness that you Sullivans carry around with you. And don't be dragging other folks into your life without your cleaning house first. Think I don't know what's happening in my own parish? Caitlin is a good woman, but she's as fragile as angel hair."

Sullivan fidgeted behind the wheel of the Dodge and kept his eyes on the road. "I love her." The words escaped from his mouth as if they came from somewhere else. "I mean, I think I could."

"You don't know what you're thinking with a head full of brain cells swimming in alcohol." O'Malley let his eyes burn on Sullivan's flushed face. "You remember this, Nick Sullivan. Folks here have invested their love and friendship in you, and when you let yourself down, you hurt more than just yourself. But a selfish man can't see that. And that's what you are, a selfish man."

When Sullivan pulled into Lochinver Harbour with Father O'Malley, he guessed that almost fifty people, and one German shepherd, were gathered around the *Jessica Elaine*. Father O'Malley sprinkled holy water over the ketch and gave a blessing for the boat and Sullivan too. D leaned over the bow and broke a bottle of faux-champagne on the hull. Sullivan made a brief speech thanking all those that had helped in the restoration of the ketch and bringing his uncle's dream to fruition.

Sullivan looked at his surroundings. It was as if he was in a glass bottle, capped and filled with fog, the view disengaged and surreal.

John Sylliboy was there with his wife and their daughter. Sullivan had met Sylliboy's wife at their Christmas party. She was petite, brunette, pretty and younger than Sullivan had remembered.

And Young Willie had come too, announcing his engagement to a tall thin girl with long red hair who held a baby in her arms. Heads turned when Paddy arrived with his wife and son, each holding one of the boy's hands.

D's band played Celtic music, and town folk, many of whom worked pro bono on the *Jessica Elaine*, feasted on pork, tasty side dishes and desserts and emptied the two kegs of beer on hand. Calum seemed to be truly enjoying himself too. Todd Sipu's wife and girls arrived later. Sipu's wife was shy and quiet and attentive to her children and husband.

Sullivan's eyes drifted often toward the only road into Lochinver Harbour, looking for Caitlin's Jeep. Father O'Malley was the first to leave. D's boyfriend had to leave too, and he dropped the priest off at the rectory on his way back to Yarmouth where the boat he crewed on would be soon departing.

Esherick put his hand on Sullivan's shoulder. "Nice party, Nick. Walk me to my car, won't you?"

Sullivan followed along like a zombie. As they walked Esherick said, "I met some nice people today. You're lucky to have such good friends. Thanks for again inviting me."

"Thanks for everything, Doc." Sullivan's voice was disembodied, mechanical and painted with finality.

"No problem, Nick. That's what we do as soldiers, we watch each other's back."

Sullivan remembered hearing Capello say the same thing.

"Next time you're planning on coming down Sydney way give me a shout ahead of time. A bunch of us that served together in Afghanistan get together every couple of weeks and try out different restaurants or get together at the Legion," Esherick said. "You'd like them."

Sullivan nodded.

It was about half past three when D walked over to Sullivan. She slipped the cell phone that was in her hand into her purse. "Caitlin called," D said loudly enough so those around her could hear. "I guess she isn't feeling well. A twenty-four hour stomach bug or something I guess. She sends her regrets to everyone."

Sullivan nodded, wondering what Caitlin had told D.

By five o'clock, people were filling doggy bags with leftover pork. An hour later, the pig roaster followed Todd Sipu's truck out of the parking lot. D dropped Calum off at his house and returned to Lochinver Harbour. She found Sullivan lying on the settee on the *Jessica Elaine* rubbing Dutch's ears. D took a seat at the galley.

"Nice party," D said.

"I'm glad it's over."

"You weren't looking your best in church, and when I didn't see Caitlin, I kind of thought your day was on a downward slide."

"Caitlin. What did she say when she called?" Sullivan asked.

"Only that she didn't feel well and wouldn't be coming. A girl knows how to read between the lines, so I didn't ask for details. I figure that was between you and her." D leaned forward. "So what happened?"

"It's personal. And I could ask you the same thing."

"Ooh," D chirped. "Pointing fingers are we?"

"I don't want to discuss it."

"Hey, I can't help you here if I don't have details."

Sullivan gave her a cold stare.

"Okay, I can take a hint. You coming home?"

Sullivan sat up and let out a sigh. "I guess. I'll clean up a bit," he said, looking around the cabin, "and meet you there."

Sullivan put the cabin back in order, readied the *Jessica Elaine* for sea trials the next day and drove to the house. He confided in Dutch, bringing him up to date on the events of the prior night. Dutch looked at Sullivan, listened attentively and then turned his head to look out the window.

When Sullivan arrived home, the sun was bent over Aspy Bay. He took a chair on the deck to watch the sky blend into the sea. It was a spectacular sight and he went inside to search for a friend to share it with, but the kitchen was dry except for a few bottles of beer and a half-empty bottle of wine. Any port in a storm, Sullivan thought. Besides he hadn't had much to drink all day except for a few beers and a bottled Long Island iced tea. It was amazing what a drink could do to heighten the colours and smooth out the mood. He felt guilty letting Doc Esherick down, and he'd give his words some thought but not today, not now. Now he just needed an attitude adjustment.

He walked into the kitchen when his friends went dry. Sullivan found D looking in the refrigerator. Sullivan didn't stagger, he was a practiced drunk.

"I helped myself to some wine. I didn't think you'd mind."

D bit her lower lip. She opened her mouth to speak, but instead she just stood silently staring at the floor.

"I think I'll go to bed now," she whispered.

During the blush between twilights, Sullivan had walked the road from hope to despair. He was on the edge of the precipice again, not caring which way he fell. He slid behind the wheel of the Dodge and pointed it toward the Celtic Pub for the company of a tall glass and Jackie and his friends.

Chapter 21

The alarm buzzed as promised, not that he remembered it going off or that he had pushed the snooze button. Fifteen minutes later when the alarm sounded again, he ignored it until Dutch began barking and pulling the covers off his bed. D knocked on the door and then stuck her head in.

"I thought you were supposed to meet Calum at seven. It's six thirty."

Sullivan tried to mouth an "okay," but his tongue felt like a cotton ball. He slipped into a pair of shorts and a T-shirt that he grabbed from the drawer and ran out the door. Dutch was running behind him.

D shouted, "Remember, I'm going on a gig."

Sullivan ran back to the house and grabbed Dutch's bowls and dog food and then sprinted for his uncle's Chevy.

Calum was waiting on his porch when Sullivan arrived. He had on a black North Sea style cap, a white T-shirt with a breast pocket and trousers held up with suspenders that stretched over his belly. His pipe was blowing smoke like a steam locomotive.

Calum looked at his watch. "Any later and we'll miss the tide. We barely have time for breakfast."

Luckily the café was slow and their orders came quickly. Sullivan asked the waitress to bring over a pot of coffee, and he was well into it when his breakfast came.

Calum pointed to the coffee pot. "It's blowing a bit today and we'll be beating right into it. You load up your kidneys with that stuff and you'll be pissing in the wind all day. Nothing makes the kidneys work like caffeine."

"I had a late night. I just need a kick-start."

Calum let out a sigh and shook his head. "Everyone's knowing you fell off your horse. Have you lost your senses, lad?"

"I've got a handle on it."

"Ain't no such thing, and you'd be knowing it too."

The waitress brought their orders to the table, putting a cap on the conversation. From where Sullivan stood, he could see Caitlin's Jeep parked in front of the chandlery and his eyes settled there like steel on a magnet. He could see Calum watching him.

Calum raised his hands. "I'm not saying any more, but mind you, I could."

Calum finished his breakfast and excused himself to the restroom while Sullivan ordered sandwiches for lunch and another cup of coffee to go.

It was nearly eight o'clock when Sullivan turned over the *Jessica Elaine*'s engine and steered the ketch out of the harbour. The sky was the colour of tinfoil with the sun trying to burn through the shrouded overcast and promise light.

Calum took the helm and Sullivan ran up the mainsail while the ketch was still in the harbour and out of the ocean breeze. Outside the breakwater, the mainsail caught the wind. Sullivan cut the engine and winched in the main sheet and then set the ketch mizzen. The *Jessica Elaine* heeled over and raced ahead on a close reach.

"Watch the telltales for the apparent wind," Calum said, pointing to the small ribbons fluttering on the lower shrouds and at the masthead. "Now close your eyes, face the bow and tell me what side of your face the wind is on."

"It's coming from the same direction the telltales are indicating," Sullivan answered.

"Right, lad. And is the wind forward or abaft the beam of the boat?"

"Forward."

"Good. That means the apparent wind is stronger than the true wind. Now, put up the working jib and let's see what it'll do to the knot meter."

Dutch stood with his front paws resting on the cabin combing as Sullivan moved forward, clipped his safety harness into the safety line running along the edge of the deck and hoisted a working jib. When he was finished, Sullivan held onto a stay and looked out over the bow. The wind ruffled his hair. The only sound he heard was the hiss of the hull as it sliced through a steely sea crowned with tresses of white curls. He made his way back to the cockpit and sat on the starboard sail locker opposite Calum. Calum watched the smile on Sullivan's face as Sullivan gazed up at the telltales and adjusted the sheets. Calum was smiling too.

"She's a fine boat, Nick. Rides as smooth as a good whisky. And she's quick, as fast as any racing yawl her size, I imagine. The stays are new and may stretch a hair, but we'll get them tuned after a few more runs, hey. Now, winch the mizzen sheet in just a hair and then take a peek at the charts. "

Sullivan nodded. "Where are we headed?"

"Saint Paul Island," Calum said pointing the stem of his pipe to a spot on the chart. "About twenty-four kilometres from the mainland and just seventy kilometres from the coast of Newfoundland – about a three-hour run," he said looking at the knot metre.

"I remember going there as a boy on my uncle's lobster boat a year or so after the light station was abandoned." Sullivan adjusted a protractor on the chart. "That would be a compass course of about sixty degrees with the wind almost dead on."

"Now you've got it. We'd be needing to tack then. That's the weak point of a ketch rig – she's not efficient to windward so you'll want to fall off some. Call it out then."

Sullivan sheeted in the main and wound the hawser from the mainsheet into a loose coil. "Ready to jibe!" Sullivan called out. "Jibe-oh!"

The ketch swung her stern through the wind and heeled when the wind filled her sails. Calum had Sullivan practice coming about and jibing a few times and made him reef and unfurl the main too. Then the *Jessica Elaine* sailed a steady course.

Calum lifted one leg up with his hand onto the port sail locker seat and slipped the handle of his cane into his pantleg and lifted up the other leg. Then he laid his head down on a sail bag with a sigh. He stared up at the rigging.

After several minutes Sullivan asked, "What are you thinking about?"

"I was just remembering when I was a lad. Got my first job on a fishing schooner when I was fourteen, just for the summer mind you, but it was one summer I'll never forget.

"You know the best part of fishing, Nick?"

"I'd guess catching fish," Sullivan answered.

Calum shook his head. "No, it's about casting out your nets and not knowing if you'll be coming up with fish or not. It's what makes you haul in and cast out over and over again. It's all about hope, Nick. It's all about not giving up, you see.

"During those summers, I learned about lassies, tobacco and how to tell the difference between good whisky and rot gut. And I learned how to fish too. Got to working full time on the same boat at seventeen and worked aboard her until the war came. My folks moved back to Scotland later that year, but I stayed. Been here ever since. But I miss Scotland."

"Have you been back?"

"A few times. When my folks died and once with my wife. And I stayed in a hospital in England for a spell, during the war, and took time afterward to visit family in Scotland before shipping home."

"I didn't know you were wounded."

"Shrapnel in two places. Some of it's still in my thigh, at least that's what they told me. You?"

"No, never got shot. Broken bones and a collapsed lung though."

Calum coughed. Sullivan could hear his lungs wheeze as he tried to catch his breath.

"A prison camp was no place to be in my war either."

"Did you go back to visit the battlefields of France?"

Calum shook his head.

"Why not?"

"No reason," Calum said, "except to say goodbye to me good friend Seumas, and graves registration said they never found his body. His bones are still out there in the mud I guess. You ever go back?"

"No, same reason as you. But I visited the wall in DC. It was about as close as I could come."

Calum turned his head toward Sullivan. "You want to tell me about it?"

"It was a few months after the official dedication of the Vietnam Memorial," Sullivan said. "I'd returned home to Connecticut. My mother was ill with pancreatic cancer. Three months later I buried her next to my father. During those three months I had idle time – time to dwell on the past, time to recall earlier days, better days."

"Aye," Calum said. "Even though my family struggled to put food on the table I have no bad memories of my boyhood. I remember my aunt died when I was young. After that my granddad once said that a rich man was someone who had his health and no debt. Burying your child changes how you look at things."

"Smart man, your grandfather."

"Go on, lad," Calum urged.

"Well, after the funeral, after the thank-you cards were mailed and the bills settled, I cleaned out the house. I found that my mom had saved every letter that I had sent to her from Vietnam. In the stack of withered envelopes I found one from my friend who was the cook for our unit, Modesto Martinez. He'd sent it to my mom shortly after I went MIA."

Sullivan paused trying to recall Martinez's words.

"What did it have to say, Nick?"

"Just that we were like brothers, all of us in our unit, and not to give up hope. I remember Modesto saying that there was nothing he and others wouldn't do to bring Tony and me back alive.

"I'd spoken to Mo a few times on the phone after I returned home from Nam. He attended my commissioning ceremony as a pilot and then we lost touch. It wasn't until I found Mo's letter that we made contact again.

"Mo had finished thirty years with the Air Force and opened a restaurant in Albuquerque that specialized in brick oven barbecue ribs. I propositioned him on the phone with a trip to DC – Mo was excited about it. He caught a military hop to Dover, Delaware, where I picked him up. Mo was more than a few pounds heavier than when I last saw him."

Calum laughed. "I remember trying on my old uniform twenty years ago. I couldn't get the top of my shirt buttoned."

Sullivan laughed too.

"So, you met up."

"Yeah. I had cash from my flying jobs and had paid for two rooms at the Renaissance Hotel that was within walking distance of the wall. We had dinner and then we watered our horses." Sullivan smiled. "We had to help each other get back to the hotel."

Calum slapped his knee. "Aye. I remember being pulled back to the rear in France. Me and the boys found a deserted tavern and drank it dry. It's a good memory mixed in with all the bad. So you woke up with a headache," Calum said.

"As I recall, Mo was in pretty good shape when I met him for breakfast. He was decked out in his dress uniform with the buttons loose on his jacket. I had on my bush hat with my silver wings pinned on it along with some ribbons."

Sullivan closed his eyes.

"What is it, lad?"

Sullivan let out a sigh. "Shit, I was shaking. Mo grabbed my arm and said that it was alright, that it was only a stone wall with names, but we both knew better."

Calum put his hand on Sullivan's arm and felt it tremble.

"We walked to the wall, didn't say another word to each other. You know, the air smelled of engine exhaust and curb-rotting garbage, like it had smelled when an F-4 came in low over a Vietnamese village, its jet fumes settling just before the napalm burned flesh to the bone.

"From a distance, the wall seemed huge, stretching the width of over fifty-eight thousand names. The enormity of that loss – my knees shook and I was sweating bullets. You know what I remember most?"

"What's that, Nick?"

"The air. It smelled like a gravesite from flowers propped against the wall. As we stepped closer, we could see our images reflected off the black marble. I found Tony's name and traced it with my finger."

Sullivan went silent. Tears ran down his face and spotted dark on his shirt.

Calum's hand was still on Sullivan's arm. "Go on with it, lad."

Sullivan sniffed. "We both wept. We found other names we knew. When we stepped away from the wall, it was like tearing ourselves back into the world of mortals. Then I got drunk.

"I was a mess the next morning – didn't remember a damn thing. My room was filled with the smell of vomit, but I was covered with clean linen. Soiled bed sheets were rolled into a bundle and tossed in a corner. Mo was dozing in a lounge chair.

"Mo made me take a hot shower and called room service for coffee. Then he dragged me for a walk."

"And what did he say?"

Sullivan shook his head.

"I'm guessing he told you to get some help with your bad habit."

Sullivan sniffed again. "That was the last time I saw him. He called a few times."

Calum had the brim of his cap pulled over his eyes. He took his hand off Sullivan's arm. "Your friend loved you, and he gave you some good advice. You think you have some sort of right on suffering? No one gets a free pass. Sometimes what's good in life travels in a straight line and it's forgotten, and what's not good collects in a pool of bad thinking that will drown you if you let it. And there's times that life is so heavy on you that hope is just knowing you'll never live forever. But the Scots have a saying: 'There's nothing so bad that it couldn't be worse.' Your self-pity is what stifles your hope. Then one day you wake up and find that all that sorrow you were feeling was a waste and you hate yourself for it. You see, lad, it can all change in an instant. Some use a curve in the road as an excuse to feel sorry for themselves so they could go and tip the bottle and feel that it's alright."

Calum became silent, and when Sullivan looked over at him he was asleep.

An hour later, the *Jessica Elaine* rounded the old lighthouse keeper's home and the solar-powered beacon on the southwestern tip of St. Paul Island and made her way toward Atlantic Cove. Sullivan tacked the ketch. The sound of rigging and sail woke Calum. He sat up and blinked his eyes. Sullivan took in the jib and lowered the main and the ketch mizzen and then started the diesel.

"I'll take the helm while you tend to the anchor," Calum said.

Dutch followed Sullivan to the bow. Calum slowed the forward motion of the boat as the anchor was lowered into the water. Then the prop spun in reverse until the anchor took hold. Sullivan tied off the anchor line and joined Calum in the cockpit.

"Ready for lunch?" Sullivan asked.

"I'm always ready for lunch."

Sullivan smiled and went below to the galley. He returned with the sandwiches the café had prepared, paper plates, a bag of chips and two bottles of beer. He ducked below again for a bowl of water for Dutch that he placed on the deck.

The sun leaked from behind thick clouds as the *Jessica Elaine* bobbed in the lee of the protective cove. Dutch watched, hoping that something tasty would spill from the sandwich rolls, which were stacked with ham, Swiss cheese, tomato, lettuce and black olives.

Between bites Sullivan asked, "How well do you know old man Boudreau?"

"We've lived in the same town all of our lives, but I've never broken bread with the man if that's what you'd be meaning."

Sullivan said, "I was just wondering why it is he shows so much animosity towards me. More than once he's made it clear that I'm lower than swamp bottom."

Calum finished chewing the morsel of food in his mouth. Then he said, "Maybe he's just trying to iron out your wrinkles. You know, his son was a bit of a problem when he was a lad and needed some straightening out."

"His son the lawyer?" Sullivan asked.

"No, his older boy, I think he teaches college out in Vancouver. Anyway, the lad was in with the wrong crowd: petty vandalism, underage drinking, that sort of stuff. According to your uncle, he caught the boy leaving his boat one night with some electronics. Sean gave him a choice: he could beat the daylights out of him and then call the police or the lad could work for him all summer for the going wage. The lad was not galoot, so he worked for your uncle and he was worked hard. I guess when you're working from sunrise to sunset there's not much opportunity for shenanigans. And the way I heard it, Sean straightened the lad out."

"So maybe I'm reading old man Boudreau incorrectly? Maybe he's trying to straighten me out?"

"For certain he's not approving of what he sees in you," Calum said.

"Why make the effort?" Sullivan asked.

Calum put his sandwich down on the paper plate and wiped his mouth with a napkin. "He'd be doing it for the same reason that all those folk helped you out with the *Jessica Elaine* and, I'm thinking, it's the same reason that you helped out Paddy the way you did with the mortgage on his house, except Boudreau's using a stick instead of a carrot."

"So, there's a lesson in all of this?"

"Maybe you've learned something about life since you've come back to Dingwall?" Calum raised his eyebrows. Sullivan thought for a minute. He thought about the stipulations in his uncle's will, how he was baited by Boudreau to stay and complete the restoration of the *Jessica Elaine*, how the community watched over him like a lost child and how Boudreau prodded him. Sullivan nodded. Calum nodded too and finished his sandwich.

After lunch Sullivan lowered the inflatable dingy, which hung from davits at the stern of the boat. He loaded Dutch into the dingy, fired up the outboard and headed toward the beach. The tall grass, baked cinnamon by summer, billowed like ocean swells in the wind. The old oil shack on the island lay in burnt ruins, and the large duplex house sagged with age – mortal wounds gaping from missing windows and a holed roof. Keeping watch nearby were the graves of the five-month-old Laing twins, the wireless operator's children that died in 1936. The ancient light-keeper's home, abandoned for forty years, was in danger of collapse, and the graves of other children watched from there too. Sullivan looked at his watch and walked back to the beach.

It was nearly five in the afternoon when the *Jessica Elaine* slipped into Lochinver Harbour past the longliners, draggers and lobster boats. Sullivan secured the ketch to the wharf and began scrubbing and hosing the deck and topsides while Calum went to the men's room at the café and Dutch watched from the front seat of the Chevy.

After the ketch was secure, Sullivan pointed the Chevy toward the Celtic Pub. He slowed as he passed the chandlery. Caitlin's Jeep was nowhere to be seen.

Calum caught Sullivan's gaze. "She's not there," Calum said. "She's gone to Montreal."

"Did she say anything to you?"

"She's in need of figuring things out. To me it sounded like she may not be coming back."

Sullivan felt something unravel like a broken spring on a windup toy.

Sullivan emptied three bottles of beer over shepherd's pie at the pub and then sat at the bar and finished four glasses of Glenora. Before he could order a fifth, Calum asked for a lift home while Sullivan could still drive.

It was raining when they left the pub. On the way back to Sullivan's house, Dutch nestled on the seat of the truck close to Sullivan. Sullivan stared manically through the windshield. The gas pedal of the Chevy was pressed against the floorboard. Sullivan let up on the gas when the truck skidded on two wheels through a curve. Sullivan laughed and his demons laughed with him all the way back to the house.

———

D sat at the kitchen table across from John Sylliboy.

"When I drove in, he was just sitting in the truck staring through the windshield at the rain, not moving, not even blinking his eyes," Sylliboy said, "like something sucked the life out of him and left him freeze-dried. I tapped on the window, and when he didn't respond I tried the door handle. It was locked. Dutch was sitting next to him."

D wrapped her hand tightly around a cup of tea. "Like sometimes he seems normal and then all of sudden he slips away someplace that you can't see."

D looked at her reflection in the kitchen window and watched the rain drip down the glass. "I'm afraid that someday he won't come back from wherever his mind goes. Whatever happened with Caitlin has devastated him. It's so much worse when he drinks, and he's drinking now more than ever."

Sylliboy looked down at the checkerboard pattern of the table-cloth. "He goes someplace where we can't reach him, someplace safe were life can't hurt him."

"Like being unconscious, I guess."

Sylliboy nodded. "All we can do is let him know that we care, that we're here for him."

"Love is medicine for the soul," D said. "I just hope he knows that."

Chapter 22

The next two weeks were made up of days that were facsimiles of one another. The text of those days held the certainty of the sea and of endless tacks, sail changes and practice with the *Jessica Elaine*'s electronics. But there were blank paragraphs when rivers of eighty-proof spirits spilled into lakes of lager and ale. Old demons whispered sweet promises, and Sullivan listened to their counsel.

September was on the horizon. D's summer season with the band had ended with the tourist season, and she was preparing to leave for Connecticut to find an apartment near Hartt College, her application having been accepted. She spent every other weekend with Scott who flew in on a private plane. In between, D walked the beach and soaked in images and sounds and smells of Cape Breton until they were indelible in her memory.

John Sylliboy had visited to ask Sullivan if he wanted to crew on the next turnaround of the *Aspy Lady*, hoping he would agree so that he and the crew could keep a watchful eye over him. But Sullivan declined, saying that he would be sailing south within a month and had much to do.

Todd Sipu had stopped in too, repeating the offer, and also invited Sullivan to a spiritual revival at Wagmatcook First Nation, but Sullivan's spirit was inconsolable. His demons had cleaned house and moved in.

Sullivan stopped looking for Caitlin's Jeep to appear in front of the chandlery. He spent time pouring over charts and plotting courses for points south when he wasn't holding court with his demons.

Calum was always there, in the background, mentoring and admonishing. There was a sparkle in his eye each morning when he set out with Sullivan in the *Jessica Elaine*, but there were days when that sparkle weakened and he willed himself aboard the ketch. Now the lessons were over, and Nick's next excursion in the *Jessica Elaine* was an overnight solo voyage.

Sullivan looked out the kitchen window, watching the gulls circle around the sand dunes, soaring and then slipping away beyond sight. D was at the kitchen table reading a college brochure. She closed the pamphlet and leaned back in her chair.

"Let's do something special," D said.

"Like what?" he said, still looking out the window.

D said, "It has been a remarkable summer. I keep on thinking that if I leave here, the bubble will burst. So I don't want to celebrate our final days here. That would be like dancing at a funeral, you know? Let's be spontaneous and do something now. I mean right now, just the two of us. We'll go out and buy some lobsters and clams and anything that catches our appetite. We'll cook all day and eat all night and then celebrate some more. Maybe we'll go to the pub after or just sit home and talk about stuff."

Sullivan thought about it for a minute. A soft whisper spoke of finality – a last supper. "Okay," he said.

They left in separate vehicles: Sullivan to Lochinver Harbour to see his wholesale seafood connection and D to the market. Two hours later, pots were boiling and skillets sizzling with lobsters, clams, scallops and garden vegetables. A bottle of wine disappeared during the culinary preparation and another over dinner.

D made coffee and served rhubarb pie in the living room when the dishes were washed and pots and pans stacked in a drying rack. Later, Sullivan sat in the lounge chair with his feet on an ottoman. D was curled up on the couch, and Dutch was sprawled on his bed in between.

"God, that was good. I'm glad we did it," D said.

"Me too," Sullivan replied.

"It doesn't get any better than this, and I don't mean that as a cliché. This is what makes life good, just being alive and appreciating the little things, which aren't so little. Thanks for giving me such a wonderful moment in my life."

Sullivan said nothing.

Sullivan's demons hissed. Unforgettable moments? We have lots of those, don't we, Nick? Letting your best friend die and then walking away? It doesn't get any better than that.

Sullivan took a deep breath and cleared his head. "Thanks, Raindrop. Thanks for trying to bring me sunshine when the clouds were dark."

D blinked her eyes dry. "I remember when you first called me Raindrop. God, so much has happened, and now it's over."

Sullivan's demons laughed. It's all over. Tell her, Nick.

An arrow of certainty sent a shiver through Sullivan so that he actually trembled. He fought for control.

He said, "Hey, you'll be back. This house will be waiting for you anytime you want."

"I'd love to visit next summer, if you'll have me?"

"You can come back anytime you want."

The demons whispered, You're not coming back.

D sobbed as if she knew the truth. Sullivan sat next to her and gave her a hug. It wasn't until the phone rang that she stopped crying.

The strained voice Sullivan heard on the other end of the line promised bad news. His mind reached for a bottle of Glenora single malt waiting for an excuse in the kitchen cabinet.

"Hi, Joe," he said. "It's good to hear your voice."

Joe said, "Ma's in the hospital ICU. She had a heart attack. She's too weak for bypass surgery, but she's stable. She wanted me to call you."

"Can I speak with her?"

"No calls into the ICU, but I'll tell her you asked for her."

"Tell her that I love her, Joe, will you do that?"

"Sure, buddy," said Joe. "Gotta go."

Sullivan went out to the beach and took the bottle of Glenora with him. A few minutes later D sat next to him.

"Bad news?" she asked.

"Ma is in the hospital. It doesn't sound good."

"Want me to stay?"

"No thanks. I'd rather spend some time alone."

"Okay." D kissed him on the cheek and went inside.

Caitlin, Ma, D. There's nothing left, Sullivan thought. He took a long pull from the bottle of Glenora and stretched out in the sand. Then he took another, and another. The sand was still wet from the afternoon rainstorm. Black clouds raced across a slice of orange moon. The horizon was purple and the sky blue-grey. The single malt painted over Sullivan's world in vivid colours. It cleared his head too, so he could think and plan.

How will I do it? Should I leave a note?

A voice, not his, hissed, *Only wimps leave notes.*

"Where and when?"

Far from here, maybe off the coast of Little Creek where your body will wash up on the beach. That will show those bastards who deserted you.

"What about Dutch?"

He's only a dog. He doesn't care. Put him ashore. He'll forget about you in a minute.

A while later Sullivan recoiled at a warm, wet lick on his face. Dutch placed his front legs and torso over Sullivan's body to warm him. Sullivan was shivering and chilled to the bone.

—

The tide was high and the sky was still stained black when he awoke. Dutch was still protecting him, and now shivering himself. Sullivan stood up. He grew dizzy, vomited and fell back onto the sand. He laid there for a moment, caught his breath and then crawled to the steps of the house. The next thing he remembered was waking up again on the kitchen floor. His miserable life swarmed over him.

A drink will calm things down, make the world right again. Sullivan found a beer in the refrigerator. Between gulps he caressed the bottle in both hands. He found the stairs and the bathroom where he pulled off his shoes and ran a hot shower over his still-clothed body. After peeling out of his wet clothes and making an attempt to dry himself, he stumbled naked into bed.

It was one in the afternoon when Sullivan squinted at the daylight, his mouth dry and tasting of vomit. He tried to go back to sleep, but he was head-throbbing awake. He staggered to the bathroom and purged his mouth with mouthwash. The bathroom mirror showed sand still caked on his forehead and in his hair.

Sullivan took a long shower, pulled on jeans and a sweatshirt and went downstairs. The house was empty and the Dodge was gone. A note on the refrigerator door said that D had given Dutch a bath and taken him for a ride. There was coffee in the carafe of the Mr. Coffee machine. Sullivan filled a cup and took a few sips, managing to keep the coffee down, taking small swallows until the cup was dry. Then he went out on the deck and slumped into a chair.

When he woke up, the sun was nearly spent. He squinted and saw D sitting in one of the old wooden deck chairs with a sunglass-tinted stare toward the ocean. Dutch was at her side watching Sullivan. Sullivan struggled to raise himself into a sitting position.

D said, "It was a wonderful day. Too bad you missed it." She turned her head toward him.

Sullivan raised a cautionary hand and shuffled off to the bathroom to urinate. He grabbed a handful of Aspirin and went downstairs to wash them down with a beer. There was no beer in the Frigidaire. Sullivan slammed the refrigerator door. Yanking open kitchen cabinets he looked for a drink – nothing. He wasn't sure if D had removed all traces of booze from the house or if he had consumed it. A shout began to grow in his throat as he headed toward the door to confront her, but a wave of pain shot through his head that stopped him cold. The Aspirin was flushed down with a glass of water.

D came into the kitchen. "Want me to fix something to eat?"

Sullivan shook his head.

D sighed noticeably. "Anything I can do?"

"Yeah, stop asking me questions!"

D's face fell.

The demons cheered. *That a boy, Nick. You tell that bitch to mind her own business.*

Sullivan was shaking with anger now. He stormed out the door to the Dodge and sped down the driveway to the main road toward the pub. Halfway there he noticed that he didn't have his wallet. The wheels of the Dodge squealed as the truck spun around and headed instead to the *Jessica Elaine*.

Sullivan parked the Dodge out of sight behind the boat repair facility at the harbour. Aboard the ketch, he closed the cabin hatch, went up on deck through the forward hatch and padlocked the cabin hatch so it would appear the ketch was unoccupied. Closed curtains kept the dim light from a single lamp from spilling from the cabin.

There was a six-pack of beer in the boat's refrigerator. Sullivan grabbed one, took a long swallow and sat down on the galley settee before downing the beer in a gulp. No anger now – he was relaxed, back in his element. While he was up getting another cold one, he rummaged through the galley and came up with a box of crackers, a wedge of cheddar, a Snickers candy bar and a can of vegetable soup. While the soup was warming on the galley stove, Sullivan nibbled at the cheese and crackers. The throbbing in his head was reduced to a dull buzz by the time he drained the soup directly from the pan. He savoured the Snickers bar and then washed the remnants of peanuts, caramel and chocolate from his mouth with another beer.

Sullivan's eye caught the burl wood turtle that Todd had given him. It swayed from its perch on the light fixture with the gentle rocking of the ketch. He retrieved it and hung it around his neck, admiring its beauty and craftsmanship.

Reclining on the galley settee, he watched the lamplight scatter shapes overhead as he sipped on the beer. The food and alcohol made him sleepy. When he closed his eyes, he listened for his demons to share their wisdom, to keep him company, but even when he called them out loud, they didn't answer. There was another presence deep in the land where the hobgoblins patrolled the approaches to his soul. It was kind and spoke softly, although Sullivan could only hear unintelligible whispers.

"You there, Cappy?"

No answer.

Sullivan finished the beer. Lonely, he listened for his demons, but they were hushed and, he sensed, afraid of what had invaded their territory.

The sound of men and boat engines yanked Sullivan from his sleep. His Timex said it was five in the morning, and his stomach said it had been ignored and otherwise abused for thirty-six hours. Sullivan showered, shaved and pulled on a spare set of clothes he kept onboard in a gym bag. In the bottom of the bag he found ten bucks and change – more than enough for a good breakfast.

The café had only a handful of patrons. He looked around at the few familiar though nameless faces he had seen around the harbour or at the pub. Those would nod but otherwise leave him alone. He ordered breakfast, lots of coffee.

An hour later he was on the road headed toward the house. Dutch ran to greet him at the door. D was in the kitchen.

"Hey," Sullivan said.

"Hey," D replied distantly.

Sullivan made his way to the Mr. Coffee machine and then sat at the kitchen table across from D. She sighed and stared into the morning paper.

Sullivan fractured the silence. "What's going on today?"

D looked up from the paper. "Tying up loose ends. I'm going to go shopping in Sydney later today to get some clothes and stuff for school. I'll fly to meet Scott in Boston and we'll drive down to Connecticut. I think I found an apartment off-campus."

"It's Tuesday," Sullivan said. "I'm leaving on Thursday for a solo to Saint-Pierre and Miquelon. I'll be back before you leave."

D nodded.

Sullivan took a deep breath. "Look, I'm sorry if I've been a bit testy lately, but I've had things on my mind."

D sighed. "We know something is troubling you, but all we can do is speculate."

"We?"

"Me, Calum, John, Father O'Malley, everyone who cares."

"So, it's a conspiracy."

D just shook her head.

Sullivan's eyes widened, his right eye twitched, his jaw was clamped tight. "What are they saying about me?"

"We're all concerned. We thought maybe it was Caitlin or maybe post-traumatic stress from falling overboard last summer, but whatever it is, it's changed you, Nick. You're not the same person I used to know. That person had at some grip on his life, as imperfect as it may have been. You seemed like a new person for a while after your accident, but that person is gone, and someone else is occupying his body, someone dark and full of anger. And he gets worse when he drinks, and he hurts the people that love him. Nick, you're out of control. Whatever is happening to you, we can't fix it. You need help from people that know about these things."

A chuckle began in Sullivan's throat that grew into fit of laughter that brought tears to his eyes. When the laughter ebbed he said, "That's precious. Okay, sometimes I drink too much. And sometimes I get a bit edgy. Who doesn't go on a bender once in awhile? Sylliboy, Calum, you? Even Father O'Malley has his moments. At least I never shoved things up my nose."

D recoiled, her eyes filling with tears. She went upstairs and returned ten minutes later with an overnight bag packed with clothes. She made a quick telephone call and then headed for the door.

"Where are you going?"

"I can't stay here anymore," D said. "I'll pick up the rest of my things tomorrow."

"Look, I'm not good company right now. I'll stay on the boat. You can stay here."

D pushed past him. He watched her walk out the door and down the long driveway to the main road.

Dutch was looking at Sullivan – ears down, sorrow in his eyes. "What we need is a drink, Dutch boy. Come on, let's go to the pub."

Sullivan arrived at the pub when it opened for lunch and left after dinner. Staggering through the door of the house, his arms were around the shoulders of his demons.

He made himself a nightcap and took it outside. The night was clear and full of stars that flickered in booze-tainted splendor. Dutch followed him to the barn and watched as Sullivan climbed the rickety wooden ladder to the loft under the still-unfinished roof. Dutch looked up at Sullivan from the foot of the ladder. Sullivan pushed open the loft door and gazed out at the ocean. And, in the sound of hissing surf, he heard a voice telling him to spread his wings and fly away.

Chapter 23

Morning spilled liquid gold over Aspy Bay. Sullivan packed clothes in a gym bag and loaded Dutch into the Dodge. He drove to the bank to make a withdrawal and stopped at the village store for food and dog chow. On the way to Lochinver Harbour, he loaded up with beer and whisky at the liquor store and then drove to Calum's to see if he wanted to go to breakfast. Sullivan knocked on the door and waited. He knocked again and peered through the windows. The house looked empty, so Sullivan drove to the café hoping to find him there.

Sullivan took his regular table next to a window in the corner of the café where he had a view of the harbour. He scanned the café for Calum, and when he came up empty, he asked the waitress if she had seen him – she hadn't.

Sullivan watched the harbour as he waited for his breakfast. The sun was summer hot and the sky reminded Sullivan of the view out of the cockpit window of an F-4 touching the approaches to heaven, where the air was innocent of human effluence. In the morning, before his demons awoke, before his body craved an eighty-proof fix, there were moments of clarity. Sullivan thought about D and how he had taken pleasure in her pain, and he hated himself.

After breakfast Sullivan provisioned the *Jessica Elaine* and turned on the single sideband radio for a weather report. The forecast called for promising skies. Rather than wait another day, Sullivan wrapped Dutch in a canine floatation vest, turned over the diesel and slipped the lines.

Outside the breakwater, Sullivan put on a personal floatation device and a safety harness, hoisted sail and entered the coordinates of Saint-Pierre and Miquelon into the GPS. Even with a number four genoa jib, the ketch was cruising at only four knots. The GPS system calculated that the *Jessica Elaine* would make landfall in the middle of the night. Sullivan made a check of all the thru-hull fittings and then settled into the helm chair. As the familiarity of shoreline gave way to the sea with its endless horizon, there was a sense of excitement for the unfettered freedom from man-made rules. But the uniqueness of sailing was quickly lost in a becalmed sea. The autopilot, which was interfaced with the GPS, gave the *Jessica Elaine* a brain of her own and Sullivan became just a passenger.

Sullivan reviewed the charts and memorized the approach to the islands, the only French possession in North America. He contacted the harbourmaster at Saint-Pierre on the frequency listed in his cruising guide and made arrangements for a slip in the harbour. After the sails were trimmed for what seemed the hundredth time, after he had checked the radar and noted the progress of the ketch in his log, he made lunch and opened a box of biscuits for Dutch to snack on.

Midday was the official commencement of cocktail hour among some cruising sailors, and Sullivan, being one to respect such imperatives, cracked open the first beer of the day. But to Sullivan, piloting a sailboat instilled a sense of order that was etched into his psyche as a military pilot. He drank his beer slowly and waited before he opened a second one. He needed his senses when he navigated the harbour at night, at least enough of them to ensure that his honour would remain intact.

By late afternoon the wind picked up. Sullivan tethered Dutch's safety harness to a cleat and attached his own to the boat's safety line before he walked to the bow to change the genoa to a working jib. When he finished, he steadied his six-pack buzz by holding onto the forestay as the deck pitched and yawed. The sea was now white-capped and gilded by the sunset. And except for the rattle of rigging and a gentle whisper as the bow skimmed across the water, there was silence. There were moments like this when he thought that maybe there was a God. He remembered climbing high above the clouds in his F-4 to pray, in his way. He thought there might have been a God then, too. He prayed for one, but he never got an answer, at least not the one he was hoping for.

Sullivan went below to check the radar. Two blips showed up on his screen twenty-five kilometres away. A call to Calum on the ship-to-shore came back with only the hum of static. He made a sandwich for dinner and made another just in case he got hungry later and poured a cup of coffee from a thermos he had filled at the café before he left.

Sullivan climbed the stairs to the cockpit and sat at the helm. Dutch sniffed at the sandwich. Sullivan convinced Dutch that is was okay to urinate in the cockpit where the deck could be washed and drained through the scuppers.

Dressed now in a sweatshirt and a windbreaker, Sullivan fed Dutch and then poured two fingers of Glenora whisky into his steel coffee cup and settled into the helm chair. The spreader lights lit up the white mainsail, dumping dim light over the boat. Red and green running lights at the bow and masthead reminded Sullivan of Christmas decorations. As he sailed closer to landfall there were more lights: a freighter eastbound and fishing boats hauling nets or perhaps just drifting while the crew slept.

The harbour lights at Saint-Pierre winked at the *Jessica Elaine* just shy of three in the morning. Half an hour later the GPS alarm bleated a warning at the harbour entrance. Sullivan lowered sail and turned over the diesel. He scanned the harbour for the customs dock, finding it quickly.

The village was still nocturnal as Sullivan ran a yellow quarantine and French tricolour flag up the mast. After the boat was secured, he went below, gulped down a short glass of whisky and settled into his berth.

The sounds of a revving engine and Dutch's bark roused Sullivan. He pulled on his clothes and slid open the cabin hatchway, squinting into the early morning sunlight at the custom official waiting at dockside. After checking the boat's papers and Dutch's vaccination certificate, the *Jessica Elaine* was moved to the town marina.

After taking Dutch for his morning constitutional, Sullivan showered while a pot of coffee percolated on the stove, and then he and Dutch had breakfast in the cockpit.

Later, Sullivan tethered Dutch with a leash and walked narrow streets past shops and houses of stone, wood and stucco brushed with the vibrant reds and greens of an artist's palette. It was as if a piece of Brittany had floated loose from the French mainland and come aground here, lost and forgotten.

The town was busier than he had expected, as the population of over six thousand began their day. The aroma of fresh baked goods and meats beckoned from open storefronts. Restaurants posted daily fare in curtain-clad windows. People nodded in greeting. Dutch let them stroke his head for the price of a smile. The villagers knew that they were from away by the cut of Sullivan clothes and the baseball cap that touted the name of a sailmaker.

The farther they walked, the more the streets widened. Homes and fishing shacks rose from the water's edge and climbed hillsides. Sullivan backtracked through the centre of town, stopping at a shop to buy D a souvenir sweater and a French beret – a small gesture that begged at forgiveness. The aromas of a bakery and butcher shop they had passed earlier summoned the senses to make a stop too. Back onboard the *Jessica Elaine*, Sullivan spread slabs of spicy sandwich meat on slices of bread still oven warm.

After a nap below deck, Sullivan lowered the inflatable and secured Dutch and a cooler inside. The wind was just a whisper. The small boat skimmed over the water toward the small island of Ile-aux-Marins that once had been a fishing village but now was a living museum.

Sullivan then turned the tiller on the outboard toward Miquelon and motored along the twelve kilometres of dunes and sandbars that connect Saint-Pierre with Miquelon. On the south side of Miquelon, the inflatable slowed as he took in the ambiance of the quiet village. The wind began to freshen and the cooler was nearly empty, signalling a return to the harbour.

The afternoon was gone when the inflatable was secured to its davits aboard the *Jessica Elaine*. Sullivan's internal hydrometer signalled that it was the time of day for pursuits of a higher proof. He poured whisky in a small glass and downed it before he showered, taking off the burl wood turtle and hanging it from a bulk-head lamp. The bottle of Glenora and his head were lightened a bit more as he settled Dutch in for the night and navigated toward a restaurant that had caught his eye that morning.

La Voilerie was nearly empty at five thirty in the evening, keeping to the European panache of an early afternoon dinner hour. Sullivan ordered a carafe of white house wine that he sipped as he waited for an appetizer of snow crab–scallop chowder flavoured with dandelion liqueur.

He could see the *Jessica Elaine* from his seat by the window. He watched, too, as people passed by on the sidewalk intent on some purpose. From their body language and expressions, Sullivan imagined what they were feeling and where they were going: home to warm embraces, or to domestic tedium, or perhaps to unfinished work, or to a shade-drawn affair. He stopped wondering when dinner arrived and he stopped thinking when the wine bottle was inert and dessert arrived with a cup of café de Bancs .

Leaving La Voilerie, Sullivan ambled in the glow of streetlights muted by a blanket of fog. There was fifty dollars and change crumpled in his pants pocket. He remembered a tavern down a side street not far away and headed in that direction.

The smoke-filled bar was indiscernible from the fog outside. Sweet pipe tobacco congealed with blue plumes of smouldering cigarettes and kitchen smells. Sullivan sat at the bar. The patrons were all local, working class, and most had the silver hair and wrinkles of those that were on the downward slope of life. The tavern was probably a second home for most of them. Some sat at tables drinking their beer. Others slurped from bowls of chowder and didn't look beyond a spoon's breadth of their space, as if they knew there was nothing there to see anymore.

Sullivan pointed at a bottle behind the bar and the bartender obliged him with a glass of cognac.

"You are Canadian?" the bartender asked.

"No, an American disguised as a Canadian." Sullivan smiled at his attempt at humour.

"Long way from 'owme," the bartender said.

Sullivan nodded.

"Euh. Where in deez United States is 'owme?"

Sullivan looked into his glass as if it held the answer. "I don't have a home."

"Euh, no? Deez boat your 'owme. I geez sailor man no 'owme free drink, euh."

"Thank you." No home, Sullivan thought to himself.

He sat and listened to the rhythmic conversation, the sweet sound of vowels and consonants rolling from tongues that he could not understand. But there were other voices too, faint and in his head.

Sullivan pointed to a box of cigars. The bartended handed him one and held a match until the tobacco was stoked. Sullivan nodded a thanks. The cigar lasted through three more cognacs. He felt drunk and lonely and stood up to leave.

Where you going, Nick? We just got here. His boys were back.

Sullivan moved toward the door.

The night is young. Live it up. Sullivan moved outside. The voices murmured, angry now for Sullivan's disregard.

In the darkness and fog, he had no sense of direction other than right or left. He chose left, down side streets until he came into an area of lights and traffic sounds. He needed to rest, to get a sense of direction back to the marina. There was an open area with trees and a tall building. As he grew closer, he could see the tall spires of a church. He walked up the steps and tested the door. It swung heavily on its hinges and closed behind him with an echo.

Sullivan found a rear pew abutting the church's stone wall that was washed in shadows. Votive candles, glowing red, blue and white, reminded Sullivan of the wooden facades of Cape Breton. The room spun when he closed his eyes. The stone wall of the church felt cold as he rested his head against it. The church was void of sound and human presence, and the voices in his head were quiet. He felt himself falling asleep.

—

Sullivan awoke more sober. The Timex hinted that he had been out for about thirty minutes. He rubbed his eyes and blinked them into focus. Outside the fog had lifted, swept away in a strong breeze. A passerby directed him to the docks.

Dutch greeted Sullivan with tail wags and whines when Sullivan slid open the cabin hatchway. Dutch leaned against his master's leg and was treated to a gentle rub of his head and ears. Sullivan walked him and then settled back into the *Jessica Elaine*'s cabin while a pot of coffee perked on the stove. The sideband came to life with a press of the power button. Sullivan threw out Calum's call letters over the airwaves. Calum answered on the fourth try.

Sullivan slurred his words. "I've been trying to reach you for the last two days. I stopped by the house and asked around, but no one had seen you. Rumour has it that it must be a woman."

Calum's chortle turned into a raspy cough. He caught his breath and his voice was a whisper. "Haven't been at the top of my game for a couple of days."

He paused with his microphone still open. "Where are you, Nick?"

"Saint-Pierre. I'm short on cash, probably leave in the morning."

"Sounds like you might be needing a long nap to get your head on straight enough to do that. They're saying some dreich of weather is heading your way. Best you stay over another day or two, wait things out."

Sullivan didn't answer.

"You hear what I'm saying?"

"Yes, I hear you."

"Give me a shout when you leave, and when you make Lochinver Harbour come by and see me as soon as you can. Will you do that for me?"

"Sure, Calum. Everything okay?"

"I will be soon. Don't forget. Best I sign out now. X-ray, Romeo, Sierra, clear."

Sullivan listened to the static for a moment before he switched frequencies for a weather report. The marine forecast was for heavy weather: a local low combining with high winds and storm surge racing north from a hurricane east of the Carolinas promised wave heights of up to three metres. Nothing that the old ketch couldn't handle, but no picnic either. Sullivan decided to get a few hours of sleep and let the buzz clear before setting sail before dawn.

Chapter 24

The alarm on Sullivan's Timex beeped him awake at four. He rubbed the sleep from his eyes and listened to the wind chime rattle of the rigging against the mast for a few minutes before he swung his legs over the edge of his berth. Saint-Pierre was still asleep when he warmed the pot of coffee leftover from the night before and prepared enough sandwiches to sustain himself for his return trip. The pastry he picked up at the bakery the day before made for a quick breakfast. He fed and walked Dutch, secured the cabin and hatches and set out his foul weather gear. A storm jib was readied on deck as the diesel warmed up. At six o'clock, the *Jessica Elaine* made for the open sea.

Just outside the harbour, Sullivan headed into the wind and raised the main and mizzen, double-reefing both. The storm jib went up and snapped full in a gust of wind. The *Jessica Elaine* was close-hauled on a course for home, the sea fighting her even while the breakwater was still in sight.

Sullivan looked over the cabin hatch splash boards at Dutch who was curled on his bed in the cabin at the bottom of the stairs. The wind was blowing more than twenty knots. An hour later, all traces of Saint-Pierre had disappeared. A storm-filled sky had fallen to meet raindrop-pocked waves. Sullivan ducked below to put on his rain gear. The pitch and yaw of the boat rattled the contents of storage cabinets like castanets and gave Sullivan vertigo.

Sullivan tried to contact Calum on the radio, and when there was no reply, he turned the dial to the frequency monitored by the Coast Guard who was broadcasting a message warning all mariners of a storm warning for waters north and east of the Gulf of Maine. Sullivan studied the barometer and made a note of the time and millibars on a pad of paper.

His nerve endings felt raw. He needed a fix. Glenora spilled over the lip of a paper cup that Sullivan tried to steady in his hand, so instead he took a swig from the bottle and brought it up on deck. The liquor warmed him and smoothed his nerves.

Sullivan settled into the helm chair. The autopilot was working overtime trying to keep the ketch on course while he took swigs from the bottle. The air was dark and so heavy that his chest and eardrums felt taut. The wind hummed a lullaby through the rigging as the booze worked its way into his head. Pitching and rolling like a baby's cradle, the ketch rocked Sullivan to sleep.

Music. Not of this world, but beautiful, so very beautiful, played from his dream. Suddenly it was cold – the kind of cold that numbs you with needle pricks and leaves you breathless. He was floating now and something was tearing at him and trying to lift him higher. Sullivan awoke with water swirling around him. The line attached to his safety harness was straining to keep him from being swept into the sea. He watched as the near empty liquor bottle was ripped from his hand and floated past his head. The *Jessica Elaine* shuddered as another wave smashed broadside against the hull, keeling the vessel over on its side and slamming Sullivan down on the deck. Sparks of pain ripped through the shoulder that was injured a year before on the *Aspy Lady*, and blood seeped from a deep cut in his head.

Sullivan's military instincts battled millions of damaged brain cells, trying to process what was happening. He glanced at the wheel – locked tight, not moving. It should be moving, he thought. Sullivan disengaged the autopilot and fought the helm to bring the bow of the boat head-on into the sea. The bow swung around slowly.

Sullivan put the boat in irons by steering it directly into the wind and arresting all forward motion. The boat rocked almost gently, giving him an opportunity to compose himself. He took in the mizzen, rigged a sea anchor and inspected the boat.

He glanced around the deck. In the fading light, he couldn't see any damage. The wind plucked pizzicato at the rigging. Sullivan reached over to a bank of switches mounted on the helm station and flicked on the running lights. Nothing. He moved the switch back and forth. When that didn't work, he turned the ignition key to start the diesel. The alternator gauge was flatlined. Then it occurred to him that he hadn't charged the batteries. With no DC power, the autopilot was unable to keep the ketch on a course, bow into the waves.

A whine came from the cabin. Sullivan slid open the splash boards. Dutch was standing, fear filled and shaking, trying to keep his balance. His bed had been thrown across the cabin.

"It's okay now," Sullivan said in a voice so calm it surprised him.

He adjusted a locking stud on the wheel to keep it from moving and went below. In the cabin he gave Dutch a reassuring rub on his head and then removed the engine room hatch. On his hands and knees inside the engine compartment, he wiped away blood that was dripping into his eyes. His fears were confirmed: the switches to the boat's two batteries were both open, meaning they were both dead, or nearly so.

The vulgar smell of diesel fuel and bilge crude worked with the rocking of the boat to make Sullivan retch. He crawled out of the engine room and nearly landed in the noxious remnants of Dutch's breakfast. He retched again.

Then Sullivan went about bandaging his head wound and cleaning up the mess. The carved wooden turtle that Todd Sipu had given him had fallen on the deck and he put it in his shirt pocket. A check of the bilge showed it was relatively dry. The clock on the bulkhead said it was seven o'clock. That meant he had been in booze-induced sleep for three hours.

He made a note of the time and checked the barometer, which registered 965 millibars. It occurred to him that he had no idea where he was. Without electrical power from the batteries, the GPS and other electronics were useless.

Pulling out a chart, Sullivan sat at the navigation station. Given the time underway and approximate course travelled, Sullivan drew a line of position on a chart and made an educated guess that the *Jessica Elaine* was still eight to twelve hours from Dingwall. He made a notation on the chart and entered the boat's estimated position in the log. Before going back on deck, Sullivan tossed pillows and a sleeping bag on either side of Dutch to cushion him against the sudden lurching of the boat.

He gave Dutch a hug. "Don't worry, I'm going to get us home soon, I promise."

Manoeuvring sail and rudder, Sullivan coaxed the *Jessica Elaine* out of iron. The sea was boiling and confused, but there was still a prevailing southeasterly wave pattern. He guessed the waves to be about four to five metres, based upon the distance from the top of the mast to the crest of the waves. The ketch slid down the huge surf, corkscrewed slightly, and wallowed in the trough, with sails luffing until the ketch crawled up the back of the next wave. Sullivan gripped the wheel tightly with both hands, knowing that if the boat slipped off course fifteen degrees in either direction, it would broach.

As he wrestled with the helm, he wrestled too with his torment. In a heartbeat, it could be over. He could escape. He thought of Dutch. If he was alone, if he wasn't harnessed by commitment or affection, he wouldn't care. But there was something else – a sliver of pride in delivering the *Jessica Elaine* back home intact. Home. He remembered how the folks in Dingwall welcomed him home when he arrived. Maybe it wasn't pride that was urging him to survive. Maybe it was something else.

The ashen cloud of daytime that had enveloped the *Jessica Elaine* was now replaced with the colourlessness of night. Sullivan fumbled for a flashlight in the storage cabinet beneath the helm station. The narrow beam of light was focused on the compass with one hand, as Sullivan gripped the wheel in the other, making constant adjustments in heading as the ketch thrashed about in the storm.

Sullivan was tired. His brain, still awash with booze, begged for sleep. He drank coffee, pinched himself, sang out loud and talked to Dutch – anything to stay awake. The wind changed from a howl to a scream, and although he couldn't see the sea battering the boat with sledgehammer blows, he knew the storm was intensifying and that the easterly course required to keep the boat intact was taking them further out into the Atlantic.

Sheets of water were swept off wave tops and hurled across the deck and into the cockpit where it whipped at Sullivan. He rotated his injured shoulder, intentionally sending sparks of pain through his limb. Maybe he could fend off sleep until morning, but not indefinitely. He imagined the ketch broaching, rolling over and demasting as he gained a hold on Dutch and maybe a bottle of whisky for company as he swam clear of tangled rigging.

He could hear his demons calling out from the storm. *Nick. It's just a waste of time. Grab a bottle and enjoy the show. It's going to be spectacular, Nick. Let's close the curtain with a standing ovation.*

Sullivan gritted his teeth and screamed over the taunting howl of the storm. "You're not going to take us, you bastard." Then he laughed as he shook his middle finger in the face of the storm.

The hands on his watch pointed to one-twenty in the morning. Sullivan slid open the splashboards slightly and illuminated Dutch with the flashlight. His eyes looked up at Sullivan as if at a god capable of all things.

Sullivan closed his eyes. A moment later his chin fell against his chest, waking him from a micro-second of sleep. He craved it, wanted it more, even more than he wanted a drink.

Let it go, Nick, let it go.

"No!" Sullivan yelled. "I'm not going. I'm staying here. Dutch, we're staying here."

A bark followed by an encore of barks burst from the cabin as if to say "That a boy, Nick."

Sullivan spoke to Dutch, gained resolve from his whines and woofs and howls, but the demons were right – it was time. Sullivan tried praying but couldn't finish a single prayer. Muscles became relaxed. His breathing became shallow – inhaling defeat, exhaling resolve. Calm now. Maybe death was sweet after all. He said goodbye to D and Calum and Ma Puglise, John Sylliboy, Todd Sipu, Mo, his daughter and everyone he loved on this earth. Yes, he loved them. Love. Love was what he would miss most. Finally, he said goodbye to Dutch. Sullivan found himself standing up and saluting the storm. The son of a bitch had finally won.

Later he wouldn't be able to explain why, but he grabbed the ignition key to the engine and turned it. The diesel roared into life. The last thing he remembered was dialing the boat's proper heading into the autopilot.

———

"Covey one, Hornet. Sit rep. Covey one, this is Hornet. Come back, Covey one."

Brass casings from Sullivan's M-14 spun into the air. Flashes of dazzling light spit from the flash suppressor of his rifle. He was on his feet now, running. Capello. He had to save Tony. He loved Tony. The chopper was overhead. He could feel the downdraft of the rotors. The acrid taste of gunpowder that spewed from the door gunner's M-60 machine gun mixed with the Jolly Green's engine exhaust, burning his eyes and lungs. He had Tony over his shoulder now, running, his hand reaching, so close now. Sullivan willed his legs to move faster. Strong hands pulled Capello and then himself into the Jolly Green. Bullets pinged against the airframe as the chopper gained altitude. The M-60 silent now. Tony saying, "We're safe. Everything's going to be okay."

———

"Hello, sailing vessel *Jessica Elaine*. Do you require assistance?"

Sullivan blinked awake. "No, safe now, safe," Sullivan mumbled to himself. His eyes took inventory of his surroundings, told him where he was, what had happened. It was daylight and the rain had stopped. The deck of the *Jessica Elaine* was pitching and yawing, but not as bad as the night before. Sullivan's head and shoulder ached. Standing up, he waved to the Coast Guard helicopter with his good arm and went below to switch on the sideband.

"Coast Guard, *Jessica Elaine*."

"We hear you, *Jessica Elaine*. What is your condition and how many aboard?"

Sullivan looked around the cabin. Dutch was curled up in the corner, dizzied but alert. A cabinet door had sprung open, spilling its contents, but the boat was dry and sound. The diesel idled noisily in the background. It was just after seven in the morning according to the clock on the bulkhead.

"One aboard. No, two including my canine. The vessel seems to be sound, and I think we can make it back to Dingwall."

There was a pause. "Your destination, say again?"

"Dingwall, Nova Scotia."

"Cap, do you know where you are?"

"Not exactly. We got blown off course."

"We have you two hundred nautical miles east northeast of Halifax. You copy that?"

"I read you. We'll correct our course accordingly."

The Coast Guard gave him a navigational fix and then said, "The weather has moved off to northeast of Labrador and should improve gradually. Anything else we can do for you today?"

"No thanks, Coast Guard."

Sullivan signed off the radio and looked over at Dutch. "We're going home."

The weather did improve enough for Sullivan to clean up the boat and make a light meal for himself and Dutch and put on a pot of coffee. He tried to raise Calum on the radio, but there was no reply.

Later, Sullivan took in the sea anchor and raised a shortened mizzen. He brought Dutch into the cockpit and hooked his canine life preserver onto the safety line. The sea now was a series of widely spaced big rollers. Settling into the helm, Sullivan relaxed. The ketch was sailing itself, and he allowed himself time to just think.

The images of his dream the night before had been knocking on the door of his consciousness since he awoke. The dream had been so real. The clatter of the battlefield still rang in his ears. His muscles ached just as they had that day as he carried Capello over his shoulder. The touch and feel of weaponry and flesh were still fresh on his fingertips. The mordant taste of cordite and napalm still made his eyes tear and throat raspy. The last scene of the last act of the endless loop that had played in the war-torn cinema of his nightmares had always ended as it had played out in real life, but not this time. Perhaps it had been Capello who had been trying to rescue *him* all these years. And maybe it might be okay someday, just like he said.

Nova Scotia came into view hours before the *Jessica Elaine* reached Lochinver Harbour. Waves were crashing against the breakwater, throwing water into the afternoon sky. The *Aspy Lady* was tethered to the dock, empty of crew. The harbour parking lot looked like a ghost town – no boat would be going out until the storm cleared. Sullivan motored to the dock and secured the ketch. Dutch tumbled onto dry land right behind Sullivan. They both staggered as their brains adjusted to the equilibrium of a landlocked world. Sullivan sat on the dock. Dutch buried his head in Sullivan's chest as Sullivan stroked his back.

Sullivan started up the dock toward the parking lot and home for a shower, a meal, sleep and to apologize to the people that he loved. It took a moment to register that someone was standing at the top of the dock. Wisps of short blond hair floated in the wind. Caitlin's hand trembled as she wiped a tear from her eye. Her lips formed words that were muted and stretched as if she was speaking through a long tube.

"Calum is dead."

Chapter 25

Sullivan sat in a folding chair behind the counter in the chandlery. He had a buzz in his ears and still felt dizzy. Caitlin sat face to face with him.

Caitlin said, "We were so worried about you. Calum said he talked with you on the ship-to-shore before you left Saint-Pierre. Then the storm worsened. The crew of the Lady wanted to go out looking for you, but John couldn't risk the boat and crew in the storm, so he notified the Coast Guard that you were overdue."

"Yes. They paid me a visit," Sullivan said.

Caitlin nodded and let out a sigh. "I hadn't seen Calum. He knew I was back in town, and he's here every morning like clockwork when I'm in the shop. That's when I went to his house. No one answered the door. It was unlocked, so I went in and that's when I found him."

"He was gone?"

"No, he was on the floor still alive and saying he didn't want to go to the hospital. I called the ambulance, but by the time they got there, he had died."

Sullivan took in a lung full of air and exhaled a sigh. "Did he say anything?"

Caitlin's lip quivered and she nodded. She wiped away a new flood of tears and let out a sob. Then she said, "Personal things. He knew he was dying and had started writing notes to some people a few days before. He left a note for you and asked me to give it to you."

Caitlin got up and walked over to the coffee maker and filled a cup. When she sat back down she was more composed. She handed Sullivan a sealed envelope.

"You may want to wait until you're alone before you read that," she said. "The funeral is scheduled for the day after tomorrow. Father O'Malley was going to ask you to serve as a pallbearer. Calum was very fond of you, Nick. I'm sure you know that."

It was Sullivan's turn to nod. He sniffed and stared at the floor.

There was a pause. Then Caitlin said, "Nick, there are some things I need to say."

"Maybe now's not the best time to—"

She put her hand on his and then took it away. "Please, Nick. It will just take a moment, and I'm not sure I'll have the courage later."

Sullivan let out another sigh. His hands were trembling. "Okay."

"That night, on your boat, I was trying to say goodbye to my husband. When someone dies at sea, there is no funeral, no body to grieve over, no gravestone that tells you the person you had loved, made sacred vows with, is gone. After the memorial service is over, you still hold hope, you still expect him to walk through the door, throw his arms around you and say it was just a bad dream.

"A week goes by then a month and a year and you still watch that door, half hoping, half expecting, that every time it opens, he'll be standing there. And all the while, you ache just for the warmth of a human touch, a moment of affection, the chance to love and be loved back. But it doesn't come and the need grows larger, and you look for something just to take the hurt away, if just for a second. Nick, that night on the boat, I needed someone to give me all of that, but I wasn't ready. Yes, the hurt went away for that brief moment, but then it was replaced with the remorse that you feel when you've cheated on someone who had trusted and loved you. And then you realize that you've sinned twice. Nick, I know I hurt you, and I'm sorry. I'm very sorry."

Sullivan started to speak, but Caitlin raised her hand. "Please. Let me finish. I'm leaving, Nick. I'm putting the business up for sale, but I'm not waiting. I'm leaving right after Calum's funeral.

"I'm going to Montreal – a change of scenery and maybe a chance for closure. That's what Calum talked to me about – the promise that tomorrow brings. But know that I care for you deeply, and that I will always be grateful to you for helping me along in my journey. Please, don't hate me."

Sullivan shook his head. He stood and walked out the door.

Dutch watched Caitlin follow Sullivan out the chandlery from the open window of the Dodge. He listened as she stopped and called out the name of the one he loved most. And then Dutch watched Sullivan collapse on the pavement.

Dutch squeezed out the open window of the Dodge and ran over to Sullivan. He gave Sullivan's face a lick and settled put his paws over Sullivan's lap to protect him from the hurt, all those terrible things that humans do to one another and to themselves.

Strangers came. Dutch sniffed at their intent and watched as they lifted Sullivan. Dutch whined and pulled against the leash that restrained him as the ambulance took Sullivan away.

—

Sullivan's consciousness evolved into flashes of light and sounds and touches. The touches were sometimes probing and callous, and at other times they were soft and caring. His eyes blinked on a world out of focus. He could not speak – something was in his throat.

A hand, soft and warm and full of love caressed his. Sullivan blinked again. Features barely lucent ripened into someone: blond haired, fair-skinned and blue-eyed. The eyes sparkled with a familiarity that arose from somewhere deep in his memory. He examined the face not believing, but his suspicions were confirmed with a single word.

"Daddy."

Sullivan tried to speak. Jessica placed the tip of her index finger on his lip.

"Don't try to speak now. There's an endotracheal tube in your throat," she said.

Sullivan had always wondered what his daughter's voice would sound like. She began to speak, but a doctor came, examined the monitor wired to Sullivan's body and placed a cold stethoscope on his chest. Sullivan pushed the doctor's hand away.

"Jessica," he whispered.

"You need to behave," Jessica said.

Sullivan nodded.

The doctor asked Sullivan a series of questions, which he answered with grunts or a shake of his head. The doctor removed the breathing tube.

"Doctor Sullivan. Ten minutes and we need to do another MRI," his physician said.

"Doctor?" Sullivan whispered.

"I'm in my first year of residency at the University of Southern California, Daddy. The last MRI they did showed minor encephalo edema, and you were positive for hydrocephalus. You should make a full recovery, but you do have a concussion and you're going to require surgery to repair a torn rotator cuff."

Sullivan managed a smile. "Am I in good hands?"

"And not just mine. You have a lot of good friends that care very much for you, Daddy. I've had a chance to talk with them over the last few days."

"Days?"

"Yes, three to be exact, not including the brief stay in the hospital in Cape Breton. You were placed in a medically induced coma. You're in Halifax now. They have specialists here."

Sullivan, exhausted now, closed his eyes. Then he opened them again and turned to look at Jessica. He balked at the thought of closing his eyes again only to discover that the vision before him had been just a dream.

As if reading his thoughts she said, "I'm here, Daddy, and I'm not going to leave until you're well again." She wiped the tears from his eyes with her index finger.

Two orderlies pushed a gurney through the door.

"I've got to go now."

Sullivan grasped her hand.

"I'll be here. I made a promise to you, and I never break a promise."

Later, after machines whirled and hummed and images were analyzed, Sullivan was wheeled back to his hospital room. And as promised, Jessica was waiting.

"How?" Sullivan asked.

"That's a long story."

Jessica unravelled Sullivan's questions later in his room. The story was a curious melding of one part chance and one part circumstance.

"Mom never told me about you until my sixteenth birthday. I was mad as hell, so mad I ran away for a month to Colorado. They, Mom and my stepdad, they're divorced now, hired a private detective when the police couldn't find me. I was pretty proud of that."

Sullivan smiled – Daddy's girl. Jessica – Jess, as she liked to be called – smiled back.

"When I asked about you, all Mom said was that you were a POW in Vietnam and that you came back all messed up. She said that you became a drifter and never really cared about us. It wasn't until my twenty-first birthday, one of those landmark birthdays that makes you introspective, that I made some inquiries of my own. I wrote to the Department of Defense under freedom of information and that's when I found out that you came home a decorated hero, finished college and became a fighter pilot. I thought that was so cool."

Sullivan smiled again.

"That's when I changed my name to Sullivan. Anyway, about a year ago I hired a private detective who recently tracked you to Virginia. That was a dead end. I guess you have friends there that know how to keep a secret. And then I received a Christmas card from you."

Sullivan remembered. He had wept when he'd written a card to Jessica last Christmas. The letter folded inside was a cloud-burst of emotion.

"The card was postmarked 'Sydney, Nova Scotia.' But again, my detective came up cold. There are hundreds of Sullivans that live in Cape Breton, and no one with the given name Nicholas . Finally this retired attorney from Nova Scotia, I think his name was French – Boudreau – found me through court records in the States. My private detective talked with him. Quite the guy, I'm told."

Sullivan nodded.

"So, that's how I found out where you were. I called your house and D introduced herself to me and told me you were out sailing around in a storm. My travel agent booked the first avail-able flight to Halifax and I rented a car."

Sullivan looked at his daughter and nodded. He pointed to a glass of water on the food cart next to his bed. Jessica put a straw in the glass and helped raise his head as he sipped the water. Then he rested his head on the pillow. Sullivan put his hand over the bandage on his head.

"Does it hurt?"

"No. Not much anyway." Sullivan went silent.

"You were very lucky that storm didn't kill you."

Sullivan remembered the wooden turtle that he had stuffed in his pocket while he was fighting the sea on the *Jessica Elaine*.

He reached over for Jessica's hand. A diamond ring sparkled from her finger.

"Who's the lucky guy?"

"I've got so much to tell you."

And she did.

Chapter 26

The Wednesday after Labour Day, summer was in denial. Aspy Bay was still. The tourists had returned to lesser places, taking with them digital cards with burned in memories that they could visit through their pixel glass or Bluetooth printer .

D was upstairs in her bedroom pouring over textbooks that Scott had picked up at Hartt College so she could get a head start on her academics. She was leaving for school on Friday.

Sullivan was sitting in one of the slat chairs tossing a ball with his good arm to Dutch who chased primal visions of birds and squirrels and retrieved them for the price of a smile and a soft spoken word.

Jess came out and sat next to Sullivan. Dutch abandoned his ball and scurried up to her for a pat on the head and then took a spot on the deck between them.

"I expected it to be much cooler here," she said. "Canada conjures up images of polar bears and icebergs for us Californians. I packed too many sweaters and long pants."

"The icebergs won't reach the northern shores of Newfoundland until spring," Sullivan said, "and they melt before they reach our coast, although a few years ago a berg showed up in Halifax with a polar bear on it ."

Sullivan slipped off his sunglasses. The last of the summer's sun tilted toward the western sky where autumn was waiting. Waves, little more than pregnant ripples, washed against the beach and slid back into the sea again. Installed on the cheap by a friend of Sylliboy, a new roof on the barn budded green against the sky.

"Cheap ride for the bear, but lousy accommodations," she said.

"And no restaurant on board."

"There's that, too," she said.

She followed Sullivan's gaze. "I understand now why people here love this place so much. We have our Big Sur, and the southern coast of California is special, but there's a magic here I can't quite put into words."

"Magical says it fairly well," Sullivan said. "Sometimes I think God cut a little piece of the world out to try to save it from human corruption and pasted it here. And the people that call it home tend to it like it was their first-born."

"I'd like to bring Len here and spend some time."

"I'd like to meet your fiancé. Must be a smart guy – a Harvard Business School grad and a fund manager."

Jess grabbed her father's hand. "Daddy, I'm concerned about you sailing alone."

Sullivan looked at Dutch. "I've got my stalwart crew."

Dutch raised his ears.

"He loves you," Jess said.

"Back at him."

"I've got to get back to California," Jess said. "Are you sure you're feeling okay?"

He squeezed Jess's hand. "Never better."

"And I'll fly down to wherever the *Jessica Elaine* is this winter for a visit."

The screen door to the kitchen opened and then fell back on its hinges.

"You guys have an appetite?" D asked.

"If it's your turn to cook, yes. If I'm up at bat, I feel like finger food," Sullivan said.

"Your lucky day," D replied. "Jess lit the burners last night and you fed the masses the night before. But you and Jess get to deal with the aftermath of my culinary creations."

Jess smiled. "She's like the sister I never had."

Lobster meat swimming in a sour cream and wine sauce over rice with asparagus smothered in hollandaise sauce and a Greek salad. Cleanup was easy.

D was out on the deck as the last of the dinnerware was dried and put away. "You guys have got to see this," she said.

Jess and Sullivan stepped outside. A harvest moon filled the sky with crimson as if some divine hand had grasped it and moved it so close that you could clearly see ridges and valleys on its dimpled complexion.

"I've never seen anything like it," Jess said.

"Let's take a walk," D suggested.

The sand was cool on bare feet. Dutch nipped gently at D's ankle, coaxing her for a game of run and chase. D sprinted ahead and Dutch rocketed passed her, running in circles, waiting for her to catch up.

They caught up to D. She was out of breath. "What's doin' tomorrow?"

"I've got a doctor's appointment in Sydney," Sullivan said.

"Let's all go," D said. "Jess and I can go shopping while you do your thing and then we'll meet up later and have lunch."

"Why not," Sullivan said. "We'll make it a big lunch and have something light for supper."

D crossed her arms and gave Sullivan a look that reminded him of Sister Rosemary when he got caught chewing gum in parochial school. "And whose turn is it to prepare supper tomorrow?"

"You don't miss much, do you?" Sullivan asked.

Jess and D dropped Sullivan off at the hospital the next morning at nine thirty. At ten fifteen he left radiology and walked up the stairs to Dr. Esherick's office. Sullivan met Esherick in the waiting room and followed him into his office.

Sullivan examined the furniture. "No couch."

Esherick shrugged. "Budget cuts."

Sullivan nodded.

"So, tell me how you're doing," Esherick said.

"Can't complain."

"The anti-depressant doing its job?" Esherick asked.

"Just like the advertisement says."

Esherick nodded. "But the blues are still playing."

"Sometimes like B.B. King. Sometimes not."

"We've made progress. We know survivor's guilt is your nemesis. Talk therapy is the other piece of the puzzle," Esherick said. "Let's begin where we left off."

Sullivan took a deep breath and read another page from the story of his life.

Lunch was oversized and everyone seemed sleepy on the drive back to Dingwall.

Sullivan dropped D and Jess off at the house and then drove with Dutch to check on the boat. As Sullivan pulled into Loch-inver Harbour, he could see Caitlin's Jeep parked in front of the chandlery. Dutch followed Sullivan out of the truck, looked at the chandlery and then at Sullivan.

Sullivan shook his head. "Come on, buddy. Can't go there."

The ketch was nearly ready. They would slip the lines and head south in mid-October when hurricane season was over. Sullivan put a pot of decaf coffee on.

A faint knock caused Sullivan to look out through the open hatch. He climbed into the cockpit.

"Hi," Caitlin said timidly.

Sullivan nodded.

Caitlin looked at Sullivan for a long while then looked away.

Sullivan sighed. "You can sit if you want," he said pointing to the cushions on the sail locker.

She climbed over the combing and sat down. Her hands were clasped together.

"Coffee?" Sullivan asked.

Cailtin shook her head. "I just wanted to see how you were." She paused, her voice soft and uncertain. "Sometimes I'm just one big mistake."

"It happens," Sullivan said. "I'm living proof."

He ducked into the cabin and returned with a cup that exuded curls of steaming neutered Columbian bean.

"How's Montreal?"

Caitlin shifted in her seat. "I'm a little homesick for Cape Breton, I guess. I've had time to think. I have an offer on the store. Montreal is a big move. I'm not so sure it's the right one."

Sullivan took a sip of coffee and watched a herring boat clear the breakwater. The sea was oily and still and reflective.

She said, "I visited Calum's grave. Someone had put flowers there recently – a bouquet arranged to look like a sailboat. I thought it might be you."

"I guess the sailboat was a giveaway," Sullivan said.

"No. It was the kindness." Caitlin lowered her eyes. "Well, I'll be in town for awhile. Maybe we could go for coffee or something."

"I'd like that," he said.

Epilogue

The *Jessica Elaine* glided through the mist-covered waters of the Gulf of Maine. The October sun, still rising, spoke of promise. Sullivan sat at the helm of the ketch and watched the sails billow in a light wind. Dutch looked up as seabirds hovered hoping for a handout. The aroma of coffee and fresh baked muffins spilled from the galley. Sullivan smiled as a blond-haired, blue-eyed vision of beauty sat next to him.

"Coffee is on. The muffins will be done in a few minutes – cranberry with white chocolate."

Sullivan had been drinking a lot of coffee since he started rehab. He learned to turn a deaf ear to his demons. There would be meetings to attend and a prescription for the depressive illness, but he felt as if the dots of his life were finally being connected.

Sullivan put his arm around Caitlin and she nestled her head against his shoulder.

"I'm glad you decided to come along as far as Portland," Sullivan said.

"Me too. Who would have thought," she said. "I think I understand why your uncle wanted you to go on this journey – it's a perfect place for dreaming and self-discovery. You're fulfilling your uncle's final dream. He wanted to share that with you because he loved you."

"He didn't blame me."

Caitlin looked at him questioningly.

"I think he wanted me to know that he didn't blame me for Richie's death – and that I shouldn't blame myself either."

It had been his uncle's death that brought him back to Cape Breton, back to people that would make a difference in his life. Perhaps his Uncle Sean knew that he would never embark on a journey in the old ketch himself, that it was just the reverie of an old man counting time, marching in place. Perhaps he knew it all along. Sullivan looked up at the telltales and trimmed the sails. Then he grew quiet.

"What are you thinking about?" she asked.

"Oh, something reminded me of Calum."

"You never got to say goodbye to him."

"Not in the way that I should have. I think about him a lot."

"Then he'll never be far away."

"I guess."

"You never told me what was in his letter."

Sullivan looked away for a moment before he could answer. "He said a lot of things about the times we spent together. He said a lot of things about hope too."

"Do you think he was right?"

"He was never wrong," Sullivan said.

Later, as coffee and muffins settled, Caitlin laid down on the port sail locker and gazed at the sky.

"Cape Breton and everything that happened there seems a world away," she said. "Do you miss it?"

Sullivan nodded. "I miss everything about it: waking up to the surf rushing against the shore, the sounds of Celtic music through open windows, the Aspy River when it shines silver in the afternoon sun, the beach under a blanket of stars. But I miss our friends the most."

"Like they say, 'Great minds think alike.'" Caitlin squeezed Sullivan's hand. "I'm so glad we're giving it a second chance. Thanks for being so patient with me."

Sullivan squeezed her hand back. "Ditto."

"I can't wait until I catch up with you in St. Christopher."

"Me too," Sullivan said. "And then we'll sail back with plenty of time to get ready for Jess's wedding next June."

"And D's engagement party too," Caitlin said.

"It'll be like giving away another daughter."

Sullivan adjusted the jib sheet as the *Jessica Elaine* made good on a course for Portland, Maine, where they would clear customs and Caitlin would catch a flight back to Halifax.

He pulled out the telescope that Calum had willed to him – his eye squinted through the lens. In the boat's wake to the north, the sea bent to meet the curve of the horizon and Cape Breton beyond. Then Sullivan looked past the bow of the *Jessica Elaine* and remembered Calum's words, when they first met – about the wonder of life.

Fin

www.ingramcontent.com/pod-product-compliance
Lightning Source LLC
Chambersburg PA
CBHW022001010726
47494CB00003B/840